AMARA

AMARA

Richard Laymon

headline

First published in Great Britain in 2003
by HEADLINE BOOK PUBLISHING

10 9 8 7 6 5 4 3 2 1

Cataloguing in Publication Data is available from the British Library

ISBN 0 7472 6932 7

Typeset in Times by Palimpsest Book Production Limited,
Polmont, Stirlingshire
Printed and bound in Great Britain by
Mackays of Chatham plc, Chatham, Kent

HEADLINE BOOK PUBLISHING
A division of Hodder Headline
338 Euston Road
London NW1 3BH

www.headline.co.uk
www.hodderheadline.com

What may this mean
That thou, dead corse
Revisits thus the glimpses of the moon,
Making night hideous?

William Shakespeare
Hamlet: Act I, Scene iv

Introduction

By Dean Koontz

As long as I have been on Earth, which is longer than Microsoft Word 5.0 but not longer than the English language, I've been involved in only two traffic accidents. They occurred a little more than a year apart, and the circumstances were eerily the same; I should not have survived either incident, and certainly should not have survived unscathed, but I did.

In the first instance, my wife and I were in a large sedan, stopped at a controlled intersection, on our way to dinner, when a car hit us from behind at (the police estimated) 55 mph, without braking. That day, with spring approaching, I'd had the snow tires taken off the rear wheels and replaced with springtime rubber. The snow tires had been stored temporarily in the trunk of the car until I could tuck them aside in a corner of the garage for use the next winter. When we were hit from behind, the stored tires were two enormous shock absorbers; however, even with the protection they provided, the rear half of the sedan was spectacularly crushed, compacted into about two feet of mangled ruins that were shoved against our headrests. The back doors folded like accordions. The front doors buckled and would not open. The gasoline tank ruptured and sprayed fuel into the passenger's compartment. Incredibly, the engine was still running – and wouldn't shut off. Expecting fire or explosion, I needed perhaps a frantic half minute to wrench open a buckled door. Our sedan was totaled, but the car that hit us was totaled and *squashed*. We thought the driver of the other vehicle must be dead, but to our amazement, as we hurried to him, he struggled out of his demolished coupe, as unharmed as we were. As it turned out, he was a sixteen-year-old boy who had gotten his driver's license a month previous; he had bought his first car *that morning*. Regarding the wreckage with disgust, he looked at us and said, 'I didn't *need* this,' as though he suspected that we, unlike him, had been driving around with no sane purpose but with the mad hope of being hit from behind and killed. We had just paid off our car loan that day.

Fourteen months later, having moved three thousand miles from Pennsylvania to California, we were stopped at a traffic light, on our way to dinner (going out to a restaurant is seldom viewed as the extremely dangerous undertaking our experience has proved it to be) when a car hit us from behind at (the police estimated) 55 mph, without braking. This time we were in a small sports car, a Mercedes 450 SL, which had no backseat. Because the Mercedes was solidly constructed and brilliantly engineered, the fuel tank didn't rupture and the doors didn't buckle; we got out of the vehicle unscratched. The car that had hit us, a large sedan, looked as if it had been nuked. We were sure the occupant must be dead or seriously injured. We hurried to the driver's door. The window was broken out. The door had buckled. The woman inside was alive – but obviously intoxicated. When we told her to stay calm, that we would get her out, she cursed us and said, 'I didn't *need* this,' putting the emphasis on the word *need*, precisely as the young driver had done fourteen months ago in Pennsylvania. I couldn't get her out of the car, and even the police, who arrived within two minutes, had trouble extracting the woman, not because she was pinned in the wreckage but because she was determined to stay in there rather than get out and have to face a breathalyzer test. As had happened fourteen months earlier in Pennsylvania, Gerda had made the final payment on our car loan that very morning.

The uncanny similarity of the details of these two accidents suggests to me – as do so many other things in life – a world that operates not always according to the predictable laws of physics and chance, but also and perhaps as often under the influence of a mysterious power with a delightfully byzantine sense of *story* and with an agenda that is, though perhaps not inscrutable, challenging to analyze and understand. Pondering the significance of these two accidents, Gerda and I posited all sorts of possible meanings and messages to be derived from our experiences. I thought it logical, for example, never to halt at another traffic light or stop sign, but to cruise blithely through the intersection with the expectation that to stop would be to invite an inevitable read-end collision. Eventually, however, we made only one change in our lives due to these events at opposite ends of the continent: Because we were finally able to afford to do so, we thereafter never took out another car loan but paid cash for each new vehicle we acquired. Granted, on any day that we paid for a new car, we assumed that we were at risk till midnight, but when we made it to that witching hour, the suspense was over!

One evening a few years after the second of these two accidents, Gerda and I went to dinner with Dick and Ann Laymon. In our flivver, we picked them up at their house and buzzed off into the glamorous Angelean night, which glitters with film stars and carjackers, movie moguls and diseased streetwalkers, pop music divas and babbling urine-soaked hobos (some of whom had no doubt once *been* pop music divas). We had reservations at a sixteen-star restaurant, outside which even the richest titans of industry wrestle in the street like hooligans over a suddenly available table. We were exuberant at the prospect of superb food, fine wine, and the chance to share dozens of hilarious personal anecdotes about such subjects as the publishing business and dental surgery. Nothing, we thought, could taint this spectacular evening – and then I missed our freeway exit.

As a driver, one of my hallmarks is missing freeway exits, but only when chauffeuring particularly interesting and voluble people. Dick and Ann were so interesting and voluble on this occasion that Gerda was preparing syringes full of Thorazine to calm them down, and I suppose that rolled up sock in her left hand was meant for my mouth. Anyway, as I regaled Dick and Ann with the story of our two nearly identical accidents, fourteen months apart, I zipped by our freeway exit *and past another one* before any of us realized what I had done. After consultation, we agreed that by switching freeways, we could eventually get back around to where we needed to be, so I switched, and switched again . . . and by some means that was mysterious to all of us, we found ourselves on what seemed to be an unopened section of an uncompleted freeway – and shortly thereafter on a surface street in a neighbourhood so grim and forbidding that even the attack-trained pit bulls carried semiautomatic pistols and kept their heads down.

We were familiar with the maze of streets and highways that form an all but infinite Gordian knot binding the limbs and bowels of this great city, yet we were uncertain of our location and flummoxed as to how to find our way out of what seemed about to become a vortex of terror. In a baffling and unconventional move, Gerda consulted a map, as if that would be of any help. Dick and I, on the other hand, voted for the sober and sensible approach: cruising at random into ever meaner streets, in the hope that we would stumble upon a freeway sign and a hasty exit route before we were all shot, stabbed, throttled, dismembered, set on fire, and offered up to the Beast of

Beasts on a satanic altar. Naturally, as we were both writers who had been born with a generous measure of imagination, we saw threats at every turn, which we excitedly pointed out to each other, and we were able to envision – and vividly describe – a virtually endless series of hideous fates that might very well befall us before we found an escape route. Ann, for reasons beyond my comprehension, chose to lean forward from the backseat and consult with Gerda over the stupid map. Anyway, by eventually executing a series of turns that Gerda suggested based on – I suppose – her superior female intuition, we found a freeway and were able to arrive at dinner a tad late but with all of our extremities intact.

After a delicious dinner accompanied by a superb Cabernet, after desserts even more likely than any Barney the Dinosaur performance to trigger a diabetic coma, and after many hilarious anecdotes about the publishing business and dental surgery, the four of us departed the restaurant, stepping between the wrestling titans of industry who thrashed upon the sidewalk, and presented our car check to the valet-parking attendant. Since I had begun the evening talking about our two strangely similar accidents at opposite ends of the country and then had driven the Laymons deep into harm's way, it seemed fitting that the car should be returned with a long, deep scratch/crease on the passenger's side, from front fender to rear – and that the valet-parking attendant should, instead of apologising, say, 'I didn't *need* this.'

Dick and I exchanged a look, and neither of us needed to say that one of the greatest problems for novelists is that reality is not only stranger than fiction but generally funnier and more deeply disturbing. To get the true flavor of life, it seems to me, a writer has to let his imagination cruise not merely through the precincts of realism where you might find Hemingway but, more important, also into neighborhoods of the fantastic. Dick and I are radically different writers, but what I love about his work is his willingness to drive at high speed into the fantastic – and make it seem, for all its flamboyant qualities, as real as tomorrow's newspaper. *Amara* is one such. Enjoy.

Prologue

Emil Saladat leaped down from the cab of the U-Haul van and rushed to the cover of bushes near the wall. He watched Metar run to join him. The van moved away, its taillights disappearing around a bend.

Emil stepped into Metar's cupped hands for a boost. He clutched the top of the brick wall and flung himself onto it.

This was so easy.

This American was a cinch.

No broken bottles embedded in the wall. No electrified wire. No armed guards.

This American, Callahan, was making it so easy that Emil should be ashamed to take money from his people. He would take it, though, just as he had always taken it before, no matter how simple the job. A man must put food into his belly. A man must buy fine gifts for his women.

He reached down. Metar handed him the backpack. He set it on top of the wall, lowered his arms again, and this time pulled the smaller man off the ground.

From his perch on the wall, Emil looked toward the house. He couldn't see it. Too many trees in the way. He knew it was there, however. He and Metar had paid it a visit, just last week.

He leaped from the wall. Metar dropped the pack down to him, then jumped. He held the pack while Metar slipped it on. Turning away from the wall, they started toward the trees.

Out of the darkness sprinted a Doberman, its feet silent on the summer grass.

This is Callahan's security?

It was laughable.

The dog yelped and tripped over itself as a .22 caliber hollow-point slug crashed through its skull.

Then three more Dobermans raced out of the darkness. Emil fired his silenced automatic, knocking a foreleg from under the lead dog. As it tumbled, the one beside it leaped at him, teeth bared. He stepped

1

toward it, ignoring Metar's cry of pain. The dog snapped, its teeth clattering on the silencer. With quick twitches of his index finger, Emil pumped two bullets into its mouth. He sidestepped away from the lunging, dying animal, swung his pistol from its mouth, and dropped the dog he had previously hit in the leg.

Then he whirled around. Metar, the incompetent fool, was on the ground, fighting for his life as the last surviving dog savaged his arm, trying to get through it to his neck.

Emil fired.

The dog yelped as the bullet tore through its spinal cord.

Then jerked and died.

Metar rolled out from under the heavy body and stood up. He raised his bloody arm for Emil to see, like a child showing a scraped elbow to his mother for sympathy.

Emil turned away in disgust. He hurried through the stand of pine, and saw the Callahan house across fifty yards of neatly groomed lawn. Floodlights illuminated the colonial's pillared veranda. All the windows Emil could see, however, were dark. He ran to the left side of the house, staying far from the lighted front, and leaned against a wall.

Metar, a handkerchief tied around his wounded forearm, ran to join him.

With friction tape, Emil reinforced a panel of the window. His glasscutter bit into the glass. He cut a rectangle.

A neat job. A good job. That was why his clients paid him well.

Holding the rectangle in place with tape, he pounded it loose and withdrew it. He gave the neatly cut geometric lozenge of glass to Metar, then reached into the gap. Unlatched the window.

It slid upward easily.

Quietly.

Emil climbed through. As planned, he found himself in Callahan's study. He sat on a corner of the teak desk, and watched Metar climb awkwardly through the window.

They crossed the study to the door. Emil eased it open. He peered into the dark hallway, and gestured for Metar to follow.

In the foyer, Metar's rubber-soled shoes made squeaking sounds on the marble. Emil glanced sharply at his young partner. The man shrugged, crouched. Removed his shoes.

Emil flashed the beam of a small flashlight toward the front door. Next to it, on the wall, he found the speaker box and remote-control button.

He pushed the button.

*   *   *

2

In the U-Haul van parked nearby, Steve Bailey squinted through a haze of cigarette smoke at the iron gate. It began to swing open.

Very good.

In ten minutes, he would be done with this business. He would be away from the house, and on the freeway to the airport. In a couple of hours or so, he'd be with Carla. It was always best with her, right after a job when he knew he was finally safe, and the fear was gone, and he had money . . . good money . . . in his pocket. His cock knew it was time to come out of hiding and celebrate.

Easing his foot off the clutch, he rolled through the open gate. He steered up the driveway, swung left, and drove over the grass to the veranda.

With a hissing sputter, the acetylene torch came alive. Emil watched his partner shoot its flame against the lock panel of the steel door. The metal bubbled and peeled back like the lips of a knife wound.

Raising the goggles to his forehead, Emil stepped silently down the hall to the foyer. He squinted up the stairway.

Perhaps he should go up and put a bullet into Callahan's head? Then he could go about his work untroubled by the man's presence. Murder, however, would increase official interest in the case. That was to be avoided, if possible.

As long as the old man didn't interfere, Emil would allow him to live.

The torch shut off. Sparks winked out.

Emil returned to the door and helped Metar remove the severed lock panel. As he set it aside, Metar loaded the torch into the backpack and slung the straps onto his shoulders.

Slowly, Emil pushed the metal door open.

Robert Callahan, asleep in his upstairs room, heard the quiet drone of his alarm and dreamed of sirens. An ambulance was bearing down on a heap of torn cars. Sarah, lying in the road, raised her bloody head and cried for help.

'There she is,' shouted the ambulance driver.

Robert, for some reason dreaming that he was sitting in the passenger seat, said, 'Thank God she's alive.'

'We'll soon fix that,' said the driver.

The ambulance sped toward her. Lethal as a bullet.

'Stop!'

'It's her due.'

'No!'

She stared with pleading eyes into the headlights. Stared into the face of death.

Robert felt the vehicle jolt as it struck her.

Suddenly wide-awake and panting with fear, he realized the siren was the burglar alarm amplifier by his bed. Someone had penetrated the collection room.

Emil entered the room, Metar at his side. Walking close to the wall, he shined his light on the statuettes of gold and ivory, on gold necklaces heavy with precious jewels, on scarabs and brooches and glistening rings.

To see so many antiquities in a man's private collection disgusted him. If he had time, he would clean out the entire collection of this grave robber.

But Emil had come only for Amara.

The thin beam of his light found a stone vase, its lid decorated with the jackal head of the god Anubis. Beside it stood a similar container, this with the head of a hawk. His light fell swiftly across two more vases. These were the canopic jars holding the embalmed organs of Amara – heart, lungs, kidneys. Her womb. He must take the jars tonight.

Swinging his flashlight, he found the coffin.

It was the wooden, inner coffin of Amara. The outer coffins and massive stone sarcophagus had never left Egypt. The thieves had taken this only, and the canopic jars. And Amara herself.

Stepping close to the coffin, Emil shined his light onto a golden disk on the edge of its lid. He was thankful to find the sacred seal in place.

Though vermin, Callahan was not a fool.

Leaning across the lid, Emil inspected the second seal. It, too, appeared to be intact.

Reassured, he allowed himself to look down at the carved face of Amara. It was a face of rare beauty, a face that might have shamed Nefertiti herself, had the ladies' paths ever crossed. But their paths were separated by centuries. Amara belonged to the long-dead era of the eleventh dynasty, when Mentuhotep I ruled and gods were young in the memory of the people.

Emil glanced at Metar, who stared as if hypnotized by the beautiful image. With a tap on the arm he caught his partner's attention. He pointed to the foot of the coffin.

Together, each at one end, they lifted it. They carried the

deadweight of it across the room, through the doorway, down the dark hall. Emil's powerful arms strained with the weight. Metar whimpered as wounds from the dog's bite stretched, reopened, bled. At the end of the hall, the carpet ended. He felt the marble of the foyer floor under his feet.

A few more steps, then they could set down the coffin while Metar opened the door.

It was good to accomplish the hardest part first. The canopic jars would be easy after this.

Emil nodded for Metar to stop.

A quick blast shattered the silence. In the muzzle flash, he saw Metar slammed backwards, dropping the end of the coffin. Mist jetted from between the casket and the lid. Dust of the ages. Corpse dust. Even as he looked toward the stairway, a second flash and explosion filled the darkness. He had no time to duck.

Steve Bailey, in the U-Haul van just outside the door, heard the shots.

Holy shit.

They hadn't come from a .22.

They'd come from a high-powered sucker, like maybe a .12 gauge.

Emil and Metar only carried peashooters.

So who had the cannon?

Bailey didn't wait to find out. He dropped the emergency brake lever, rammed the shift to first, floored the gas pedal and popped the clutch.

Callahan lowered the shotgun. His shoulder was numb from the kicking stock. His ears rang as if they'd been slapped.

Stepping down the stairs, he heard an engine just outside the door. It roared, then faded with distance.

Callahan stepped across the dark foyer, careful not to trip over the bodies or the coffin. Near the door, he found the light switch. Flicked it on.

Both the bastards looked dead. One had caught it in the chest. The other had lost most of his forehead.

He turned his eyes to the coffin. It had landed on its side. Bending down, he saw a crack across one of the golden seals.

'Robert!'

He glanced up the stairway. His small, swarthy friend looked confused and frightened.

'Give me a hand with this, Imad.'

'Robert, what happened?'

'These bastards tried to make off with Amara. Same two guys who were here last week wanting to do landscape work.'

As Imad reached the bottom of the stairs, his mouth dropped open. 'The Seal of Osiris,' he muttered.

'I'm not blind. Give me a hand, we'll see how the other one looks.'

Together, they crouched and rolled the coffin off its side. On the marble underneath lay two chunks of gold from the second seal.

Gasping, Imad stepped back.

'Forget it,' Callahan said. 'We'll take care of it later.'

Imad shook his head, his eyes large with fear.

'Let's just get these guys out of here, first. We'll plant them in the garden.'

Still shaking his head, Imad stepped backwards toward the door. He spun around. His trembling hands fumbled with the locks, then he flung the door open, and ran into the night.

Callahan watched him dash across the lawn, white robe fluttering.

'Imad!' The man kept running. 'Better off,' Callahan muttered, and pushed the door shut.

He slept soundly after the hard work of burying the men and cleaning up the mess they'd left in the foyer. Bloodstains were the worst. His snoring was loud in the darkness.

The figure entering the doorway didn't disturb him. He continued to snore peacefully as it crossed the room. He moaned once as it raised the covers on the empty side of the bed.

It climbed in beside him and he knew, vaguely, that he was no longer alone. Sarah must have come back from the bathroom. He was glad to have her back. The bed felt so empty without her.

Rolling toward her, he put a hand out. It would be so good to touch her skin. Sarah had always felt so soft, so smooth. Hungry for her warm, supple body he reached out, searching for her. His fingers found the figure. Touched. Caressed.

If felt wrong, all wrong. He touched skin that was hard, wrinkled. Cold.

With a nauseating jolt, he remembered that Sarah was dead.

The shock woke him. At that instant he found himself gazing into eyeless sockets and a leathery, shrunken face.

Something under the sheet touched his bare leg.

Slowly, the mouth opened.

Callahan started to scream

The head jerked forward, jaws snapping shut, teeth barely missing his throat.

Callahan rolled off the bed. His knees hit the floor. He scrambled, naked, trying to get on his feet. As he started to rise, the mummy pounced upon his back. 'Get off!' he shrieked.

Its dry fingers clutched him by the shoulders.

He heard the clatter of its snapping teeth.

'Get off! No!'

Callahan got to his feet, but the thing kept its grip and stayed on his back as he ran across the room.

Its teeth tore the side of his neck. Its head jerked savagely, ripping.

Callahan dropped to his knees. He reached behind him, hoping to free himself from the creature. He gripped its hair. He jerked. Tresses pulled loose in his hand.

The mouth kept biting and tearing long after he was dead.

Chapter One

Susan Connors, assistant curator of the Charles Ward Museum, was dead. Dead on her feet, that was. She'd been standing all day, directing the two workmen who uncrated the collection, marking her checklist, pointing out where she wished the dozens of ancient artifacts placed for display.

She hadn't been on her feet this long since the day she'd worked a double shift at the Wagon Train restaurant, bussing barbecue ribs and cheeseburgers for conventioneers. Some treat that was. Man, oh man . . . That was – what? – six years ago? She'd been an undergraduate then. A senior.

That seemed like a long time ago.

Aeons.

Almost as long ago as eight o'clock this morning.

One of the workmen, the one called Top, lifted a canopic jar out of its packing case. It was made from alabaster, a stone that looked like fresh, white milk that had been transformed into something hard. Brittle. A sculptured head of a jackal formed the lid. Susan marked her checklist.

'That goes with the others.' She pointed to the stand beside the mummiform coffin where three other stone jars had already been placed. Top carried it across the room. Its weight didn't seem to bother him, though he looked frail and old enough to be the father of the other man. As he set down the jar, he said, 'That about does it, miss. The whole kit 'n caboodle. Wanta sign here?'

She scribbled her initials on the invoice. Top tore off a copy, gave it to her.

'All set,' he said.

When he and the younger man were gone, Susan sat on a folding chair – the only piece of furniture in the room that was less than two thousand years old, certainly the only piece that hadn't come from the Callahan Collection. Leaning back, she crossed her right foot over her knee and sighed with pleasure. The aches seemed to flow out of her. When that leg felt almost normal, she lowered it and raised the other. The relief!

'Your meditation hour?' a voice asked.

'Tag?' She looked around and saw Taggart Parker standing in the doorway. 'What are . . . ?' Then she remembered. Her car had treated her to a flat tire this morning. Tag had given her a lift to work. 'Come on in,' she said, getting up.

Tag unhooked one end of the plush cordon from its post and stepped forward through the doorway.

Into Susan's arms. She kissed him. The day's growth of whiskers was scratchy against her face, but she didn't mind. She pressed herself tightly to him, stroking the soft fabric of his corduroy jacket. She felt a hard shape against her belly.

'Is that a gun?' she asked, trying to sound like Mae West. 'Or are ya glad to see me?'

'Both,' Tag said.

Reaching down, Susan stroked the walnut grips of his Colt Python. 'You've got a hell of a pistol, fella.'

'And I'm good with it.'

'Braggart.' She kissed him again. 'Hey, we'd better knock it off before the boss walks in.' She stepped away, but kept hold of his hand. 'How was your day?'

'Improving.'

'Mine, too.' She swept an arm around to indicate the room. 'Look what I did today. It's the Callahan Collection.'

He scanned the room and his gaze settled on the single coffin. 'What's that, a mummy?'

'Sure is.'

'How about giving me a peek? I've never seen a real live mummy before.'

'Are you sure you want to?'

'I'd love to.'

'She's been dead a while.'

'Is that right?'

'The better part of four thousand years.'

'That long?'

'We don't know much about this gal yet: just what we got from the list Callahan left. Her name is Amara.'

'Amara? That's a beautiful name.' He smiled, teasing.

'And she was a wife of Pharaoh Mentuhotep the First. He ruled Egypt during the eleventh dynasty, about 2,000 BC.'

'Well, let's have a look.'

'Promise not to touch?'

'You don't trust me with strange women?'

'Especially not when you say they have a beautiful name.'

'And so it is . . . Amara, Amara, Amara. A guy can fall in love with a name like that.'

'Okay, promise not to touch. It's extremely fragile.'

'Cross my heart.' He patted Susan's rump. 'Actually, I doubt if I'd want to.'

Together they raised the lid. Susan, who had seen the mummy only for a moment that morning, gave it a closer inspection. The hair was a sweep of shining red, the only part of the once-young woman that had apparently defied time. It must have been elaborately coiffed at the time of entombment. Those who unwrapped her had probably also removed the jeweled hairpins. Her eye sockets were empty. No valuable stones inside, as imitation eyes, as was the ancient funerary practice. No onions to mask the smell of corruption, like they found in Rameses IV. No bags of frankincense and myrrh in the body cavities, either. Robbers had undoubtedly made off with those. Valuable spices were still valuable spices even after they had been drawn from their grisly container. Across the abdomen was a diagonal cut nearly a foot long that had been crudely stitched with twine. The breasts had shriveled into puckered bags. The pubic region had been shaved, probably by the ancient morticians after the young woman died.

Susan realized that Tag was looking away.

They closed the lid, covering that awful face.

'Do mummies all look like that?' Tag asked. His new, pasty complexion worried Susan.

'Are you all right?' she asked.

'I've felt better, on occasion.'

'Ready to leave?'

'I wish we'd left five minutes ago.'

In the subterranean parking area beneath the Marina Towers apartment complex, Tag drove slowly past Susan's Jaguar.

'It's fixed!' she blurted.

'I had a few minutes to kill after I got home from work, so I put on the spare for you.'

'Oh, you're a sweetheart.'

'Somebody isn't. Your tire didn't go flat all by itself. It had help. Somebody with a knife, I'd say.'

'You mean someone intentionally . . . ?'

Tag nodded. 'It might've been random, but I doubt it. I think you've made yourself an enemy, Susan.'

She shook her head.

10

'What about Larry?'

'He wouldn't do that. I mean, that's the last thing he would do. He *paid* for the car, he wouldn't try to damage it.'

'Unless he doesn't appreciate the fact that it now belongs to you.' Tag swung into his own parking space. In spite of his low speed, the tires sighed on the slick concrete.

'I don't think it was Larry.'

'Just a suggestion.'

Their doors banged shut and echoed.

'How about coming in for a drink?' Susan asked.

'Sounds good.'

They took an elevator to the third floor, and walked along the narrow, carpeted hall. At her apartment, Susan opened the door to the warm, rich odors she recognized as enchilada sauce.

'Evening, Maria,' she greeted the chubby, smiling woman in the kitchen.

Maria nodded eagerly.

'Everything go all right today?'

'*Si*. All right.' Her bright eyes turned to Tag. 'Ah, Senor Taggart. Margarita, *si*?'

'Right.'

Susan left them, and went into the small bedroom that she used for a nursery. Geoffrey, who was busy inspecting his toes, looked up as she entered. He grinned and gurgled.

'Hi there, little guy,' she said. 'Have yourself a good day?' She picked up the baby, kissed his cheek, and pulled out the front of his diapers. They were definitely damp to the touch. She stripped him, dried him, powdered him, and put a new diaper on him. After a brief struggle, she managed to maneuver him into a pair of tiny brown corduroy pants. Then a yellow T-shirt that read *Slippery When Wet*. 'There you go, my little man.' Hefting him, she carried him into the living room.

Tag came in. He handed Susan a bottle of ProSobee, and a glass of Perrier. 'Cocktails for everyone,' he said. Sitting across from her, he sipped his margarita.

Maria entered and placed a bowl of taco chips in front of him. '*Gracias*,' he said.

'*De nada*.'

He watched her walk away. 'I sure wish I had one of those,' he said.

'I wish I didn't.'

'What would you want to do, stay home all day?'

11

'Wouldn't mind. After Geoffrey was born I did it for three months and loved it.'

'What about the museum?'

'It'd still be there when I'm ready for it again. But like they say, the bills won't pay themselves. So I guess I stay with the museum and Maria stays with Geoffrey.'

'With what Larry makes—'

'I don't want anything more from him. It's bad enough I have to take the child support.' Looking down at the baby, Susan said, 'I'm sure glad Geoffrey doesn't know what a creep his father is.' She smiled at the boy, who stopped sucking long enough to grin. White formula trickled from the corner of his mouth. She dabbed it away with a soft tissue, then looked up at Tag. 'How about staying for dinner?'

'I'd sure like to. I have to get out of here, though. Class tonight. Crowd Management Techniques.'

'You still have to eat.'

'I'll grab something in my apartment.'

When he finished his margarita, he went to Susan and kissed her. 'How about later?' he asked.

'How much later?'

'Ten-thirty, eleven.'

'That's my bedtime,' Susan said.

Tag grinned. 'I know.'

'I didn't get much sleep last night.'

'Me neither.'

'That's for sure.'

'How about it?' Tag asked, smiling.

'How can I refuse?'

He kissed her again. 'See you later, alligator.' He rubbed Geoffrey's head.

Geoffrey belched.

'Excuse yourself, kid.'

As Tag took the elevator to the fifth floor, he considered skipping class and taking up Susan on her dinner invitation. He needed the class, though; with the sergeant's exam scheduled for next month, he needed all the help he could get.

The doors slid open and he stepped into the hallway. He turned left. The corridor stretched out silent and narrow. Though he'd never been in a submarine, he often thought of them when he walked these halls.

A guy could get claustrophobia. A guy could get short of air. So short he finds himself rubbing his throat, his breath coming in short, painful tugs.

As he stepped around the corner, he saw something heaped on the floor. Something the size of a body, covered by faded, grimy cloth.

In front of his door.

He moved toward it, hand darting to the firearm at his waist.

Chapter Two

The heap in front of Tag's apartment door moved. A head appeared, hair slicked down with filth, face bloated, blotchy and pale.

Tag recognized it at once. He stopped running. Took his hand away from the pistol. 'Mable,' he said.

She smiled by raising her lip. More of a canine snarl than a human smile. From the look of her mouth, her missing teeth were the lucky ones. She rolled until she was sitting up, her back against the door. She straightened the dress over her thick thighs.

'I come to see you, babes,' she murmured.

'How did you find me?'

'Got your name offa your name tag, you know? Got it right offa your tag. That little plastic gadget on your uniform. Then I looked you up.'

'What for?'

''Cause you're my kinda guy. Give a gal a lift, would ya?' She reached out her hand. Tag didn't want to touch the blotchy mitt. Refusing would be awkward, though. Besides, he felt sorry for Mable. She was forty years old and lived with her mother, a slovenly woman who could pass for Mable's old sister, if she stood on the kind side of the street light, that was. Last week, Mable ran into half a dozen members of the Braves, a Pony League team sponsored by a local hardware store. It started with name-calling. Ended with a gang bang.

'When did they let you out of the hospital?' Tag asked. Taking the offered hand, he helped her up.

'Yesterday. First thing I says to myself, I says "Mable, that nice officer Parker is your kinda guy." So I looked you up and come right over here just to see ya. Ya gonna let a girl in?'

'I have to go out tonight, Mable.'

'I'll go with you, hmmm?'

He opened his door. 'Can't,' he said.

She followed him into his apartment, gave it a quick inspection with dreamy Demerol eyes, and whistled. 'Say, this is some nice place.'

14

'Thank you.'

'Won't hurt me at all, waiting here. Hmm?'

'Waiting?'

'Sure. You come back, I'll show you a time and a half, babes.'

'I don't think that's a good idea, Mable.' He went into the kitchen. Mable didn't follow, so he quickly took a handful of sliced salami and American cheese from his refrigerator, stuffed it all into a baggie and hurried back to the living room.

Mable's dress lay on the floor.

She was on the couch, naked but for black briefs and a red brassiere that barely cupped all she had to offer. Leering, she slid her tongue over her thick lips. One hand stroked a thick, blotched thigh. Cellulite rippled.

'Aw, Mable.'

'Put it right here,' she said. 'Come on, babes, don't be shy.'

Jeez. Shyness had little to do with it.

'I really shouldn't,' Tag said, trying to look only at her face. 'You're not ready for those kind of games just yet.'

'I'm tougher than I look. Come on, Tag, hold me tight for a little. I won't bite.'

No, maybe not, but I'd wager there's plenty in that tangle of hair that'd bite good and hard.

'Babes,' she cooed. 'I can take you places you've never been before.'

Damned right. The clap clinic. Front of the line. Pants down.

'I'm sorry, Mable.' He picked up her dress and tossed it to her. 'Thanks for your kind offer, but I have an important class tonight. Now get dressed. I'll walk you downstairs.'

'I ain't good enough for you, that it?'

'No, that's not it. I'm in a hurry, that's all.'

'I could have shown you a real good time. Hot and spicy, you dig?'

'I appreciate the offer.'

'Well, I'm staying put till you give me the goodies. Hmm?'

Tag groaned. He couldn't leave, not with Mable still in the apartment. The alternative? Tease those black panties down over her thighs, then . . . oh, man, no. She wasn't a bad person, just more than a little mad.

Mad. Sad. Horny. Hell, what a combination. 'Do you want some money?'

'What do you want me to do for money?'

'Nothing.'

15

'I'd do anything for you for free, babes.'

'Mable, listen to me, I'll give you money.'

'What for?'

'To leave,' he said. Blunt, okay, and he saw the pain in her eyes. 'I'm sorry, but I have no intention of making out with you. I have an important place I have to be in about five minutes. I'm already going to be late and I can't leave till you're out of here, so please get dressed and go.'

'I ain't good enough for you, that's it. I ain't pretty and cultivated like that whore downstairs.'

He glared, but said nothing.

'Sure . . . sure, I know all about you and her; how you stayed at her place last night, and me waiting for you here all cold and lonesome.'

'You're the one.'

'She's a scrawny nothing, babes. You just climb on here.'

'*You*'re the one who did it.'

'You're not gonna believe what I can do with my tongue.'

'You flattened her tire, didn't you?'

'Me? Not me. No sir, officer.'

'That was a rotten thing to do, Mable. Now get your dress on or I'll run you in.'

'What for?' A brassiere strap slipped, exposing a fat brown nipple.

'Indecent exposure.'

'Oh yeah?'

'That's right,' Tag said. 'Maybe a little trespass, too.'

'Okay, okay,' Mable hoisted up the strap cupping the dollop of breast. 'Hand me up my dress, will you?'

As Tag crouched beside the sofa to pick up the pile of dirty cloth, Mable grabbed him. She tugged his arm. Off balance, he fell onto her. Her arms clutched him tightly. Those hefty breasts felt like twin cushions against him. Sour breath rushed into his face. Her arms clutched him.

'Mable!' he snapped. 'Damn it, you'd better . . . !'

Her mouth pressed against his. Her tongue prodded his tightly sealed lips. Something warm and wet dribbled down his chin.

Trying to push away, his hands sank into those twin mounds of soft flesh beneath the brassiere. She moaned with excitement. 'Oh, that's it, Babes . . .'

'Mable . . . let go . . .'

Mable rolled. Both tumbled onto the floor.

'Get—'

16

Her thick tongue penetrated his mouth. The sour-milk odor made him gag. A hand pushed roughly under his belt, searching . . .

'No!'

He jerked his head back sharply, gasping for clean air. At the same moment, he tugged the roving hand from out of his pants and bent it backward at the wrist until Mable cried out. Using the hand for leverage, he forced her to roll off. He stood up, still keeping the hand bent.

'Okay,' he panted. 'On your feet.'

He helped her by twisting the arm.

'Bastard!' she cried out. 'Cocksucker!'

'Shut up, Mable.'

'Motherfu—' she yelped in pain as he gave the arm a quick turn.

'I said *shut up*.'

Using the twisted arm, he steered her toward the door. 'I don't want any more trouble from you, do you understand? I want you to go home.'

'No, I want—'

'I want you to go home and never pull this kind of stunt again. If you bother Susan or me, know what I'll do?'

'What?'

'I'll tell your mother.'

She jerked her head sideways and glared at him. 'You better not.'

'I will.'

'You better not,' she repeated. This time frightened.

'You be a good girl from now on, or I will.'

'All I wanted was to be nice to you. That's all I wanted. What's wrong with that?'

'The way you went about it. Now, I'll let go of you and I want you to get dressed, then go straight home. Okay?'

'Okay.' Her swollen lips formed a sulky pout.

He let go of her arm. She leaned heavily against the door, arms hanging at her sides, head down, mess of hair dangling across her eyes. Tag turned away. He picked up her dress, handed it to her, and turned his face away as she hauled it over herself. Then he opened the door.

He watched her walk slowly down the hall. Thirty years ago she'd have been a cute kid. Nice. Friendly. Polite in class. At night she'd have heard her mother going down on any guy with a dollar in the next room. It's hard to grow up decent . . . hard to grow up

17

sane . . . after a childhood like that. 'Good-bye, Mable. You take care of yourself, do you hear?'

She looked over her shoulder. He saw tears on her face. Sniffing loudly, she wiped her nose with the back of her hand, turned sadly away.

Tag shut the door. Locked it.

He glanced at his wristwatch.

Too late to bother with the damned class.

Feeling tired and bruised and dirty . . . like something thirty years dead had just crawled over his face . . . he went to the bathroom, turned on the shower. When it was scalding he stood under it, his face up to receive the driving jets.

Chapter Three

April Vallsarra, hands resting on the stone balustrade, enjoyed the cooling breeze playing against her cheek after the heat of the day.

She loved to stand here at night. The air was cool. She took pleasure from the sound of the crickets. The scent of the wildflowers out in the woods reached into her, calming her.

She listened to the music the trees made as air currents ran along the canyon. The surging hiss that would fall away to a whisper. It reminded her of the time she lived in the beach house with her father. The sound of the surf. Especially at night when she lay warm and safe in her bed. Then the waves would surge across the beach.

She stood listening to the sounds in the outside world. The breeze moved across the rooftop terrace, swirled round her bare calves and ankles, tugged at her dress, at her hair.

Often she tried to imagine what those trees looked like. They would move, she decided, like she'd heard how herds of elephants move. She could never know exactly, of course. She'd been born blind. Had to leave home at six years old to attend a school for the blind in San Francisco. That was when her world fell apart. Her parents' marriage broke up. Her mother moved to Canada and she never heard from her again.

She was so miserable at school that at the age of eleven years she tried to take her own life. Tying a noose from panty hose, she knotted it to the shower rail and jumped off the edge of the tub. The rail didn't take her weight; it snapped; she fell to the bathroom floor and broke her wrist.

Her father was the one who saved her.

After a long talk in the hospital, as she waited for her arm to receive the cast, he realized how unhappy she was at the school.

He brought her home.

It wasn't to the beach house, though.

The new home was here in the canyon. In one of the passes that snake between Hollywood and Burbank. Even though you were in the midst of three million people, here was an oasis of calm.

The canyon contained no other houses. Only this one. Her father built the house to his own design. His 'sneakaway', he called it. It was two-storied, built of brick. There was a huge rooftop terrace where her father could barbecue the biggest steaks. Where he could host the coolest parties that were the talk of LA. The guest list would read like the contents of *Rolling Stone* magazine.

By day her father recorded music in his own studio in the basement. And, Jeez, what a studio. John Lennon, dropping by for cocktails, announced, 'Sweet God in heaven, you could put the London Philharmonic Orchestra in here and still have room for the bloody performing elephants.'

The wind sighed in the trees. April tilted her head to one side. The air played on her neck, toying with her hair.

A beautiful place. Peaceful.

Away from everyone. Away from city noise and smog.

She considered what she could have for supper. A salad with shrimp. An ice-cold glass of white wine. Yes, that would be nice.

For a second she thought she heard the scrunch of a foot on the gravel path.

'Dad?'

The word reached her lips before she could stop it.

No.

Couldn't be.

Her father was dead. Shot by a pair of thugs he'd found breaking into his car. He'd been staying in a motel coming back from Nashville. He'd glanced out the window, seen the two morons cracking open his car like a money box. When he'd gone out to challenge them, one had pulled a pistol and . . .

Her hands tightened on the balustrade.

No. Not tonight.

She wouldn't replay the incident. That was ten years ago.

So now I'm here alone. She'd no sooner thought the word *alone* than the sound came again.

Feet on gravel.

But who's there at this time? No one would make the long drive out of town up here to see me in the middle of the night.

'Hello, who's there?'

Her blind eyes moved as if looking down onto the driveway below. She listened.

The wind cried through the trees. Leaves rustled.

'Anyone there?'

No answer. But the sound of a zipper being pulled slowly down.

20

'There *is* someone there.' Her heart raced. 'What do you want?'
She listened again, heart pounding.

What if it's an intruder?

I'm all alone here.

Lettie came out during the day to bring her groceries, help her clean the house and keep her company for a while. But Lettie was long gone now. Maybe she should phone—

That sound again. Feet on gravel.

Slowly she backed away from the balustrade toward the center of the roof terrace. It was dark. Yet, she knew sighted people still might be able to see her standing on top of the house. Here in the center, though, she'd be out of sight.

But what if they should break in?

Nothing she could do would stop them then. Even if she could reach the phone it would take a while for the police to reach this remote part of the canyon.

She was thirty-three years old. Men had told her how pretty she was. That her shoulder-length hair was glossy. She had a slim figure. Tanned arms and legs.

So whoever broke into the house might not be here for money or the TV.

But her.

A scrunching sound came again. Maybe they were trying to find a window without a steel shutter or an unlocked door.

Her father had been thorough. All the downstairs windows were sealed with steel mesh. After all, she didn't require daylight. Or *any* light, come to that.

The doors were of hardwood. The locks substantial. What was more, each one was covered by a wrought-iron screen.

Maybe they will try and climb up the wall? They'd find me alone on the roof.

Now, in the open, she felt vulnerable. She wished she had a companion to share her home. Someone strong to keep her safe.

She backed into a potted shrub. The leaves prickled her hip through the flimsy material of her dress.

She caught her breath.

Stay calm . . . stay calm. He cannot climb up here. I'm safe.

But was she?

April reached the barbecue and crouched down beside it, her arms clasped around her knees, trying to make herself small as possible.

For a long time she waited, hunched beneath the night sky. For a while the sounds beyond the house haunted her. She imagined a man scaling the outside with a ladder. Or finding an unshuttered window. She imagined the sound of footsteps. She even gasped out loud as she imagined rough hands on her. A fist grabbing her hair, another hand finding her breasts. The sound of the man's hoarse panting.

Shaking, her breath coming in frightened gasps, she waited and waited.

At last, when she heard no more sounds, she felt her way back down to her bedroom.

'Please, God,' she whispered after she climbed into bed. 'Please bring me a companion. Please bring someone to me. I don't want to be lonely anymore.'

Chapter Four

Barney Quinn, night watchman, didn't care much for the museum. It always seemed too damned stuffy, as if every piece of ancient junk was quietly giving off a stink. Going home in the morning, he smelled the same stink on himself. An old tomb stink. The stink of three-thousand-year-old skulls.

The same stink oozed from those shitty old stone statues in the Greek collection. *Jesus H*. Pretty soon, if he didn't watch out, he'd turn into one himself. And wouldn't that be dandy? Every last one of those buggers had an arm off, or a head, or even a pecker.

They'll open up one fine morning and say, 'Where's old Barney Quinn?' Won't find him till they look in the Greek room and count up the statues. One too many. And here's a statue in a shitty brown uniform. Maybe they'll just leave him standing there, save his family the price of a funeral. Spend that insurance on a new TV. Damn squat for old Barney Quinn. Leave him here in the statue morgue until some clumsy cleaner knocks his pecker clean off. RIP old Barney Quinn.

'Shit,' he muttered.

Need some fresh air. Need some time outta here. Besides, it was about time to visit George.

Crossing the lobby, he went to a metal fire door, shoved it open. The landing was lighted by a bulb over the door. He started down the stairs. *Damn*: the light at the next landing was out. He stepped down into the darkness. At the bottom, he pushed open the outer door. He stepped outside and leaned against the door, propping it open with his back.

The employees' parking lot was empty except for his old Grand Prix. Used to be a good car. Used to be his pride and joy back when he bought it. Everything was good in those days. Before the brass got wind of the Fun House and kicked his ass off the force.

Well, shit, can't win 'em all, can ya?

He lit a cigarette. As he dragged on it, filling his lungs with sweet blue tobacco smoke that went a-tingling and a-singing to his fingertips, he saw the dog near the edge of the lot. Old George, right on time. Pinching the cigarette between his lips, he crouched and clapped his hands. 'Here, boy,' he called. 'Come on. Come to Barney.'

The dog loped toward him, its collar tags jangling.

'Yeah, there's a good guy.'

George ran into his arms, licking his face, damn near knocking the cigarette out of his mouth. 'Yeah, that's my good boy. Sure you are. Bet you're hungry, huh?'

The thick, brown tail swished.

'Come on, then. See what Barney's got fer yer.' After propping the museum door open, Barney walked to his car. The dog kept ahead of him, glancing back impatiently, brown eyes twinkling in the meager street light.

'Hold your horses, boy.'

Barney unlocked his car. Reaching into the glove compartment, he took out a cellophane bag containing a ball of raw hamburger. 'Isn't much, fella,' he apologized. 'You like it, though, don't you? Sure. You keep coming back for more. A satisfied customer.'

He opened the bag. The hamburger was still partly frozen, but it was soft enough to break up. He twisted off chunks and gave them to George. Some he tossed for the dog to catch, enjoying the quick snap that snatched the pieces out of the air. Others he held in his hand. George took these like a gentleman, lifting them delicately away with his front teeth before swallowing.

'That's all, pal,' Barney said, smiling.

George looked up, eyes wide, hopeful.

'All she wrote, fella.'

Kneeling, Barney let the dog lick his fingers. 'Yep. All gone. You come back tomorrow night, though. I'll have some more tasty bits and pieces for you.'

He walked back to the open door of the museum, George prancing beside him.

'Gotta say goodnight, George old pal.'

He patted the brown fur of the dog's back and pulled the door shut. Then he turned on his flashlight and climbed the stairs. Would have to leave maintenance a note about the bulb down there. A guy could break his back there in the dark. Only took one little slip.

At the first landing, he pushed open the metal door and stepped into the lobby. It was dimly lighted. Switching off the flashlight, he hung it back on his belt, then headed for the front doors. Better be certain they're still secure before making the tour of the main floor.

24

As he turned away from them he heard the *thump.*

Like something wooden falling to the floor. He listened for more sounds, but the museum was silent.

He thought: *That's grave silence, Barney*: a silence to be *felt.*

It had probably been nothing, that thump: a shelf giving way upstairs, or a wire snapping so a piece of that ancient junk fell to the floor. On the other hand . . .

Damn it – he should have kept an eye on the door while he was out feeding George. Some kids might have sneaked in. Or some bum looking for a place to sleep. Or even a damn cat.

Silently, he walked to the main stairway. As he climbed, he scanned the second-floor balcony through the rods of its railing. The area looked clear.

He wished he had his piece, just in case. Damned museum wouldn't let him carry a gun; said they didn't want anybody hurt. 'If there's trouble, Barney, call the cops.' *Sure. I call the cops, and they find a pussy cat in the Callahan Collection.* That'd confirm to everyone down at the station that old Barney was a washed-up piece of horseshit all right. Calling out a SWAT team to save Barney from some liddle puddy cat. *Yeah, right.*

Hell.

Did seem like the noise came from there. He wondered how he got that impression: just because the Callahan Room was closer to the stairway than the others? He stepped to the entrance. Peered in. Dark. Very dark. No light in the room. He could only see vague shapes. Reaching down, he unhooked the cordon and let it hang. His fingers found the switches. *Snick.* A dozen bulbs, concealed above tinted ceiling panels, filled the room with soft light.

Well, how'd that happen?

The lid of the mummy's coffin lay on the floor.

Barney, standing motionless, scanned the room: the display case full of jewelry that was a mass of golds and sky blues, the chariot wheel, the dozens of statuettes, the stone jars, the coffin.

No one there.

Unless some intruder was crouched at the far end of the display case? *They can see me but I can't see them. Are they watching me standing there? Hoping that I shrug and turn away.* Nothing doing. Time to move on to the next floor.

No. Barney, with all those years on the force, wasn't going to be fooled so easily.

Silently, he walked along the case to its end. It concealed nobody.

25

Okay, so how did the coffin lid get on the floor?
Disturbed by a cat?
Hardly.
Toppled by kids?
Maybe.
Wish I'd got my piece.
Colt .38. Hollow-nose slugs. *Pop one of those caps and the perp's going down.*

He pushed the coffin lid with his toe. Heavy sucker. Stepping over it, he looked into the coffin. He stared at the mummy, feeling a tightness of nausea in his throat.

Hell . . . she looked like *hell.*

Once, when Barney was still a rookie cop, he helped a fireman drag a charred body from the debris of a burned apartment house. A crispy critter, the fireman called it.

This gal wasn't a crispy critter, but she didn't look any better than one. Looked worse, for that matter. Like someone had let the air out of her tits.

He didn't like seeing that red hair on her head, either – how glossy, even how beautiful it looked – not when the rest of her body was such a wreck.

Glancing down her naked body, he saw that she had no pubic hair. Well, damned if he was going to dwell on it. Best put it out of sight.

He crouched. Lifted the coffin lid. Heavy as a door. *Christ.* But he managed to get it onto the coffin.

Turning away, Barney swept his gaze around the room. Everything appeared fine. He walked to the doorway, turned off the lights; darkness swooped back into the room . . . and he jumped at the crash of wood behind him.

Barney whirled round. In the gloom he could make out that the coffin lid was on the floor again.

'Holy shit,' he muttered.

He stared at the lid. Felt sick and chilled . . . and for some reason his balls seemed to shrivel up into the pit of his stomach. A prickling sensation ran up his forearms as the hairs stood on end, feeling for all the world like a hideous spider had dropped from the darkness onto his bare arm and was scurrying up toward his head, determined to climb into his mouth. He rubbed his face. It felt cold. It felt numb, too, as if his nerve endings were in retreat from that awful darkness.

He wanted out; he wanted out fast. But he was afraid to turn his back on the coffin. Afraid, if he turned away . . .

26

It happened.
The thing he dreaded in the pit of bones that was his skeleton.
It happened like deep down he knew it would.
Swift as someone startled from sleep, the mummy sat up.

Chapter Five

'Hey, A-rab . . . move your ass.'

Imad sipped his neat gin; didn't acknowledge the man.

'You hear me? Move your ass. My lady friend wants that stool.'

'Sir,' Imad intoned, 'your lady friend *is* that stool.'

'Yeah, what's that supposed to mean?'

Imad looked at the girl. She wore tight, faded jeans and a dirty T-shirt. The T-shirt only half there; cut off just below the breasts. The breasts were tiny with points like nails.

Her eyes, with half-shut lids, had a lazy and insolent look.

Imad sipped his drink. 'Does my meaning evade you, sir?'

'Huh.'

'Your lady friend is shit . . . and you're a fly.'

The fist slammed the side of Imad's head, knocking him off the barstool. His back hit the floor. Shouts filled the bar.

The man had him by the wrists, was dragging him across the floor, was pumped up with fury. The girl in jeans hopped alongside him. Imad could see up her shirt. Saw the two small mounds of breast had no jiggle. A shame. He liked a little jiggle. These were made of stone; hardly arousing at all.

The man flung open a side door. 'Gimme a hand,' he snapped.

'Sure, Blaze.'

Blaze? A cute name. A name for a horse.

The girl bent down and helped lift Imad. He staggered between them. Raising his head, he saw that they had brought him into a deserted alley. The walls of the building pressed close. Far down the narrow passageway, cars passed on the street. The alley smelled ripe with garbage.

'Now we'll see who's a fly on shit, camel-fucker.'

Blaze jerked Imad away from the girl. Shoved him against a garbage can. The ripe, fetid smell leaped into his sensitive nostrils with every breath.

The girl giggled. 'Blaze on him!'

As Blaze gripped the back of his collar, Imad reached deep into

28

the sweating garbage. He found a beer bottle. As Blaze jerked him round he swung the bottle and broke it against Blaze's head.

The girl went silent. Now the lazy eyes snapped suddenly wide. Wondering what was coming next.

Blaze dropped to his knees, then fell forward, his face hitting the ground with a *slap*.

Imad turned to the girl.

She laughed once through her nose. One side of her mouth smiled. 'Guess you fixed *him*.' She tried the door of the bar. It was locked.

Softly he spoke. 'Come here.'

'You better not try nuthin'.'

'Come here.'

She took a hesitant step toward him, then stopped. 'Say, mister . . . you wouldn't hurt a girl, would you?'

'Come here.'

She glanced up the alley. Laughed quietly. ''Bout time somebody fixed Blaze,' she said, stepping toward him. 'He's such a prick.'

She flinched as Imad touched her cheek.

'You are a beautiful woman,' Imad told her.

'Me? Hell, you called me shit – I've got ears.'

He slid a hand under her T-shirt. Her small breasts felt firm, but not like concrete. Not at all. The turgid nipples were pliant under his fingers.

Her smile trembled.

'You are a flower,' Imad murmured. 'A lovely, fragile flower.'

'Yeah?' She shook her head.

'Come with me.'

She looked down at Blaze who was still motionless in the ripe goo that dripped from the trashcan. 'Just a sec,' she whispered. Crouching, she shoved a hand into a front pocket of Blaze's jeans. It returned with a pack of bills fastened into a thick, square mat with paper clips.

'Two hundred bucks,' she said. 'We'll split it even-steven, okay?'

'Is it yours?'

'Is now.'

'Did this man take it from you?'

'Hell, no. It's what's left of his pay from Market King.'

'Market King?'

'You know? The grocery store? He's a checker. That's how we met.'

'Let Mr Blaze keep his money,' Imad told her.

29

'No.'

'I do not countenance theft.'

'Huh?'

'I won't allow it. Return the money.'

'Aw, shit.'

'At once.'

'Please, mister?'

'At once,' he commanded.

With a frown over her shoulder at Imad, she tucked the pack of bills back into Blaze's pocket.

Imad held out his hand. She went to it. Took it.

'Where we going?' she asked, walking with him down the alley.

'To my home.'

'Yeah? Where's that?'

'In Greenside.'

'Greenside *Estates*? In Burlingdale?'

He nodded.

'Sure. I'll believe that when I see it.'

When they reached his gray Mercedes, she looked at him with suspicion. 'This yours?'

'Certainly.' He opened the door for her and she climbed in.

Imad went to the other side to slip into the driver's seat. As he started the car the girl said, 'You must be one of them Arab oil bastards, huh?'

'Wrong. My parents were Egyptian. I have nothing to do with oil. In addition, my birth was entirely legitimate.'

'Yeah? How you come to live in a ritzy place like Greenside?'

'How come you don't?'

She laughed. 'Shit, who's got that kind of money?'

'I do.'

'You're so loaded, how come you were over at a dump like Shannon's?'

'One meets an interesting set,' he told her.

'Set, huh?' She leaned against him. 'How's mine?'

'Just fine,' he said. Putting an arm behind her, he slipped his hand under her T-shirt. He stroked the smooth skin of her side. Stretching, he reached the breast.

He'd had many women in the months since Callahan's death. He'd met them at parties, in bars, at a university class in anthropology that he took only for that purpose, at church. Whenever possible, he brought them home for the night. He didn't like being alone in the house he'd inherited.

30

Not at all. It held too much pain for him.

His shame at running away.

His confusion at Callahan staying to be killed.

The memories of the terrible morning when he returned to the house. Finding Callahan naked on the bedroom floor, his skin tattered, chunks torn from him and scattered about as if a beast had tried to devour him but found his flesh unsavory and spit out mouthfuls on the carpet.

The hunt for the mummy. Finding it, at last, wedged behind the refrigerator. Glossy red hair hanging down. Eyeless sockets in the face: twin pits of darkness. Shriveled lips. White teeth.

Nailing it into its coffin.

Then the grim business of the dogs. Carrying them, one at a time, upstairs to Callahan's bedroom. Using their teeth on the grotesque body, tearing the dead flesh until all traces of human teeth were obliterated. The police interrogation. Always back to the gun. Where's the gun, the .22 Callahan used on the attacking dogs? Imad only shrugged. The cops knew it was all wrong: no gun, not nearly enough blood in the room. They suspected Imad. Guessed he'd had a hand in all this. After all, he would inherit the estate. Without evidence, though, they never arrested him.

Alone in the house, he felt haunted by what had happened there. With a woman he had little trouble keeping the memories away.

This one looked at him, half grinning, as the iron gate swung open.

'I got it,' she said. 'You're the chauffeur.'

He began, as usual, with a tour of the house. Though the girl was obviously awestruck by the lavishly furnished rooms, she kept grinning wryly, shaking her head, making sarcastic remarks.

Until they reached the master bedroom.

That was when Imad turned her to face him. He pulled the T-shirt over her head, enjoying the way her small breasts moved as she raised her arms. He unfastened the waist of her jeans. The open zipper revealed a deep V of pale skin, curls of pubic hair, no panties. He peeled the jeans down her legs. She kicked off her sandals and stepped out of the jeans.

She moved back, fixing him with a crooked smile. 'Find what you're looking for?' she asked.

'I believe so, yes.'

'Know what to do with it?'

31

'The bathtub's that way.' He pointed to a door behind him. 'You may have half an hour.'

'What for?'

'To bathe.'

She laughed. 'Afraid you'll get your pretty hands dirty?'

'I do not intend to wallow in the residue left by my predecessors.'

'Huh?' The heavy-lidded stare again. Insolent. Ignorant somehow.

'Take your bath. I'll shower in the other room and prepare drinks for us. What do you prefer?'

'Rum and Coke.'

Imad grinned. 'Certainly.'

Wrapped in a towel, she entered the bedroom. Her wet hair clung to her head; her skin rosy.

'You look delightful,' Imad told her. He handed her the drink.

'Here's how,' she said.

They drank. Imad's neat gin tasted fine. He put down his glass and reached for the girl.

'Not so fast,' she said. 'We've got a little matter to settle first.'

'Ah.' Imad smiled, hoping to hide his disappointment. 'A financial matter, I assume.'

'You're quick on your feet.'

'Would a hundred dollars be appropriate?'

'Two hundred.'

Imad laughed. 'In that case, you'd best get dressed. I'll call you a cab.' He turned toward the door.

'Hundred-fifty,' she offered.

'I'll make the call.'

'One-thirty.'

'One hundred . . . with a bonus if you deserve it.'

'Who decides *that*?'

'I do, of course.'

'How much bonus?'

'Whatever I think suitable. Agreed?'

'But a hundred for sure?'

'One hundred for sure.'

'Why not?' She plucked a corner of the towel. It dropped away.

Imad stepped close to her. She slipped open his cloth belt. Parted the bathrobe. Her eyes widened. 'God Almighty, where'd you get a thing like that?'

'I inherited it from my father.'

She took it in her hands and it grew mightily. 'Who was your father? Babe Ruth?' She laughed at her joke. 'Bet you've hit a lot of homers with this.'

He nodded. 'Yes, indeed, I have frequently scored.' He arched his back, trembling with pleasure, as she drew her tongue up the underside of his erect shaft.

Chapter Six

Susan was watching the TV news when her doorbell rang. 'Who is it?' she asked.

'Tag.'

She let him in. 'So how was your class?'

'I didn't go.' They sat down together on the couch. 'Turned out there's this girl who finds me irresistible.'

'It's your aftershave,' Susan said.

'I don't know what it is, but she showed up in front of my door.'

'Who? I thought you meant me.' Susan felt a knot of anxiety. Here it comes . . . so long . . . thanks for everything . . . stay just good friends, huh?

He shook his head. 'Mable Rudge. Took me a while to get rid of her.'

'Three hours?'

'Ten, fifteen minutes. Seemed like hours, though. Then I had a shower.'

'Together?'

'Jeez, no. She was the other side of a locked door by then. But I didn't feel much like facing anyone, you know?'

'Pretty bad, huh?'

'Awful.'

'Recovered?'

'Better all the time.'

'Maybe this will help.' She kissed him on the lips.

'It's a start,' Tag admitted, taking her into his arms. 'It's most definitely a start.'

In the morning, during breakfast, Tag offered to drive her to work.

'I don't have another flat, do I?'

'Not that I know of. I'd just like to drive you to work. It's my day off. Besides, it'll give me an excuse to pick you up this afternoon.'

'Sounds good to me.'

'How does dinner sound?'

'Great.'

Later, in the parking lot, Tag didn't head directly for the exit. Instead, he circled and drove past Susan's car. 'See?' he said. 'No flat.'

'You expected one, didn't you?'

'Let's say it wouldn't have surprised me much. My charming friend Mable is a very jealous lady.'

'Is she the one who did it yesterday?'

Tag nodded. 'With any luck, we've seen the last of her. She knows she'll be in big trouble if she pulls any more stunts.'

'Hope so.'

The drive from Susan's apartment to the museum usually took just over fifteen minutes on the Santa Monica Freeway. Tag made it in twelve.

'You've got a heavy foot there, bud,' Susan said.

'Force of habit.'

'Do you drive that way in your patrol car?'

'Faster, when I can. Nothing better than a Code Three. Really let her rip.'

He turned onto the road leading to the museum. Ahead of them, several police cars were parked near the entrance. Tag pulled alongside one of them. Like the other cars, it was empty. Tag and Susan got out. He took her hand and they hurried up the concrete steps toward the museum's main door.

A white-haired woman reached the top before them.

'I'm sorry, ma'am,' said the patrolman guarding the doors. 'You won't be able to go in, just now.'

'Of course I will.'

'It's a crime scene. Unless you're an employee of the museum, I'll have to ask you to leave. If you want to come back in an hour or so . . .'

'I'm here now, young man. I have no intention of going away.'

'I'm afraid I can't let you in.'

'You most certainly can. What's more, you *will*. This is a public museum. I am a member of the public. I have every right to visit the museum.'

'It's a crime scene, ma'am.'

'That's no concern of mine. Did I commit the crime? No, I should say not. So you just step aside, like a good fellow.'

He didn't step aside.

35

'Out of my way.'

'Ma'am,' the patrolman said, 'we think that perpetrator might still be inside.'

'Oh? *Oh!*' The old woman hurried away with fearful backward glances at the building.

'Nice touch, Henderson,' Tag said.

Henderson grinned.

Tag turned to Susan. 'Susan, this smooth-tongued devil is Manny Henderson. Manny, Susan.'

'Nice to meet you,' she said, offering her hand. As Henderson shook it, his eyes dropped briefly to her breasts.

'What happened here?' Tag asked.

'Huh?'

'You told the gal it's a crime scene.'

'Oh. Right. The night watchman turned up dead. Looks like he took a header down the stairs, broke his neck. Homicide's checking it out. They seem to think he walked into a burglary. Either he tripped over himself trying to get away, or they grabbed him and gave him the heave-ho.'

'Who was the watchman?' Susan asked.

'Quinn. Barney Quinn.'

Susan nodded, relieved that she didn't know the dead man. 'Was anything stolen?' she asked.

'Looks like they made off with a mummy.'

'Amara?'

'A mummy,' Henderson repeated.

'Amara,' Tag said. 'That's its name.'

'What?'

'The mummy's name is Amara.'

'Hell, you mean they give 'em names?'

'They're dead people, Henderson.'

'I know that. Hey, do you want to go in or something?'

'Trying to get rid of us?' Tag asked.

'Just you.' He turned to Susan. 'You should stay away from this guy, you know. He'll get you in all kinds of jams.'

'I'll be careful,' Susan assured him. 'See you later.'

They entered the museum. Across the lobby, the body of the night watchman lay at the foot of the main stairway. Susan saw how his left leg hung sideways below the knee, and how his head had a crooked tilt. How the eyes stared. A horrible sight. A flash unit blinked. The photographer stepped over one of the outstretched arms, and crouched for a shot from a different angle.

36

Beyond where the body lay, she saw Blumgard, the museum director, talking to a man in a brown suit. A detective, probably. Blumgard looked pale. Jumpy. Even from this distance, she could see the stem of his pipe shaking as he raised it to his lips.

Tag led her toward the body. 'Morning, Farley,' he greeted the photographer.

'Hi, Parker. Isn't this your day off?'

'I'm ever-vigilant. All right if we go upstairs?'

'Help yourselves.'

They climbed the stairway. As they entered the Callahan Room, a small, pale man glanced at them from where he crouched by the coffin lid. He lowered his eyes again and finished pressing a strip of cellophane to an index card.

'Getting some good latents off there?' Tag asked.

'Quite a bunch.'

'A few belong to me and the lady here.'

'That so? You're Porter?'

'Parker.'

He wrote the name down. 'And?'

'Susan Connors,' Tag told him. 'She works here.'

'What department?'

'I'm an assistant curator,' she explained. 'This room's my responsibility.'

'Then you must know the missing mummy. Have you talked to Vasquez?'

She shook her head.

Tag turned to her. 'Why don't you have a look round and see if anything else is missing?'

'I have a checklist in my office.'

'Let's get it.'

'Whoa. Before you take off for parts unknown, I want your prints. It'll speed things up for me. You first, Potter. Give me your hand.'

Farley climbed to the second floor. He took a downward shot of the stairs; the body sprawled at the bottom. From his angle, framed by the camera, the stairs looked damned steep. The poor guy must've had quite a time of it. Probably headfirst.

Farley was having quite a time of it himself. Those three glazed doughnuts on his way over had nearly run their course. If he didn't get to the men's room pretty soon . . . somewhere up here, there had to be one. He walked to the right, checking each door as he approached it. Near the end of the hall, he found one marked *Women*.

A good omen.

Sure enough, the next door was the one he wanted. He shoved it open, hurried across the tile floor. This one was a three-stall job. He rushed to the first, started to push its door. He met unexpected resistance. Surprised, he took his hand away. The door bumped shut.

'Ooops, sorry.'

He waited for someone to reply.

No one did.

'Y' ought to latch the door, you know, buddy. Hey, you all right in there? Huh?' He waited. 'Anyone in there? Hello?' Squatting, he ducked his head low enough to see under the door. Instead of Florsheims, he found a pair of brown withered feet. Brown shriveled toenails. Brown bone-thin shins.

He shoved the door open, flinging the mummy backwards. Its head thumped the tile wall behind the toilet, and it slid down, bare feet skidding towards Farley like a mannequin trying to sit down.

Tag jumped aside as the bathroom door shot open and Farley ran out. The photographer stopped short. His face had a sick, gray look.

'What's wrong?' Tag asked.

'I found the missing mummy. In there.'

'I'll go tell Susan.'

They walked up the hallway. Tag noticed how Farley's hand trembled. 'That mummy's a real charmer, isn't she?'

'You've seen her?' Farley asked.

'All of her.'

Farley ran a hand over the sleek top of his head. 'Jeepers creepers. I've photographed all kinds . . . you name it. Gunshot victims, slice and dice, torched corpses, gals with their guts stuffed in their mouths, guys who've been buried in all kinds of shit for years on end . . . but that one?'

'She has that effect on people, doesn't she?'

'Seen prettier.'

'You okay?'

'Sure, just caught me by surprise.' He ran his hand over his head again like he was trying to wipe the image from his brain. 'Aren't mummies supposed to be to be wrapped? Those ones in the movies, they're always bandaged up nice, you know?'

'This one's a stripper.'

38

'She looks like crap.'

'The years haven't been kind to her,' Tag admitted, grinning.

He found Susan in the Callahan Room, checking exhibits against the inventory list on her clipboard.

'How goes it?' he asked.

'Looks like everything is here but Amara.'

'She's not far,' Tag said.

'You found her?'

'Farley did.'

'She's all right?'

Farley shook his head. 'She looked like . . . looked terrible. All that red hair. That looks great, but it's how it seems to grow out of the skull . . . makes your stomach . . .' Gulping, he clutched his belly, turned away and wished to God he'd passed on those doughnuts.

Susan hurried down the hall ahead of them. When she reached the restroom door, however, she stopped. She turned to wait for Tag. 'Maybe you should go in first. I mean . . . make sure the coast is clear.'

Farley groaned. 'Miss, the coast won't be clear till she's outta there and I'm afraid I can't wait all day.'

'There's a toilet on the ground floor,' Susan told him. 'Just to the left as you come in.'

'Thanks. Enjoy yourselves.' He hurried to the stairway.

'I'll have a look,' Tag said. He pushed open the door, stepped inside. Nobody at the sinks. Nobody at the urinals. One body in the first stall, its feet visible just below the door. 'Okay,' Tag called. 'You can come in now.'

Susan entered, looking slightly embarrassed. She glanced from the sinks to the urinals.

'Don't believe me, huh?'

'Just checking.'

She walked ahead of Tag to the stall. He watched her crouch and peer under the door, the fabric of her blouse pulling taut across her back, coming untucked from the skirt, showing a band of smooth skin.

'That's Amara, all right,' she said. Standing, she eased open the door.

Tag, just behind her, looked in. The mummy lay straight as a slab of wood with her head against the pipes, her back on the toilet seat, her legs stretched toward the open door, her red hair tumbling down onto the tiles.

'What'll we do with her?' Tag asked.

'Pick her up.'

'Us? Don't you have maintenance men or something?'

'We're the something. Ready?'

'Well . . .'

'Scared?'

'Who, me?'

'We should wear gloves, so our skin moisture won't . . .'

'Great! Good idea! I'm all for gloves!'

'Back in a flash.' Susan smiled a knowing smile. 'You stay here and keep an eye on her.'

He followed Susan to the door, but stayed inside when she left. Turning, he looked at the stall. He could see the mummy's dark feet and ankles. They were brown. A shiny glossy brown that reminded him of chocolate bars. *Great. Won't want to eat another Hershey bar for a long time coming. Every time I bite into chocolate I'll imagine I'm running my tongue over that four-thousand-year-old foot with its evil-looking toenails. Hell, won't eat almond flakes, come to that.*

He glanced at his wristwatch, hoping Susan would hurry. This was his day off, after all, and standing watch over a withered corpse with brown paper tits wasn't his idea of a good time. He could do that at work; often had.

In fact, this reminded him a lot of his first dead body. It had been in a john, too. Houston, his partner, laughed himself sick at how they found the fat old gal, butt to the wind, head jammed in the waste basket. Said she must be an acrobat. As it turned out, she'd had a heart attack while she was taking a leak and tumbled forward until her head stuck in the waste basket. Tag never could see the humor in it, but Houston wouldn't let it go. Recently, he'd started tying it in with a Polack joke about burying stiffs with their butts up, for parking bikes.

The bathroom door shot open, missing Tag by inches. He stepped out of the way as Maurice Henderson hurried in. 'Parker,' Henderson said, barely giving him a glance as he hurried by.

'How's it going out front?'

'A pain.' At the first urinal, he unzipped his fly.

'You sure you want to do that?' Tag asked.

'Huh?'

'We've got a visitor.' Tag pointed at the stall.

Henderson looked. His face wrinkled as if he smelled something foul. Quickly, he zipped up.

'Meet Amara.'

'Holy Jesus.' Henderson stepped cautiously toward the stall and pushed open its door. For a long time, he stared. 'What the hell's she doing here?'

'Apparently she can't read.'

'Funny. Ha ha. Good God, did you get a look at those tits? Look like flapjacks.'

Someone knocked on the door. 'Come on in, we're all decent,' Tag called.

Susan entered and smiled a greeting at Henderson. 'Glad you're here, Maurice. You wouldn't mind giving us a hand, would you?'

'A hand with what?'

'Amara. We have to move her back to her own room.'

'You mean, *touch* her?'

'That shouldn't bother a couple of tough cops like you.' She held out a pair of gloves to each of them. 'I'll supervise.' Smiling, she stepped to the stall door, pushed it open, and held it in place. 'Once you've snapped on the latex, one of you take her shoulders, one her feet, and we'll just ease her out of here nice and steady.'

'We'd better call in the homicide boys first.' Tag grinned, glad he'd found a delaying tactic.

'Yeah, Christ. If we screw around with this gal before they've got their pictures and shit . . .' Henderson shook his head.

The homicide team spent less than half an hour in the men's room. They took statements and photographs, made sketches, lifted fingerprints, vacuumed the tiles under the stall, then left.

'Your turn,' Susan said.

Tag gripped the mummy's thin ankles; Henderson took the shoulders.

'You sure she won't break in half?' Tag asked.

'Maybe you should get her higher on the legs. At the knees?'

'All set,' Tag said.

'All set.' Henderson nodded.

They both lifted.

'She's sure light,' Henderson said, surprised.

'She's been dehydrated,' Susan explained. 'Hollowed out, too.'

'How do you mean?' Henderson asked.

Susan opened the bathroom door and they carried the mummy into the hall. 'They start by removing the brain,' she said. 'They run a probe through the nose, and break through the ethmoid bone into the cranial cavity. Then they use a little hooking device to bring out the brain through the nostrils, piece by piece.'

'Who *is* this woman?' Henderson asked Tag.

'My sweetheart.'

'Lucky you.'

She grinned. 'Once the cranial cavity was cleaned out, they cut into the torso and removed all the organs except the heart. During some dynasties the heart went, too. That's what you'll find in those stone canopic jars beside her coffin: her stomach, liver, kidneys, intes—'

'Susan.'

'You wanted to know why she's light.'

'Now we know,' Tag said.

'How come she isn't wrapped in bandages?' Henderson asked, unable to take his eyes from the shriveled torso. 'I thought they were supposed to wrap these things.'

'They did.' Susan walked ahead of them into the Callahan room. 'Somewhere along the line, someone removed them from this one.'

'For God's sake, why?'

'We don't know,' Susan replied. 'Okay, you can lower her now. Nice and gently does it. Good. Fine.'

Tag was glad to be rid of the body. He stepped away from the coffin to peel off his gloves.

'Grave robbers might have unwrapped her for her jewelry,' Susan said. 'Or the bandages might have been used to make paper or even medicine.'

'She's making this up,' Tag warned.

Henderson shook his head. 'The sweet nothings she must whisper into your ear at nights, old buddy. It'd give me the heebie-jeebies.'

Susan smiled. 'The paper bit isn't likely. It used to happen, though. In fact, there was an American who got involved in that. A guy named Stanwood, who had a paper mill in Maine. He used mummy wrappings in the nineteenth century for the rag content of his paper. He couldn't get it white, so he sold it to some local butchers for meat wrapping . . . it started a cholera epidemic.'

'A storehouse of knowledge,' Tag said. He turned to the finger-print man, who was now gaping into the coffin. 'Can we put the lid on now? I guess the old gal could use her privacy.'

The fingerprint man nodded. 'Sure. I'll give you a hand.'

The three men lifted it. As they set it into place on the coffin, Tag saw Susan crouch and pick up a bright chunk of metal. It looked like gold.

'What's that?'

'Part of a seal.' She showed how it fit, like a bit of a jigsaw puzzle into a broken disk of gold on the lid. 'See?'

'It looks like gold.'

'I'm sure it is gold,' she said.

'Right out in the open?'

'This section'll be closed to the public, at least for the time being. We're having a special display case made up for the coffin – with temperature and humidity controls, and a burglar alarm.'

'When will that be ready?'

'In about a week.'

'Hope you still have something to put in it.'

Chapter Seven

Imad woke the girl with his tongue. He licked her breasts, leaving the nipples slick and erect. He licked a trail down her belly. He probed her navel, then the moist cleft between her legs. She stroked his hair as his tongue darted. Soon, her chest was heaving. Her fingers twisted his hair. Her knees lifted and she writhed, rubbing herself against his mouth.

Without stopping, Imad pulled her by the legs. He knelt on the floor at the foot of the bed. He kept pulling. Her buttocks came off the mattress and she slid down, crying out as his stout penis impaled her.

They fell and tumbled. On top of her, Imad finished with quick, hard thrusts that jolted her whole body beneath him.

She hugged him tightly, panting.

'You've earned the bonus,' Imad said.

'Have I?' she gasped.

He pulled slowly out of her, stood up, slipped on his robe.

The girl sat up, her hand against her tingling groin. 'Does that mean we're done?'

He answered with a nod.

'I can stay, if you want.'

'Stay?'

'Sure. One night, maybe, if you want?'

'You can cook?'

'Sure. Want me to make breakfast. I can fix that?'

'All right,' Imad said. 'For the time being, I'll allow you to stay.'

They went downstairs. Imad showed the girl through the kitchen. The vast refrigerator that contained nothing but a bag of salad and a dozen eggs. While she made omelets, Imad went outside and down the long driveway for the newspaper.

The girl turned down the burner under the skillet. She stepped quickly across the kitchen to a telephone. She dialed. Listened to the quiet ringing. The ringing went on for a long time and all the time she listened for the return of the Egyptian who moved like some damned spook.

Hurry up, answer . . . answer . . . he'll be back any moment. If he catches me he'll—

'Yeah?'

'Blaze honey, it's me.'

'Hydra? Where the fuck are you?'

'I went home with the camel-jumper.'

'*You what?*'

'Listen. He's got a regular mansion out here in Greenside. I mean, you wouldn't believe it. All these rooms, marble bathrooms, huge TVs. This guy's got so much money it's running out his poop chute. You better haul over.'

'All right!'

'His place is at 285 Greenside Lane. It's got this big wall around it, so you better park outside and climb over.'

'Got it. I'll be over tonight.'

'Why wait?'

'It'll be dark, shithead.'

Hydra heard him laugh. 'What's so funny?'

'What I'm gonna do to that fucking A-rab, that's what. Hope he ain't got claustrophobia, 'cause I'm gonna shove his stinking greaseball head up his ass for him. By the time I've finished with him he's—'

'Blaze. Gotta go. I can hear him coming back. See ya tonight.'

Chapter Eight

Shortly before noon, Blumgard called a meeting of the museum staff. Susan took a seat at the long, mahogany table in the conference room. Her stomach rumbled. She glanced sideways at Esther Plum. The prim, silver-haired archivist showed no sign of hearing the noise. If she had heard it, she was the type to pretend she hadn't.

It growled again. More loudly this time. Esther stared at her folded hands.

'Excuse me,' Susan said.

'It's quite all right, my dear.'

'I haven't eaten since seven.'

'I'm sure I couldn't eat a bite, myself, after what happened to that poor man.'

Blumgard entered, shut the door. He stepped to the head of the table.

Susan liked the man. Though he conducted himself with strict formality, he was never quite able to conceal his shyness or his enthusiasm. He loved his work. He cared for those who worked with him, as if they were all partners in a wonderful, shining quest. His eyes were red-rimmed behind his glasses. His hand trembled as he lit his pipe.

'I'm certain,' he began, 'that we're all aware of the tragedy that struck here last night. Barney Quinn was a fine man, a loyal and trusted member of our staff. Many of you never had the pleasure of meeting Barney, since he worked the graveyard shift.' Blumgard's eyes showed that he regretted his choice of words. 'Those of us who did know Barney will miss him.'

He cleared his throat, relieved to be done with that part of the business.

'The police tell me that Barney apparently died of injuries sustained by falling down the central stairway. Whether he fell accidentally or was pushed, they won't say. Or they don't know. Neither do they know how the burglars entered our facility. They found no evidence of forced entry. Therefore, we may assume one of two possibilities: either the robber used a key to gain entry, or they entered with the public and secreted themselves before closing time. I, personally, think the latter possibility the more likely.' He cleared his throat again. 'I also think it likely they will return.'

Esther murmured, 'Oh dear.' Several others at the table frowned and muttered.

'The police suspect youthful vandals may have been responsible. Who else, they said, would attempt to steal a mummy? While their position seems reasonable, in some respects, I have made known my reservations.'

His forefinger curled over the bowl of his pipe and tamped down the loose ashes. 'As many of you know, there has been a recent increase worldwide in thefts of Egyptian antiquities. Some, no doubt, were committed by the same breed who plundered tombs down through the ages in search of personal wealth. This is not the majority, however. It has become increasingly apparent that a great number of these robberies were committed by professionals – Egyptian patriots. Many priceless objects stolen from museums and private collections have been reappearing in Egypt. It's quite possible that those responsible for last night's tragedy had such a destination in mind for our collection . . . a misguided effort to return the mummy, Amara, to her homeland.'

Susan raised a finger, catching Blumgard's attention. 'Yes, Mrs Connors?'

'I think it odd that men like that would remove the mummy from its coffin. From what I've heard of their operations, they'd be more likely to take the coffin – and the whole collection, for that matter.'

'I certainly agree with you. I have no idea why they should see fit to take only the mummy. Nor do I understand why they left so abruptly, taking nothing. Perhaps the police are right in suspecting vandals. I would like us all to assume, however, that this was the work of professional thieves who may return to finish the job they began last night.

'All of us must be on our guard. A word to the docents would certainly be in order. We must keep our eyes open for suspicious behavior, especially as we approach closing time. If you see anything out of the ordinary report it at once to Hank.'

Hank, the daytime security guard, nodded confidently. He looked as if he wanted to grin, but knew it would be out of place at that particular time, with his nighttime counterpart lying cold on the mortuary slab.

'I have contacted the Haymer Security Agency. They will be sending us two armed guards tonight. Hopefully, their presence will discourage any further robbery attempts.'

Blumgard tapped the bit of his pipe against his front teeth. 'Are there any questions or comments regarding this matter?'

Nobody spoke up.

'All right, then. We'll reopen our doors at one p.m.'

Susan bit into her sandwich. The tangy egg-salad filling tasted marvelous. Just enough mustard, just enough ground pepper. Turning the sandwich, she licked the edge where a dollop had squeezed out.

A sound of footsteps made her look up. *Damn.*

She quickly looked away, pretended to concentrate on her sandwich.

Just make eye contact with one of these people and you've had it. They'll hit you up for a quarter, or start jabbering nonsense, or God knows what.

It was the only drawback to eating lunch in the museum park: you had to contend with an assortment of beggars and crazies.

She studied chunks of egg white and pepper in her sandwich as the footsteps came closer. The steps, slow, uneven. In front of her, they stopped.

She didn't look up. Bit into her sandwich. Stared at the woman's black shoes. Broken laces, knotted in a few places. Toes scuffed. Dog turd crusting one heel. Green socks hung limply around her ankles. The ankles looked thick and gray; crimson blotches . . . *Great, my sandwich . . . once it had tasted delicious, but now . . . uh . . .*

Is that ulcer on her shin leaking yellow pus?

'That's it,' snapped a woman's voice. 'Look me over, why don't you?'

Susan raised her eyes to the woman's glowering face. 'I wasn't . . .'

'You're a real petunia, you know that?'

Susan chewed her mouthful, but had a hard time swallowing.

'Think you're prime stuff, don't you?'

'I just want to eat my lunch, thank—'

'Look at you. Look at them clothes. You're a real petunia. Think you're special, don't you? A real princess?'

Susan shook her head, wishing the woman would disappear. 'I don't think anything. I just want to finish my lunch, okay?'

'Where do you get off?'

'Right here,' Susan retorted. Angry, helpless, she stuffed the remaining half of her sandwich into her bag and stood up.

'You ain't going nowhere.'

'I sure am, lady. There's no law I have to sit here and take abuse. So, if you'll—'

She clutched Susan's arm with her big gray paw.

'Damn it! You let go of me!'

The woman's hand shot out, slapping Susan's cheek. 'How's that, huh?' She slapped again. 'How's that? How's a taste of knuckle sandwich for a change?'

Susan's sleeve ripped as she wrenched her arm free. She pushed. The heavy woman stumbled backwards, arms windmilling, a strange growl in her throat. Susan saw the pain on her face as her rump hit the path.

Made her hesitate.

'You okay?' she asked.

The woman kept growling. Lip rising like a canine snarl, exposing gaps where teeth should be, and lousy chunks of enamel and decay where teeth were still rooted into the unhealthy-looking gums.

Susan looked around, feeling guilty, wondering if anyone had witnessed the struggle. Nobody was nearby. She turned again to the woman. 'I'm sorry,' she said, 'but you shouldn't have—'

'Ain't you something?' The woman muttered. 'Knock a person down.' Rolling over, she got to her hands and knees. She stood, brushing leaves from her shabby dress. 'What'd I ever do to you, huh?'

'You hit me for starters. Tore my blouse . . . You ought to be locked up.'

Susan started to leave. Hearing rapid footsteps behind her, she looked back and saw the woman charging. She tried to run, but a hand gripped her collar. It tugged backwards, pulling her off balance. She felt herself hit the concrete. It didn't hurt much, but then the big woman was on her – sitting on her, the big buttocks crushing down on her stomach; the woman pinned down her arms.

'Get off!' Susan twisted, trying to throw the woman off.

'Lay still.'

She began to yell for help, but the woman let go of one arm long enough to smash her in the face.

'Listen here, princess.'

Susan stared at the pale, bloated face, with its cluster of pimples around her mouth, like spotty lipstick. The face broke into an ugly smile, revealing more of those brown teeth stubs.

'You just keep your dirty whore hands off my guy, you hear? You

49

got no right. Keep off. You don't, I'm gonna do a job on you . . .
a real thorough job, you understand?'

'You're Mable.'

'That's me, honey.'

'Tag's going to hear about this.'

'He does and you're fer it. You and your runt.' With a smile, she
started working her mouth.

Susan knew what was coming. Couldn't believe it. The last person
to try such a thing was her older brother when they were little kids,
and he'd missed on purpose. Just planning to gross her out a little.

Mable, she realized, didn't plan to miss.

She bucked and twisted as a stream of drool spilled from Mable's
mouth. Pressing her lips shut, she turned her head away and closed
her eyes. The sticky wetness dropped onto her cheek and rolled
toward her ear. She felt its crawling path across her skin.

With a harsh laugh, Mable climbed off.

Susan used her sleeve to wipe away the gelatinous mass. Sitting
up, she watched Mable limp away, heavy arms swinging.

Susan got to her feet. Her wet sleeve clung to her arm. Some hair
close to her ear was matted. As she bent down to pick up her lunch
bag, she caught the sour-milk stench of the woman's spit.

Gagging, she rushed into the bushes.

Chapter Nine

Tag climbed the stairs, careful not to touch the railing. If he could have stopped breathing the moment he entered the building, he would have preferred it; the place smelled like a garbage can. His foot slid as it mashed something on the step. He didn't look down to see what it was. When he reached the second floor, he headed down a hallway to apartment 202.

He couldn't knock on the door without touching it, so he thumped it with the toe of his shoe.

'What you want?'

'Mrs Rudge? This is Officer Parker from the police. I'd like to speak to you.'

'Hang on.'

He waited. The door opened.

Mable's obese mother stood blocking the entry, a cigarette hanging out of her mouth, fists on hips. Her T-shirt and boxer shorts revealed more than Tag ever wanted to see.

'What's your story?' she asked, squinting through the smoke.

'May I come in?'

'Suit yourself. Got nothing to hide.' She stepped backwards, the motion rippling her flesh.

'Is Mable here?'

'See for yourself.'

'I asked you: is she here?'

'I don't see her, do you?'

'Are you aware of her recent activities, Mrs Rudge?'

'You mean do I know you been pronging her? Sure. She's my girl. She don't keep secrets.'

'I haven't been "pronging" her.'

'That ain't what I hear. What I hear, you can't get enough of her.'

'That's not true.'

'That you beg her to do it without no protection.'

'I wouldn't—'

'You should wear protection, you know? Sheaths don't cost the earth.'

'Listen to me—'

'And that you force her to do things that aren't nat-chral for a girl.'

'I've done nothing.'

'From what she says you prong her like some guys prong a farmyard animal.'

'*Listen to me.*'

'Gettin' bloodstains out of underpants ain't no picnic, I can tell you.'

'Listen. I've never had intimate relations with your daughter.'

'Inta-which?'

'I've never pronged her.'

'That a fact?'

'It's a fact.' Tag said, his skin crawling at the thought of it. Him and Mable . . . *hell.*

'Horseshit. Can't trick me. You been layin' it to her, sure as you're standing here. Made her bleed time and again, too, and not jus' from her womanly parts.' A column of ash dropped from the cigarette in Mrs Rudge's mouth. It crumbled to powder on a huge hill of breast, adding a patch of gray to her grimy T-shirt. She batted the ashes off, setting the breast in motion. 'Don't bother me where you stick it. You can stick Mable from now till your dick curls up and drops off, don't offend me. But wear a sheath. I don't want her knocking up. We don't want us a brat around here, crapping the place up.'

'Mrs Rudge. Do you want Mable busted?'

She blew smoke out of her nose. Least, she tried. One nostril must have been blocked. Smoke jetted thinly from her left nostril only.

'Mrs Rudge, in the past two days Mable has flattened a tire, assaulted a lady friend of mine, and assaulted me.'

'You?' She grinned.

'That's right.'

'You like the rough stuff? Mable's the girl to dish it.'

'I don't want to arrest her, Mrs Rudge. That's why I came over. I want you to talk to her, explain I'm not interested in having a relationship with her, and let her know she'll be thrown in jail if she pulls one more stunt.'

'How'd you mean that you don't want a relationship with her?'

'I don't want to prong her, screw her, poke her, pork her, touch her. I want her to leave me alone.'

'Yeah?'

'Yes.'

'So you're dumping her?'

'I've never had a relationship with her in the first place.'

'What the matter with you? You queer?'

'I already have a lady friend.'

'No law you can't have two.'

'Thanks, but no, thanks.'

Her eyes narrowed through the billowing smoke that began to burn Tag's throat. 'You telling me you don't like my Mable?'

'Not as a lover.'

'That so?'

'That *is* so.'

'I can see you never done her, then, or you'd be whistling a different tune. You go on and let her show you a time before you start bad-mouthing her.'

'I'd rather not.'

'Social services guy who had her case couldn't get enough of her. Bought her chocolates for her fifteenth.'

'Mrs Rudge, I'm not interested. Understand that.'

'My Mable, she wants you.'

'Well . . .'

'I like to see her get what she wants.'

'She won't get me,' Tag said.

'Don't go counting on that.' She laughed. 'Shoot, maybe we'll both get you. Good-looking hunk like you. Young and strong. We could make ourselves a cop sandwich, with you in the middle . . . yeah.' She gave him a long look-over. 'I bet you could make us both plenty happy.'

'Give her my message, please.'

'I guess she'll get back any minute now. How about you wait, tell her yourself? Beer in the cooler?'

'No, thanks.'

A mean look turned her eyes to slits. 'Don't, then. Who wants you, anyhow?' She flicked her cigarette butt at his face.

Tag flinched away. The burning stub nicked his ear.

'Good-bye, Mrs Rudge,' he said. 'Please remember to pass on what I've told you to Mable.'

On his way out he noticed the cigarette smoldering a black hole in the carpet. He mashed it dead with his heel, then walked away without looking back.

Chapter Ten

'How did it go?' Susan asked.

'Not so good. Old Mother Rudge thinks Mable and I would make a handsome couple.'

Susan grinned. The bruised side of her face felt stiff, but didn't hurt much.

'You could simplify things by pressing charges.' Tag said.

'I know, I know.' She bounced Geoffrey on her knee. He grinned and giggled.

'You shouldn't feel sorry for Mable.'

'I can't help it.'

Maria came into the room, beaming and carrying a margarita. She handed it to Tag. 'You make the best in the world,' he told her.

'The best! *Si. Gracias*, senor Tag.'

When she left, Susan said. 'Can you imagine what it must be like being Mable?'

'I'd rather not.'

'What does a woman like that have to look forward to?'

'Prison, more than likely.'

'I mean it. She hasn't got a thing going for her. I had a friend like that in college. She wasn't mean like Mable, but she looked exactly like her. We were roommates my first year at Weston and I got a pretty good idea what it must be like. Everybody stared at her all the time. She was the butt of a thousand awful jokes, mostly behind her back, but she knew what was going on. When it came time to rush, she gave it a try, but none of the sororities would touch her. That's the main reason I didn't pledge. If they could be that cruel, I wanted nothing to do with them.

'She never had a boyfriend. Guys dated her, sometimes.' Susan shook her head. Anger and sadness. 'It was just like a big joke to them, though. None of them gave a damn about her. They just knew she was an easy screw. They didn't care how ugly she was, as long as she put out. They treated her horribly. One night, some guys got her drunk and passed her round. When she came back to the room she could hardly walk. She was bleeding. She couldn't stop crying. I stayed up with her, the whole night, because I was afraid she might do something. You know, slash her wrists or something?

'The next day, I helped take her things to the railroad station. She got on the train and she never came back.'

Tag frowned, staring at the drink. 'What happened to her?'

'I don't know. I never heard from her again. But Mable makes me think of her, you know? I figure her life is tough enough without me trying to get her locked up.'

'Know something, Susan?'

'What?'

'You're a pretty nice lady.'

'Am I?'

'I want to take the nice lady out to dinner.'

'Sounds good.'

'I'll go upstairs and get into a suit.'

'Ah, a *dinner* dinner.'

'Right. Complete with necktie.'

'A necktie party! How exciting. I'd better make myself spiffy, then.'

'I'll give you fifteen minutes.'

'Half an hour.'

'Twenty minutes.'

'You're driving a hard bargain, Parker.'

A red-coated teenager was waiting in the restaurant's driveway. 'He's not gonna get his hands on *my* car,' Tag said and kept driving. He found an empty stretch of curb a block away.

In the restaurant, the maitre d' led them to a corner table.

'A libation?' Tag asked. 'Pepsi, Perrier, Mountain Dew?'

'I think I'll break down and have a real drink.'

'Don't break down at my table.'

A waiter came. Susan ordered a vodka gimlet, Tag a margarita. The waiter returned quickly with the drinks.

'To the most beautiful mummy in town,' Tag said.

'Amara?'

'You.'

They sipped their drinks. It was a good gimlet: strong, and easy on the Roses lime. 'Hmmm, this's my first in over a year,' Susan admitted.

'See what you've missed.'

'It'll probably go straight to my head, and I'll get giggly.'

'I've never seen you giggly.'

'Not a pretty sight.'

'I can't believe that.'

'Shameless flatterer.'

'I don't want this going to your head, but I think you're the most beautiful, charming, intelligent and sensitive woman I've known since my childhood sweetheart, Gretchen Stump.'

'Gretchen, heh? You always keep throwing her in my face.'

'She's hard to forget. You run a close second, though. Really. And you do have an advantage over her.'

'I'm honored you should think so.'

'She had one flaw.'

'You never let on.'

'Yes. Gretchen had a backwards eye. Looked in, not out. She was always fond of it, said it helped her see what was on her mind. Hideous to look at, though. Looked like a peeled tomato with a piece of spaghetti dangling down.'

'That's disgusting.'

'You should see what we had to do to keep it moist.'

'That's *really* disgusting.'

'I would've married her, except for the eye. Yours look fine, though.'

'Thanks.'

'So . . .' He shook his head. Even though he was still smiling the glint of mischief left his eyes.

'So?' Susan asked.

'Have you decided what to order?'

'What were you about to say?'

'Well, it would've been tacky under the circumstances. I mean . . . I shouldn't have brought Gretchen into it.'

'Into what?'

'Susan, how would you like to marry me?'

She sat back, stunned. She stared at him. 'You mean, you want . . .'

Tag nodded. 'Since you don't have a backwards eye . . .'

She laughed, but the laughter sounded strange and far away in her ears, and then Tag was blurry and she realized she was crying.

He started to talk. 'Of course, we'll have to wait for your divorce to become final, but that shouldn't be more than a few weeks. What do you think?'

'I . . . I . . . well, it's such a . . . Are you sure?'

'I'm sure I want to spend my life with you.'

'Oh Tag.' She grabbed her napkin. 'I'm sorry. I . . . here I am, falling apart . . . and you . . . you told me not to break down at your table.'

'I'll forgive you this time.'

'What . . . what about Geoffrey?'

'I'll be the best father I can.'

'Tag, jeez . . .'

'How about it?'

'Are you sure? I mean you . . . do you know what you're getting into?'

'Does that mean your answer is yes?'

'I suppose it does, huh? Yes. My God! I can't . . . Wow! I don't know what to say.'

'I think you've already said it.' He picked up his margarita. 'To us.'

'Mr and Mrs Taggart Parker.'

They drank. Then Susan sat down her gimlet and wiped her eyes. 'I must look a fright.'

'You look fine. Ready to order?'

'Not till I've . . . sheesh, my hands won't stop shaking. Why don't you get us another round of drinks? I'll go freshen up.'

During dinner they made plans. Both wanted a simple wedding. Both wanted only a family and a few close friends attending. They decided to move into Susan's apartment, since it was larger than Tag's. They would keep his bed; it was larger. Her chest of drawers; his was decrepit. His stereo system; her CD player skipped tracks all of its own accord. Both TV sets, both VCRs, both cars; neither microwave oven (both were glitchy as hell). They pretended to argue about Tag's favorite chair, a maroon monster that dropped stuffing from its tattered cushion.

'I won't let it inside till it's housebroken,' she said.

'We can put newspapers under it.'

'You have to promise to clean up after it.'

Susan finished her last bite of prime rib and excused herself.

'Going to freshen up again?' Tag asked.

She nodded. Instead of freshening up, however, she went to the cashier. Through the glass of the display case, she studied an array of cigars. She decided on an Anthony and Cleopatra because of its romantic name.

Back at the table, she presented it to Tag. 'To go with your coffee,' she said.

He turned the cigar slowly in his fingers, smelt it appreciatively, then looked at Susan and beamed. 'I think we'll get along just fine,' he said.

They took the elevator to the third floor of the Marina Towers. Holding hands, they walked down the narrow corridor to Susan's room.

A dead cat was hanging from her doorknob by a hind leg. Blood still trickled from its neck. It had no head.

Crooked words on the door dripped like wet paint:

THIS PUSSY STANK
YOU DO TOO
SEE YOU DED PITUNYA

Chapter Eleven

Such a bitch! And what a bitch. A Grade A bitch. A gold-medal bitch. An Oscar-winning bitch . . . he couldn't believe what he was hearing.

'Wait a minute, Janey. Let me get this straight.'

'There's nothing to get straight, Ed!'

'But—'

'No buts, no excuses.'

'Janey, I never even touched her, never mind—'

'Screwed her?'

'Yes.'

'So you admit it?'

'No, of course not.'

'Liar.'

'Listen, Janey, someone's been *lying* to you. I love you. I—'

'Yeah, some way to show it.'

'It's true.'

'The moment my back's turned . . .'

'Janey.'

'. . . You screw my best friend.'

'She's making it up.'

'Yeah, as if.'

'She is. Listen, Janey, she's been trying to break us up.'

'Why would she do a thing like that?'

'Because she's jealous.'

'Oh, right.'

'She was always hanging out with you. Now we are together, she's been pushed out. At least, that's what she thinks.'

'The phrase is "*were* together," Ed.'

'So you are dumping me?'

'See, you are smarter than you look.'

'But out here?'

'Yep.'

'Aw, come on, Janey. We're miles out of town.'

'Should have thought of that before you got all sticky-dicky with Pamela.'

'Jesus, I've told you. I never.'

'Like she made up that mole on your inner thigh?'

'Hell, Janey. She could have seen that in the pool.'

'Yeah, like she'd stare at your legs through binoculars when you go swimming.'

'Might've done.'

'Might've nothing, you two-timing rat.'

'Janey?'

'Enjoy the walk, rat boy.'

'Janey, this is insane – you can't just dump me out here. Janey! *Janey!*'

Ed Lake was conversing with dust. Janey slammed down on the gas in her open-top 4X4; she was gone. Dust showed as a white billowing cloud in the moonlight and all Ed could see of the car were its lights traveling like a fireball down the canyon.

Great, oh great. Not only does she dump me, she dumps me here.

And 'here' was a barren hillside road ten miles from home.

Got to do some walking, Eddie boy.

'Don't call me, Eddie,' Ed grunted under his breath. 'Whatever you do, don't call me Eddie.'

The moon lit the blacktop in front of him. At least he could see. His sense of direction should get him home before sunup.

But, hell, there was some walking to do.

No time like the present, Eddie boy.

He set off. With the time close to midnight it was silent. There were no cars. No houses that he could make out. Just road, dusty hillside, stars, a moon. And Eddie Lake. Just been dumped by the girl he loved.

Ouch. Just thinking that made him hurt inside.

Don't it sting, Eddie boy? Rejection? Being dumped?

'Don't call me, Eddie,' he grunted to himself.

And walked.

Walked fast. Angry. Angry at being dumped. Angry at Pamela, Janey's so-called best friend, who'd been spoon-feeding the lies. Those damn lies that Janey had swallowed so easily.

Damn.

Ouch – being dumped hurt. And so unfair. He couldn't believe it.

Janey had been nice earlier, so sexily nice. Whispering into his ear that they should drive out here where it was quiet. She'd suggested that before. They'd made out in her open-topped car, her long legs wrapped around his back. Her soft lips finding his in the dark and pressing passionately, her tongue working, while he stroked her bare breasts, running his fingertips over her nipples, feeling her body encircle his . . .

No, don't think that now. Concentrate on following the road home. He walked angrily again. She'd lured him out here just to dump him out in the wilds.

Ed Lake had just finished his sophomore year at Riverside High. He was sixteen. The proud owner of a VW Bug that he was carefully resurrecting nut by bolt in his parents' garage. And yes: deeply in love for the first time. Now the bitch had gone and . . . hell, the bitch had dumped him right there in the . . .

Uh, hello. What's that?

He stopped. Stared.

That didn't make sense. The hillside was strewn with big boulders. Now two of the boulders were moving.

He strained his eyes at the pale bumps and shaded hollows. He tried to make the most of the moonlight, but apart from the straight man-made lines of the road everything at either side of it was a random jumble of shapes.

But he'd swear to it. Two of those boulders were moving. They weren't rolling either like in a landslide, but sliding along . . . almost creeping.

Boulders? Boulders didn't creep.

People crept. Murderers crept.

Eddie, don't let your imagination fool with you.

'Don't call me Eddie.' He tried to sound flippant enough to stop the shivers but it didn't work.

The shivers came. His stomach felt as if it shriveled in on itself.

Janey didn't seem that important anymore.

All of a sudden he realized it was more than just annoying to be dumped out in the wilderness.

Heck, it might be dangerous, too. He wore expensive clothes. The watch on his wrist flashed in the moonlight.

A mugger might just want to check out whether or not it was a Rolex.

Ed walked.

The hunched boulder-shapes moved, too. Now he convinced himself that they were a pair of muggers.

But muggers don't hang around out on barren mountainsides, do they? They lurk in city alleyways or haunt movie-theater parking lots where there are people to prey on.

Here, there was nothing to mug apart from rabbits.

He walked faster . . . worked hard to stop running. Once you run they know they've spooked you. That's when they start running, too. Running to pounce on their victim.

And you're the victim, Eddie boy. That was the voice inside his head reinforcing the obvious.

The hill road angled downward now. Ahead the barren hillside gave way to lower-lying land filled with scrub. Beyond that were trees; the makings of a wood.

He walked, feeling perspiration roll across his skin beneath his shirt. He loosened a couple of buttons. But the night was too hot to cool him.

Hell, I'm gonna give Janey a piece of my mind. Pamela's not going to get away scot-free, either. I'm gonna get my own back for this one.

If I ever get the opportunity.

He glanced to his right up the hill as the two hunched figures moved toward him. They moved faster now, aiming to cut him off.

Probably gonna cut you up, too.

Now he did start to run, his feet slapping down against the blacktop, his arms flailing. Breath came in spurts through his throat.

He looked up at the jumble of shadows. He couldn't make out details, but the two shapes sped down at him. They were too fast. He couldn't outrun them. Jesus, he couldn't even scream to anyone nearby for help. He'd be at their mercy.

Jesus H. I'm only sixteen. Sixteen! I only lost my cherry three months ago. They're gonna bury my bones in the dirt at the side of the road, I'm never gonna—

'Leave me alone!' he yelled as the figures broke out from the shadows.

He stopped as the pair ran in front of him, cutting off his escape route.

He stared.

Rubbed his eyes.

Then laughed out loud.

A pair of goats ran across the road, hooves clattering, their horns glinting in the moonlight.

Christ, he really was out in the wilderness. Wild goats! They were as scared as he was. They ran, kicking their back legs, stirring up puffs of dust as they vanished under the bushes.

Now, when you're sixteen there are certain things you don't want people to see. One is what you do in the bath. Another is blushing when a girl speaks to you. Another is the diary you keep hidden under the bed. And then there's this one. Running in terror from a couple of runty little goats.

Jeez. He could just imagine his friends falling around laughing if they ever heard about this.

Not that they would.

This is just between me and you two goats, he thought to himself, grinning. *I won't tell if you don't. Scaring each other in the middle of the night, huh? What a trio of saps.*

Easier in his mind now, Ed carried on walking, this time with a hand casually in his pocket and sometimes whistling a few notes from a song. The air was still. There wasn't a sound, and the moon still burned with a bright cold witch-fire in the sky.

The road leveled out. Soon the boulders were gone, then it was scrubby bushes. Half a mile after that came the trees that crept closer to the road, shutting it in until only a split full of stars showed overhead.

He glanced at his watch. One a.m. His parents might have woken up and realized he wasn't at home. But they treated him like a mature adult. They trusted he wouldn't do anything stupid. So maybe they wouldn't worry yet. He hoped not.

His feet whispered across the road surface. He was maybe averaging four miles an hour. He guessed eight miles separated him from home. If he kept up this speed then two hours from now would see him slipping his key into the front door.

That didn't seem so bad.

Ed Lake heard the whisper of leaves.

Then he heard another whispery sound.

This was someone breathing.

Someone close by.

He sensed a presence right behind him.

Turning, he saw a shadow there.

The shadow swung an object.

One that hurt far more than the pain of being dumped by Janey.

He just had time to clutch the side of his head before the shadows swamped him.

Ed Lake opened his eyes. There were bars. Bars going up and

down with thinner bars running from left to right. It looked like a fisherman's net made out of steel.

The first phrase that went through his mind was *Holy Shit!*

He reached out to touch the bars. Bad move. Any kind of movement made his head hurt like hell. He touched his temple. Felt crisped stuff there. It matted his hair.

Dried blood. He figured that much.

This time he kept his head still and allowed his eyes to do all the moving.

Still hurt his head, though.

But he persisted.

Through the bars he saw white-painted walls. Light came from fluorescent strips in the ceiling. So he was in a room.

In a cage.

Holy shit. I've been knocked unconscious and dumped in a freaking cage. Now what?

His mouth tasted like a hog had crapped in it. His watch had gone from his wrist . . . mugged . . . *But why put me in a cage?*

Fresh meat for the tiger.

This thought made Ed sit up. His mind spiraled. He wanted to vomit. The pain rocketed through his skull . . . but he had to check.

See that there weren't any hungry tigers in the cage with him.

Already he could feel their teeth in him. Chomping down. Tearing. Ripping. The pain . . .

'Yeee-ow! Take it easy.'

'What?'

'You got yourself a nice whacko on the skull there, buddy. You should lie down for a while.'

'W-what'd y . . . ya do that for?' Ed's words came stuttering out as his head spun.

'I ain't done nothing, buddy. I'm just your roomie.'

'Where . . .'

'Here. Next pen to yours.'

Ed took a deep breath. The room slowed its spinning. His eyes focused and he found himself looking through the bars of the cage at an another cage identical to his. Eight by four, while maybe six feet high. Steel bars. Objects dangled by cords from the roof bars. His eyes located its occupant.

A guy of around twenty with blue eyes and blond dreadlocks grinned back at him. The guy lay on his side, one elbow propping him up. There was a match gripped between his teeth.

64

The blond guy lay grinning at Ed for a while. Then he said, 'Well, buddy . . . welcome to the beast house.'

'Beast house?'

'We're the beasts.'

'I don't understand.' His head ached so much he wanted to vomit. 'Beast house?'

The blond guy leisurely slapped the bars of his cage. 'We're in the pens, buddy, so we must be the beasts.'

'Shit.'

'Head sore?'

'Like you wouldn't believe.' Groaning, Ed sat up.

'It'll pass.'

'Yeah?'

'Did for me.' The other prisoner used his fist to mimic a clubbing motion against his blond head. 'I got double whacko. Here and here.' He pointed. 'They had to stitch my scalp. You got off lightly, pal.'

'Yeah, feels like it.' Ed retched.

'Clean it up with toilet tissue and dump it in the bowl.'

'Huh?'

'The plastic bowl there in the corner of your penthouse suite, sir. That's the bathroom facility.'

'You said "they had to stitch my scalp". Who are *they?*'

The blond guy didn't answer. 'Speak a little lower. Sleeping beauty gets grumpy if you wake her.'

Still dazed, Ed looked round. Another cage around three feet from the end of the one he occupied was separated from it by a walkway of sorts. Angling his head, he saw a mound beneath a red blanket. A hand attached to a slender wrist protruded. From one end coils of heavy red hair spilled over the foam mattress and onto the floor. Ed looked at the contours of the blanket, guessed there was a curving hip under there that shaped it.

Girl, he told himself. A girl with exotic red hair.

I wonder what she looks like . . .

He pulled back from his own curiosity.

Inappropriate or what, Eddie? You're in a cage. It's not the time to think woman, *it's time to think* out!

'Don't call me Eddie,' he murmured to himself.

'What's that you say, buddy?'

Ed looked at the blond dreadlocks. They reached down the guy's back to his rump. Dazed, Ed shook his head.

'Nothing.'

The guy gave an easy wave. 'The name's Marco. You?'

'Ed Lake.'

'Yo, Eddie. Welcome aboard.'

With a groan Ed lay down on the foam mattress. His head ached.

'You best get some rest while you can, Eddie boy,' Marco told him.

'Why? We going somewhere?'

'Nope.' The guy grinned. 'But you're sure to get a visitor soon.'

'What kind of visitor?' Ed didn't like the sound of that.

'You'll see.'

'Yeah.'

'So rest. Get your strength back.' The grin widened. 'Believe me, you're gonna need it. You're gonna need every drop.' The last sentence amused the guy and he began to chuckle.

He was still chuckling when the lights went out, plunging the room into darkness.

Chapter Twelve

The dog howled at the moon. Every night the old man had come to the parking lot, called softly, 'George . . . where are you, boy? Here, George. See what I've got for you.' The dog would speed out of the shadows across the lot, past the single car that still carried the odor of the old man, and to the foot of the fire-escape steps.

There the old man would open up a bag. Inside would be chop bones, the remains of cold cuts or even raw hamburger. This had gone on longer than the dog could remember.

Night after night. The old man smelling of strange odors like ancient bones. The man would feed him there at the back of the museum, make a fuss of him. But he wasn't there tonight. There were more lights in the building than usual. The dog's keen ears picked up voices where there were usually none. Even though the big brown dog could clearly make out the voices of the strangers he couldn't understand the words.

Certainly none of the all-important words in his vocabulary. *George. Food. Walk. Play. Here, boy. Good boy. Roll over.* Instead:

'They're paying us to do what?'

'See that no one makes off with some old dame in the coffin.'

'Jesus H . . . Amara? That her name?'

'Search me.'

'This place is like a tomb anyway.'

'Say that again. Those stone statues are creeping me out.'

'Did you know the guy?'

'Who?'

'Guy who took a dive down the stairs.'

'Uh-huh – Barney Quinn.'

'Wasn't he on the force?'

'Sure, but they kicked his sorry butt out.'

'So, what'd he do?'

'Got careless.'

67

'What? Poked the Police Chief's wife?'

'Nah, not even the Chief'd do a thing like that.'

'That ugly?'

'Hell, yes.'

'What this Quinn do, then?'

'Accepted a little cash here and there in return for turning a blind eye to some whorehouses.'

'Hard darts.'

'Could happen to anyone.'

'Whoa, Beckerman, sounds close to home.'

'None of your business. Go check on the Greek room again.'

'I was only—'

'Yeah, only poking your great schnozzola in deep where it doesn't belong.'

Tilting his head to one side, the dog out in the lot heard the voices recede with the footsteps. Two men walking in the building. One small and thin. One thickset and limping.

The dog padded up to the rear doors, put his nose to the crack between door and jamb and sniffed hard, pulling the cool air from inside the big stone pile into his sensitive nostrils. George smelled the musty odors again. Ancient bones. Stone and wood artifacts from faraway places. Faraway times. Handled by many different hands.

George smelled the two strangers patrolling the museum in place of his old friend who'd appear every night with food. The strangers smelled of the tortillas they'd wolfed down before the start of the shift. The dog even smelled the scent of woman on the fingers of one of them where he'd rolled his wife's sister during a little afternoon delight.

George's sense of smell was keen, picking up the scent of three-thousand-year-old goatskin on which was inscribed verses from the Egyptian *Book of the Dead*. His hearing was phenomenal. Heard the tick of the clock in Blumgard's office. Heard the two guards' footsteps on the upper floor. His eyesight was good too, far better than humans allowed. He could see the flutter of tiny moths against lighted windows three stories above his own shaggy brown head.

But there was more.

Much more.

A sense humans could only guess at.

Not identify. Not prove.

George possessed a sixth sense. Inside the building he sensed something stir. Something dark. Something terrible. Something vengeful. Something with the capacity to terrify, maim. Kill.

He sensed it stir again. Sensed dark purpose. He sensed it ready to move again soon.

The dog threw back his head and howled at the cold moon.

Chapter Thirteen

'Don't waste your time. They're set in concrete.'

Ed Lake glanced up at Marco as the blond-haired man shook his head.

'They're set in tight. The doors are double-padlocked. All the bars are welded together . . .'

Ed heaved at a bar.

'. . . So you won't be able to even bend one.'

Damn. The man was right. But it wouldn't stop Ed from trying. After a while Marco shook his head. 'You should listen to me.'

'Why? I want out, don't you?'

'You should save your strength like I told you, buddy. You're going to need it.'

Ed tried kicking at the bars but whoever had dumped him here had removed his shoes. All he did was hurt his toes. The bars didn't budge.

'Save your strength,' Marco repeated. Then he sat down, with his back to Ed.

In frustration Ed slammed the cage door with his hand. It made a ringing sound. Fuming, he stood for a moment, but could only straighten so far because of the height of the cage ceiling. He had to stoop. His back began to ache. The pain started in his head again, too, where he'd been struck.

Ed took stock.

I was walking along the woodland road. Someone sockoed me. Out cold, I was brought to the building, dumped in the cage. When I came to I talked to my roomie who looks a little kooky to me. Then the lights went out. I slept. I woke hours later when the lights came back on. How many hours I don't know.

So, I'm looking at the cage again. It's around eight feet by four. Six high. Welded steel bars set in concrete. Sawdust bowl for a toilet. Foam mattress is a bed. Otherwise bare as a rhino's butt. Hanging from cords tied to the cage roof bars are your fundamental toilet items: hairbrush, toothbrush, mirror (the kid's kind, made from harmfree plastic); then there's a water bottle (also plastic), mouthwash, deodorant, talcum powder, facecloth and Bible.

The cage's appearance with all those items tied to the cords made Ed think of fruit hanging on vines.

When he crossed the cage he had to push them aside so he left a path of toiletries and the Holy Bible swinging backward and forwards.

He looked up. A narrow walkway with a handrail ran around the wall some six feet off the ground. That would allow a person to simply step from the walkway onto the roof of the cage.

The cage ceiling's strange as well.

Half of it, where there were no bars, was clear Perspex. Very thick.

Certainly couldn't put my fist through it. Probably bulletproof.

'Wasting your time, Eddie . . . no way out.'

'At least I'm trying, Marco.'

'Your funeral, bud.'

'Yeah?'

'Should save your strength.'

'Why?'

''S gonna be put to the test soon.'

'How?'

Marco shrugged and went back to examining the end of the match he was chewing.

'What's going to happen, Marco?'

'You don't listen to my advice, bud, so why should I waste my breath?'

Restless, Ed examined the cage again. He'd not noticed earlier but there was a section of false Perspex ceiling. This lay just a few inches beneath the roof proper of the cage. This chunk of Perspex was maybe two inches thick, seven feet long and just over two wide. It was suspended from the cage roof by what looked like a substantial bolt in each corner. Looking at them more closely he saw something like windlasses connected to each bolt. The windlass mechanism sat on top of the cage roof. He recalled the windlasses he'd seen on his uncle's sailboat. You turned the handle to raise and lower the main sail.

'Hey . . . hey, Marco, can this section of Perspex be raised and lowered by turning the handles?'

'That's what you figure?'

'Yes.'

'You figure right, Eddie.'

71

'And what's this aperture in the roof of the cage?'

'Figure it out.'

'I'm asking you, Marco.'

Marco said nothing but sat with his back to Ed, his spine up against the cage bars.

'Marco . . . Marco?'

Marco didn't reply.

Just kept that broad back of his turned to Ed.

'Marco, why won't you answer? Marco?'

'He won't answer because he's saving his strength. He might be next.'

Ed turned to see who spoke. He saw that in the next cage a figure had partly emerged from beneath the red blanket. He found himself looking at a high-cheekboned face. Green eyes gleamed at him, while tumbling down over shoulders – *bare shoulders* – was thick red hair.

Ed caught his breath. Sheesh, the woman was beautiful.

Around twenty-five years of age, he guessed. There was something about the firm shape of her lips that suggested experience. The directness of her gaze reinforced that line of thought.

She stared back at him. 'You ask questions. You rattle the bars of the cage. You don't give anyone a chance to get some shut-eye, do you?'

'Who are you?'

'More questions.'

'You'd be the same . . . I – I mean what are we doing here? Who brought us here? What—'

She touched her lips. 'Shh. You should listen to Marco. Get some rest.'

'But why? What's—'

'Why, what, when? There you go again.'

'But what is—'

'Listen to me. It could be your turn next. You'll need your strength.'

She lay there raised up on one elbow, the blanket covering her.

Ed walked to the end of the cage that was nearest to hers, squatted down. The eyes burned back into his; beads of green ice. 'But how long have you been here?' he asked.

'Hard to tell. We've no way of telling the time. Can't tell night from day.'

'But you've seen who's holding you here?'

'Sort of.'

'Jesus.' He ran his fingers through his hair. 'This is kidnap. They can't do this.'

'I know.' She spoke casually, almost disdainfully. 'The cops would arrest, the courts would convict. But until they're caught what're we gonna do?'

Marco spoke up. 'What we gonna do? I'll tell you what we *have* to do. Play their game the way they want it played, otherwise we're dead.' He lay down on the mattress and covered himself with a blanket.

'Marco's right,' she said. 'Play along.'

She moved on the mattress to get comfortable. The blanket slipped down, exposing the top of her breast. Ed saw the smooth, milk-white mound. Found himself trying to catch a glimpse of nipple. She looked *great*. Even in this deepest of deep crocks of shit he saw that. She saw Ed's interest. He blushed, looked back up into her face. Her gaze searched his face, appraising him.

'You ever acted in a play?' she asked.

Strange thing to ask in a situation like this.

'Ever been in a play?'

He nodded. '*Dracula*. We staged it in school last year.'

'Good. If you can act you've got a chance to survive when it's your turn.'

'Chance to survive. Why? What's going to happen?'

'Questions again. We're not here as schoolteachers. We're victims. Do you understand that? We're—'

'Please tell me,' he said. 'If I'm going to get through whatever this is, I need your help.'

She sighed. 'It doesn't happen every day but from time to time we—'

'Hey!'

The suddenness of the lights going out again caught Ed by surprise. In the darkness he heard the woman catch her breath. From behind him Marco spoke, 'Whatever's going to happen's going to happen now, buddy. Prepare yourself.'

Ed Lake shivered as he crouched there. The darkness suddenly seemed cold against his skin. Drafts stirred through his hair. He looked round with wide eyes.

Saw nothing.

The darkness was total.

Air played over his skin again. Shivers ran down his back. His whole body seemed to shrivel inside.

73

What was happening?

More importantly, what would happen to him?

Not to be able to see. Hell, he didn't like this.

There could be anyone out there in the room. Guys with guns. Guys with knives. Or maybe a noose to slip round his neck.

The drafts came again. A sense of movement from above. Door opening. But still no light.

Door closing.

Footsteps.

Footsteps descending stairs.

His own breathing grew loud. Jerky. Frightened gasps. His heart hammered loud in his chest.

Holy Christ. What's gonna happen? What they gonna do to me?

Rustling sounds. The sound of clothes?

He didn't know. But it seemed close.

Maybe they'd open the door of his cage. Could he strike out, then run?

But where? This darkness. He couldn't see a thing. But how could the person who entered the room see where they were going? Nightscope goggles, maybe.

They'd see Ed crouching there, looking right and left, up and down, his eyes gleaming silver disks in the infrared light, his lips a black slash across his face. Using nightscope goggles they'd see him, all right. But he couldn't see them.

He hugged his knees close into his chest. His muscles ached with the tension. His teeth chattered.

Then he heard a whispering voice. He was sure it wasn't the girl or Marco. No . . . wait . . . he tried to make out if . . . no, he couldn't even tell if it were male or female.

The whisper continued. It seemed to be giving instructions to someone.

Maybe to him.

But he couldn't make out the words. The whisperer was very low, hoarse-sounding.

Wait. He heard the girl speak.

'Yes.' At least, that was what he thought he heard her say, but her voice was low, too. There was something intimate about the conversation between the two. They talked as if to keep it private from Marco and himself.

Maybe he should speak up?

No.

Don't do that.

74

Keep out of it, otherwise it might bring the whisperer to you. And there was something about the whisperer that made his skin crawl.

This was bad. Baaa-aaad.

The whispering voice was terrifying. It whispered instructions. Orders. Commands.

Something had to be obeyed.

The . . .

Silence.

All Ed could hear was his own respiration.

In.

Out.

In.

Out . . .

And his heartbeat. Pounding.

He struggled to slow his breathing. Struggled to listen.

Had the whisperer gone? There was no movement. No sounds. Certainly no more whispered commands.

Maybe he should speak now? Ask the other two what had happened. The whisperer had vanished. They were alone now.

The sudden shriek rocked him backwards.

It came again. He covered his ears. Tried to shut it out.

Silence.

Then another scream. A sighing one that started high then descended into a low moan.

He turned to the source of the sound. But there was only velvet darkness pressing against his eyes.

Jesus, sweet Jesus, what's happening?

A cry. Then three more in quick succession. *Ah! Ah! Ah!*

That was the green-eyed girl. Had to be. He recognized the voice.

Then: *'Please!'*

Sure, it had to be her.

'Please!'

Then another cry.

Was she in pain?

Or was someone screwing her?

Because he heard her breathy moans. Heard a loud intake of breath, then another cry followed by a quivering. *'Oh, God, please . . . please!'*

He sat in the darkness, listening. But not sure what it was that he was hearing. OK, it could be pain.

But it sounded like sex. He remembered Janey's panting cries

75

when he thrust into her. Those moans of pleasure when he worked his tongue around her nipples; her breathless *Please* when she begged for more. She'd pull his head to her breasts, panting, *'Please . . . suck harder.'*

'Oh . . . oh . . . I – I *please!'*

This 'please' came, he imagined, through gritted teeth. A *please* pushed out as sensation overwhelmed her.

God, yes, this sounded like sex.

His heart beat faster. For a different reason now.

A warm flush spread through him. He felt himself hardening.

He couldn't believe his reaction. Felt betrayed by it. Embarrassed.

But the beautiful woman with the erotic green eyes had aroused him when her blanket had slid down to expose part of her bare breast.

Now that he heard her experiencing a white-knuckle ride of sex in the raw . . . this was something else. With her every pant, every cry, he felt himself harden to the point where he needed to do something about it.

He imagined her full white breast quivering. Her hair lashing as her head whipped from side to side in the throes of ecstasy.

Jesus . . .

Oh, Jesus.

Sweet, sweet Jesus.

If she didn't stop making those sounds soon he'd explode.

Panting, moaning, gasping cries, shrill squeals. It made him tingle all over. He wanted—

Christ, he wanted—

Then it was suddenly over.

Silence.

For moments nothing, but the sound of his heart seemed to come right back at him from the walls.

A moment after that the lights came on.

Ed blinked.

Straightaway, his eyes went to the cage that contained the woman.

And there she was.

He looked, unable to stop his gaze darting all over her, taking in every tiny detail. He leaned forward until his face pressed against the bars, staring at her, trying to process and understand what he now saw in front of him.

His gaze traveled down her from head to toe. Her back was to him. She knelt on the floor, her face to the bars.

She was naked apart from a pair of denim cut-offs. These were cut high, revealing the swelling mounds of her buttocks. The back pocket had been torn almost off and dangled down, reaching the back of her leg. Her legs were long and shapely. Even from this angle he could tell that. With white skin. Milk-white.

He found his gaze travelling up from the bare soles of her feet, the toes resting against the floor, up her thighs, up over the smooth curve of her buttocks, tightly clad by pale denim. Then to her bare back. The toned skin that looked so smooth and flawless. A little further up it disappeared beneath a swathe of copper hair.

She did not move. She didn't make a sound; she just knelt there, her face pressed against the bars of the cage. Her two slender arms were raised above her head. Her fingers curled about the rounded shaft of the bars. There was something erotic about the grip. Gently encircling. He shivered with pleasure.

Unable to take his eyes from her, he watched.

This went on for whole moments.

Then she moved.

Turning, she faced him, still in that kneeling position. She looked exhausted.

His gaze traveled up from her cut-off jeans. The fastening button was gone. The zipper had slipped down a little in a V of soft blue material, exposing creamy skin. His gaze caressed her flat stomach. Then he was seeing her breasts.

No!

He looked at her in shock . . . for a moment he didn't believe what he saw.

But then he did see.

And only too clearly.

They'd cut her breasts. Thin slits radiated from the nipples. It was like a child's picture of the sun done in blood. The roundness of the nipple. Then the sunburst effect of cuts from a sharp blade.

As he watched in horror he saw blood swell proud of the cuts, bead, then trickle downward. A drip from the tip of a puckered nipple.

She folded her arms in such a way that they cradled her breasts from beneath, supporting.

She looked up at him. Her green eyes were rimmed red. Her lips were full and moist. She was breathing deeply. She gazed into his eyes. For a while she stayed like that, allowing her heavy breathing to settle and quieten.

He didn't know what to say . . . What could he say that would be of help? Even though the cuts in the skin looked superficial her breasts must have been excruciatingly painful.

As he watched, she licked the tip of her middle finger, then tenderly wiped the blood from a cut. She did this again and again. Licking her finger. Stroking a cut in the skin. Soon her lips were slicked red with blood.

From time to time she glanced up at Ed as she worked. Her eyes large now.

When she'd done, she said in a calm, strong voice, 'Don't worry yourself on my account.' Her lips twitched to form a ghost of a smile. 'You see, I'm tougher than I look.'

With that she lay down on the foam mattress and covered herself with the blanket.

Chapter Fourteen

Imad pushed the button on the control box on his dashboard, and watched the gate swing open. He drove through slowly, one hand caressing Hydra's bare shoulder.

She leaned against him.

He parked, and walked her to the front door. In the moonlight her evening gown looked as sleek as the surface of a lake. It was a low-cut, backless dress. He'd bought it for her that afternoon at La Mers.

'I'll take you out for a wonderful dinner tonight,' he'd said earlier.

'In my T-shirt?'

'No, of course not. We'll go to Beverly Hills and buy you something appropriate – an evening gown fit for a princess.'

'Princess, huh?' She smirked and shook her head.

She looked marvelous in the dress. During dinner at Henri's, he'd hardly been able to keep his hands off her. Now there was no longer any need to.

He opened the door. Led her into the foyer, locked the door, pulled her into his arms.

'You're so gorgeous,' he murmured.

He kissed her, tongue pushing into the moist warmth of her mouth. She sucked it down more deeply into her. His hands slid down the curves of her back. They glided over her buttocks, feeling their small, firm mounds through the expensive fabric of the dress. She had no underwear on; he had bought her none. He found the dress's slit that had kept him breathless all evening with glimpses of bare flesh. Inserting a hand, he caressed the back of her leg, the slope of her rump. He slipped his hand to the front and stroked upwards, pressed the crisp thatch of hair, the wetness between her legs. She writhed, moaning, as his fingers went into her. Sliding, moving, caressing, rubbing.

He was hard and aching.

She rubbed the front of his pants. Opened them. Freed his engorged organ. Slid her hand along the thick shaft.

Lowering herself to the marble floor, she pulled him down on her.

With one hand, Imad managed to untie the strap behind her neck. He swept the filmy bodice away from her breasts. He gnawed the turgid nipples. Clutching her shoulder, he held her in place while he rammed.

He suddenly jumped in pain. Reaching back, he touched his stinging buttock and winced.

Blaze crouched behind him. A cigarette in one hand. A .22 caliber pistol in the other.

'Hurt?' Blaze asked with a leer. He sucked on his cigarette, tapped off the ash, and jabbed the red tip into Imad's other buttock. Again, it burned like a hornet sting. 'Get up, camel-humper.'

Imad stood. Pulled up his pants. As he zipped them he looked at Hydra. She lay on her back, knees up, crotch slick. Her eyes were shut. 'Bitch,' he said.

Her lips curled in a smile.

'Take me to your safe,' Blaze ordered.

'Safe? I have no safe.'

'Don't shit me, man. Just take me to it, and open it up. The sooner I've got what I want, the sooner I'll get out of here.'

'But I cannot take you to a safe if there is none, can I?'

'A house like this *always* has a safe. I can find it myself if I have to.'

'It's in the bedroom closet,' Hydra said. Imad looked at her, stunned. She grinned and sat up. 'So I'm a snoop,' she said. 'Sue the pants off me, why don't you?'

'There's nothing in it,' Imad protested.

'Sure,' Blaze breathed.

'I speak the truth.'

'Sure you do.'

'It is the truth.'

'Let's go up and see.'

'Hang on.' Hydra tied the dress behind her neck. The beautiful dress Imad had bought for her. He wanted to tear it from the ungrateful bitch, rip it to pieces; let her wear the soiled rags that matched her filthy soul.

'Okay,' she said. 'Let's roll.'

They followed Imad up the stairway and into the master bedroom.

'Right in there,' Hydra intoned, pointing at the closet.

Imad opened the door. Turned on the closet light and pushed aside his hanging clothes, revealing the face of the wall safe.

'Open it,' Blaze hissed, eyes gleaming.

'I assure you . . .'

'Shut the fuck up! Open the safe! Now!'

He spun the dial. It whirred quietly under the touch of his trembling fingers. When he'd finished the combination, he turned the handle and pulled open the door.

'Step back, asshole.'

Imad backed out of the closet. Blaze stepped in. Greedy face eager.

'Damn!'

'I told you . . .'

Blaze came out, shaking a thin notebook. He flipped it open. 'A fuckin' diary.' He flung it to the floor. He aimed the pistol at Imad's face. 'Okay. You've got five seconds. Where's your money?'

'In the bank.'

'Don't shit me, A-rab.' He cocked the pistol.

'Don't, please. I will tell you.'

'Spit it out.'

'There's a secret compartment in the safe. I keep my valuables there. It's at the back. You simply push the upper left-hand corner of the rear panel.'

'Okay, that's more like it.' Blaze stepped into the closet. He turned to the safe.

Lunging forward, Imad swung the closet door shut.

Hydra reached for it, trying to tug it open. He jabbed his elbow into her stomach, grabbed her, flung her backward against the door. He pressed her against it.

The door jerked, but held.

'Open up!' Blaze yelled. 'Okay. Okay, you asked for it asshole!'

Hydra called out in panic. 'Blaze, no. Don't shoot. He's holding me against the—'

Three gunshots made quick flat *bangs*. Hydra screamed in pain, her body twitching with each shot; her face twisted, flushed bright red then drained to a waxy white color.

'Shit!' Blaze cried out.

The door jumped, but Imad held it shut, pressing himself against Hydra's convulsing body. He glanced to the side. Four feet away stood a straight-backed chair. If he could get to it . . .

Another shot cracked out. Hydra's head dropped forward onto Imad's shoulder. Behind her, the door was punctured by a tiny, splintered hole.

'See what you've done?' Imad yelled.

81

Clutching Hydra with one arm, he pulled her aside. He threw open the door, shoved her at the startled man, and slammed the door. Spinning away, he grabbed the chair. Thrust its back under the knob.

With a crash the door shook but held.

'Let me outta here, shit face!'

The gun popped two new holes through the wood; bullets whined through the air near Imad's head.

From its place behind the bedroom door. He took Callahan's .12 gauge Browning shotgun. He pumped a cartridge into the breech, stepped toward the closet. Aimed.

Fired. The gun jumped, slamming pain through his shoulder. It knocked a four-inch hole in the closet door. He pumped, and fired again.

Through the gaping hole in the door, he saw Blaze and Hydra on the floor. Blaze's chest was a sheet of flowing blood. The left side of Hydra's face was gone – as if a beast had bitten it off, bones and all.

Chapter Fifteen

April Vallsarra moved through the house easily. She didn't bump into furniture or knock against walls. She knew every inch of the building. Anyone who didn't know her would have sworn that she wasn't blind.

She glided from the kitchen to the lounge with a glass of milk in her hand. With an unerring sense of direction she made for the armchair in the center of the room, sat down, and lightly touched a remote control. Music filled the room.

This was her father's music. She listened to it often. On good days it was as reassuring as him actually being there. Bad days it made her cry. She'd think about the thugs that took his life away.

Tonight the music helped comfort her. She'd been so lonely today she'd felt a physical ache in her bones. Thirty-three years old and living alone in a big house out in this remote canyon.

Her home was her entire world. There was no world beyond this one. Two floors, five bedrooms, three bathrooms, a kitchen, a lounge, a dining room, a roof terrace, a vast studio basement.

That was it. April Vallsara's universe.

She wished she could find someone to love to share it with her.

Someone who loved her.

Thirty-three years old. Single.

Alone.

Aching for a loving companion.

Why had life dealt her this blow?

She wished she had a lover tonight.

She sipped the milk as she listened to the music that her father had created single-handed. Years ago he'd worked alone in the basement studio. First he'd recorded the bass guitar line. A rhythm that was solid enough to anchor the other instruments. Then, painstakingly, he had overdubbed the electric guitar and keyboard parts. Track by track. Layer by layer. Then he'd mixed the sound on the vast mixing desk there.

Months later he had the finished music. A huge symphony played by an orchestra of electric guitars, computers and synthesized percussion. At times he'd replayed it so loudly that she'd had to clamp her hands over her ears and leave the studio.

But the studio underground was so perfectly soundproofed that she couldn't hear the music once the series of three doors had been closed in the corridor that led to the stairwell that, in turn, led to the ground floor.

Her father would invite his friends across to listen to the music. Sometimes he'd debut a piece on the rooftop patio. Many times April had joined them there, sipping drinks on comfortable loungers, enjoying the cooling breeze after the heat of the day. And from the sophisticated sound system installed there they'd listen in awe to the music as it swooped and soared, filling the night air with the shimmering tones of guitars.

Afterwards, her father's friends would congratulate him. Although she could never see their faces of course she recognized the voices. There'd be a sprinkling of Hollywood actors, a band member or two from The Grateful Dead, Jefferson Starship, The Eagles, Talking Heads. Later years would find representatives from newer bands such as REM, Grandaddy and Krakow.

She listened to the pitter-patter of guitar notes. Keyboards swirled like restless spirits, whooshing round the room from speaker to speaker.

That hollowness came to her again. That sense of loneliness that was so great it felt as if a cavern had formed inside her. Empty. A vacuum.

Her hand rested on the cool silk of her dress. She felt her thigh beneath.

She imagined that it was a lover's hand squeezing her leg before gently gliding upwards, up over her stomach, up to her throat where it would slide round the side of her neck, then pull her gently toward her lover's lips.

But who could love a girl like me? I'm blind. Most men wouldn't be interested.

Oh, yes, they'd be interested in the sex. In years past she'd had many lovers who'd stayed a few weeks before dumping her.

But was there anyone out beyond those walls who would commit to loving her forever? To make her a wife?

She had money. Royalties from her father's albums saw to that. She could hire more help around the house. Even a nanny if children came along.

But how could she reach out there into the city and make a man notice her? How could she make him fall in love with her and care for her?

She finished the milk and set the glass down on the table beside the chair. Music filled the room. But it was no longer a comfort.

She needed a companion now. Right now. But she knew that she couldn't conjure a lover out of thin air. Equally, that craving for companionship was near-overwhelming. She wanted to cry out. Wanted to beat the walls with her fists. Wanted to push her fists into that empty ache in her stomach.

Even pain would be preferable to that gnawing emptiness.

This was the time of night when desperation grew intense.

A desperation that often led to shameful thoughts. Even more shameful deeds. But what could she do?

If only a knock on the door would sound right now. And she could open that door and welcome in a stranger who would take away this ache of loneliness.

Chapter Sixteen

Beckerman watched the flashlight beam shoot through the dimly lighted room and sweep up a pair of pale legs. The gal had a hand over her crotch. She had a knocker missing, like someone might have hacked it off with a cleaver before doing the same to her nose. Maybe took them home for souvenirs.

'Turn you on, Gonzalez?' he asked.

'Up yours, man.' The younger watchman swung his beam to another statue: a nude, armless male.

'Look at that, will you? Damned Greeks don't show diddly on the gals, but they've got the guys hanging out all over the place. That seem fair to you? Huh, Gonzalez?'

Gonzalez didn't answer. He turned his flashlight to another statue, then another.

Beckerman suddenly understood. 'Christ, Gonzalez, you take a prize.'

'Hey, man, you can't be too careful in this line of work.'

'Careful, right. You gotta be real careful you don't die of boredom. You're new, you'll see.'

Gonzalez checked another statue. 'You're the soul of respect. Quinn died here last night.'

'Proves my point. The guy died of boredom. Fell asleep on the stairs.'

'You think that's funny, Beckerman?'

'It ain't as funny as a shit attack in a whorehouse, but it'll do.'

'I don't think that's fu—'

'Holy shit!' Beckerman grabbed Gonzalez's arm. 'That one moved!'

'Huh? Which?'

The pale beam jerked from statue to statue.

'There! See?'

'Where?'

'Yeek! Here it comes!'

Gonzalez wrenched his arm away. He shoved Beckerman. 'You think that's funny, man?'

'I *theeenk* so,' Beckerman said, mimicking him.

'I'm gonna break your face.' He shoved Beckerman again.

'Hey, lay off. Can't you take a joke?'

'That ain't no joke.' He raised his flashlight like a club. 'This is a joke?'

'Calm down, hombre. For Christ's sake. You want to—'

The sound of a thud interrupted him. 'What the hell was *that*?'

Gonzalez was already running for the doorway.

'Wait up, damn it!' Beckerman called, keeping his voice a loud, hoarse whisper. He rushed into the hallway and found Gonzalez standing motionless, gaze searching the poorly lighted area ahead, revolver out.

'Don't be so eager, kid. Let's stay cool, and take it slow and easy . . . and stay alive. If we've got bandits we'll contain 'em and call the cops. No fancy shit, right?'

Gonzalez nodded.

'Okay, let's have a look.'

They stepped forward silently. As they approached the entrance to the Callahan Room, Beckerman saw that the cordon was hanging loose. He could remember hooking it into place himself, after an earlier inspection of the room. He pointed at it. Gonzalez nodded.

Crouching by the entry, Beckerman looked inside. Nobody in view. But the lid of the mummy's coffin lay on the floor.

It hadn't been there earlier.

He straightened up. 'I'll stay here,' he whispered. 'Go phone the cops.'

'Forget it, man. We can take 'em.'

'Do what I said, okay?'

'*Su madre*,' Gonzalez muttered, then rushed in.

Beckerman pulled his revolver. Followed. Their light beams criss-crossed the room. Strange shadows lurched on the walls, jumped, writhed; phantom shapes. Beckerman kept his finger off the trigger to stop himself from snapping off shots at them.

Then the overhead lights came on, killing the shadows. Beckerman took in every corner. He found no one. Gonzalez, hand on the light switch, grinned nervously at him.

They went to the coffin and looked in. It was empty.

'Oh shit,' Beckerman muttered.

'Hey, man, maybe they moved it?'

'Someone did.'

'I mean, the museum people put it someplace else, you know?'

'You're an optimist, kid. Face it, we've been ripped off. Let's get it in gear.' He was already running as fast as his limp would allow. 'You secure the front door, I'll check the rear.'

They split up. Beckerman ran down the hall to a fire door at the far end. He pushed the metal door open gently, trying not to make a sound. For a few moments, he listened. He heard nothing. Stepping onto the landing, he eased the door shut.

A single dim bulb above the door provided the only light. Sidestepping, he looked up the stairwell toward the third floor. The light didn't carry far. As he stared at the dark upper stairs, his tense excitement changed.

Changed to fear.

He raised his flashlight. His thumb poised on the switch, ready to send a beam into the darkness above him, but he didn't dare; couldn't bear to push the switch.

Hadn't felt like this since he was a kid. A kid lying in bed, rigid with terror, staring across the room at the black opening of the closet. That yawning maw. Nothing inside the closet. Nothing harmful. Nothing to hurt a kid. Okay? He could prove it by turning on a light. To turn on the light, though, he would have to get out of bed. If he moved, *IT* would leap out, grab him, gnaw the life out of him.

Lowering the flashlight, he turned away. He took two steps across the landing, wanted to look back over his shoulder – just to make sure – but didn't because it would be too much like gazing into that closet once again.

He started slowly downward. The bulb from the landing threw his huge shadow on the wall ahead. He felt nervous, looking at it. What if a second shadow suddenly appeared beside it?

You're going nuts, he told himself.

He was glad when he turned at the next landing. No more shadow. Below him, the light of the first floor looked like an old friend.

He hurried down to it.

Yeah, and you know you're following Quinn's footsteps; just don't go tripping over your own feet, okay?

He opened the door, looked out. No sign of anyone. Careful to avoid turning his gaze toward the upper stairs, he crossed the landing and stared down toward the basement.

He had a new shadow. He watched his feet to keep from seeing it. At the next landing it disappeared. But there was no friendly light shining below. Only hostile darkness. That same hostile darkness that once occupied his open closet.

Where was that light? Why was it no longer shining? The damn thing must have burned out. Shit.

Or did someone take care of it?

He turned his flashlight on. No hesitation. He was beginning to feel some of his old confidence.

That all changed, halfway down the steps, when he heard a sound behind him. Scraping sounds like a dead, windblown leaf skidding across concrete. A dry sound.

He whirled around.

He stared.

The thing was standing half a dozen steps above him. In the bright beam of his flashlight, he saw more than he wanted to: arms and legs like sticks, bulging joints, red hair falling in glossy swathes; a gaunt and eyeless face.

Its mouth opened wide.

He screamed as it leaped down at him, red hair billowing.

Gonzalez heard the scream. He ran across the lobby, flung open the metal door of the fire exit.

'Beckerman!'

From below, he heard faint sounds. Splashing sounds like water spattering concrete. He rushed down the stairs. At the landing, he shone his light into the darkness. Something was on Beckerman, hunched over his sprawled body, head jerking like a dog tearing meat from a carcass, only he couldn't see clearly because of the mane of hair that blazed fiery red in the beam of the flashlight.

It wasn't a dog.

It had red hair like a woman.

It was working on Beckerman's neck. Blood flew, raining against the walls and floor. Crimson. Liquid. Rivulets of gore.

With alarming speed, the creature scurried off the bloody body and turned. The light beam hit its face.

Gonzalez went numb. He wet himself. Warm liquid ran down his leg. As it drenched his socks and pooled in his boots it helped bring him back to reality.

'Freeze!' he shouted.

The creature attacked, arms reaching out, mouth gaping, eyes twin pits of darkness that seemed to plunge into eternity.

Those teeth.

Those god-awful white teeth.

Framed by black, dead lips.

Gonzalez reacted. Dropped the flashlight. Clutched his right wrist. Aimed. Snapped off four shots, the blasts coming so fast they sounded like one continuous, terrible explosion.

He knew the bullets hit the target. They had to. The range was nothing. An arm's length. But did they stop the thing?

Did they hell.

It rushed against him. Red hair, a billowing mass around the shriveled face. Good God, it looked as if the creature's head had burst into flame. Swirling reds, golds; the hair seemed to double the size of the body.

At that moment it struck. He jammed the muzzle to its chest, fired his last two rounds.

Their impact hardly made the thing twitch. Like shooting a cardboard box. Cordite smoke billowed.

Fingers clutched his face and hair. Claw fingers. Fingers with curling, misshapen fingernails. Gonzalez stumbled backwards, fell onto the landing, lost the revolver; it went skittering across the floor, sending out sparks as gunmetal collided with marble.

The face pressed toward him, mouth snapping; its eyeless sockets eager somehow. Those voids filled with something more than darkness. Something unseen, hungry, evil, murderous.

He tried to shove the snapping mouth away. The dry stick tongue worked behind the teeth. Raising his hands, he pushed at the shriveled head, trying to force it back. The head twisted quickly, shaking the mass of hair that tumbled over his own face; ancient tresses fell into his mouth; dusty curls reached the back of his throat. He convulsed, gagging at the mouthful of hair.

He lost his grip on the twisting head. Its teeth caught two of his fingers. He felt the bite, heard the crunch of bone, saw his hand come back with finger stubs dripping.

The thing clawed his face. He cried out as it pierced his left eye.

He heard teeth snapping.

He heard flesh rip as they found his throat.

He heard . . .

. . . Nothing . . .

Chapter Seventeen

The girl with red hair and green eyes was watching Ed when he woke up. She lay on her side, gazing through the bars of the cage.

Ed Lake waited for her to speak.

She didn't.

Didn't move either.

Merely watched his face.

Ed remembered how he'd heard her being tortured in the dark just a few hours ago. He burned inside, outraged that someone could do such a terrible thing and . . .

. . . And he burned because he remembered something else. He remembered how the cries she made had turned him on.

Christ, he thought she'd been having sex. That she was enjoying. Not hurting.

But that didn't make it all right, did it? He remembered how he couldn't take his eyes off her naked back when the light came on. It was only when she turned that he'd seen how the skin around her nipples had been sliced in a sunburst effect of radiating cuts.

Now . . .

Well, now she just stared at him with those green eyes.

So what do you say in a situation like this? When you're in a cage? When the stranger in the next cage has just had her breasts sliced?

Hi ho, honey. You're looking chipper.

Hardly.

Those nipples of hers must be aflame with pain.

Not that she showed the hurt, though. Her gaze was steady.

At last he had to say something, even if totally lame-brain: 'Are you okay?'

She didn't answer. Just kept on staring.

'I'm sorry what they did to you. It was terrible. I mean it must have . . .'

Her eyes looked into his.

He clenched his fists. 'The motherfucker should have his heart ripped out . . . ripped right out, the bastard.'

She gazed at him. Then: 'Don't become too involved with what happened.'

'But . . . hell, it was barbaric . . . the way you bled.'

'I can take it.'

'Take that mutilation, but—'

'Listen, do you know what the alternative is?'

'The alternative?'

'The alternative is far worse. Ask Marco.'

'That's right.' Marco's voice came from behind. Ed glanced back at the blond guy in the next cage. 'The alternative is . . . *grrch*.' As he made the noise he drew his finger across his throat.

'They've killed people?'

'Then where you goes nobody knows.'

'But you people talk like this is normal. That this is how the entire world is.' Ed couldn't believe how the pair accepted the situation. 'Remember who you are. You've been kidnapped by crazies, put in cages and now you're being tortured.'

Marco said. 'You learn to adapt.'

'It's out of our hands,' she said.

'If you don't accept that this is your life now you'll crack up.'

She nodded. 'Then you're as good as dead.'

'Jesus H. Christ,' breathed Ed. 'I'm not going to surrender to this. I'm not.'

'Your funeral, bud.' Marco lay back down on his mattress. 'Wonder when they'll bring breakfast today?'

'Soon,' she said.

'Hope it's not hard-boiled eggs. They lock me up tight.'

She shrugged. 'Might be bacon sandwiches. We haven't had those for a while.'

'I hope the coffee's hot. It's been tepid the last couple of days. Boy oh boy, that's one thing I hate. Tepid coffee.'

Jesus H. Get this! They're talking like a couple of people staying in a cheap hotel. Not a godforsaken torture chamber. Ed wanted out. This was madness. Maybe these two were mad?

Hell, maybe *he* was mad?

Imagining this.

Maybe he was in a psychiatric ward somewhere.

The shock of being dumped by Janey was too much.

Now he was in a rubber room; he was shot full of lithium, drooling, kacking his diaper, whining for Mom. But not here. Not in this beast house. Where bad things happened to decent people. Where invisible torturers came in the dark.

'Hello . . . hell . . . owe.'

He snapped out of it. Looked across at the girl.

She held her hand out through the bars. The blanket was pulled up over her breasts, preserving her modesty.

'Hello,' she repeated. 'Anyone home?'

She smiled, straightened her fingers. They were just inches from his cage. 'Guess we haven't been properly introduced. My name is Virginia.' Her eyes were solemn. 'Don't laugh. My parents told me I was conceived there.'

Marco chuckled. 'Count yourself lucky your mother wasn't screwed in Nantucket.'

She sneered, 'Thank you, Marco Polo.'

'It's not Marco Polo, it's Marco *Paulo*.'

'Like who cares?' She looked at Ed. 'So? What do you want me to call you? Mister?'

He reached out. Took her hand in his. He felt her fingers squeeze his fingers. It seemed like a gesture of affection. An electric thrill ran through him.

Hell, what a way to shake hands. What a situation!

But she was beautiful to look at.

Beautiful to touch.

Before he could stop himself, he pictured himself embracing her, burying his face in that thick, copper hair. *Jeez, what's wrong with me?*

Those thoughts zipped through his head in a flash. He found himself saying, 'I'm Ed Lake.' She still held his hand so he found himself adding lamely, 'I go to school at Riverside High.'

'You don't say.' She smiled. 'I went there, too. A few years before you, though.'

'Great,' Marco said. 'The perfect place for a high-school reunion. In a cage.'

At last she withdrew her hand.

Don't do that, he thought. *Don't. I like touching your skin.*

But she lay back down on the mattress on her side with the blanket pulled up over her breasts. Her shoulders were bare, though. The skin was smooth, flawless. And despite her injury, and the strain she must be under, she looked good. Sort of glowed. An erotic power shone in her eyes.

'I'd lay off chumming up together across there, Eddie boy.'

'I'm not chumming up.' Ed was annoyed by Marco's tone. The guy sounded jealous.

'Looks pretty chummy from the deluxe suite over here.'

'Knock it off, Marco,' Virginia told him. 'He's just being nice.'

'Just being stoopid.'

'Hey!'

'Like I said, Eddie.'

'Don't call me Eddie.'

'Like I said, *Eddie*, you've gotta save your strength.'

'There you go again, why do I have to save my strength?'

He gloated now. 'You'll find out. So save your strength. Save every drop.'

A kind of sullen silence settled over the room. No one spoke. Virginia and Marco retreated under their blankets. Ed didn't know if they were sleeping or not. He glared at the humped mound where Marco lay. Why did he keep talking about 'saving your strength'? What was all this? The guy wouldn't elaborate. Neither would Virginia, come to that. So, Jesus H. Christ, why? What kind of test would he face? The thoughts were still running hot through his skull when the lights went out.

Oh God. Here we go again. This time it's my turn. His belly shriveled. The strength bled out of him.

He turned his head left and right.

Too dark.

Saw nothing.

Heard nothing.

Just like last time.

Then he'd realized someone had entered the room. Then had come cries from Virginia as the sadist ran a card-cutter along her tit.

Bastards. If he could get his hands on them.

Wait . . . it's happening. He sensed movement. Heard a rustle. Felt a whisper of a draft across his bare arms. The hairs stood upright on the back of his neck. Shivers spiked his back. He clenched his fists.

Coming for you, Eddie boy.

Gonna get you good and hard. Maybe do a little blade work on your face in the dark.

No, they won't. I'm going to punch out.

Fists clenched, he waited.

Waited.

He pictured the sadist in the night-vision goggles.

He can see you. You can't see him. He has power over you. You see nothing in the dark.

But, yeah, Eddie boy, he sees all right. He sees victims.

Maybe they're going to work on Virginia. Maybe cut her again. She'll start crying out. Start panting.

You'd like that, wouldn't you, Eddie?

Don't call me Eddie.

Wanna hear her squeal? Wanna hear her say 'Please' *again in that way that makes you throb between your legs?*

Christ, why did the mind chatter always run away with him? He couldn't stop those tormenting thoughts. Devil thoughts. He pictured Virginia near-naked beneath the blanket. Maybe stuff was happening to her again . . . maybe she felt the cold—

Uh.

He blinked as the lights flickered on. He looked round. This time he expected to see their captor. But the room was empty again. Empty apart from the three cages with their three occupants.

Virginia sat up blinking. She held the blanket high up her chest.

Marco made a hoot. 'All right! Breakfast time!'

Ed's eyes swiveled. A tray had been left outside the bars of his cage. It was one of those molded ones they give you on airlines. In one hollow was an English muffin, in another scrambled egg. In the third strips of bacon. Beside the tray, a cup of black coffee.

'Ed. Eat everything,' she told him.

'My appetite isn't what it was.' He gave a grim smile.

'Eat everything. Force yourself. Keep your strength, Ed. For Godsakes, keep your strength.'

Why?

What's going to happen to me?

He nearly asked the questions but something reined them back in.

Anyway, he had a suspicion that he'd find out real soon.

Over in his cage Marco had slid the tray through the gap in the bars and had begun to eat. 'Not hot, but good,' he sang. 'Hmm, smoked bacon.'

Now Ed saw the reason for the airline-style trays. They were narrow enough to pass through the bars. The English muffin was surprisingly good. Someone had been generous with a splash of melted butter. The scrambled eggs were mixed with ground black pepper the way he liked it. Spicy. Gave a little heat, too, to the otherwise lukewarm egg. The bacon had cooled during the journey from the kitchen to the cages. But it was okay. The coffee was tepid but strong. With no forks he followed his two roomies, eating with his fingers and using the English muffin to mop the tray. He noticed the other two ate hungrily, enjoying the simple meal. He glanced at Virginia. She ate, sitting with her back to him.

Her back was bare. With a free hand she flicked back the long

95

copper hair so it wouldn't trail into the food. That bare back. It was beautiful. When she reached for her coffee he saw the pale orb of her breast jiggle a bit.

Just a little bit. But it was sexy enough to warm his loins.

Marco sang out again, 'Eat up, eat up, Eddie, old buddy. Food equals energy, you know. You're gonna need it soon.'

Chapter Eighteen

The rear door of the museum opened.

Amara stepped out into the warm night. She stood motionless, head tilted back as if taking in the beauty of the pale moon.

Then she started across the asphalt of the parking lot.

From the edge of the field, George watched. His ears heard the dry skin of the creature's feet whisper against the blacktop. His sensitive nose picked up odors, too. Sweet spicy odors that didn't quite mask the smell of ancient bone and flesh. The scent of the tomb still clung to the mass of hair that seemed to possess a life of its own. One moment it hung in heavy swathes down the hard glossy skin of the back, the next a warm up-current of air caught it, lifted it, bore it upward so individual hairs separated and floated around the skull-like head.

A red mist.

A mist like airborne droplets of blood.

The dog watched.

Never seen anything like this before.

Never encountered such a figure.

Yet deep down sensed its nature. A dead thing walking. He sensed its dark and terrible power.

Amara paused. Turned her dark, rounded head; hair floating around it. Each strand swimming in the night air.

The dog sensed life in the strands of hair that reached down beyond the crust of the corpse's buttocks, down to the back of its legs. He watched the hairs writhe and dance in the moonlight. Although the dog could not put into words what he witnessed, the image that came into his canine brain was of snakes.

As if each red hair was a blood-red snake, only as thin as a fiber. Each one malevolent. Each one possessing eyes. Each one of the thousands of hairs seeing the brown dog shivering at the edge of the parking lot.

Amara saw, too.

She walked in the direction of the frightened dog.

So frightened he stood as still as one of the statues in the museum. So frightened he could hardly breathe.

The creature moved toward him. Its naked body gleamed like hard black resin in the moonlight. Black tarry lips parted. White teeth glinted.

The dog wanted to run. Wanted to turn tail. Wanted to kick up dust with his paws. Gone. History. Back across town where this dreadful thing could never find him.

But he couldn't move. He could only stand, panting hard until his lungs hurt inside his ribs.

He watched the creature quicken its pace toward him. Although it had no eyes he knew it saw him perfectly. A brown dog shivering with fear. Vulnerable. Unable to save itself. A small life soon snuffed out. Dog bones broken. Brown fur scattered to the winds.

A whimper reached the dog's throat. Nothing more.

It could do nothing. Move nowhere.

His eyes rolled upward to see the figure loom over him. With the moon behind, it stood in silhouette. A hard outline revealing bone-thin limbs; a hard rounded head covered with hard skin. And, surrounding the head, a vast halo of floating hair through which the moonlight burned in a bloody flame.

It extended its arms, hands hooking, fingers turning to claws.

The bat flew into Amara's hair. Leathery wings beat the curls, bat claws became entangled in red tresses as it struggled to free itself. As Amara's hands went to tear the tiny struggling creature from her hair, the spell was broken.

George barked once at the strange creature, then dashed away.

Chapter Nineteen

Imad wrapped the bodies in plastic garbage bags and maneuvered them downstairs. Hydra was easy to carry. Blaze, however, weighed far too much and had to be dragged.

He left them on the rear sundeck. In the tool shed he found a shovel. He walked across the moonlit lawn to the flower garden. Began to dig. Dig deep.

Perhaps he was digging near the very spot where Callahan had buried the other intruders so many weeks ago?

The thought unsettled him.

Callahan had killed with the same shotgun. He'd no doubt used the same shovel, dug in the same vicinity, the metal blade chopping in the soil with the same awful crunching sound like an ax through firm flesh.

Callahan had died that night.

Perhaps . . .

Imad shivered, wiped the sweat from his face, kept on digging.

He kept on digging until a hand swung up from the soil to slap the shovel. With a scream he leaped back. The hand dropped out of sight into the darkened pit.

He stepped cautiously to the edge of the hole, and peered in. An arm was exposed from the shoulder to the fingertips. The edge of his shovel, he realized, had probably caught it in the elbow join, making it jump like that. *And slap the shovel like that!*

Nevertheless, he couldn't bring himself to dig anymore.

He filled the hole.

Hiding the rotting corpse once more.

The smell . . .

Imad retched.

With great effort, he dragged the bodies through the house and out the front door. One by one, he swung them into the trunk of his Mercedes.

Then he drove for miles.

In the darkness of a wooded road, he unloaded them. He returned the plastic bags to his trunk, fearing that they had his fingerprints. Then he climbed into his car. As he backed away, his headlights shone on the green of Hydra's dress.

Someone might remember the dress. Expensive. Exclusive. Not many of them about. They might remember the couple who bought it: the dark little man with the girl young enough to be his daughter, but obviously not his daughter because she was light-skinned. No. They had a different relationship; even the dumbest could guess what that relationship was.

He climbed from the car. He removed her dress, being careful not to look at the awful gap where part of her face had been.

He backed away. In the harsh beams of the headlights, her skin looked like raw dough.

Imad remembered the pleasure he had taken from her body. How she had moaned and writhed beneath him. Her pointed nipples. How they'd hardened beneath his probing tongue.

Such a waste.

But she had been greedy and stupid . . . and careless about her friends. She had done this to herself. If it had not ended now, it could only have ended at the side of a different deserted road, on a different midnight, with a different set of wounds.

He backed the car away.

The headlights retreated, leaving her in darkness.

Chapter Twenty

Tag woke up in a sunny bedroom, a sheet keeping him warm against the fresh morning breeze. He lay on his side, his back to Susan. Her hand was on his upthrust hip.

'Morning,' he said.

'Hi.'

She moved, fitting herself against him, breasts pushing against his back, lap warm against his rump, thighs against the backs of his legs. He felt her lips on the nape of his neck.

'Sleep well?' she asked.

'Mmmm.'

He rolled over and held her. She was incredibly smooth and warm. He kissed the curve of her neck, the hollow of her throat. He lingered over her nipples, taking each in his mouth, rolling them with his tongue. His hand slipped between her legs. The telephone rang.

'Damn,' she muttered. She turned away, picked up. 'Hello?'

She listened.

'Oh my God! I see . . . sure . . . yes, okay . . . I'll be right over.' She hung up.

'What happened?'

'The guards. They were killed last night. Two of them.' Her face looked as though she smelled something bad. 'Their throats were ripped out.'

'Their throats? That's how Callahan died. These guards, did they have dogs with them.'

'I don't think so.'

'Let's get over there and see what's up.'

'That's why they called. They want me to inventory the Callahan Collection again to see if anything's missing but the mummy.'

'It's gone again?'

She nodded. 'They've already searched the museum.'

'Did they check the men's john?'

'First, probably.'

She sat up. Tag watched, warmed by the sight of Susan's body

101

as she swung her legs off the bed and stood up. She disappeared into the bathroom.

Tag dressed, thinking. This was Saturday, the only time this week in which his day off coincided with hers. He'd planned, vaguely, on taking Susan and Geoffrey to the beach. Since she had to go to the museum, though, he would go along. The inventory shouldn't take long. Besides, this would give him a chance to check out the killings. He picked up his Colt Python, clipped its holster to his belt.

As he was tying his shoelaces, Susan came out of the bathroom, still naked.

'All finished,' she said.

Tag knew he should wash his face, shave, brush his teeth, comb his hair. Instead, he took pleasure watching Susan step into her brief black panties. He moved in behind her. Reaching around, he cupped her breasts in his hands.

'Aren't you going to shave or something?' she asked.

'Can't tear myself away.'

She turned to him. They kissed. He slid his hands down the smoothness of her back, pushed them under the slick sheath of her panties, caressed her buttocks. Skin silky, oh-so-smooth . . . hell, oh-so-desirable. He wanted to ease them down then—

'We have to go,' she whispered against his mouth.

'I know, I know.'

Reluctantly, he took his hands away. He went to the bathroom. By the time he'd chased the heat of sheer lust away, he found Susan dressed in slacks and a loose-fitting white blouse.

On the way out, she looked into Geoffrey's room.

'He's sleeping,' she said.

They told Maria good-bye, explaining they had to go out in a hurry and, no, they'd have to skip breakfast. Tag eyed the fresh pancakes and syrup regretfully. All his appetites were keen this morning.

Susan stepped back as Tag opened the front door. Stains still showed on the hall carpet, though Tag had scrubbed it last night after men from the Department of Animal Regulation had taken away the cat's body. The door was stained, too, but the words were no longer legible.

'Hallway's clear,' he said.

He took her hand; they walked to the elevator.

'You'll be coming in?' Susan asked.

Tag nodded.

'Might as well park out back, then. We can use my regular space.' She directed him to turn left near the museum entrance where three police cars were parked. At the corner, the road curved to the right. 'Follow it to the rear,' she said.

In the back of the museum, they came to a sign that read *Employees Parking Only.* She pointed out her reserved space. At its head, *S. Connors* was painted on a low concrete curb.

'They'll have to change that "S. Parker,"' she said.

'Soon, I hope.'

'Can't till the divorce is final. That'd be bigamy.'

'Also bad form,' Tag added.

He parked and they got out. The sun was a heavy, pleasant pressure on Tag's face. He took a deep breath of air rich with the scent of flowers. At the sound of yelling, whooping kids, he turned his eyes to the field beyond the parking lot.

A boy in the weeds took a combat stance, aimed his pistol at a running suspect, and yelled, 'Blam!'

'The kid's good,' Tag commented.

'Maybe you should go over and recruit him.'

'I'd rather play along.'

'No fair. You'd use real bullets.'

'Sure, but I'd only shoot to wound.'

Susan took hold of his arm, laughing. It was a tense laugh. Tag looked into her eyes; saw fear. 'What's wrong?' he asked.

She smiled, shrugged, and shook her head sharply. 'Nothing.'

'You're really upset.'

'I'm okay. Just a little scared, that's all. Anything wrong with that?'

'No, it's—'

'I mean, I'm trying to handle all this. Right? I'm okay . . . haven't broken down yet. Kept my head, so far. I'm keeping it all together, aren't I, Tag?'

'Sure.'

'I shrugged it off when that first watchman got killed, didn't make a fuss about messing with that damned mummy in the john, didn't crack when that disgusting Mable beat me up or killed that poor little kitten and hung it outside my home.' She swallowed. Her face was fixed rigidly, but her eyes filled with tears. 'And now there are two dead men in there and I don't even know them, and I've got to go in . . . *must* go in . . . only the last thing I want is to go in there. *I don't want to.*'

103

All her control broke. She flung herself against Tag, hugging him tightly, crying like a lost child.

He held her. 'It'll be all right, Susan,' he said, soothingly. 'Please don't cry. It'll be all right. It'll be all right, believe me.'

Chapter Twenty-one

'So, how long have you been here?'

'Doesn't the guy ever stop asking questions?' Marco complained.

Ed Lake sat on the foam mattress in the center of the cage. He'd been talking to Virginia but Marco lobbed in comments. Virginia sat with the blanket round her, facing Ed. Marco lay on his back, feet crossed, and resting them on one of the horizontal bars of the cage so that they were higher than his body.

'How long?' Virginia shrugged. 'Hard to tell.'

'Days? Weeks?'

'Weeks, I guess.'

'And you, Marco?'

'Always. I've been here always.'

'Always?'

'That's what it feels like.'

Virginia nodded. 'You can't tell night from day in here. We guess the lights go on for around six hours, then off for four. It's a completely artificial day-night cycle.'

Marco laughed. 'If we weren't tough cookies it could screw us up.'

Ed rubbed his jaw. 'How did you get here?'

'Don't remember,' Marco said.

'You must remember something.'

'Not me. You might say I'm of no fixed abode. I moved from place to place. I'd been staying with a girl over near the beach until she threw me out. Then I took to sleeping on a bench outside a shopping mall.'

'Can't have been easy?'

'I made it easy, brother. I took the girl's stash of weed. I got mellow every night. Hours just seemed to float away on a summer breeze.'

'Then what?'

'I went to sleep on my bench one night. When I woke up, here I was in the beast house. Someone had whammoed me as I slept. Easy-peasy.'

. Ed looked at Virginia. 'You?'

'It seems so stupid.' She looked embarrassed.

'No more stupid than I felt.' Ed smiled. He remembered being dumped in the wilds by Janey.

'I'd been to a party,' she said. 'Drank too much, then I walked home.'

'Now that was stupid.'

'Tell me about it. But I lived just down the street. A three-minute walk at most. So, there I am alone in the middle of the night in a quiet neighborhood when all of a sudden – wham.'

'Knock on the head.' Ed touched his still-matted hair.

'No, a stun gun, I figured. Didn't see anyone, just felt a jolt like someone had kicked me in the small of the back.' She shrugged. 'Woke up here with Marco as my neighborino.'

'And we've been inseparable ever since.'

'Yeah, inseparable.' She didn't smile.

Ed looked round. 'And you've never heard any noises from outside? Anything to tell you where you might be?'

'Look at the white panels on the walls.' Marco pointed with his bare toe.

'Soundproofing,' Virginia added.

'Yeah,' Marco chuckled. 'In this place no one can hear you scream.'

'That's not funny.'

'Sure is. Remember George? That guy who split his sides laughing?'

Ed lifted his head. 'George?'

'An ex-roomie,' Marco said.

Ed looked at Virginia. 'There have been others here?'

'Some.'

'What happened to them?'

Marco wriggled his bare toes. 'They come . . . they go.'

'Jeez.'

'So it's best to play the game to their rules,' Virginia said meaningfully. 'They ask, you *do*. Got that?'

Ed still couldn't believe they took this lying down. They sounded so damn passive, so damn *accepting*. Like the fight had gone out of them.

'But surely the cops are out searching for us?'

Even Virginia laughed at that one.

Marco knelt up. 'Now that kind of doofus talk makes me need to take a leak.' He pulled down his zipper. 'Watch out, you folks in the front row. *You will get wet.*'

106

He knelt up and pointed himself in the direction of the bowl full of sawdust. His aim, Ed saw, wasn't all that it should be.

Jesus Christ. It can't get any worse than this.

Wrong, Eddie.

It's just about to do exactly that.

The lights got killed. That same instantaneous plunge into darkness. Maybe this was the lights-out phase for sleep. But Ed doubted it. Surely the period of light had been too short.

He heard Marco murmur. 'Ladies and gentlemen. Fun in the beast house is just about to begin.'

Ed's scalp tingled. Suddenly it felt cooler in the room. He looked round but as before he couldn't see a thing in that total darkness.

Here it comes, he told himself.

Here it comes, Eddie boy.

Did you keep your strength like Marco said? Or did you drizzle it all away asking questions?

But what will they make me do? What kind of challenge am I going to face?

Maybe it won't be me.

Maybe Virginia? Might be Marco?

It doesn't have to be me this time. They might not be interested in me and—

'Lake.'

Holy shit, they're talking to me.

'Lake.'

But how do they know my name?

Marco told.

Hey, maybe Marco's in on this. When the lights go out how do I know that Marco doesn't simply unlatch the cage door and come out to do his funky stuff? He might have sliced Virginia's breasts. He's got the night-vision goggles hidden somewhere.

He walks round. Seeing us. We don't see him.

The thoughts blasted through Ed's brain. They were paranoid thoughts but, hell . . . Maybe they were *both* in on this. Both Marco and Virginia could be his captors. This could be their game.

Pretend to be captives in cages. Pretend they were just like him.

But why?

To get inside his head, of course. Enjoy his fear close up. Watch his face when he reacted.

Marco went on and on about keeping his strength up. Working on him. Working on the scare centers of his brain. Maybe that was it.

But what about Virginia's injuries?

Self-inflicted.

But, hell, that must hurt.

Maybe moviemakers' fake blood?

'*Lake.*' The voice came again. It was a man's deep voice. Eerily slow, too. Inhuman-sounding.

It sent ice down his spine.

'*Lake. In a moment. I will give you instructions. You will follow those instructions to the letter. Otherwise you will be punished. Do you understand?*'

He remained in the same frozen crouch position, not moving so much as a finger.

'*Nod if you understand, Lake.*'

So they do see me? Jesus H. Christ. He'd never been so scared.

'*Nod if you understand, Lake.*'

He nodded.

'*When the lights are switched on again go immediately to the panel that is suspended beneath the roof of the cage. Lie flat on your back on it. Then present your penis.*'

'What!'

'*Present your penis. Present it in such a way that it will pass through the aperture in the top of the cage.*'

'No way. I'm not sticking my cock through no goddamn hole!'

Virginia hissed: 'You've got to, Ed. Remember, play by their rules.'

'But, shit . . . I can't. I mean I really—'

The deep bass voice continued calmly. '*Lay on the panel. Present your penis. This is a matter that requires no further discussion.*'

The light flickered on. He glanced at Virginia. Solemn, she nodded. *Do it, Ed.* Marco had retreated under the blanket as if he didn't want to witness what happened next.

Holy shit.

What were they going to do?

To take his dick out of his pants and push it through a hole in that Perspex. Jesus.

What's wrong, Eddie? Afraid of runaway lawn mowers?

The thought escaped before he could rein it in. Lawn mowers and penises. They were three words that didn't belong in the same sentence. No way.

But what choice did he have?

Skin crawling like a jug full of ants had been poured onto him, he made his way across the cage. In front of him the transparent panel was at eye level as he crouched there. Maybe ten inches or so separated it from the transparent roof of the cage. It would be like lying on a bunk bed that nearly touched the bedroom ceiling.

Virginia whispered. 'Use the bars at the side to climb up, then slide onto it on your back . . . that's it. Now push your feet against the bars to move yourself along.'

It wasn't easy. He yanked his back muscles working his way onto the panel. His forehead butted the Perspex top of the cage. He couldn't raise his knees to use his feet so he had to worm his way further along, pressing his palms against the panel.

Jesus H. He felt like he'd become a sandwich filling now, with the glass panels forming the two slices of bread.

Present your penis.

That's what the deep voice had told him. *Present? What a way to phrase it.*

But, good God, what would they do to his dick once it was poking up in the fresh air? You couldn't feel any more vulnerable than this. That's why guys outdoors took a leak facing a wall or a tree. You felt uncomfortable exposing your cock to the wilderness. It felt so unnatural.

A passing eagle might mistake it for a tasty snake.

It wasn't easy in that confined space but at last he took his dick from his pants and . . . yes . . . *presented* it. Gritting his teeth, he poked the head up through the hole in the Perspex. Fortunately, the hole was smooth round the edges, so there should be no nasty cuts. He tried to lift his head to see how much of itself it did *present*. Only he couldn't lift his head on account of the sheet of Perspex above his face.

Was Virginia watching?

Was Marco?!

He didn't know whether to feel terrified or embarrassed. Mortally embarrassed.

Terminally embarrassed.

Shoot.

Then the worst thing happened.

The worst he could imagine.

The thing he didn't want to happen just went and happened anyway.

The damn lights . . . they went out. It was dark again.

And here I am lying with my dick pushed through a hole in

the Perspex. He swallowed, gritted his teeth, waited for the next installment.

OK, buddy. You can pause the tape now. I've seen enough . . . The mind chatter didn't help. Especially when it began talking about runaway lawn mowers.

Swirling blades. A soft column of flesh. *Who's gonna win that wrestling bout, Eddie boy?* He closed his eyes. Not that it mattered. He wouldn't see what happened next in the dark anyway.

He waited.

Waited.

Minutes sneaked by in no particular hurry.

Maybe this was the test . . . to lie there with his dick poking up above the Perspex. This could be a psychological challenge. Not physical.

A rustle sounded close by.

The drafts came again. Cool air played over the end of his manhood. A manhood that wanted to shrivel back into his body where it would be safe from whatever lay out there.

He pressed his lips together. A cry tried its darnedest to escape.

He wanted to yell: NO! NO! NO!

But he must keep quiet.

Revealing his fear might only excite his captor into . . . no, he didn't want to speculate any further than that.

The sensation came that somebody was moving above him. He heard a whispering sound. Feet moving across the floor.

Holy shit!

The Perspex floor flexed above him. Had someone stepped from the elevated catwalk onto the cage roof?

Moments later came a faint squeaking sound.

Oiling the lawn-mower blades . . .

No. Someone was tightening the bolt arrangement that supported the panel that held him. Slowly he was being raised up toward the underside of the cage.

This went on for several minutes.

Inch by inch he felt himself being winched up tight to the roof of the cage. He felt his entire body pressed hard against it. His hips were crushed full against it; his skin burned with the pressure.

Was the intention merely to crush the life out of him?

But just as the pressure against his ribs made it difficult to breathe it stopped.

Then came the next shock.

Something touched his penis.

110

He could see nothing in the darkness. And right now he didn't want to. What if it was a blade? *Remember the cuts on Virginia's breasts?*

Was it his turn?

But this was light. A feathering motion. Faster.

It was a tongue!

Someone's tongue flickered lightly against the end of his cock.

He remembered the man's deep voice . . . *oh, holy Christ, not that!*

His reflex action was to recoil but the panel he lay on held him firmly against the underside of the roof. He couldn't move even a fraction of an inch. He was wedged tight against the Perspex. Only his cock was free and that was being . . . well, he couldn't believe it but it was being licked with a rapidly flickering tongue. First the very tip. Then down the shaft.

Now fingers . . . encircling. Gentle, tentative.

But then firmly. Holding his cock upright so the whole mouth could slip over it, gorging, swallowing.

Teeth next. Leastways, that's what his runaway imagination anticipated. Teeth clamping hard. Biting. Rending. Ripping.

He could hardly keep from screaming. But somehow he held the scream inside his body. He sensed his survival depended on it.

And then came something even more shocking.

The ultimate betrayal.

In utter disbelief he realized his body was responding to that sucking mouth. Felt himself stiffen, felt himself rise, growing big in the mouth.

The Perspex flexed above him.

Whoever was above him was getting excited. They were moving, getting in a better position to suck at him.

What had happened to him? Why was his body becoming excited by the attentions his penis was receiving?

He felt disgust . . .

Worse, he felt turned on. With involuntary movements he tried to thrust his hips forward into the face of his abuser. His heart hammered. He wanted to writhe in pleasure, only he was constricted by the two sheets of Perspex that held him sandwiched so tightly.

Then the mouth was gone.

Relief.

Disappointment.

He didn't know which emotion was the strongest. Saliva cooled on the end of his penis. It throbbed as it stood erect above the Perspex.

111

Then it happened so fast.

He gasped with disbelief. Understanding only too well what was happening to him now.

More importantly, what was happening to his cock.

He clenched his hands. Gritted his teeth. Curled his toes so tightly that his feet ached.

Someone had slid onto him. The sensation was different. He knew that someone now knelt on the Perspex above him. Taking his cock into them. Inside.

But inside what?

He felt a slick encircling.

Felt the motion, too, as they lowered themselves, then raised a little before sliding slowly . . . slowly down his erect shaft.

Please – he wanted his cock to shrivel back.

But the perfidious hank of meat wouldn't. It became so swollen that it felt as if it would burst. He'd never been as hard as this. Or as thick. He felt himself penetrate deep into this captor's body.

But what was he penetrating?

He could feel the moist lips, the clenching muscles.

It reminded him of when Janey sat on him and impaled herself on his cock.

But there was that man's deep voice . . . *Dear God* – and here he was enjoying this . . . no, *loving* this sensation.

It didn't take long before he felt himself ready to ejaculate.

But he remembered Marco's talk of saving his strength. He knew he must hold back until his captor had been satisfied.

Still the motion continued. The rising, falling. The tightly encircling collar of flesh about his flesh.

He must delay. He couldn't permit himself release.

They were insatiable. His captor rose and fell above him for hours. He heard them panting. But they said nothing.

They were inexhaustible. A squeaking sound came to him and he realized it must have been their perspiring hands taking the weight against the Perspex and slipping backwards and forward.

He centered himself on the pain as the Perspex squeezed his ribs. The pain distracted him from coming to orgasm.

His captor must be satisfied first.

Punishment would follow if he disappointed.

The Perspex flexed above him. In the darkness he saw nothing. Heard nothing but the squeak of moist palms against Perspex and muffled panting. No words.

This won't end . . . this will never end.

On and on. The perpetual motion of flesh against his flesh.

But then it changed. Louder panting, convulsive movement from above. Spasms.

Then the body was gone from his. He heard the bolts turn and the panel lowered. In a moment he'd slithered off, soaked in perspiration. He thought he'd have orgasmed with his captor but sheer willpower on his part had prevented his release.

Still hard and still slick from his encounter he crawled on his hands and knees across his cage. Found his mattress in the dark. Curled up tight on it. Kept his eyes shut. Waited for the hours to pass.

Chapter Twenty-two

Imad woke up late in the morning, still tired. Bone weary. He had not fallen asleep until dawn and feverish dreams had made the sleep a broken, frightening business. Flashes of dream returned to him. A woman weeping brokenhearted in the closet. A grimy hand slapping lifelessly at his windowpane. The green dress, torn and bloody, whirling around his bedroom; falling on his face, smothering . . .

Dreams.

They can't hurt.

But they can torment. They can haunt.

Tonight, he would find himself a woman for comfort.

He thought of Hydra spiked on his erection, writhing on it, head thrown back, small breasts thrust out. Hydra twitching as the small bullets pierced her back through the closed door as Blaze had fired from within the closet. Hydra, half her face gone, a dark cavity where there ought to be a cheek and a cynical eye and a glossy forehead . . . and a hole where part of her brain should have been, and . . . He clenched his fist, perspiring.

She was like Amara, that way.

Amara.

That fiend had caused all this – filled him with fear and guilt, started him searching the low parts of town for women. Certainly, there had been women before. Many of them. But there had never been the desperation. There had never been a Hydra.

She was Amara's fault.

He should go to the museum and defecate at Amara's feet. Throw hog fat onto the wizened corpse. For ancient Egyptians, like Jews and Moslems, pigs were unclean animals. Long ago in Egypt criminals were sometimes sewn into pigskins and buried alive. It killed their spirit and deprived the man of his afterlife with the gods.

He was tempted to take Callahan's memoir along, too. It would be a relief to be rid of it.

No.

114

Callahan had said to keep it in the safe unless Amara walked. So far, all seemed well.

So far.

Perhaps she had only walked that night to avenge herself on Callahan.

Perhaps.

In any case, he would return the memoir to the safe and go to the museum without it to defecate at Amara's feet. A ripe offering of turd for her late Egyptian majesty.

Laughing sourly, Imad climbed out of bed. He would not defecate at Amara's feet today. Nor tomorrow. The farther he remained from the hideous thing the better.

He put on his robe and slippers, then went downstairs. Outside, the morning was sunny and hot. A wonderful day for the beach. Perhaps he would go there later. Perhaps he would find a lovely young woman, ripe and golden in a bikini. And willing. She must be willing, of course. If Imad's good looks and charm and mammoth bulge at the crotch were insufficient to woo her, his wealth would likely accomplish the task.

He picked up the morning paper. As he walked back to the house between beds of sweetly scented flowers he slipped off its string and opened it. On the front page, he saw no mention of bodies being found in remote woodland. He waited until he was inside before studying the paper more thoroughly. He checked each page. As he progressed he began to realize that there would be no mention of the bodies of Blaze and Hydra. After all, didn't the paper go to press late in the night? At perhaps two or three a.m.?

Nothing would appear, he realized, until tomorrow morning's edition. Assuming the bodies would be found by then.

He was about to fold the paper shut when an article caught his eye. Merely a single column beneath a blurry photograph of a middle-aged man in a uniform.

WARD WATCHMAN KILLED IN FALL

The night watchman at the Charles Ward Museum fell to his death late Thursday night, police officials stated. According to a police spokesman, the watchman, Barney Quinn, 53, sustained severe neck injuries in his plunge down the main staircase to the museum's lobby. The cause of death is under investigation.

Quinn, a former police officer with the . . .

115

Imad skipped the biographical details, but returned to read the first paragraph again and again. *The Charles Ward Museum . . . severe neck injuries . . .* It told him little. Even so, it frightened him. There was more meaning in that dark print for Imad than he dared to imagine.

Amara . . .

Chapter Twenty-three

'Blam, blam!' Toby yelled.

Byron kept running. If he could just get to the clump of bushes, he'd circle around and ambush Toby.

'Hey! I gotcha!'

'Did not,' Byron shouted over his shoulder.

'No fair! I gotcha right in the heart!'

'I've got a bulletproof vest!'

'Do not!'

'Do so!' Byron ducked behind the bushes. Looking back, he saw Toby walking slowly toward him through the high, brown weeds. The boy's lips were sticking out.

'I *got* you!' Toby called. 'No bulletproof vests. We agreed.'

'Okay, I'll take it off.' Byron sneaked sideways, staying low behind the bushes. Then sprang out. '*Ker-plam! Plam, plam!*'

Toby turned to him, startled.

'Three shots right in the heart.'

'Ha, ha. I'm wearing a bulletproof vest, too.'

'Yeah, but I've got armor-piercing bullets!'

'Do not!' Toby raised his plastic pistol. 'Blam! Right in the puss!'

Byron grabbed his face, spun around, flopped to the ground. When he opened his eyes he found himself staring into a leathery, eyeless face. He scrambled to his knees and peered at it. Then at the rest of the body. All that hair . . . red like the red foil you sometimes get on chocolates . . . and skin. Dry. Hard. A glossy look. For some reason it reminded him of the skin of a melon, only dark brown. He could even smell it. A spicy smell. Like a deli store. One that needed airing out badly. The spicy odors settled thickly in the back of his throat.

'Wow,' he whispered. 'Toby . . . hey, Toby!'

'You're dead.'

'Toby . . .'

'At least you're supposed to be.'

117

'No. Come here.'

'Gotcha right in the puss.'

'Come here and take a look!'

'I know that trick, so no can do.'

'Toby. Take a look! This is really cool! Quick!'

Toby, holstering the made-in-Hong-Kong weapon, ran through the weeds to join Byron.

As they both stared at the dark face, a spider crawled out of its left eye socket, scurried down its ruined cheek that was as ridged and wrinkled as a 3D relief of the Rockies.

At last Toby managed to ask, 'What is it?'

'A body.'

'I saw my Uncle Frank's body. Looked nothing like this critter.'

'Maybe this one's older?' Byron suggested.

'Maybe it isn't even a body. Maybe it's a dummy. Somebody put it here to scare us.'

'Looks like a body to me, a naked body,' Byron said. 'A real old one. Like maybe an Indian that got killed a hundred years ago.'

'What are those?' Toby asked, pointing.

'Her tits, stupid.'

'Yuck.'

'See that? She's a girl.'

'You sure?'

'Geez, Toby, don't you know nothing? If it hasn't got a whang, it's a girl. That's how you tell.'

'I knew that.'

'Sure you did. *Sure.*'

'I *did.*'

'The only way it isn't a girl is if a guy gets his whang cut off with a knife. Then he turns into a girl, anyway. They call 'em trans-sectionals.'

'Sure. I knew that. Everyone knows that.'

'Yeah.' Reaching out, Byron touched the brown skin of the body's shoulder. It felt dry and wrinkled, like beef jerky, before smoothing out across the chest to that melon skin effect, then rising to hollow breasts that looked like . . . well, they just looked gross. 'Oooh, you oughtta feel it.'

Toby nodded. He looked pale, but he knelt in the weeds, poked a finger into the mass of red hair. It scrunched dry as the weeds themselves that were under his knees. The hair felt springy at first but his finger got entangled with it the deeper he pushed. For some irrational reason he thought something would be in the

118

hair. Something that'd *bite*. He withdrew his finger and touched the same shoulder as Byron now pawed. 'I don't think it's real.'

'Sure it is.'

'We better tell our folks.'

'Are you kidding? They'd take it away from us.'

'It isn't ours anyway.'

'Is now. Finders keepers.'

'What do you want it for?'

Byron shrugged. 'Come on, let's take it over to my house.'

'This way,' Byron said, leading the group of children across his backyard. There were five of them: Barbara and Tina, who'd been skipping rope in Tina's driveway; Hank Greenberg, found shooting baskets alone; and the Watson twins, picked up on their return from the A&W. He could have dug up half a dozen more neighborhood kids, but Barbara was getting impatient and she was a big mouth. Big, *loud* mouth. After the group was finished, he'd have Barbara out of his hair. He could take his time and round up a bigger bunch. Guaranteed no big mouths.

'It better be good,' Barbara said, 'or you've gotta give us our money back.'

'Oh-ho no,' Byron told her. 'It's fifty cents a look and you can't have your money back, no matter what.'

'I'm not gonna look, then.'

'Okay. Get outta here.'

'No.'

'Want to get pounded?'

'Give him his money,' Tina said. 'If it ain't any good, I'll get my brother on him.'

At the corner of the garage Byron halted the group and took the admission fees. The Watson twins paid with a fresh, stiff dollar bill. The others paid in quarters. He counted the take: $2.50.

Pretty good.

But that's only the start.

This's gonna make me rich.

'Okay,' he told them. 'Follow me.'

He led them behind the garage where Toby was waiting.

'Feast your eyes,' Byron announced, trying to sound like a ringmaster. He swept his hand toward a long shape propped against the garage wall. A white sheet shrouded it from top to bottom.

'Bet it's Tommy Jones,' Barbara said, sarcastic, and reached for the sheet.

119

Byron shoved her away.

'Hey!' she snapped.

'Don't you touch it.'

'It's just Tommy Jones. And this is just a rip-off. Come out, Tommy.'

'If it is,' Tina said, 'I'm going to fetch my brother and there's gonna be some busted noses round here.'

'It isn't Tommy, it's . . .' Byron paused for dramatic effect. 'It's the body of an ancient Apache squaw.'

'Oh, sure.'

'Everyone stand back,' Byron advised. 'You don't want to be standing too close.'

Barbara stepped away. She folded her arms across her T-shirt. Her face wore a smirk.

'Ready?' Toby asked.

'Wait.' Byron turned to his audience. 'You've gotta promise to keep it a secret and never tell a soul.'

'It's something dirty,' Barbara muttered.

Tina giggled. 'Tommy's probably in his birthday suit.'

'Cross your hearts and hope to die,' Byron said.

They all crossed their hearts except Barbara. 'I'm not gonna hope to die. It's against my religion.'

'Okay. But you've got to promise. If you tell anyone, we'll pound you.'

'You and who else, doofus?'

'Jeez, Barbara,' Tina said. 'Let's see what it is.'

'I know what it is. It's Tommy Jones with his peter out.'

The Watson twins giggled.

'Tommy's in Yosemite,' said Hank Greenberg. 'His uncle's gotta place up there. They go fishing in the—'

'Hey! You guys want to see this or don't you?' Byron sounded short of patience now.

'Sure,' Barbara said, arms still crossed, still belligerent. 'Let's see what the big deal is.'

Byron nodded to Toby.

Toby tugged the sheet. As the sheet pulled loose, revealing the dried body, the figure tipped forward. The girls screamed. They leaped out of the way as it fell into their midst, hair flaring out, sightless eyes staring into their faces. Still screaming, they ran. Didn't stop running. Piercing screams faded into the distance.

Hank, pale and shaking his head, backed away. 'You guys are

120

nuts,' he muttered. Then he ran, too. Made it as far as the driveway, tossed his cookies, then carried on running.

'They're gonna tell,' Toby said.

'Let 'em . . . just let 'em. We'll just say they lied.' He felt the money in his pocket. $2.50. This was just a start. He was gonna be the richest kid in town.

'But what about *her*?' Toby pointed at the mummy lying face down, its hair covering its back in a swathe of tumbling curls.

Byron stared at her, frowning. This was his cash cow. He wasn't losing it for nothing. 'I've got it! We'll hide her someplace. In my bedroom. Under my bed. They'll never think of looking there.'

'Is anybody home?' Toby asked.

Byron shook his head. 'Mom took the baby with her when she went shopping. Come on. Take the head.'

Chapter Twenty-four

'I feel so grubby,' Susan said as they left the museum later that morning. Tag held her hand. They walked down the broad, concrete stairs. 'Like I've been touched by something really disgusting.'

'Not my hand, is it? I swear I washed it this morning.'

She laughed softly. 'No, it's not your hand. I'm sure your hand is immaculate.'

'It's not *that* clean.'

'No, but don't you ever feel that way? Like you're contaminated from just being close to where such awful things have happened?'

'I feel that way a lot. You know what takes care of it? A long hot shower, strong soap, a couple of drinks, a good meal, clever conversation – preferably not alone. A little siesta.'

'Preferably not alone,' Susan repeated, the smile still playing on her lips. 'Sounds like it might do the trick. I really have to spend more time with Geoffrey today, though. We don't see enough of each other as it is.'

'We've got the whole day ahead of us,' Tag said.

'I'm feeling less grubby by the second.'

'Just doing my job, ma'am.'

They went to Tag's apartment. The siesta came first, but they didn't sleep. Then they took a long hot shower, soaping each other, growing excited by the feel of slippery skin, and making love awkwardly in the tub with water pelting them like hot rain. When they were dry and dressed, they took the elevator down to Susan's apartment.

She made Tag a Bloody Mary. She drank Perrier and played with the baby while Maria made tacos for lunch.

'This has turned into a pretty decent day,' Tag said.

'Not half bad,' Susan agreed. She felt good. Her skin tingled. She felt warm inside, pleasantly satisfied. The horrors at the museum, the threat of Mable, seemed far away.

After lunch, they took Geoffrey outside for a stroll in the sun. Tag looked happy pushing the baby carriage. They walked for blocks, finally arriving at a municipal park where they sat in the bleachers and watched kids playing softball.

'Geoffrey's going to be a real slugger,' Tag told her.

'What makes you think so?'

'I'm gonna teach him.'

Geoffrey turned his wide eyes on Tag and grinned as if he understood.

When a foul ball shot toward his face, he blinked, kept grinning. Susan gasped with fright. Tag flung out a hand, caught the ball, tossed it back to the kids with a good-natured, 'Here you are.'

'I think it's time to leave,' Susan said quickly.

They were watching television later that afternoon when the telephone rang. Susan picked it up. 'Hello?'

'Hello? Miss Connors? Is Taggart Parker in?'

'Yes, he is. Just a moment, I'll see if I can tear him away from the game.' She waved the phone at him. 'For you.'

'Marty Benson?'

She shrugged.

Tag took the phone. 'Hello . . . ah, Marty. What've you come up with?' He listened for a long time, nodding at first, then frowning. Finally, he said, 'Okay, thanks a lot.' Hanging up, he turned to Susan. 'Marty's with the Medical Examiner's Office. I asked him to call me when they finished with Becker and Gonzalez.'

'That was quick.'

'They put a rush on.' He sat down and stared at the television. The crowd went wild but he didn't react. He was lost in thought, frowning.

'Well?' Susan asked.

'The wounds on both men match. They weren't made by dog teeth.'

'Then by what?'

'By a human.'

'*Jesus.*'

'Gonzalez got off some shots before he was killed. He hit something and knocked out plenty of tissue and bone. They analyzed it . . . and it was old, real old. Dead tissue. Traces of natron, some chemical they used to . . .'

'I know. Part of the mummification process. They used it to speed up the dehydration which in turn halted decay of the flesh.'

'The upshot is, they're pretty sure the tissue came from the mummy.'

123

'He was shooting at Amara?'

Tag sighed into his folded hands. 'It sure looks that way. And get this: they found scrapings of the same flesh under Beckerman's fingernails. Also long red hairs on the body that matched those found in Amara's coffin.'

'What does that mean?'

'If I threw you down on the floor right now and ripped off your clothes . . .'

'You wouldn't dare.'

'And you tried to fight me off . . .'

'Which I would, since Maria's in the kitchen.'

Tag grinned, but he looked tired. 'You might scratch me. You'd likely end up with some of my skin under your nails. Maybe some of my hair lying around.'

'And they found Amara's skin under Beckerman's nails, and some of her hair on his clothes, which means he was fighting with her?'

'That's how it looks. It's impossible, of course.'

'Ever heard of a guy by the name of Lazarus?' Susan asked.

'Sure. I've also heard of little green men from Mars.' He shook his head. 'Maybe Beckerman and Gonzalez ran into robbers in the stairwell, and one used the mummy as a shield. That could explain how she got shot. Then the guy flung her at Beckerman and he scratched.'

'Okay, but they were killed by human teeth.'

'The robbers could have done it.'

'Oh? How?'

'They subdued Beckerman and Gonzales and used the mummy's teeth to finish the job.'

Susan's eyes widened. *'Manually?'*

'Like this.' One hand holding his forehead, he used his other hand to work the jaw.

'That's pretty far-fetched,' Susan told him.

'Considerably less far-fetched than a living mummy.'

'Suppose Amara did kill them?'

'That's pretty hard to suppose.'

'It would explain a lot, though, wouldn't it?'

Tag grinned, shaking his head. 'Sure. It would explain everything. Only problem is, dead people don't walk. Dead people don't bite.'

124

Chapter Twenty-five

'You'll never make it into pictures.'

'Says who?'

'You've gotta have an agent.'

'I'll get one.'

'How?'

'They'll be listed in the phone book. I'll call them up.'

'Yeah, right. As if that doesn't happen a hundred times a day.'

'I've got experience; they'll see me.'

'Showing your jugs on a hardware poster isn't much experience.'

'I've done TV ads.'

'When you were fifteen.'

'I'm only seventeen now.'

'TV ads for a burger joint that no one's ever heard of outta North Carolina.'

'And corporates . . . I've done corporate video.'

'That's not the movies, is it? Charlottesville ain't Hollywood and you know it, Grace.'

'No one asked you to come.'

'I'm not staying to get boned by old Joe now you've gone.'

'Pix! You said you wouldn't bring that up again. *You promised.*'

Cody slammed the steering wheel with his palm. 'Pix. You keep quiet about that now.'

'It's the truth,' Pix protested.

'I don't care if is the truth. We agreed that's history. We wouldn't talk about Joe again. Okay?'

Pix was sixteen years old. She chewed a strand of her long blonde hair; face sullen, she stared out the window at passing traffic.

He slammed the steering wheel again.

'*Okay?*'

By way of reply: 'I'm hungry, Cody.'

'We'll eat soon,' Grace said. 'We'll be in LA in a couple of hours.'

'I want something now. I'll start feeling sick if I don't eat soon.'

'Want an apple?' Grace sounded tired. This journey was taking it out of her.

'I don't like apples.'

'You ate one this morning, Pix.'

'That's 'cos there was nothing else.'

Cody aimed to be diplomatic. He couldn't stand another row after driving near-nonstop for the last three days. 'I'll find a diner.'

Grace shook her head. 'No diners. The police'll be looking for the truck.'

'Don't worry,' he told her. 'I'll park up then walk. No one will recognize me.'

'Yah,' Pix sneered. 'You're hardly America's most wanted, Cody.'

'You lay off that.'

'The FBI are sure going to put every man they've got on the case,' Pix said, then held her nose so when she talked it sounded like a police radio. 'Attention. Attention. Be on the lookout for Cody Wilde, eighteen years of age, gas-station jockey from Going-Nowheresville, suspected of stealing fifteen-year-old Ford pick-up, worth approximately one hundred and three dollars, eighteen cents. Shoot on sight. I repeat. Shoot on sight.'

'Pix, will you quit it?' Cody fumed. *Would you believe it? Who runs away from home with their girlfriend only to take the kid sister along? A kid sister from hell who's whined, who's kvetched, who's complained for the last two thousand miles straight.* Still, better that she came along than being left home with Joe.

He glanced at Grace sitting beside him. She was beautiful. Dark Latino eyes. She had a great body. The body of a dancer. He knew he was in love with her, and he knew they were doing the right thing, escaping that hell-hole where she lived with her indolent mother and Joe who was . . . hell, who was no great shakes as a human being, never mind a stepfather.

The plan was to shoot for Hollywood. They both knew she could make it into movies if she got the right breaks. She *could* dance. She *could* act. A couple of years ago she'd starred in a whole string of TV ads for Chucky Burger in their hometown. She'd made good money, which she'd set aside for college.

Wise kid.

But she hadn't banked on Old Joe moving in.

Huh, the college fund?

126

Joe found it, took it, spent it.

Grace's mother never even roused herself from in front of the TV. Never accused Joe. Most she whined was: 'Grace. I'm sure he had his reasons . . .'

Pix sang out. 'There's a diner. Hey, stupid. A diner!'

'I see it.'

'You've gone right past it.'

'I know. I'm going to park up, then walk back.'

Grace looked uneasy. 'The road's awful busy. What if there's cop—'

'Don't worry.' He pulled off along a dirt track that led into the desert. 'We can't be seen from the road here.' Parking the truck behind a mound of tires that some litter-louse had dumped, he switched off the motor. The relief of silence after hours of hearing the roar of the engine. Boy, Cody loved the sweet silence.

Not that it would last.

'I'm so hungry I could choke,' Pix said, winding down the window. 'Gee, it's so hot I could choke.'

Grace gritted her teeth. 'You want to choke? Be my guest.'

'Some sister you are.'

'Some sister *you* are, Pix. You begged to come with us, now you bug us nonstop.'

'Well, Hollywood's a stupid choice. You'll never get into pictures.'

'So what do you suggest, Pix?'

'New York.'

'New York?'

'We could've got work there!'

'Pix!' Cody slammed the steering wheel with his hand again. Sweat burned his eyes. His back ached from driving clean across the country. He felt dirty. Needed a shower. Needed a drink; a cold, cold beer. This endless arguing he *didn't* need. He took a deep breath to steady his temper. 'Pix. What can I get you to eat?'

When he took the orders he told them to stay put until he came back. 'I'll be twenty minutes, tops,' he told them.

'Ice cream . . . bring some ice cream.' Pix leaned out the window.

'It'll melt,' he told her, then walked away.

Grace watched Cody go. He walked like a Wild West hero along the desert track back to the highway. His brown cowboy boots raised dust with that nice even stride of his. She watched the way his lean

127

body in the denim jeans and jacket moved. There was a confident rhythm there. He glanced back at her and smiled that easy smile that she loved so much.

In her ear Pix humphed. 'I bet he takes ages. And he bet he forgets the mayonnaise.'

Grace hoped this was for the best. Maybe she should have stuck it out back home a little longer?

I could have married Cody. Found a place of our own. Being a teen runaway sounded glamorous. But these long hours on the road in a stolen truck were taking their toll.

Sure the truck was stolen from Mom's boyfriend.

And, for sure, the truck had been bought using *her* money for the TV work she'd done.

But she was certain that Joe would have reported it as stolen. And stolen by his girlfriend's daughter and lover. And maybe he would claim that they'd kidnaped Pix, too. Just to add a little more seasoning to the charge sheet. Cody could get time for this. Even though everyone knew that Cody was the gentlest, kindest guy you could ever meet. Okay, so he didn't shine bright at school where she'd first met him more than five years ago. But he was the last man on Earth to pull a mean stunt or bad-mouth anyone behind their back.

She didn't want to see him in trouble with the cops.

Maybe she could have stayed?

Maybe.

Maybe gone to her own private hell, too.

It all went crazy last week.

Joe had leered at her plenty. He even took to fingering her underwear in the laundry basket and making cheap comments. 'Bet Cody likes you in this. You dance for him like they do down at the Snake Pit? Dance with your back to him and rub your butt in his crotch, huh?'

Then last week she'd been woken by hands touching her under the sheet. She'd smelled beery breath panting into her face. Heard grunting. 'Your Mom's sick. I haven't nailed her in a week. Looks like your lucky night, Grace.'

'Joe?'

'Old Joe, friendly old Joe,' he slurred. 'Now pull up that nightie . . . up over your hips . . . there's a good girl.'

'Get off me . . .'

'C'mon, Joe ain't gonna hurt you.'

'No.'

'Nothing you ain't done before plenty, I bet.'

She reached out, yanked the light cord.

In the blaze of light she looked up to see Joe kneeling on the bed, pawing the sheet from her, his chin slick with saliva. With his other hand he was working himself hard. Panting. Face nearer crimson than red. Watery-eyed stare fixed excitedly on her body.

'Nice tits. Nice and firm. Big, too,' he muttered in surprise. 'Bigger than I thought . . . never would have guessed.'

'No, please, Joe.'

'Joe won't hurt yer.'

'*Get off—*'

'Might even enjoy it. Might want more in a day or so.'

'Don't touch me. Ow!'

Joe had clamped his thick fingers on her breast. Squeezed hard.

'Gonna get those nipples all pert and erect. Little nip'll do the trick.'

She took a deep breath, ready to scream the walls down.

'You do, you little bitch and I'll bang your little sister, so you be nice to me and your sis stays virgo intacto. You follow?'

Grace had frozen then. She knew that he would. Mom wouldn't do anything. Maybe she could hear now as she lay there in her own bed, shutting out the sounds, thinking about the lives of the soap stars who she cared about so much more than her real family.

'That's it. You lay nice and still, Grace. Oooh-ay, have you ever seen a boner as big as that?'

'Joe,' she whispered. 'Please don't do this to me.'

'Once this baby goes inside, 's gonna stir your brains some.'

'Don't . . . please.'

She looked down as his hand went to her throat. He squeezed. A message: *Don't mess with me, or else.*

Then his hand went down.

Down.

Down to her breasts again. They formed hard mounds in the cool air.

He kneaded them. Squeezed. Pinched nipples between nicotine-stained finger and thumb. Pinched hard until it brought a cry to the back of her throat. But she clamped her lips to stop the cry escaping with the ferocity it demanded.

'Good girl. You know when to keep your mouth shut.' He pinched

129

her nipple until it turned black and congested. 'Although I like it when a girl knows to open her mouth when the time's right. Know what I mean?'

In terror she looked up at his beer-sodden face. His jaw stubbled with gray.

He's going to rape me.

He's going to rape me and I can't stop it. He'll do the same to Pix if I resist. Oh, Mom, how could you?

She'd lain there. Looked up at the ceiling. Those rough hands squeezing, stroking, probing. She looked at the posters of pop groups on the walls. Tried to concentrate on them. Block it out. She focused on the picture of James Dean tacked to the back of the door.

Joe's fingers reached down to the cleft between her legs. Fingers pushed hard.

'*Stop it.*' Her arm swung up and she scratched the side of his face. She couldn't take this anymore.

Joe looked down at her in fury. Bloodshot eyes grew to the size of eggs in his face.

'I was tryin' to be nice . . . if you don't want nice you can have rough.' He slapped her.

Her head whipped back against the pillow. Her face felt numb; her mind swam, dazed.

'Now I'm gonna flip you over . . . I'm gonna nail you in the ass . . . teach you a little respect.'

Grace felt his hands on her body, turning her over. A second later she lay on her stomach, her bare bottom upward. Then he was on her. The weight of him pushing so hard in the small of her back she felt her spine would snap.

Agony.

Unbearable agony.

Got to shout. Got to scream.

But he pushed her face into the pillow. Now she couldn't even breathe.

'Gonna show you. Once this baby goes in, 's gonna split you like a melon.'

She felt him pushing at her. Trying to force his penis into her, but she was too dry. He couldn't slip inside.

'Got a little trick of my own,' he panted in triumph. 'This does the trick.'

He shifted his weight off her but still pushed with one hand in the middle of her shoulder blades, holding her down. She lifted her head, turned it.

In the mirror of the dressing table she saw what he did next.

Her stomach turned in disgust.

He hawked wetly before spitting a great mouthful of sputum into his cupped hand. Then he rubbed it onto the bulbous swelling on the end of his penis.

'Lubrication.' He grinned. 'Good ol' slippery lube.'

She felt him lower himself back . . .

No . . . can't . . . won't . . .

With his weight shifted from her top half she pushed herself up onto her left elbow while with her right hand she reached back. Grabbed his balls in her fist.

'Don't you dare,' he snarled. 'I'll beat you—'

With all her strength she squeezed . . . twisted . . . pulled.

His scream set all the dogs in the neighborhood barking.

Now a week later, here by the pile of tires in the desert, Joe was thousands of miles away.

Pix was safe.

Although that didn't stop her complaints. Complaints about the long journey. Complaints about sleeping in the truck. Complaints about an uncomfortable this . . . an irritating that . . .

After Grace had cooled Joe's ardor she'd grabbed what she could, including Pix, then fled the house in Joe's truck. There came a confused whirl of telling Cody everything. Then the crazy dash out of town at the dead of night.

Now here.

'Here' was a desert.

With the sun going down. And with stumpy trees that looked like zombies from some bloodthirsty horror film.

She'd switched on the radio for a while. Surfed the stations. One carried a news report of two guys being killed at a museum; the theft of a mummy . . .

She found a music channel. Flamenco music . . . she liked that . . . made her think of faraway places. Mexico . . . beautiful dancers whirling in brightly colored skirts beneath starry skies.

'I hate that music,' Pix said. 'Find some rock.'

Thud.

At that moment a hand struck the windshield. Grace started. In the back Pix gave a yelp of fright.

She looked out to see three guys. They weren't old. Could have

131

been high-school dropouts. They chewed gum and smoked black stumps of cigars. The one who'd thumped the glass looked at her through mean eyes. Grinned.

'It's Christmas, guys,' he told his buddies. 'Christmas come early.'

Chapter Twenty-six

While his parents were off in their bedroom getting dressed for a party, Byron ate his hamburger in the den. He watched a rerun of *Superman*. Then the news came on.

He was stuffing the final chunk of toasted bun into his mouth when the blonde newswoman said, 'Closer to home, our own Charles Ward Museum was the scene last night of a brutal double killing. Two security guards from the Haymer Agency, Arnulfo Gonzalez and Ernest Beckerman, were found slain in the museum when it opened this morning – this, on the heels of the death of guard Barney Quinn on the previous night. Lenny Farrel was on the scene this morning with our live-action mini-cam to give us this report.'

The picture changed to a curly-haired man holding a microphone. Byron recognized the museum's main entrance behind the man. 'With me is Lieutenant Carlos Vasquez, the officer in charge of the investigation.' He turned to the broad-faced man. 'Lieutenant, there's been a great deal of rumor afloat regarding the manner in which the two guards met their deaths. Can you shed some light in that direction?'

'Until the medical examiner has completed his investigation, Lenny, I'd prefer not to speculate.'

'We have information that they appeared to have been mauled by an animal.'

'I'd prefer not to speculate on the cause of death.'

'According to an earlier police statement, Lieutenant, the men were killed while trying to foil a robbery attempt. Was anything, in fact, stolen?'

Vasquez nodded. 'A portion of the Egyptian collection does appear to be missing. We assume it was taken by the perpetrators.'

'By "missing portion", are you referring to the mummy?'

'Yes. A mummy does appear to have gone.'

'A mummy?' Byron muttered. He stared at the television.

'Are other items missing?'

'Not to our knowledge.'

133

'Thank you, Lieutenant.' The reporter gestured to someone off at the side. The camera turned, showing a young woman who looked awfully pretty – even prettier than Byron's favorite teacher, Miss Bloom. She had soft hair, bright blue eyes. The neck of her blouse was open. Her skin looked like gold. One side of her face was bruised. Maybe someone had tried to punch her out. But who'd do something like that to such a pretty woman?

'Susan Connors is assistant curator here at the museum, and in charge of the Egyptian collection. Miss Connors, can you speculate as to the motive for the robbery? The missing mummy? Was it worth killing for?'

'I suppose it must be in some eyes. Three men are dead.'

'How much intrinsic value does a mummy have?'

'Normally, not more than a few thousand dollars. Their chief value – the reason they've been the targets of robbers through the centuries – is the objects buried along with them, either in the coffin or wrapped inside the linen bandages. This one had already been plundered . . . unwrapped. If she was buried with jewelry and precious artifacts it was stolen long ago. She's really nothing more than a pile of skin and bones.'

The reporter nodded. 'So you see little reason for stealing her?'

'She's a significant piece of historical heritage. That alone gives her a certain value. Some collectors would go to great lengths to have her.'

'Her? You will know her name, then?'

'Yes, hieroglyphs on the mummy case tell us her name was Amara.'

'And so people have gone to murderous lengths to steal Amara.' The reporter's face filled the television screen. 'Two men dead of causes the police refuse to disclose. Another killed in a mysterious fall, Thursday night. Amara, the missing mummy. The police appear to be baffled. This is Lenny Farrel, reporting to you from the Charles Ward Museum. Back to you, Bonnie.'

Nervously, Byron looked out the den window at the street. An hour had gone by since the newscast. Any second, the cops were sure to show up, blue lights flashing, sirens whooping. Cops with guns drawn. A bullhorn crackling. *'Come on out, kid, we know you're in there . . .'*

But maybe none of the other kids had seen the news. Maybe he was safe from arrest.

'You okay?' Karen asked, looking up from Jane as she peeled off soiled diapers.

He smiled for her. 'Sure.'

'You look kind of sick.'

'I'm okay.'

'Sure?'

'Yeah.'

He wished he could tell Karen about the mummy. It would make him feel better, talking to someone. She was nice. She was his favorite baby-sitter. Sometimes she let him stay up late to watch some creature feature. If he showed her the mummy, though, she'd probably tell on him.

The cops would take him away.

There I am in the cuffs. The cop's hand pressing down on my head as I climb into the back of the cruiser with its flashing blue lights. And there would be Barbara, ringside, grinning. *Hell.*

The cops might bust him for killing those guards. They'd be sure to think he did it. His prints would be all over the mummy. Maybe he'd get the gas chamber. In his mind's eye he saw Barbara, in the ringside seat again, right at the front where she could look through the glass panel of the chamber. Grinning all over her face. Grinning as he choked. Blue lips . . . bulging eyes. And the last thing he'd see would be Barbara's grin. *Hell.*

A black and white patrol car appeared on the street. Byron's stomach knotted.

They're here.

Come for me.

No messing.

Maybe one of the dead guards was a buddy of the cop?

'Don't bother with the arrest on this one, Bill . . . this one's personal . . . this kid killed my best friend . . . Just blow the little freak away the second he shows his face . . .'

Oh, Holy Christ on a motorcycle. Byron's chest turned slick with sweat under his shirt. He craved the john . . . fear did that to people . . . he'd crave the john in the gas chamber. Barbara would scream with laughter when he peed himself . . .

Holy Jesus.

The car kept moving. The cops seemed more interested in chatting to each other. Hadn't even looked in his direction. As he breathed a sigh of relief as the black and white car cruised out of sight, a bicycle turned up along the driveway. A girl climbed off.

Barbara!

She tipped the bike onto its side, leaving the back wheel turning, then came up the driveway with long, self-important strides.

'Karen, can I go out for a second?'

'Your mother said to stay inside.'

'Just on the porch, okay? Somebody's here. I've gotta talk to her.'

'*Her,* huh?' She gave a knowing smile. 'Okay, but don't leave the porch, do you hear, Bryon?'

'I won't.'

Byron opened the door as Barbara was reaching toward the bell. He stepped out quickly, let the screen bang behind him.

'What do you want?' he asked.

Folding her arms, she grinned in her stuck-up way. 'I know.'

'Know what?'

'Whatcha think?'

'Search me.'

'I know your secret?'

'Yeah?' His mouth went dry.

'I know all about you and that mummy.'

'You don't know nothing.'

'Oh, yeah? I watch *Eyewitness News* every night. A young lady has to keep herself informed.'

'So?'

'I know all about it.'

'Like what?'

'Like it was stolen from the museum.' Barbara's eyes gleamed. This was pure candy for her. 'Like the guards were slaughtered like sheep.'

'So what?'

'I'm going to tell.'

'Tell who?'

'Who else? The cops.'

'You better not,' Byron warned. He took a threatening step toward her, but she held her ground.

'You don't scare me,' she told him.

'You'd better not tell.'

'I won't. But only if you let me see it again.'

'I haven't got it.'

'I bet.'

'I haven't. We took it back where we found it and left it there. Honest.'

'Then you won't mind the cops searching the house?'

136

'No. Why should I? I haven't got it.'

'Sure.' She scratched her thigh, then turned away. 'See you tomorrow, Byron. On *Eyewitness News*.'

He watched her walk toward her bike. With her short hair and T-shirt and shorts, she didn't look much like a girl. She didn't act like one, either. But she *was* a girl. Byron had a policy not to beat them up. You might threaten to pound them, but that was only talk.

It's chickenshit to beat up girls.

Guys didn't do that.

Not real guys, anyway.

He wished Barbara was a boy. He'd knock the daylights out of her.

'Okay,' he said. 'I've got it.'

She turned round, grinning. Came back to him. 'Let's see.'

'You can't come in.'

'Then bring it out.'

'Yeah, I can just walk through the house with it.'

'So?'

'The baby-sitter will see it, brain-box. How about tomorrow?'

'No dice. Show me, or I'll blow the whistle.'

'Whistle?' Startled, he looked at her hands.

'That's just an expression . . . a figure of speech. Don't you know *anything*, Byron? Now let's go in and have a look.'

'Okay. Come on. But keep your mouth shut. I'll do all the talking. Got that?'

'Just get on with it, Byron.'

Feeling humiliated, manipulated, he led her into the living room. 'Karen, this is my friend Barbara. I have to show her something in my room.'

Karen smiled strangely. Knowingly. 'In your bedroom?'

Byron nodded.

'This is a new one. What do you want to show her?'

'Nothing much.'

'Oh, you're just being modest,' Karen said, the smile broadening. 'Huh?'

'Okay, go ahead. But leave your door open.'

'Sure.'

They went down the long hallway to Byron's bedroom. The room was dim in the light of the evening sun, but Byron didn't bother with a lamp. Kneeling, he reached under his bed. Grunted. Started to pull. 'Help me, will you?'

137

'I should say not. Imagine the germs.'

He managed to slide the mummy out by himself. 'There,' he panted.

Barbara peered at it. Her nose wrinkled. 'That's disgusting.'

'Sort of.'

'She's naked.'

'Whatcha want me to do? Put her in panties and a bra?'

'You've probably been playing with her, haven't you?'

'Have not.'

'I'll bet.'

'You can see her front bottom.'

'I haven't touched her. Not *those* places. Who'd want to?'

'Only a creepy pervert like you.'

'Oh yeah?'

'Yeah, you can see your finger marks on her butt.'

'Cannot.'

'Pervert.'

'Am not.'

'If you're not a creepy pervert, what're you keeping her for?'

'Finders keepers.'

'Are you going to give her back?'

'Why should I?'

'She belongs to the museum, that's why. She was stolen. Finders keepers doesn't work when it's stolen. You still go to jail.'

Byron shrugged. 'Well, I might give her back. I'm keeping her tonight, though. Toby's gonna bring his Polaroid over tomorrow. We're gonna take pictures of her.'

'That is gross.'

'It'll be neat. You can get in a picture with it, too, if you want.'

'Who'd want to?' Contorting her face, she touched the chocolate-brown mummy with the toe of her sneaker. The empty eyes seemed to stare into hers while the red hair formed a shining red halo around the skull-like head. And as for those teeth . . . 'Do I get to keep the picture?'

'Sure.'

'Okay, then. You can keep it till tomorrow. I'll let you. But then you've got to take it back.'

Byron nodded. He had no intention of returning the mummy, but it seemed a good idea to let Barbara think he would. That'd keep her quiet for tonight, anyway. Keep her from telling her parents who'd then tell the cops. By tomorrow, maybe he'd think of something else. He pushed the mummy under his bed, its hair crackling with static as

138

it dragged across the nylon carpet. He'd best open a window wide, too. Disperse the stale deli smell. The thing seemed to sweat garlic and onion odors.

'What time tomorrow?' Barbara asked.

'Ten. In the back of my garage.'

'And I get a picture free?' She was calculating the value of such a picture. That center-of-attention kind of value it would bring at school. 'It won't cost me anything?'

'It's free to you. But only you.'

'Byron, one more thing.'

'What?'

'Give me a buck.'

'Hey!'

'If you don't, I'll tell. Tonight.'

'You wouldn't.'

'The cops will be all over you like a rash.'

'That ain't fair!'

'It is, too. You made me pay to see it. Now you have to pay me to keep quiet.'

'You only gave me fifty cents.'

'So what? A buck or these lips start flapping.'

'Good thing you're not a guy, Barbara. I'd flatten you.'

'You and who else?' She held out her hand for the money. Grinned. 'Give.'

'You'll be sorry,' Byron muttered. He reached into a front pocket of his jeans, pulled out a crumpled bill.

'Thanks. See you tomorrow.'

He stayed in his room while she walked away. A few seconds passed. Then he heard footsteps approaching. Karen appeared in the doorway.

'Did you two fight?' she asked. 'Or . . .'

'Oh, Barbara's a creep.'

'I thought you said she's your friend.'

'Well, she isn't. She's a creeping crud. I'm going to bed.'

'All right.'

Karen paused at the doorway. 'You haven't left anything under your bed.'

He flinched. 'Like what?'

'Left something there you shouldn't?'

'Like what?'

'An old piece of pizza or garlic sausage?'

She's going to look under the bed. She'll see the mummy.

He stood by the bed with his calves hard against the bedframe side. 'Nothing's under there, my Mom made me clear everything out yesterday.' *Liar-liar-pants-on-fire.*

'It just smells a bit . . . well, spicy in here.'

'I ate a hamburger earlier. I'll brush my teeth.' He didn't know why he said that, but it sounded fairly convincing. Well, kind of.

'Best do that. And open the window wide for some fresh air.'

Karen left. Byron flopped backwards onto his bed and lay there, trying to figure a way to get his dollar back.

He dozed off.

When he woke his room was dark. He got up. On his way to the bathroom, he heard quiet voices. Karen must've had Eric come over. They were probably on the couch like the other time, kissing; other stuff, too, that made Karen pant: *Oh-oh-oh-oh-oh* . . . like she'd trapped her finger in the door.

Byron wasn't interested. In the bathroom, he washed his face, brushed his teeth, peed. He returned to his bedroom Shut the door, and stripped. The night was hot. Instead of wearing his pajamas, he put on a clean pair of jockey shorts. He climbed into bed. The sheet felt cool. A delicious ice-cream feel. He liked that. Rested the palms of his hands down on it. A second later he began to heat up again, so he tossed the top covers aside, and lay on his back, staring at the dark ceiling.

Tomorrow, maybe he and Toby could round up a whole bunch of kids. With ten kids they'd make five bucks. Ten bucks with twenty kids. That'd give them five each. For eight-fifty he could buy one of those Super Whack Slingshots. How many kids would that take? Let's see, fifty cents times . . . times . . .

He was asleep.

A night breeze disturbed the shade. A scratching sound filled the room.

Chapter Twenty-seven

Grace stared out the windshield. The three men looked in at her. Dirty, unshaven. The T-shirts they wore were ragged-looking. Oil-stained. Maybe even a little bloodstained, too. The setting sun turned their skin red. The one who'd swatted the windshield made a rotating motion with his finger.

Wind the window down.

No way.

Lock the doors.

She flicked the catches on the inside of the old truck.

The guy slapped the windshield again.

'Don't you know the meaning of the phrase "antisocial"?' He grinned. 'We only want to talk.'

She shook her head. Behind her, in the rear seat, Pix whimpered, scared.

'Hell-owe . . . hell-owe in there. Speak English?'

The guy grinned. His teeth looked as if he'd spent the day sipping road tar.

'Can you spare us all a cigarette, miss?' He grinned back at the others.

Grace caught her breath, forced herself to speak. 'Sorry. I haven't got any. I don't smoke.'

'Miss?' With exaggerated politeness, he pointed through the windshield at a pack of cigarettes on the dashboard. They'd have belonged to Joe. He called them 'Steppin' stones to heaven'.

'Miss? Aren't those cigarettes?'

The guy flicked the cigar butt at the window. It bounced. Sparking.

Nodding, frightened, she fumbled the cigarette pack from the dashboard, opened the window a crack, just wide enough to slip them through.

'Why, thank you, miss.'

'Keep them. Please.'

Now go away. Go away. The plea hammered inside her head but they didn't go away.

They sidled up to the passenger window. All three pressed forward to look through the glass at her. She was wearing shorts. Her brown legs stretched out long and enticingly into the well beneath the dash.

They grinned at each other.

Coming to a secret agreement.

'Grace?' Pix sounded strained. 'Let's get away from these men.'

'How?'

'Drive away.'

'Can't.'

'You gotta.'

'Can't. Cody took the key.'

'Sis, these guys are gonna hurt us. I know it.'

'They can't get in. The doors are looked. They'll—'

'Hey!' *Thump.* The big guy, the one who seemed to be in charge, swung his fist against the door. 'What you talking about in there?'

'Nothing.'

'Seemed like somethin'.'

'No—'

'You talkin' about us?'

'No.'

'Not nice talking about people behind their backs.' And to the other. 'Is it, fellers?'

'No, it ain't. Damn rude.'

The three laughed. One slapped the roof of the pickup, sending a thunderous clamoring round its interior. They laughed even more when they saw the frightened reaction from inside.

Where's Cody? Dear God.

Grace glanced back through the windows. The only things she saw were desert. Dry bushes. The pile of tires that was nearly the size of a house. And, dear Lord, it was getting dark. The sun sinks fast in a desert, she knew that. Plunges toward the horizon like a stone. Soon it would be dark. Soon the men would get impatient. They were horny now. They wouldn't wait.

Not when they could see the curve of her breasts through her shirt.

Didn't have time to put on a brassiere when she left home.

Didn't have time to grab much.

Only the clothes she stood up in. Truth of the matter: she wouldn't be wearing those soon if these three roughnecks had their way. And as for Pix in the back. They leered at her, angled their heads to see up

142

her tiny skirt. For a sixteen-year-old she had a full, woman's body. They could see her nipples through her T-shirt.

'C'mon, open the door.'

Thump.

'We're not going to eat you, are we?'

Grace gave a scared shake of her head.

'Aw!' They were enjoying the situation. One, in a greasy bandanna, hooted: 'Come out, come out or we'll blow your house in.'

This led to a chorus of *little piggies, little piggies* and then hog snorting.

These guys weren't just boisterous. They were buzzing on something. Maybe some of that cactus juice. The sort that gets you high . . . and dangerous.

'Now we *are* gettin' impatient,' the big one said, speaking so close to the window his breath fogged it. 'Open up.'

'No.'

'Open up or we're coming in after you.'

'Make 'em squeal like pigs,' shouted the one in the bandanna. 'Man, I love to hear 'em squeal . . . just like this . . . *heee-yeee-heee-yeee.*'

They laughed again, louder. Their leers got hornier. They were cooking now. They wanted in; they wanted body contact and heat and dirty things Grace had only heard about.

'Open the door, bitch.'

'Go away!' she yelled.

'Open the door or I start shooting.' The big guy bunched a rag round his pocket where he'd carried it through a belt loop. Poking from the rag, Grace saw a black barrel.

'Grace, he's got a gun,' Pix cried. 'You gotta open the door.'

'No.'

'They're gonna kill us if you don't.'

'They're gonna kill us if we do. When they've finished with us.'

Pix groaned. 'Oh shit. Stop them, Grace. Please . . .'

She slammed her hand onto the horn. Didn't make a sound.

Damned old truck. Did any thing work?

Outside the three guys fell about.

'What a heap of junk,' laughed one. 'Bet even the door locks don't hold.'

The tall one tugged at the passenger door handle. With a sick-sounding click the lock gave out, worn to shit by use. Grace watched in horror as the door opened.

'Oh boys—' the gang leader smiled '—it's show time.'

Grace looked up into his face as the smile turned into a grin. 'Me firsties, boys.'

The guy in the bandanna scowled. 'Hey . . . why do I always get sloppy joes?'

'You complainin'?'

'No, but—'

'Keep your mouth shut, then.' He spoke to Grace. 'Your call, girl. Make it easy on yourself or make it hard. Doesn't matter a damn either way to me.'

The third one hooted with excitement. 'Make her squeal, Joe. Just like a little pig. *Hee-yeeee! Heee-yeeee . . . uck.*'

Grace thought a big black bird had swooped down on the guy. *A tire?*

A big truck tire came out of nowhere. It sailed down out of the sky and struck the guy tread first on the shoulder. The pig squealer went down like a chunk of the moon had fallen on him.

The other two looked round in confusion. Grace leaned forward and looked at the top of the tire mound. A figure appeared in silhouette. A second later Cody ran down the slope of black rubber. Tires spilled from the mound. Cascaded down. A dark avalanche. Tires bounced. Struck the side of the truck. Bounced over it, the two guys fending them off as best they could.

Cody appeared by the side of the truck, steadying his balance. 'Okay,' he told the two guys. 'It's finished. We're moving on.'

'What about our buddy? Look what you've done to him.'

The pig squealer had managed to pull himself up onto one elbow in the dust. His head sagged. The guy was only semiconscious.

Joe, the gang leader, squared up. 'You say it's finished. We say otherwise.'

'Yeah.' The bandanna wearer backed him. 'We say when it's finished.'

'Look.' Cody held up his hands. 'Don't let this get out of control. We don't want any trouble.'

'Says you.'

'Look what you done to our buddy. Bust his shoulder, then say you're moving on.'

'Payback time.'

'Careful,' Pix warned. 'He's gotta gun.'

'Yeah.' Joe smirked. 'So you get out of here, pretty guy. We've got something that needs attending.' He winked at Grace. 'Say, you've got a nice soft mouth.'

144

'Sucks like a Hoover, I shouldn't wonder.' The guy with the bandanna chuckled.

The guy on the floor mumbled, 'Shit, my shoulder.'

Cody advanced across the sea of spilt tires. 'I'm not backing off. Quit this before someone really gets hurt.'

'Yeah, my gun can do some hurtin' if you don't do some vanishing into the desert over there.'

Grace leaned forward, looking at the bunch of rag with the black tube in Joe's fist. 'Cody?'

'You okay, Grace?'

'Cody. It's not a gun.'

'Shut your face, bitch,' Joe growled.

'It's a—'

'Bitch, shut—'

'A pen.'

Joe scowled in fury. 'So who needs a gun, Cody? Come and take the pair of us.' The guy flung the rag and pen away.

'I don't want any trouble,' Cody said. 'We'll just be on our way. Forget that—'

'No way. You're going to have to fight your way out. Or are you yellow?'

'We're leaving.' Cody made to get into the truck but the tall, mean-looking guy was on him. Dealt him punches to the side of his head. Cody tottered backwards. Steadied himself.

The guy in the bandanna grinned. 'Guy's chicken, Joe.'

'Time to deck the bastard,' Joe said as if it was a dull chore, but one that had to be done. He stepped forward, fists swinging.

Cody blocked them.

Moved forward lightning-fast.

Fists flashing in the setting sun.

Cody didn't aim for the face. Instead, landed half a dozen crunching body blows into Joe's lean frame.

Joe rolled back against the pickup, straightened, then walked forward, fists raised. Then he paused as if forgetting what he was supposed to be doing. Took another two steps before dropping into the dirt, sending up a billow of dust.

The guy in the bandanna had come round the truck, maybe figuring to do some kicking once Cody was on the ground. Only it was Joe on the ground. When he saw Cody turn to him with that look in his eye . . . that look that told you someone *meant* business, he backed off. 'It's cool, man, it's cool. I don't want no trouble.' He ran back around the truck, tripped over the guy with the bust

145

shoulder, then loped away along the track. Seconds later Joe and the other guy followed, one holding his side, the other holding his shoulder.

Five minutes later Cody sat with Grace and Pix in the pickup. He handed Pix the brown paper bag with the sandwiches. For a long time she stared into the bag. Above them the stars came out.

'I knew it.' Pix looked up. 'Cody. You've forgotten the mayonnaise.'

Chapter Twenty-eight

Neither Virginia nor Marco asked what had happened to Ed when the lights went out. He was thankful for that. Explaining any aspect of his experience would have been difficult. Explaining his fierce arousal would have been impossible.

Maybe that was how it was in the beast house, as Marco called this room full of cages. They did whatever their captor required of them, then went on with their day-to-day lives in captivity.

Certainly they wouldn't discuss it with each other. He remembered how evasive Virginia had been when he'd asked her about her injured breasts.

Now he lay on the mattress.

Tried to forget.

Failed to forget.

That sex had been so shameful. He didn't even know who he'd been screwing. Man or woman?

Trouble was: the sex was good.

No, it wasn't.

It was the best.

Best ever.

Overwhelming animal sex that had just about blown his mind.

Later the lights went out. He found himself trembling with either fear or excitement, he couldn't decide which. When they came back on again he realized there'd be no repeat of the bizarre sexual act. Instead, lunch appeared.

Same airline trays.

Same tepid coffee.

Only this time there was a sandwich and two bright red apples. His two fellow captors ate theirs immediately. As if still ashamed of what he'd done he waited under his blanket until they'd done before he ate. The sandwich was chunky turkey on wholewheat. It tasted pretty good, considering.

He realized as soon as he'd eaten that he would have to make use of the sawdust tray.

Oh, man. Just when he thought he couldn't suffer any more embarrassment it was turned up another notch.

No one watched. He found himself wiping himself with the toilet paper in such a way that the action would be as quiet as possible.

But no one commented. No one looked his way.

Later Marco spoke. He sounded pleased. 'Who's a pretty boy, then?'

'Not you, Marco,' Virginia said.

'Must be. I got a chocolate-chip cookie with my lunch. Home-baked.'

'So?'

'You two guys didn't.'

'So what does that make you?' Ed was irritated by Marco's smug attitude.

'It makes me the favorite with the big guy upstairs.'

Ed looked across to see Marco beaming through the bars of the cage. He glanced back at Virginia. She shook her head.

'Leave him, Ed. He's only trying to mess with your head.'

'Says who?'

'Says me, Marco.'

Ed looked at Marco's mouth. His lips were full and red for a man's. Even as he watched the tongue darted out to take a crumb that lodged in the corner of his mouth.

Could it be . . . ?

No. Ed's flesh crawled.

But *could* it be Marco that had abused him a few hours ago? Maybe Marco *was* his captor? He could have an accomplice who turned out the lights and operated the mechanism, raising the panel to the roof of the cage. Then all Marco had to do was unlatch the door, climb onto the cage roof and then . . . and then . . .

Ed swallowed. No, he didn't like the way those thoughts led him. That Marco was in on this . . . even the instigator.

But it could be the truth. Marco might be playing some sick game.

He glanced at Virginia. She looked back at him, green eyes cool as ice. Was she in on it, too? Two kooky kids who'd built their own fun house where they brought kidnapped men and women.

The more he thought about it the more likely it seemed. But was he just being paranoid?

'What are you thinking about, Ed?'

He colored. 'Nothing.'

'Nothing?' Virginia angled her head. 'Seemed an intense nothing.'

148

'Uh?'

'You were scowling at me.'

'Sorry.'

'Thought I'd done something wrong.'

'No.'

'That I'd offended you.'

'Not at all.'

She looked him in the eye. 'You'll let me know if I step on your toes, won't you?'

Right then she looked so vulnerable. He wished he could reach out through the bars of the cage to embrace her.

'Because,' she said, 'if you think bad things about me I'll wish you dead.'

For the next hour or so Ed Lake felt like the odd man out. A little while ago Virginia and Marco had been bickering. Now they were chatting to each other. About nothing much in particular. About vacations they'd had as kids. Seemed they'd both been to Lake Placid. Both had fathers who had fished. Both had kept hamsters. Both shared the same birth sign. Taurus. They'd swapped reminiscences. Suddenly they had *so* much in common.

They're trying to exclude me. Make me feel lonely, Ed told himself.

Mind games.

Two people buddy up. Shut the other out.

She toyed with her hair as she spoke to Marco. Once she'd let the blanket slip as if to deliberately show her breast to him. He smiled a lot, tilting his head as they spoke. Because Ed's cage was in the middle they had to look through the bars and through *him* as they talked.

The conversation was cut short.

Even though the killing of the lights usually brought a frisson of fear for Ed, this time he welcomed it. Because normally with the darkness came silence. Everyone stopped talking.

Again it was the same. Rustling sounds. Drafts, as if the door to the room had been opened, then closed.

A voice came. For a moment Ed thought he was being addressed and obeyed before he realized it was a different name.

'Paulo. Move to your right. Keep moving until you reach the cage bars . . . now turn round.'

They used Marco's surname, just as they had used Ed's.

Ed heard movement from Marco's cage. He was obeying the commands.

149

'*Let the bars of the bars of the cage take your weight. Splay your feet. Lower your body. Keep your back to the cage bars . . . now . . . bring your head back.*'

It was the same deep voice. It was loud, too, and seemed to come from no single direction.

Odd.

Then: 'Please . . . I'll do anything—'

That was Marco's voice.

'I'll do anything . . . please!'

Then the light flickered. It didn't come on completely but the fluorescent strips were strobing on-off. Ed saw a figure briefly. It was outside the cage. It was doing something to Marco. Marco's arms were outstretched, crucifixion style. His hands seemed to flutter, fingers spasming.

Then darkness.

Ed waited a long time, until he was sure their captor had left, then said, 'Marco?'

Silence.

'Marco?'

There was no reply.

Ed lay on the foam mattress. There was no other sound. Virginia didn't speak. He felt cold inside.

He tried to sleep. Couldn't. His side ached where he lay in the same position, but for some reason he couldn't bring himself to change it.

The lights went on.

Outside the cage bars there was a tray containing slices of melon and a cupcake. A carton of milk beside that.

He looked into Marco's cage.

Marco leaned against the bars, his arms straight out, wrists tied by wire to the uprights. His eyes were open. His throat had been cut. A great grinning crimson wound.

Blood pooled on the floor around him.

For a time Ed stared at the dead man. Virginia stared, too. Said nothing.

Then Ed pulled the tray through the gap in the bars and started to eat.

Chapter Twenty-nine

Karen, astride Eric's lap, rocked gently back and forth, making his thick organ move slightly inside her, rubbing just a bit in a delicious way that would make it last. It was in her deeper than seemed possible. As she rocked, eyes shut, she felt his hands inside her open blouse, stroking her back, squeezing her breasts, teasing her nipples.

The baby, in the nursery at the end of the hall, started to cry.

Karen felt like crying herself.

Just when she'd wanted to start screaming with pleasure.

'Oh, shit, shit, shit,' Eric muttered.

She kissed him. 'It's all right, honey. I'll just be a minute.'

'Come on, don't go. She'll stop pretty soon.'

'No, she won't. Not till she gets her bottle. Besides, she'll wake up Byron. Would you like him to walk in about now?'

Eric could only groan with despair.

In so deep.

In so good.

Didn't get better than that.

He helped lift Karen as she raised herself off his lap. She felt him slide out. It left her feeling empty; hollow now. 'I'll be right back,' she said. Straightening her skirt, she looked down at his erection. It stood like a wet, shiny post of flesh. Kneeling, she kissed its swollen head. 'Don't go away,' she whispered.

Buttoning her blouse, she hurried into the kitchen, took a pink bottle of formula from the refrigerator. Then went down the dark hallway. A night-light was on in the nursery. Jane was on her back inside the crib. Wailing.

'It's okay,' Karen soothed. 'Everything's okay.' She slipped the latex nipple into Jane's mouth. Tiny, eager hands clutched the bottle. 'Nighty-night,' Karen said. 'Sleep tight.' She waved to Jane and left.

Even as she hurried back to the den, she felt a tremor of anticipation. Her fingers trembled as she opened the buttons of her blouse.

*   *   *

The baby's crying had disturbed Byron's sleep. He rolled onto his back. The sheet under him felt hot and wet, so he edged sideways to find a fresh place. His foot dropped over the side of the bed. He let it hang there.

He was almost asleep when something brushed the bottom of his foot, tickling. He wondered, vaguely, what it was.

A bug, maybe.

A moth fluttering near his foot.

Suddenly the smell of spices and garlic seemed strong in the room. The blind rustled in a dead breath of night air.

Foot tickled again.

Damn bug.

Byron began to raise his foot.

Something clutched it in a tight, dry grip. He gasped with fright. Tried to kick free. Tried to pull away. The grip only tightened.

He sprang out of bed. A single dark hand had him by the ankle. A single dark hand connected to a stick-thin forearm that vanished into the darkness beneath his bed. Crying out, he lunged toward the shut door, dragging the creature from under the bed. Its hair crackled against the carpet. Flickers of blue static shimmered across its head.

A second hand grabbed his ankle. Looking down, he saw the mummy pulling itself toward the ankle like you'd pull yourself up a tree with a branch. Its elbows bending. A flash of face – eyeless sockets, teeth glinting white. It bit.

Byron cried out in pain.

Twisting, reaching for the door, he fell backwards. The thing scuttled up his body. Its fingernails cut into the flesh of his legs, tore at his genitals through his shorts, slashed gashes in his chest. Goughed furrows across his shoulders. The mouth, hideously wrinkled came down on his face. The eye sockets were huge empty craters. He turned away, but the teeth sank into his cheek. Ripped. Ripped again. Looking up, Byron screamed at the sight of his own flesh hanging from its mouth, dripping red.

'What the hell was that?!'

Karen shook her head. The baby started to cry again. 'I'd better go see.' She climbed off Eric, chilled with concern, and reached down for her blouse.

He clutched her arm. 'You stay here.' Fastening his pants, he rushed into the dark hallway.

152

Karen put on her blouse. She bent down to pick up her panties and heard Eric yell as if startled. She froze, gazing toward the hallway. Something slammed heavily against a wall or the floor. She listened for the sounds of a struggle but the cry of the baby hid any other noises.

'Eric!' she called.

Quickly, she stepped into her panties and pulled them up beneath her skirt. She took a step toward the hallway. Stopped.

Didn't want to go there.

Couldn't.

'Eric! Are you all right? Eric! If you're playing a trick on me, it's not funny.'

She took a step backward, eyes on the hallway entrance.

'Damn it, Eric!'

Out of the darkness stepped a wrinkled brown figure, clutching Jane to its chest. Its hair tumbled down in copper swathes from a skull-like head. The baby cried with wild terror.

Screaming, Karen spun around and ran to the front door. Threw it open. Dashed across the lawn to the sidewalk. With a glance over her shoulder, she saw the thing appear in the doorway with Janey. Her foot passed through an empty space as she went off the curb. Staggering forward, balance gone, she looked into dazzling headlights and felt the car break her apart.

Chapter Thirty

Cody downshifted as the traffic thickened. The pickup lumbered up the incline, the big motor taking the strain.

'You sure you two are okay?' he asked.

'Yeah, no problem,' Pix said as if the subject bored her.

'That was a close one.' Grace rested her hand on his thigh. 'Thanks, Cody.'

'What matters is we're away from them now.'

'The creeps. They must hang around out in the desert, waiting for people to come by. It makes you wonder how many women they've—'

'Hey, hey,' he said softly. 'Put it behind you. It's over . . . they're just losers.'

'Dangerous losers.'

The familiar whine came from the back. 'This is Hollywood. Where are the damn movie studios?'

'Pix, they're all over the place – behind those big walls.'

'But I can't see nuthin'.'

'You will.' Grace sounded determined. 'We're going to make it here.'

'Yeah. *Right.*'

'Hey, Pix.' Cody stopped at a red. 'Give your sister a break, can't you?'

'But it's dumb to haul out here. We should have gone to New York.'

'Pix—'

'There'd be work there . . . even for a lummox like you.'

For a moment Cody sat fuming.

Put little sister on a Greyhound bus. Send her back East. She was doing her best to break Grace's will to succeed. *Huh, talk about sibling rivalry.*

Come on lights, change.

They stayed fixed.

Red.

No go.

Don't move.

Even though it was way late he saw lights in the houses that clung to the sides of the Hollywood Hills. Along the road in front of him were restaurants, hotels, all-night stores. Lights blazed. *Here we are*, they seemed to say to him, *this is LA. The city of dreams. If you're lucky.*

A figure lurched from the shadows.

Pix screamed. 'Grace! Look out!'

The dark shape leaned forward, laid a brown hand on the part-open window where Grace sat.

Cody watched her twist round as the mummy leaned right into the car.

The light was red. Cars lined up in front of him. He couldn't move. But gunned the engine just the same.

Looked in horror as the mummy reached out a hand.

'Cody!' Grace cried.

He reached out his arm around his girlfriend's shoulders and scooped her close.

The mummy extended its brown paw toward them both.

Pix shouted, 'It's going to get Grace!'

The mummy loomed in.

Closer.

Reaching.

'Here,' it said. 'Take.'

Cody felt Grace's slender body quiver with fear against him.

'Take,' the mummy repeated. In its hand was a green card not much bigger than a cinema ticket.

The mummy pushed the bandage up where it had slid down over one eye. 'Present this at the Pyramid Diner down the road to your left. You get a free side salad.'

'Sweet Jesus,' Grace cried. 'You scared me half to death.'

'Special promotion,' monotoned the guy in the mummy costume. 'Free side salad. Set midnight feast for five ninety-nine. They got genuine Egyptian beer, too. And apple pie just like mummy used to make.'

Dazed, Grace took the card from the bandaged figure. The card bore the drawing of a mummy. *Pyramid Diner: 24/7: Why eat like a king when you can feast like a pharaoh? Entitles bearer to one free side salad.*

Cody shook his head. 'Los Angeles. City of Angels. What a place!'

155

Pix added, 'Los Angeles. City of the dead, more like.' She looked out the rear window to watch the man in the mummy costume shuffling along the line of waiting cars, handing out more of the cards.

Horns sounded.

'*Green,* Cody, you big lummox.'

As they pulled away, Grace said, 'Cody, we best find somewhere to spend the night.'

'Motel,' Pix said hopefully.

'No can do.' Cody shook his head.

'We'll have to find a parking lot,' Grace added. 'Or a quiet side street.'

'What? No motel?'

'We can't.'

'Shit.'

Grace looked back at her sister. Her arms were folded. With her mouth sulky she stared out.

'We don't have enough money for a motel, Pix.'

'How much we got? They can't be that expensive.'

Cody spoke, 'Eight dollars, thirty-three cents.'

'Oh great.' Pix shook her head in disbelief. 'We're thousands of miles from home, in Los Angeles, and we haven't even got ten lousy bucks between us.' She lay down on the back seat, glaring up at the pickup's grubby roof. 'How we gonna survive here. D' ya hear me, you two? How we gonna survive?'

Chapter Thirty-one

Ed Lake was making use of the sawdust bowl when the lights went out. Taking a leak in the dark wasn't easy. Felt weird, too.

Also, he knew what might be coming his way.

Maybe I'm next?

Is this where I get my throat slit just like Marco?

Poor kid. How would that knife blade have felt as it was dragged through his throat? Just the thought of that sawing motion of cold metal on his Adam's apple shut off the flow.

Ed shook himself. Then zipped up as fast as he could.

What now?

He waited in the dark.

Waiting for orders.

They came.

'Virginia . . . Virginia . . .'

So Virginia's favored with first-name treatment.

'Virginia. Stand up.'

Ed made his way back to his mattress by touch alone in the darkness, feeling across the concrete floor until he found the hunk of foam. He sat. Waited. Listened. His heart beating faster.

Would Virginia be killed this time? The thought of seeing her lying there with her beautiful throat gashed open made him shrivel inside.

There in the dark he could see nothing. But he heard all right. He heard Virginia's frightened breathing.

And did that panting sound loud!

He tried to block the thought, but it sounded as if she was sexually aroused. He thought about her copper hair tumbling over bare shoulders. A glimpse of her cleavage as she tried to keep the blanket high with trembling hands.

Jesus, what they gonna do to her? Please don't kill her. Please, she's so young and beautiful. She's got a whole life in front of her.

'Virginia, stand up'

So their captor would be in the room now. Looking at Virginia

157

through nightscope goggles. Seeing her skin gleam, and her eyes shine like lamps in the infrared.

Ed looked in the direction of where he imagined Virginia stood in the center of her cage. She'd be so frightened. She wouldn't know what was going to happen next. She must have been thinking about Marco, too. How he'd hung there with his throat cut. And how later the lights had been killed and they'd heard a dragging sound as his murderer dragged the body away. Following on from that were wet slicing sounds as someone worked at the bloodstained floor with sponges.

'Virginia. Drop the blanket.'

The voice was deep, masculine. But there was something strange about it. Ed listened hard. Again, it came from no single direction. It didn't even sound completely natural.

'Remove your clothes . . . now stand facing the bars . . . slip your hands through the loops.'

Ed's eyes widened in the darkness. *Loops? Some kind of restraint?*

Virginia made little gasping sounds. Whispered words that he couldn't make out. Then he heard something that made the shivers pour down his spine.

She spoke . . . a long-drawn-out 'Oooooh . . .'

He tilted his head, listening hard, trying to interpret the sound. Was it hurting? Was it pleasuring?

He sat with his knees hugged to his chest.

There was a rustling sound. Clothes? Paper?

Like the voice, the sound seemed to have no single source. It came from every direction.

Virginia's breathing quickened. She made soft 'Hmm' and 'Uh' sounds. Ed's heart thudded.

Then: 'Please . . .'

He remembered the last time when he'd heard her pant like this.

They'd cut her breasts.

If only I could get out of this cage and get my hands round the bastard's throat. I'd fucking squeeze the life right out—

But then everything changed.

Virginia gasped. 'Please . . . yes, yes . . . deeper. Put your fingers inside . . . that's it . . . deeper. Please, deeper . . . ah . . .'

Ed couldn't believe it. She wasn't in pain . . . this was pleasure for her. Overwhelming pleasure.

She was having sex with her captor. Virginia was horny. She was enjoying whatever was being done to her. How could she? Was she some kind of slut to surrender to her captor so completely, then enjoy their attentions so *completely?*

So what makes you *so squeaky clean, Eddie old buddy? You surrendered too. You enjoyed your captor's proclivities.*

He hugged his knees to his chest, hearing sounds of rapture.

Virginia's gasping for breath, her murmurs of pleasure were turning him on. He felt so horny. He sensed himself growing large, his cock straining against the fabric of his pants.

I want to join in, he thought, unable to hold back the thoughts any longer. *I want to be nailing Virginia and I want her to make those hot sounds in my ear. Sweet Jesus listen to her. She's having great sex. She's so turned on. She's so hot. She loves what's happening to her.*

In his mind's eye he saw her. She'd be standing facing the cage, her hands held high by loops that restrained her, that held her there, her nakedness pressed hard against the cage.

But what is happening to her?

Couldn't tell.

No way of knowing.

But, sheesh, it sounds good.

So good it makes my cock ache. I want to explode.

But can't get that kind of one-handed relief here in the dark.

My captor's wearing funky night-vision goggles. They'd see me jerking off. They'd have something to say about that. Might be against the rules. I might wind up with my throat cut. But listen to Virginia panting.

Just picture her. She's naked. She's shackled to the cage bars. Her head's rolling, swishing hair down her curving back, as the captor does something to her. But what a helluva something!

Finger?

Tongue?

Dildo?

'Virginia. Slide your feet further apart.'

That weird voice again. It—

Holy shit.

Suddenly he knew why it sounded strange. He knew what it reminded him of. It was the same as a recorded voice played back at a slower speed. The voice was low, manlike, but distorted. And it came from different directions because it was being broadcast over speakers placed around the room.

So maybe the guy isn't a guy after all?

Maybe it's a gal?

159

And you know what that means, Eddie?

The sounds of rapture you're hearing now are a lesbian love-fest.

Wow.

Right on!

He found himself smiling. Now this was hot. Gal on gal.

Maybe he could suggest a threesome?

Not that he got a chance.

The deep voice commanded him to lie on the platform again.

And again the same commands as he was winched up hard against the Perspex ceiling. To unzip himself. To 'present' himself. This time he didn't hesitate.

Lying flat on his back there he unzipped, then guided his penis through the hole in the Perspex. Already he was hot and erect. In fact, he felt the muscles straining against the confining skin. Wanted to explode.

Wanted to explode there and then.

For moments cool air played around the head of his cock.

This waiting's driving me insane. I can't bear it. I want to feel that soft mouth again with its busy tongue.

Movement from above. Although he saw nothing in the darkness he felt the Perspex flex slightly as a someone stepped onto it. More movement as they positioned themselves. He imagined a woman . . . a beautiful, mad woman who captured victims and kept them as sex slaves.

Right now he imagined her naked, positioning herself over him, ready to sit on his swollen, throbbing member.

And, good God, was he right!

He felt soft flesh touch the tip of his penis. Soft lips that were hot. A downward movement. A sense of parting. Slickness. An eager downward thrust, followed by a slow return upward, the lips encircling his shaft, the exquisite dragging sensation, before the next thrust down.

He moaned.

This was beautiful.

This he loved.

He was entering the body of his captor and nothing could be nicer. No way.

She must be kneeling above him on the Perspex ceiling. She straddled his cock. Impaled herself on the hard shaft. Now rose and fell, no doubt her head twisting with pleasure, a look of bliss on her face.

He felt the tight encircling flesh travelling the length of his shaft . . . Down, down, down. All the way. Then back up, up, up, until the lips nearly parted from the tip.

Only not quite.

Then down again, encircling, squeezing, stroking.

It happened.

With a yell he came fast and furious into the body, expending every drop into that moist softness. His hips bucked, pressing hard against the Perspex as he tried to gain just another quarter of an inch of penetration.

Then . . .

Over . . .

Spent . . .

Sagging . . .

'*You did not wait.*' The deep voice held cold anger. '*You should have held back, Lake. For that you will be punished.*'

Chapter Thirty-two

Ed Lake didn't have long to wait.

The lights had flickered on and he'd wormed his way from the platform with the words still ringing in his ears: '*You should have held back, Lake. You will be punished.*'

He saw Virginia standing there. She was wearing the denim cut-offs. Her arms were crossed in front of her so that they hid her naked breasts.

She was watching Ed. Her green eyes were sympathetic, her demeanor serious.

'I'm so sorry, Ed,' she whispered.

'But all I did . . .' It wasn't easy to admit. 'All I did was come too soon.'

'That's a crime . . . at least it is in their eyes.'

'But who are *they*?'

She shook her head, her eyes downcast; unhappy with the situation but powerless. 'I don't know.'

'Listen, we've got to do something to get out of here.'

'We can't.'

'But we've got to try.'

'No, Ed.'

'We can't stay locked in these cages all our lives.'

'I know. But you saw what happened to Marco.'

'We've got to fight back.'

'Don't say that, Ed.'

'Why not?'

'They might be listening.'

He looked round, then said loudly, 'I don't give a damn if they are listening. They can come and suck my big one for all I care.'

'Ed,' she warned.

'But we can't just give in and be treated like animals. We're human beings.'

'We're also caged, Ed. They call the shots.'

'You going to let them do whatever they want with your body, Virginia?'

'Oh, Ed.' She sounded pained. 'We've got to play by their rules, otherwise—'

'They kill us?'

'Yes.'

He looked at her. 'Is that what's going to happen to me now?'

'I don't know.'

'They've threatened me with punishment.'

'It might not be as bad as you think, or—'

'Or . . . *chkkk*.' He ran his finger across his throat, imitating a blade.

'It might,' she agreed.

'Then I'm going to go down fighting,' he boomed. 'D' ya hear that, whoever you are, you little creeps? I'm gonna go down fighting!'

The lights went out.

Oh shit.

Deep, deep shit.

The moment the darkness swamped them was when Ed knew they were coming for him. He, she or they . . . what did it matter now? They'd used him up. Now he was going the same way as Marco.

Throat sliced open. Then dragged somewhere. Dumped in a shallow grave, or even fed piece by piece into a furnace, for all he knew.

Leastways, this is how it ends.

After a moment or so of darkness he felt the draft as a door opened somewhere. Then the whisper of feet on concrete.

Here they came. His captor.

Or captors.

He should fight. He really should. They shouldn't be able to just stroll up and carve his trachea like that. They'd have to fight to take him.

But his insides shriveled, leaving an empty space in his gut. The strength had gone from him.

What if he was to plead for his life?

The thought of begging revolted him. But if it gave him a chance? They might leave him with a warning. *That's it. Don't do it again, Eddie boy. Beg . . . plead . . .*

If only.

163

Or should he offer up his throat? If they cut cleanly and fast then it would be over quick. No pain.

At least no more pain than need be.

The first cut is the deepest. Yeah, an old song. But there was a truth in the line. And didn't condemned criminals used to tip the executioner, way back? So they'd kill in a way that was merciful. No agony. No screaming.

'Jeez. Okay, okay. Get it over quick.'

'Lake, remove your clothes.'

He did as he was told, moving by touch in the darkness.

'Now move forward to the cage bars . . . Closer, Lake. Closer . . . move your feet until you're hard up to the bars.'

Did as he was told. Kept his eyes tight shut. Clenched his fists.

Come on, get it over with.

Do it.

Use that blade.

Then came a surprise. A terrible surprise.

'Oh, God, no.'

His heart lurched. His stomach plunged.

A hand closed round his testicles.

'Oh, please, God, no.'

He waited for the hand to grip tight. Squeeze ferociously. Then for the tingling edge of a blade against his soft scrotum.

Gonna whip off your balls, Eddie boy.

Then let's hear how you scream.

His eyes opened with shock, staring into the darkness. They'd never opened as wide as this before. He felt they'd simply pop out with the pressure inside his skull. And just for a second he did see. There was a faint reddish light coming from somewhere. He thought he saw a cowled figure – almost like a monk. And goggles of some sort.

They *were* wearing goggles. Round ones. Welder's goggles?

Then the dim red light died. Once more there was darkness.

Suddenly the grip on his balls changed. *Here comes the knife.*

Wait for it . . . wait for it. They were positioning the blade nice and close to his groin.

Suddenly the hand was gone. Maybe his captor was gone, too. That was it! Mind games again. Inflict psychological pain rather than physical. If that was the—

Then he felt a cold pressure against his foot. To be precise, against his little toe.

That was strange. *Why should—*

He didn't have any more thinking time than that. He heard a loud metallic tap – metal on metal. Then a crunch. A loud one.

After that there was no time for rational contemplation. That was out of the window, along with standing still.

A wave of agony flashed up his leg. It set his brain alight.

The next thing he knew he was rolling on the floor, screaming, holding his foot.

Only his foot no longer seemed the same.

The lights had been on for a whole hour. He lay on his side. The concrete floor must have been hard and uncomfortable but he didn't notice.

'I'm sorry what they did to you. Listen, Ed, I'm sorry.' Virginia must have repeated the words many times but when he didn't respond she let him alone.

He lay there without moving for what seemed an age. He lay looking through the bars of the cage at something that lay on the floor.

It was a small object. Almost insignificant.

It lay in a pool of blood on the concrete. A little island in a sea of blood.

'I don't believe they did that,' he said to himself at last. 'They cut it off . . . they cut off my little toe.'

Chapter Thirty-three

When Ed Lake woke his severed little toe was gone. The blood had gone, too. All that remained was a wet area of concrete.

So, like a goofy kind of Tooth Fairy, they'd come in the middle of the night.

Taken the toe. Left him nothing in return. Some Toe Fairy . . .

He laughed.

'Now that does surprise me,' Virginia said from the next cage.

'What does?'

'They cut your toe off and you find it funny.'

'Considering Marco, and what the alternative might have been, I'm damn lucky.'

'I guess you're right. Go ahead and have yourself a belly laugh.'

'Maybe it's not *that* funny.'

'Hurt?'

'Like hell.' He rubbed his head. 'Maybe it's the blood loss. I feel drunk.'

'Probably that and shock, too. Drink plenty of water.'

'Good idea.' He reached for a water bottle that hung from one of the roof bars.

She looked at his foot. 'Still bleeding?'

'Nope. I clamped a mountain of toilet tissue to it. Stopped eventually.'

'I guess it's a good sign.'

'I'll say,' he said. 'If it hadn't stopped I'd have bled out.'

'No, it's a good sign they did what they did.'

'You mean they just wanted to teach me a lesson?' He chuckled at his bloody foot. 'To toe the line?'

She nodded, her copper hair sweeping down over a bare shoulder. 'They must value you being alive.'

'Maybe I can demand better accommodation.'

She smiled. 'Wouldn't push it, buster.'

'And how's the . . .' He indicated his chest, then blushed, suddenly awkward. 'I mean have—'

'The cuts on my breasts? They're healing, Ed.'

'Was that punishment, too?'

'Nah, they did that for fun.' She flicked back her hair. 'They do all kinds of freaky things for fun.'

'Like when they made you put your hands through the loops?'

'We decided early on that it would be bad etiquette to ask each other what they did.'

'But I—'

'We decided it was a way to maintain at least some small area of privacy.'

'We?'

She sighed and shook her head. Her eyes took on a sad, downward cast as she remembered. 'There were others when I first got here. I even shared this cage with another girl. One by one they all . . .' She shrugged. 'They were all taken but me.'

'And Marco?'

'He was brought in later.'

'So you decided you wouldn't talk about how they abused you?'

'Our captors call the shots. I've told you.'

'So you go along with it?'

'Have to. If you want to live.'

He moved his foot as he sat on the mattress. It had started to throb again. Where the little toe had once connected with his foot was now a gooey red-black scab.

'They cut off my little toe,' he said.

'I know. You've already told me.'

'When they make me lie up on that shelf they tell me to put my penis through a hole in the Perspex roof of the cage. Then they—'

'Ed.' She looked at him pleadingly. 'What our captors do to us they do in the dark. It's secret.'

'Then whoever it was sucked me. Then stuck my cock inside them.'

She turned away, briefly burying her face in the blanket.

He continued. 'I was forced to have sex . . . but get this, I loved it. They excited me. It was great sex. I was really turned on.'

She sat, resting her elbow on her knee. She gazed at him with those green eyes for a moment, then shook her head. 'I know what you're doing.'

'You do?'

'You're saying we should share the experiences of what they do to us.'

'Keeping it secret doesn't help.'

'So if we share, if we confess, it makes us stronger?'

'Yes. But there's nothing to confess. *We*'ve done nothing wrong. But if we tell each other what happens to us . . . the abuse we suffer . . . then we're not so isolated. We can lend one another emotional support.'

She nodded. 'Guess we might as well. After all, the old way wasn't that effective, was it, now? Remember what happened to Marco?'

He looked at her.

She said, 'So you think I should tell you what they did to me?'

'I can't force you to talk.'

'No . . . well . . . it's . . .' She took a deep breath. Then, making a decision, she spoke in a no-nonsense way. 'The last time they made me their plaything I was ordered to stand facing the bars of the cage. In the dark they must have hooked loops to the bars. They made me put my hands in.'

'You were restrained by the loops?'

She nodded. 'Like lassos. They pulled tight round my wrists. Then they began touching me.'

'Hurting?'

'No. Gentle.'

'Was there anything about the hands?'

'You mean anything distinctive about them? Anything identifiable?

'It might help us later.'

'You mean when it comes to identifying them for the cops?' She gave a sour laugh. 'Some hope, Ed. Anyway, here comes the confession, Hollywood style. They touched my body. Stroking me up and down. Then they ran their hands up inside my thighs to between my legs. They worked at me with their fingers.' She looked at me defiantly. 'There. Does that supply the picture for you?'

'I have to ask this, Virginia. Have they raped you?'

'Direct kinda guy, huh?'

'It could be important.'

'No,' she said. 'They haven't. Always fingers.'

'Nothing else?'

'No, always fingers. But there's something else.'

'Go on.'

'They were small, slender. I'm sure they were a woman's.'

'Jesus.'

'Yeah, so you heard what you thought you heard.' She looked me in the eye. 'You heard a red-hot lesbian lust-fest.'

Ed blushed.

168

'Does that turn you on?' Her voice sounded hard. 'Did you get all horny as you listened in the dark?'

'Virginia, I didn't—'

'Course you heard. That's what made you pop your cap too soon. But more fool you – they hacked off your toe for that mistake.'

'Virginia, I'm sorry.'

'Sorry for what? For being a horny teenager?' She pursed her lips as if ready to let fly some insults. Then she let out her pent-up breath. 'No, I'm sorry.' Her gaze softened. 'You see, I don't get out much. Makes me cranky.' Her lips twitched into a faint smile. 'Forgive me, Ed?'

'Nothing to forgive. But we've learned one thing. We need to stick together.'

Then Virginia caught him by surprise. Letting the blanket fall from her she crossed the cage to the bars nearest him. Her heavy breasts swayed. He allowed his eyes to take her in. She was naked apart from the cut-offs. Her hair coiled down; heavy strands slipped over her shoulder to brush her nipples.

Ed imagined the sensation must have been a pleasant tickle.

The cuts were healing fast now.

Boy, she looked good. Despite everything, her face glowed. She looked healthy. Vibrant.

She knelt down against the bars. Slipped her hand through. Reached out to him.

'Ed, will you hold my hand, please?'

'Be my pleasure.'

Avoiding catching the raw wound on his foot, he slid across the floor until he sat near the bars. He stretched out to her. Took her hand. She grasped his tightly. He squeezed back.

Suddenly the pressure of her hand in his became the most beautiful thing in the world.

'Partners?' she asked.

'Partners,' he agreed.

Time passed. Ed Lake's foot healed. During this time the funky games continued in the beast house. The lights would go out. Sometimes it was Virginia who got the attention. Sometimes Ed.

He kept his strength up so he could perform.

And performances went on for hours. He'd lie on his back on the platform.

Either it was the hungry mouth that worked his cock or it was the equally ravenous orifice.

169

But he was certain it was a woman now.

Of course he never saw. Too dark.

And he never let himself orgasm until his captor had been sated.

Afterward, whatever had been done to them, Ed would talk to Virginia. They shared their experiences. They discussed every detail – what their captor did, how they smelled, how they felt. Whether their captor climaxed. Whether Virginia or Ed climaxed.

Did it feel good?

Did it feel bad?

Sometimes it was so *bad* it was great.

Talking helped. Talking made them stronger.

They began to discuss how they could strike back.

Chapter Thirty-four

It came for him. It staggered, legs moving with awkward stiffness, an arm reaching out.

He backed away, breathless with horror.

Backed into waiting arms.

Crying out, he spun and stared into Hydra's leering half-face. Naked, she fell to her knees. She clutched his erection. She guided it slowly toward her face.

'Fuck my brains out,' she said. Laughing, she eased him into her head. He felt the tissues part around his stiff organ.

Heard the *squish*.

'Hey! Hey!'

Somebody shook Imad.

'You okay?' A woman's voice asked through the darkness.

He sat up, turned on the bedside lamp. The woman beside him swung up an arm to shield her eyes. She lay on top of the sheets. She was older than Imad and bony. Her skin was slick with suntan oil – a coconut oil that smelled rich and inviting. He remembered their encounter at the beach, where he'd offered to rub the oil on her back – and she'd accepted. He remembered bringing her home, drinks, a meal, and taking her to bed where they oiled their bodies and wrestled in an endless slippery contest of lust.

'Louise,' he murmured, at last remembering her name.

She uncovered her face. A handsome face with thin lips and high cheekbones and clear blue eyes. She gave him a tentative smile. 'Are you all right?'

'I dreamed.' He smiled. Shrugged. 'It was nothing.'

'It sounded just awful.'

'We all have our crosses to bear, do we not?'

'That's for sure. Me included.'

'I apologize for waking you. However . . .' He smiled. 'Since we are both awake now and the night is young . . .' He massaged one of her small, soft breasts.

She held his hand as if she wished to keep it there always.

'The night isn't all that young, Imad. I'm afraid I have to be on my way.'

'No.'

'I really hate to go, but I've got a job to get to.'

'At this hour?' he asked. 'It's nearly eleven.'

'Yeah. I go on at twelve. Waitress over at Clyde's. You know, Clyde's? Has this dumb sign out front. "Twenty-four Hour Service Day or Night"?' She laughed softly. 'Anyway, it's been cool.'

Turning onto her side, she kissed him long and hard.

She was gone. Alone in the huge house, Imad went to the wet bar and poured himself a glass of gin. He took it to the couch, sat back, used the remote to turn on the television. He pressed the buttons, watching a few seconds of each broadcast before turning to the next.

He settled for an adventure show in which a lithe brunette was being pursued by a gunman. She wore a T-shirt and shorts. Imad was pleased to notice that she wore no bra. He watched the breasts dance as she ran.

Then she hid and knocked the gunman unconscious with a flowerpot.

Rather silly, but Imad enjoyed the view of the woman, and was disappointed to see the show end.

A frowning, white-haired man came on. 'In just a few minutes, on *Eyewitness News* at eleven, we'll tell you about a miraculous rescue at sea, the President's latest energy proposal, and a bizarre double murder at one of our local museums. This and more from Bonnie, Lenny and me after a brief time-out.'

Imad watched the museum story. The cops behind the crime-scene tape, forensic specialists moving around in their white coveralls. Views of the Callahan Room. A close-up of the empty mummy casket. Then Imad went upstairs to the safe. He opened it. Removed the small black notebook.

He glanced at the title page and shivered.

The Memoirs of Robert Callahan.

THE MEMOIRS OF ROBERT CALLAHAN

The Fearful Descent

Though I wish, for reasons that will shortly be obvious, to prevent my Egyptian activities from coming to the public's attention, I find myself compelled to record the extraordinary events surrounding the discovery of the mummy, Amara. I shall take precautions that these pages remain concealed during my lifetime and the lifetime of my dear wife, Sarah. If eyes other than my own are now reading this manuscript, it may be assumed that we have both met our final fate. Disclosure of my activities cannot harm us now and may serve to prevent further tragedies.

In the year 1926, my father and I traveled to Egypt for the purpose of lending his expert assistance to the famed Howard Carter, who had recently unearthed the tomb of the boy king, Tutankhamun.

In Luxor, we met Mr Carter. He welcomed my father heartily, for they had worked together several years earlier with Theodore Davis at the tomb of Mentuhotep I. He was not so enthusiastic, however, about my presence. He must have felt that my youthful age of eighteen years, no matter how mature my attitude to work, would prove a hindrance. I am pleased to record that his attitude in this matter changed remarkably once he saw how I aided my father in the intricate details of his work. My copious, exact notes soon earned Mr Carter's respect.

It was my bravery, however, that won the respect of the Egyptian youth, Maged. We met on a December night. Suffering from the oppressive heat, I wandered beyond the boundaries of our encampment in hopes of chancing upon a stray, cooling breeze. I longed for the winters of my Wisconsin childhood: to be sledding down a slope, a chill wind battering my face, snowflakes blowing, the night lit by a full moon! I was close to weeping with frustration when suddenly an urgent cry entered my consciousness.

Never one to flee in the face of a crisis, I rushed forward and discovered half a dozen youths engaged in battering a young fellow senseless. I attacked. In the brief affray that followed, I struck several telling blows on the bullies and sent them scurrying for safety.

Maged introduced himself, using passable English. (His father, I learned, had served with the British during the Great War.) He offered me his gratitude and his friendship.

At first, he explained that the boys had fallen upon him for the purpose of committing robbery. After our friendship had grown, however, he finally confided in me. It seems that Maged, no innocent victim, had made vile suggestions to the sister of one of the boys. When she refused him, the young Maged showed his hostility by defecating on the family's doorstep. It was no wonder that her brother and several of his comrades reacted with violence.

Over the weeks, Maged proved to be an invaluable companion. The little Egyptian led me about in the night. We found his enemies. Fought with them. Won battles with our fists. We drank stolen raki. On regular occasions we whiled away the nights in the arms of tawny, lusting women with dark orbs for eyes who showed me delights I had never known.

It was because of Maged, and the wild times we shared, that we made the discovery that has so altered my life.

On a January night, after saying goodnight to Father, I met Maged at our agreed rendezvous point. From there, we traveled a long distance on foot across the desert until we reached a village of mud-brick houses. In one of these, Maged assured me, we would find a pair of twin sisters whose beauty and sexual talents would spoil me for all other women.

I waited outside while Maged entered one of the houses to fetch them. Soon, he reappeared. The two girls following behind him were beautiful indeed, though no older than seventeen. For long moments, I stared at them in the moonlight, struck with awe. I greeted them in Arabic. They smiled lasciviously, but spoke not a word. Maged quickly informed me that they were deaf-mutes. At first, I was troubled by this revelation. I soothed my conscience, however, by reminding myself that the five piasters we intended to pay the girls for their expert services was a handsome amount for such peasants. The fellahin who worked at the tomb, after all, received only three piasters for an entire day's labor.

Taking one girl by the hand, I followed Maged into the dunes beyond the village. There we spread blankets on the sand. The girls disrobed, revealing their beauteous skin to the moonlight. Their eyes were dark, lustful, their breasts small peaks, tipped with velvety dark nipples. My whole body was a mass of scintillating sensation as I anticipated whiling away the night with these desert beauties. I was ready to take mine at once, but Maged restrained me and indicated that he and I should be seated.

The girls stepped away from us, their bare feet leaving dainty prints in the sand. With olive oil cupped in their hands, they caressed one another until their skin had a glossy sheen in the light of the moon. Then they danced. Never have I seen such a dance; never before nor since; and it has always lingered in my mind, to be recalled on balmy nights when my heart is restless. The memory is painful, as exquisite memories so often are.

I see the flow of their bodies moving as if to a wonderfully haunting, erotic melody. But there is no music. The only sound is the distant barking of pariah dogs.

I see the naked girls caressing themselves, hands rubbing pointed breasts, sliding over smooth bellies and thighs, stroking over the darkness between their legs while they turn and writhe as if spitted on great phalluses. I see them move closer to one another. Reaching out, their fingers meet. Then they are drawn together like lovers long apart, lovers starved for the touch of one another, starved for the taste.

The taste of forbidden love.

Prohibited desire.

How long they continued, I don't recall. I wanted them to dance forever, yet I wanted them to stop instantly so that I might sate the appetite that strained my entire being. At last, their bodies slid apart. They stepped toward us, chests heaving, hair wild. They had, no doubt, expended themselves several times in the course of their strange dance, but their half-shut eyes held a promise of boundless delights.

I stood motionless as one of the twins slowly removed my clothing. She smelled of far-blown sand and olive and woman. A moonlit droplet slid to the tip of her nipple, shimmered there, containing all the vibrant colors of the rainbow. I longed to lick it off, that drop of woman-heated oil. When the last of my clothes fell to the sand I leaned forward, my tongue finding that drop of oil, licking, rolling the flavor around my mouth and swallowing.

Had I been cheated out of the next few minutes, I should have counted my life a waste. But whispers of the girls' departure from the mud-brick village were tardy in reaching Kemwese, their father. Before his arrival, I spent myself with each of the girls. I was standing, a twin upside-down in my heated embrace, my head hugged by her slick, golden thighs, my tongue darting into her sweetness, my phallus throbbing within the tight constriction of

177

her mouth, when a sharp blow to the back of my leg toppled me (it was only with rare good fortune that I avoided a tragedy regarding the girl's teeth).

As I rolled in the sand, I glimpsed Maged making a dash for safety. A sandaled foot kicked my breath away. Hearing a struggle behind me, I managed to look around. The naked girls were at their father, clutching his arms and legs, fighting to save me. They proved no match for the enraged monster. He battered them aside and came at me, roaring.

His foot slashed toward my face. Catching it in both hands, I twisted, throwing Kemwese down. At this moment, I might have chosen to run and save myself. This, however, was against my combative nature.

Never one to abandon a fight, I attacked the growling savage. I fell upon him, fists pummeling his face. I heard a satisfying, gristly crunch as my knuckle smashed his nose. No sooner did blood gush from the nostrils than his arm swung up and struck my head with the force of a club. Dazed, I tumbled away.

I was only vaguely aware of the huge man lifting me. He raised me high above him, then tipped my head downward and drove me toward the sand. My neck should have snapped like a rotten twig when I hit the ground. Somehow, it didn't. The blow shocked every inch of my frame, however, and I was powerless to prevent the beast from working his will upon me.

He lifted me again. I knew, in what remained of my conscious mind, that I would soon be dead. Rather than throwing me down again, however, he began to carry me. Where he was taking me, I had no idea. Nor did I care. I only hoped, in a fogged, dreamy way, that if he continued to carry me long enough, some of my strength might return and I might yet save myself.

At length, he reached his destination. He flung me to the ground. Though I hadn't the power to raise my head, I could see that we were near the ruins of the Temple of Mentuhotep. Grunting, Kemwese pushed aside a large block of stone. I immediately recognized his intentions. Horror coursed through me, clearing my mind and giving me new strength. Raising my head, I saw a small black patch in the sand beneath where the rock had rested. A hole. A dark, shadowed hole reaching downward into the belly of the desert.

When Kemwese came for me, I threw a handful of sand into his face. Blinded and coughing, he groped for me. I rolled out of his reach. I got to my hands and knees and crawled, trying to gain my feet, but my body obeyed the commands of my mind in only the slowest fashion and soon he had me by the foot. He dragged me backwards, dragged me toward the awful hole. My fingers clawed at the sand. All sense of manhood broken by the horrible prospect awaiting me, I cried out for forgiveness. I begged him. I offered him money. At the end, I threatened him with terrible vengeance.

It was useless.

He raised me by both feet. I saw the black pit, like a tunnel to Hell, below my face. My hands dug into the sand at its edges, but to no avail.

Then he released me.

I plunged headfirst into the blackness.

Screaming.

The Awful Pit

I fell, petrified by an unreasoning fear that I might plunge forever through the lightless void. I had little time, fortunately, to dwell on the horror of that thought. Abruptly, I hit the bottom of the shaft and lost consciousness.

When my mind returned to me, the aches in every limb of my body quickly reminded me of the gravity of my situation. The darkness was so intense that I blinked several times to be certain that my eyes were indeed open. The lumpy pressure on my back told me that I was lying face upward. I raised my arms. I felt great relief and comfort in touching my still-naked body; my face, my chest and belly, my privates, my thighs. The hands, touching familiar places, gave me a warm feeling that I was not entirely alone in this strange and frightful pit. They also confirmed that I was still whole, at least as far as I could reach. I stirred my legs. They seemed unbroken.

As I lay there continuing to stroke my body and regaining a sense of reality, I began to assess my situation. The devil Kemwese had undoubtedly left me here to die. That being the case, he must have covered the opening of the pit with the enormous block of stone that had originally sealed it. Even should I succeed in climbing to the top, I would be powerless to shift the rock. My best chance of survival, however, seemed to lie in that direction.

Gazing into the black space above me, I tried to determine whether Kemwese had, indeed, rolled back the stone. If he hadn't, I should certainly be able to see the light of stars or the moon. Nothing was visible. Nothing.

I decided I must attempt to climb out, nonetheless. First, however, it would be wise to explore the confines of my prison.

As I stirred myself to sit, the uneven ground beneath me seemed to wobble. Lowering a hand to the lump beneath my bare hip, I touched a pliant surface that I immediately recognized as hide. My fingers explored further. The hide felt wrinkled, sunken. Pressing it, I felt the solid roundness of bone below the surface. With a gasp, I flung my naked body clear of the creature.

There, shivering, I huddled in the darkness and gazed in its direction. I could see nothing, of course. To confirm my fears, I finally ventured forward. My hands again encountered the dead flesh. I explored it briefly before realizing, with an agony of horror and revulsion, that my fall had been cushioned by the desiccated corpse of a man.

He, like myself, was naked. I wondered if he, too, had been caught in debauchery with the daughters of Kemwese. The thought chilled me, in spite of the pit's dreadful heat. Perhaps my end would be the same as his.

'No, damn it,' I said. The sound of my voice was dreadfully loud in the confined chamber. Silly, I know, but I feared for a moment that I had startled my deceased companion awake. I listened, half expecting him to speak. Or, worse, to advance and to lay his dead fingers on my naked body.

To my great relief, he didn't.

All I could hear was my ragged breathing.

A dry, labored sound.

From that point on, I took pains to remain silent.

Starting at the feet of the dead man, I began to inch my way along the boundary of my cell. I crawled on hands and knees across ancient dust. Dry as dead skin on the back of my throat. I let my shoulder brush along the stone wall to keep my orientation. After proceeding in this manner for no longer than a minute, I set my hand down on someone's face. I screamed.

The sound came back at me like a banshee howl.

Jabbing my eardrums so hard that they hurt.

For a long time, I crouched against the wall, panting in the hot air, struggling to regain my composure. Then I ventured forward. With hesitant hands, I familiarized myself with my new neighbor. His flesh felt stiffer than that of the other man, leading me to the assumption that his residence in the pit had been more prolonged. My hand searched along the length of a naked limb. I could not tell whether this was an arm or a leg until my fingers met a bag of shriveled skin and a hard stick of dried flesh as thick as my thumb.

Scrotum; phallus.

Both sucked dry of moisture by the desert air.

Briefly my hand roved over a sunken stomach; a chest; through skin I could feel the ridges of ribs. Then I found the husk of the throat and hard roundness of the head with cotton-candy tufts of hair.

181

I left him behind. Continued my exploration. My searching hands moving over the dust through the utter darkness. My reaction to the next body was more easily controlled. I did not scream. I merely removed my hand rapidly from his foot.

This man was fully clothed. I checked his pockets. In his shirt pocket, I found a pack of cigarettes and a small box of matches. Carefully sliding open the box, as if it contained the most valuable treasures of Egypt, my fingertips found the matches. Counted them. Eight. Eight precious matches. I struck one.

Nothing.

Duds.

Spent matches.

Was I doomed to sit out the rest of my life in this arid chamber beneath the desert?

To die slowly of thirst?

Madness claiming me first. As this all-engulfing darkness bore down on me.

Would tomorrow find me singing to my dead companions while holding their dry hands for comfort?

No . . . *take care,* I told myself. *Try the matches again.*

This time I felt the box until I found the abrasive strip. I must have run the match head along the smooth-paper side.

I struck again. The match's phosphorus head sparked in the darkness, then burst alight with such brilliance that pain shot through my eyes. In a moment, however, the pain passed, and I found myself gazing upon a horrible scene. I groaned.

For there, gathered around me in the bottom of the shaft that was no larger than a dozen feet in diameter, were the dried corpses of five men. The one in front of me, the clothed one, still held a revolver in his shrunken hand. I saw a hole in his right temple, the stain from the copious outpouring of blood and brains darkening the dust around his head where it lay.

Another corpse, across the floor, had gaping wounds in its thigh. I had little doubt how they got there. The grim thought entered my mind that I, too, might soon be driven by extremities of thirst and hunger to consider partaking of my companions.

One in particular, a bald, lean man clad only in undershorts, looked fresher than the others. I doubted that he had been dead more than a few days. Perhaps his body still retained enough moisture to quench the thirst that would shortly begin to torture me. There might be as much as half a pint in the bladder. No. That would be—

Fire scorched my fingers. I dropped the match. Darkness swallowed me and I stood motionless among the dead, considering my next course of action.

At length, I crouched beside the man who had taken his own life. Groping blindly, I found his pistol. I had the devil's own time getting it out of his hand, and finally resorted to breaking two of the fingers. With the gun free, I carefully released the cylinder catch. The cylinder swung sideways. I tipped the barrel upwards. Six loads dropped into my other palm. By touch alone in the darkness I deduced from the open ends of the cartridges that two were expended shells, while four were still whole, hence live cartridges. From their size and weight, I guessed them to be of .38 caliber. I reloaded and set the pistol aside where I would have no trouble finding it.

For the present, I had no need for the weapon. The fact of its presence, however, was a great comfort. I knew that, should circumstances offer no alternative, I need not be reduced to a groveling, inhuman beast. I would simply take my own life, as my inert companion had, and be done with it.

With that settled, I groped once more in the dark. With a new sense of assurance I stripped the man of his trousers. I found a penknife in one of his pockets. Using that, I cut his pants legs into long, narrow strips. When I had a dozen of them, I struck another precious match. Six left, I told myself. Only six. I applied its flame to the end of the strip and found that I had created a rather satisfactory source of light. Paying out fabric as needed, I made a close inspection of the chamber by the illumination of the burning cotton.

The stone wall, I noticed, sloped gradually inward above me. This ruled out the possibility of climbing to the top of the shaft. Might there be another way out? Certainly, my predecessors hadn't found one. Their failure, however, constituted no certain proof that such an exit did not, in fact, exist.

Here, my knowledge of Egyptian tombs stood me in good stead. The pit, my prison, had obviously been constructed in ancient times. Its proximity to the Temple of Mentuhotep might indicate that it had been built during his reign, possibly as a secret entrance to his tomb. It was not unusual to find such passages, often designed as elaborate mazes complicated with false entries, dead ends, and portals concealed in walls and ceilings for the purpose of foiling tomb robbers.

I exhausted most of my supply of makeshift wicks in a useless search of the walls and floor. While my flame still burned, I quickly fashioned more strips from the dead man's trousers. Then I renewed my search, looking for the slightest clue that a secret passage might lie behind the stone wall of my cell. I found no such clue. Had I a pick, I might have battered my way to freedom. With bare hands, I was powerless.

Allowing my light to die, I sank against one of the walls. I was sweaty, exhausted, coated in dust. My hopes of escape had faded to a dim prayer for a miracle.

As I sat in the blackness, surrounded by my silent companions, an idea began to form. It seemed impractical at first. It seemed less so as I thought about it. Though the top of the shaft was higher than my frail light reached, any object that might take me closer to it seemed worthwhile.

Perhaps, after all, the passage to the tomb had been placed midway up the shaft wall. Such a manner of concealment was not unknown to the wily priests of those ancient times.

Thus, with the project justified in my mind, I set about constructing a platform of the bodies. It was a ghoulish task. In the darkness, I dragged each from its place of rest. Their joints were stiff, their skin tough. I grew to know their flesh by their manner of undress, by the various configurations of their limbs. Some had died prone, others sitting. I made use of these differences in constructing my platform, often sacrificing height for sturdiness.

At last, by clever stacking of four cadavers against the wall, I had a platform as high as my chest. I lifted the last body, the one most recently dead. He seemed less brittle than the others. Also his limbs had stiffened into convenient positions. I stood him upright on top of the others, leaning him slightly backwards against the wall. When he was securely in place, I lit a strip of cloth, the upper end of which I had earlier inserted in his mouth. I adjusted the burning tip at the side of the platform so that it wouldn't hinder my progress.

Then I began the awful climb. The bodies trembled precariously under my feet, but I was careful to place my weight only on the strongest points: a hip here, a shoulder there. At last, I reached the top of my platform. I stood motionless, gripping the wall, gathering my strength for the most strenuous part of the climb.

The flame had inched slowly up the strip of cloth. As I paused, it ignited the hair of one man, blazing briefly, illuminating the chamber with flickering white light, filling my nostrils with a terrible stench. When the fire died, I inspected the end of my taper.

Half the strip yet remained. I intended to use its flame, when I reached the summit, to ignite another makeshift taper, which was wound around my neck. This would save me the use of a precious match. The matchbox was tied at my throat, however, so I wouldn't be at a loss for light should the original taper expire during my climb.

Without further hesitation, I inched sideways. I swung the burning taper away from the knees of my ghastly companion and let it hang beside him out of my way. Pressing my body to his, I began to climb him. It was a horrible business, all the more so because of my nudity.

I was perched upon his bent knees, one hand pressed to the wall, the other gripping his left shoulder, when the light failed. The sudden darkness unnerved me, but I knew that I would soon fall if I didn't continue upward. Sliding a foot up his dry leg, I sought the bony protuberance of his hip. I found it. When I felt secure there, I raised my other foot. It, too, found a hold at his hip. Perched more precariously than ever, I leaned forward, my knees gripping him as if I were a child shinnying up a tree. Carefully, I straightened up, leaning full against him. I felt his face against my belly, then against my privates. I shall not tell of the nightmarish images that passed through my mind as I made my slow way upward.

I was almost onto his shoulders when he moved. My hands sought purchase on the stone wall but found none. The corpse continued to slide out from under me. In an instant I was falling. One foot struck the top body of my grisly platform and punched through it as if it were a plank of rotten wood. From there, I tumbled backwards through the darkness.

The ground struck me a terrible blow. As I lay there, stunned, a body fell on me. Then another. I flung them aside, and scurried out of their way.

Hunched against a wall, I gazed at the darkness. I listened intently. Beyond the drumming of my own heart, beyond the windy gasping of my lungs, I heard other sounds. Muted, incoherent babbling. The papery sounds of dry flesh dragging across the gravel floor.

I knew they were coming for me.

'No!' I shrieked.

I thought I heard their sandy laughter.

With palsied hands, I unlooped the strip of cloth at my neck. I tore open the box of matches. Poised to strike one, I hesitated. Better to die in the darkness, certainly, than to look upon the creatures – the dead creatures – crawling toward me. But I had to see!

I struck a match. In its sudden glare, I saw one reaching for my foot! Another, sitting upright, grinned. The rest, still in a heap, writhed as they tried to untangle their twisted limbs. It took me several agonizing moments to realize their movements were an illusion created by the flickering light of my match.

I lit an end of my taper and watched. Finally, I convinced myself that I was in no danger from my companions – that the danger resided only within my troubled psyche. My eyes turned to the shining nickel plate of the revolver.

Time to end it all, I thought.

Time for the kindness of oblivion.

I got to my feet and realized that I had lost the matchbox. Lowering my gaze, I scanned the floor until I spotted the small box. As I crouched to pick it up, I noticed an usual shadow at the base of the wall. I dropped to my hands and knees. With my free hand I reached into the shadow . . . deeper . . . deeper . . . A hole!

It was more than two feet in diameter. Inserting my arm as far as possible, I found no obstruction. Surely this was the passage I had searched for!

Such a fool I had been! Such a timorous fool! It had never occurred to me, during my careful search, to look *behind the bodies*!

I laughed out loud. Had the others, seeking a way out, made the same mistake? Indeed, had Kemwese placed his first victim over the hole on purpose to conceal the passage from his future prey? I shouldn't have put it past the devil.

For the next few minutes, I cut new strips from what remained of the trousers. I tied them around my neck. Once more, I secured the box of matches at my throat. Then, clutching the revolver in one hand, I slithered into the hole and began my quest for freedom.

The Tomb of Amara

I made my way slowly, laboriously, through the narrow passageway. At times, the stone walls squeezed my shoulders and I feared I might become stuck. Turning back, however, was out of the question. I knew what lay behind me: certain death. Ahead, there was hope.

The rough walls pressed in on me. They scraped the naked flesh of my body. Had I been afflicted with claustrophobia, the blackness and suffocating heat and tight, constricting walls would surely have driven me mad. But I kept my sanity and pressed onward.

Finally, my outstretched arms found open space instead of confining stone. I inched forward as far as I dared. Tucking the revolver into the gap beside my chest, I used both hands to free a strip of cloth from my neck and light its end.

I found myself near the ceiling of a chamber. It appeared to be about twelve feet in length and width. The floor, however, was out of sight. Paying out my makeshift taper, I lowered the burning tip as far as possible. I was still unable to see the floor, so I pulled up the strip and tore off its last few inches. I let it drop. It fluttered downward for some distance before stopping. I watched it burn on the floor no more than twenty feet below me.

With no choice in the matter, I clutched the revolver and writhed forward. As I hung over the lip of the hole, about to fall, I pushed away from the wall with all my strength. I maneuvered myself in midair, much as a diver would, and hit the floor feet foremost. My legs buckled, of course. I tumbled forward. The ground dealt me a terrific blow. I remained conscious, however, and a quick survey of my limbs indicated that the fall had bruised and battered me, but nothing was broken.

Eagerly, I lit a match and ignited one of my cloth strips. I found, to my relief, no unwelcome company in this pit.

I also found the door of a tomb.

A strange golden disk decorated with the scepter of Osiris had been applied as a seal to the stone door and was held in place by hemp cord. My feeble light showed several kinds of hieroglyphics engraved on the door. Under my father's tutelage, I had learned to read the language as if I had been born to it. Unfortunately, someone had chiseled and scratched the glyphs, rendering them indecipherable.

I had seen such work before. This, no doubt, was the tomb of an outcast, or heretic, one whose name was anathema.

The realization made hackles rise on my naked flesh. As a skeptic in matters supernatural, I should not have been unsettled to find myself at the tomb door of one damned by the ancient priests. Unsettled I was, however: I could feel malevolence like vapor rising from ice. It chilled me to the bone.

Stepping away from the door, I began to search the walls for a way out.

There was none.

None that I could find.

This came as no great surprise; my route to this chamber was surely the only manner of entry or exit.

I was glad for the revolver. At least it would give me a speedy end, not the slow and maddening agony of death by dehydration.

I blew out the light and sat in a corner. Not yet time to end myself. There would be plenty of time for that later. I tried to push aside the grim thoughts and consider possible avenues of escape. My mind found no answers.

At last, I decided to try my luck with the tomb. Though I dreaded the thought of the place, I was quite curious about it. Besides, there was only one way to find out, with certainty, what lay beyond the sealed door. Anything was possible, even my salvation.

I moved across the black chamber to the door. Fighting my reluctance to touch it, I lit one of my tapers and set to work.

I started calmly enough. As I progressed, however, my frenzy grew. What if I should be unable to force the door? What if I should succeed, only to find myself no closer to escape? All the while, I fought against my dread of the unholy person entombed within. I wanted only to huddle in the chamber's farthest corner, but my fevered mind told me that my only chance of survival lay in opening the door. I raged as I ripped the hemp loose. I yelled and roared like a lunatic as I strained at the stone slab.

At last it groaned.

Dust fell from the sealed edges of the door.

The door moved.

Swung open.

I cringed away as a foul gust of hot air breathed into my face and extinguished my light. The rank odor made me gag. It had the smell of dead, decaying snakes. In the darkness, I pictured the tomb to be a charnel house where dying vipers waited eagerly to swarm over me. Where hooded cobras swayed. Fangs dripping venom. I knew this was impossible: the nightmare of an overwrought mind. Only renewed light could still my fears, however. With shaking hands, I struck another match. I lit my taper, and peered through the door's opening.

There were, of course, no snakes.

Gazing at the small area revealed by my light, I stepped into the tomb.

At first, I thought it was empty. Surely, robbers had cleared the room of all its treasures: the countless necessities secreted with the corpse to assure its comfort in the afterlife – the utensils, the weapons, the furniture, the effigies of servants. No doubt the sarcophagus and mummy had also been removed.

I looked round at the walls. Normally these would have been covered with paintings, depicting the life of the deceased: hunting fowl, fishing by spear for the fat fish found in the Nile; or there would be representations of the deceased with members of their family. Also there should have been hundreds of hieroglyphics describing the life of the individual entombed here, the victories, the names of their children. There should also have been prayers and verses from the great Egyptian *Book of the Dead*.

Instead, the walls had been covered entirely with some black pigment. It still contained a reddish-brown tinge. This, too, I had seen before. In the tomb of one of the priests of the Pharaoh Akhenaten, the heretic king who banished Egypt's vast family of gods in favor of a single deity, the Aten. I recalled standing in the disgraced priest's tomb and hearing Howard Carter describe how later priests would have erased the name of the evil priest, then painted the walls with the blood of pigs. An animal considered unclean by ancient Egyptians. This and the destruction of the dead priest's identity would have destroyed his soul in the afterlife.

This had happened here, too. The erased name on the tomb door. The painting over of wall paintings and hieroglyphics in the despised blood of swine.

Whoever had been buried here must have been truly hated by later generations, who had set out so thoroughly to seek vengeance on the spirit of the deceased.

I comforted myself with the thought that the evil one had long ago met the same fate as countless other mummies. Even now, perhaps, it

189

was residing in a far-off museum. Or, like so many others, it had been ground into powder by some luckless European, now long dead, as the miracle cure of his day. Or it might have simply been used as kindling for some Bedouin's fire.

As I proceeded across the chamber, however, my light fell upon a canopic jar. Nearby lay the stone lid of the sarcophagus; near that, the mummiform lid of a coffin.

A chill penetrated my body. My bowels cramped, my privates shrank as if trying to retreat into my groin. For a long time, I simply gazed at the open sarcophagus, afraid to move.

My taper grew short. I realized that if I didn't act quickly, I would be plunged into darkness. That thought quickened me to action. I unwrapped a length of cloth from my neck – the last such strip – and lit it. The dried-blood walls seemed to feed on the light, making the chamber gloomier and gloomier.

With only the slightest hesitation, I stepped to the side of the sarcophagus and gazed into it.

I wasn't shocked, at first, by the strange sight below me.

Here was a person – a dead person, to be sure – but not so different from myself. He had brown hair. He wore a shirt and trousers, a leather belt, boots with neatly tied laces. Since he was laying face down inside the inner wooden coffin, I was spared the sight of his face.

Only when I looked more closely did I notice the mummy beneath him. A portion of its head was visible. I saw its red hair, lots of red hair that filled the spaces between the body and the coffin wall. Saw its eyeless sockets. I had the impression, for a moment, that it was kissing the dead man's neck.

The odors also. Through the smoke of my burning tapers I caught musty scents of ancient spices. Probably the ones that had been placed into the body cavity of the mummy to mask the smell of post-mortem decay.

I raised the man's head. The mummy's head also lifted and I realized its teeth were buried in his throat.

Stepping away from the coffin, I put the revolver to my temple.

Pulled the trigger.

Salvation

Had the revolver discharged and ended my life at that moment in the tomb of Amara, many would have been saved from the miseries later visited upon them. But if there are gods they are wily devils, tricksters that toy with our fates. They saw fit to let the hammer drop on an empty chamber.

I drew back the hammer for a second try.

As my finger began to press the trigger, I heard the distant, echoing call of my name. It was the voice of my companion, Maged.

Backing my way out of the tomb, I turned my eyes toward the tunnel high on the chamber wall. There I saw the shaky, dancing beam of a flashlight.

'Maged?' I called.

'Robert!' The delight in his voice made me smile.

My desperation, my madness, my suicidal helplessness, fell away, vanishing as the morning mist on the Nile vanishes before the dawn sun. I felt the sudden joy of a man who, chased by nightmare demons, awakens to a golden dawn.

Finally, the light beam fell upon my face.

'Ah, my friend!' Maged called. 'Always the explorer. I thought I should never find you.'

'You certainly took your time about it.'

'I went for a rope.' It dropped from the tunnel's mouth. 'Coming up?' he asked.

'Are you alone?'

'Most surely.'

'Secure the rope, then, and come down. I've found something you ought to see.'

A few moments later, I saw my young friend sliding down the rope. He hurried to my side. His joy was such that he embraced me.

'I ought to bash your head,' I told him, grinning.

'Were not the sisters everything I promised?'

'They were marvelous, marvelous. Only you neglected to mention their father.'

'A tyrant, that man.'

'Tyrant? He's a murderous lunatic! But enough of that. Let me show you what I've found.'

I showed him the door of the tomb, with its defaced hieroglyphics. His mood turned somber. He was reluctant to enter the tomb, but I persuaded him at length. I took his flashlight and led the way. Even with his olive skin his face paled visibly when he saw what gory blacks and rust browns painted the walls.

'Truly this is the tomb of a despised one,' he said. 'Never have I seen every inch of a tomb wall painted with hog's blood before.' He made sure his body made no contact with the unclean blood of the swine.

'Come along,' I said. He joined me beside the sarcophagus. I shone the light inside and lifted the man's head so that Maged might see the mummy's teeth embedded in the throat.

He backed quickly away. 'We must go.'

'What's the hurry?' I asked, rather enjoying his fright.

'The Bride of Set,' he muttered.

'What?'

He was gone. In spite of my refreshed humor, I was not eager to remain alone with the ghastly pair. I hurried after Maged. I was no sooner outside the tomb than he began to push its door shut.

'Don't bother,' I said, stopping him. 'We'll only have to open it again.'

'Please! It must be sealed.'

'Must it?'

'She will arise from the dead to seek after the blood of her slayers.'

'Nonsense.'

'It is true, Robert.' He pointed to the defaced glyphs on the door. 'Much has been destroyed, but this was once her name. *Amara!*'

I peered at it. True, the little that remained legible may have been part of the name 'Amara'.

'We must leave at once,' Maged told me, 'and find a holy man to reseal the entrance.'

'What we *will* do, Maged,' I said firmly, 'is figure out how to take her and her coffin out of here.'

His eyes widened with fright. 'We must not. You don't understand, Robert. You have broken the seal of Osiris guarding the doorway. Its magic is destroyed. Without it, Amara will walk the night.'

'She's dead, fool.'

192

'She is of the dead who lives.' Maged pushed the tomb door shut and leaned his back against it. Perspiration glistened on his face. His eyes were large . . . frightened. I'd never seen him like this before. 'Please listen, my friend. I will explain.'

'Speak your piece,' I told him rather impatiently.

'The banished god Set, slayer of Osiris, is the one recognized by both Jew and Christian alike as the one you call Satan.' He took a breath and continued. 'Set came in the night to Amara who was the favorite wife of Pharaoh Mentuhotep. He gave her the seed of his loins, that she might bear him a son. In return for her favors, he promised Amara the gift of eternal life.'

'Bunkum,' I said in contempt.

Maged ignored my remark. 'The god Set, the evil one, he wished his son to be Pharaoh after Mentuhotep, and lead the people of Egypt to their doom. When Amara gave birth, Mentuhotep suspected treachery, for the son had wicked eyes . . . snake eyes. He put Amara to death.'

'What about the baby?'

'It too was executed, and entombed with Amara.'

'I didn't see it.'

Maged gave an elaborate shrug. 'Robbers, perhaps . . .'

'Well, your story is charming, but it's utter bunk.'

'It's true, Robert. Believe me.'

'Where'd you pick it up? I've never run across the story before.'

'When I was a child, my grandmother whispered it to me in the night. She said, if I was bad, Amara would come for me and eat my throat.'

'We wouldn't want that, would we Maged?' I said and laughed. 'Come along, let's be off.'

Vengeance

My first order of business, after recovering from the ordeal of the pit, was to deal with the villain Kemwese.

I stayed away from the Tutankhamun diggings all day so the bastard wouldn't suspect that I had escaped from his death-hole. When night came, I dined with my father. He enquired about my battered appearance and I satisfied his curiosity by explaining that I'd taken a nasty fall down the hotel stairway. The subject was dismissed.

After we separated, I went to my room. I waited there, trembling somewhat with anticipation. Shortly after dark, I heard a knocking at my door. I opened it and Carmen entered, wearing a glittering cocktail gown that revealed her milk-white shoulders. Her cleavage was breathtaking.

Carmen was her stage name – or rather bed name, if you prefer, for she was a whore. She was a fabulous whore, renowned throughout Luxor. She stood nearly six feet tall, with hair the color of wheat and breasts like the silos of her Iowa hometown. All her orifices were portals to unspeakable pleasure. But they were costly to enter, and only those of us with considerable wealth could afford to journey there.

I had been with Carmen many times. I was one of her favorites, as she told me time and again. When I spoke to her that afternoon she readily agreed to my request.

'For that kind of dough,' she had said, 'I'd blow King Tut himself.'

Naturally, I didn't explain my entire plan.

'Now let me see if I've got it straight,' she said, sitting on my bed, her long legs stretching out. 'I go to this guy's house and I say my friend and me, we got attacked by a gang of cutthroats out by the temple ruins. Right?'

'That's it.'

'And would he come and help, 'cause I think my friend's hurt real bad?'

194

'Exactly.'

'And I get him out there and get him all worked up and—'

My engorged organ stopped her words. For the next half-hour, I used her with such vigor that we both finished sweaty and exhausted. When we recovered, we dressed and set out for the home of Kemwese.

At his village, I pointed out the mud-brick house. Carmen went to it while I hurried away. I rushed through the darkness. Soon, I reached the stone slab, the entrance to Kemwese's horried prison. I hid myself in the shadows of the nearby temple ruins. There, I waited.

The wait was a lengthy one. I sat on the rough stone, watching the desolate landscape before me with its endless vista of sand. For all the world I must have looked like Ahab searching the waves for his damnable White Whale. No one can know the horrors of the charnel pit; no one can know the rapture I felt as I waited in the moonlight to take my vengeance upon the man who had put me there.

Man?

No! *Human fiend.*

My heart pounded. My hands trembled. Yes, even my teeth chattered, in spite of the night's heat. Several times I laughed, muffling the sound with my hands.

Finally, Carmen appeared. Her golden tresses cascaded down her back. Her hips swayed as she walked.

She was holding Kemwese's hand. His robe gleamed as white as bone.

'I do not see your friend,' Kemwese said.

Carmen swirled away from him, her laughter trilling through the silence.

'Where is the friend who was beaten?'

Her forefinger tapped the side of her head. 'In here, Kemwese. I made him up.'

'And why is that?' he asked. He crossed his arms over his massive chest.

'To drag you away from your village. What we're gonna do, it's got to be a big secret.'

'Kemwese does not pay for his women.'

'Course not. This isn't business, sweetheart. This is just for pleasure. My pleasure.' She went to him, long, slender arms held out, her gold bracelets glinting.

I watched from my hiding place, trembling. They embraced, they kissed. Soon Carmen was naked and standing upright as Kemwese lavished kisses on her shoulders, on the vast twin mounds that were her breasts. He fell to his knees like a worshiper at the temple of her body. As he lapped between her legs, she pulled the djellaba over his head and flung it aside. Now he was naked, his body hairy like a gorilla's. Taking his face away from her womanhood, he crawled behind her to dwell on her rear parts. He forced her down and mounted her. It surprised me not the least to discover his preference.

Once he was firmly implanted, I left my place of concealment. I made my way stealthily toward the pair. Soon, I was standing close behind Kemwese, watching the hairy mounds of his buttocks twitch and jiggle as he rutted. From the frenzy of his exertion and the rhythm of his beastly grunts, I guessed that he was on the verge of expending himself. I wanted to cheat him of that moment, so I stepped forward quickly and brought down the revolver. Its butt cracked against the bastard's skull. To my chagrin, the impact triggered a bowel movement.

I pulled the unconscious body off Carmen and saw that I hadn't prevented his climax after all.

'Damn,' Carmen muttered, getting up. 'Damn, look what he did!'

One of her calves bore a glistening dark smudge. She used Kemwese's djellaba to clean herself.

For the next few minutes I busied myself with binding the hands and feet of my quarry. I knew the hemp would not restrain him for long after his return to consciousness. I didn't intend that it should.

'All done?' Carmen asked when I finished tying him.

'Nearly.'

'Nay, now, sweetheart, you said we'd just truss him up and leave him bare-ass. If you've got any other tricks up your sleeve, you can count me out.'

'There's nothing to worry about, Carmen.'

'Not for you. You ain't the one went in his house, honey.'

'Who saw you?'

'He had these two gals with him. A couple of twins.'

'They won't tell.'

'I'll just bet.'

'They're his daughters. They hate him more that I do. Besides, they're both deaf-mutes.'

'You sure about that?'

'I'm positive. Were you seen by anyone else?'

196

She shook her head. 'I don't think so, but that don't change the picture. If you want to pull some nasty business here, I'll take a walk, thank you very much.'

'It won't take long,' I told her. 'If you prefer not to watch, go on ahead. I'll catch you up in a few minutes.'

'What're you gonna do to him? Some homosexualist thing?'

'No.'

'What, then?'

'I thought you didn't want to know.'

'I guess I don't.'

'Like I say, take a little stroll. I'll catch you up when I'm done.'

She agreed to that.

When she walked off, hips swaying, I dragged the unconscious body of Kemwese to the side of the stone slab. I pushed it away from the hole. I turned to Kemwese and slid him forward until his legs as far as the knees dropped out of sight.

I slapped his sweaty face until the eyes blinked open.

'Remember me?' I asked.

He scowled, his gaze burning into me.

'Time for a dose of your own medicine, my friend.'

I was delighted to see the terror that suddenly twisted his face as he understood what I meant, and realized that the lower half of his body had already been swallowed by the pit.

Down he went.

Down, down, down.

He cried out in pain as he hit the bottom.

'Nasty fall,' I called down.

I crouched at the edge of the pit, grinning. He cursed me and my ancestors; my sons and their sons. He threatened me. That he would peel the skin from my body; that my male member would be worn as a trophy on his belt. Finally, however, much to my satisfaction, he began to cry and plead for mercy.

I pushed the stone into place and left him there.

With great restraint, I allowed a full week to pass before returning to the pit. Maged and I went there in the dead of night. I had told my friend nothing of Kemwese. The purpose of our excursion, I'd made clear, was to determine the best way of removing the mummy and its coffin from the tomb.

Maged was against the whole affair, at first. He reminded me, at endless and tedious length, of Amara's nasty reputation – indeed, her demon-like nature. In my turn, I reminded him that dead is *dead*.

He was unconvinced. Those fright stories of his grandmother's had embedded themselves deeply into his heart and soul. Then I told him of my plans for the mummy – as well as my plans for myself. I described my family's private collection of Egyptian antiquities. I told him that we possessed no mummies, as yet, and how my heart was now set upon adding such an infamous lady as Amara to our collection.

He argued that it was silly and dangerous and impossible. Aside from the hazards of Amara herself there were laws. I was surprised by his familiarity with Egypt's restrictions on the removal of artifacts, and even more surprised by his knowledge of problems we would face with the United States authorities, who look upon mummies as little more than germ-infected corpses.

'I know ways,' I said, 'of getting around all that rubbish.'

I explained about my father's friend, the smuggler.

Maged was adamant; he wanted no part in such dealings. Then I explained that, of course, I would not only have Amara smuggled into the US, but Maged as well. He would live with my father and me, as just one of the family.

'Is this true?' he asked, dumbfounded.

'You have my word on it.'

From that moment forward, Maged was as brash and energetic about the project as if he had originated it himself.

I watched him climb down the knotted rope. He disappeared into the pit and I was glad I had not mentioned Kemwese. His surprise at meeting our old friend would be marvelous to see.

Quickly, I followed him into the darkness.

When I reached bottom, I shone my flashlight over the grim collection of corpses. Kemwese was not among them. This troubled me somewhat, in spite of my certainty that we would find his body nearby: in the tunnel, or the adjoining chamber, or Amara's tomb.

After all, no man could survive a week without water in this climate. And there was no other exit; I was reasonably certain of that.

Because of my lingering apprehension about Kemwese, I insisted on being the first to enter the connecting tunnel. In my restored condition, the narrow tunnel had little effect on my nerves. True, it was often a tight squeeze. Overall, however, the tunnel seemed less confining, less threatening, than previously. My only concern was Kemwese. What if he should squirm towards me out of the darkness? I knew this was rubbish. Nevertheless, the idea of it would not leave me.

I was greatly relieved to reach the opening at the tunnel's end. Eagerly, I searched the area below with my light.

My dread increased, however, for there was no Kemwese in the room below.

I debated whether to broach the subject to Maged and decided against it; what useful purpose could it serve? It would give him a warning to be cautious, true enough. On the other hand, it might be enough to frighten him into abandoning the project. I couldn't take a chance on that, so I kept my silence.

I secured a length of rope to a corner of the masonry, as Maged had done on the night he saved me. Then I squirmed out of the tunnel. With my legs wrapped in hemp, I lowered myself head foremost to the floor of the room. Then I helped Maged down.

The door of Amara's tomb was shut, just as we had left it.

Could Kemwese have entered and pulled it closed after him?

I drew the revolver from my pocket. I didn't fail to notice a faint smile on Maged's face.

'Dead is dead,' he whispered.

Together, we pulled open the door of Amara's tomb. We swung the beams of our lights inside.

In my memory, the next instant seems endless. And yet I know it lasted no longer than a blink or two of the eye.

I saw Kemwese on his back, gazing at us with dead eyes. The flesh of his naked body had been savagely torn.

Facing us, seated on his chest, arms resting casually on her upthrust knees, was the mummy, Amara.

As if sitting on a cushion.

Relaxing.

Patiently waiting for us.

The Living Dead

With shocking suddenness, Amara leaped from the body.

Maged hurled the flashlight at the monstrosity. It struck her head, distracting her for a moment as it entangled itself in her voluminous red hair. We leaped through the entrance. Flinging ourselves against the heavy door, we somehow managed to force it shut before the awful creature could reach us.

Despite the pressure on the other side of the door, our combined efforts were sufficient to hold it shut. The strength of Amara was such that neither of us alone could have held it closed. As we pressed our shoulders to the rough stone, I searched my mind for a method of escape.

If we simply made a dash for the rope, Amara would certainly fall upon us before we could climb to safety. If one of us stayed behind to hold the door as long as possible, the other might be able to climb to freedom. The one remaining, however, would be compelled to face the mummy alone.

At the time, I knew only that she was dead . . . and yet alive.

I had no desire to exchange blows with such a creature.

Unworthy thoughts entered my mind, thoughts of making a sudden dash for the rope, leaving Maged to face the hideous creature by himself. Ashamed, I reminded myself that he was my best friend, nay, my only friend, and that he had saved my life. I could not leave him at the mercy of the awful hag.

And yet, I knew we could not hold the door shut forever. At a loss, I asked Maged's advice.

'It is simple enough, Robert. The god Set gave Amara power only to walk the night. At dawn, she will again be as one who is dead.'

'Are you sure?'

'This is what my grandmother told me.'

'Then I hope your grandmother was right.'

Neither of us knew precisely what time dawn would arrive that morning. Shortly after five o'clock, however, the pressure on the other side of the door ceased. As a precaution, we waited until six o'clock by my watch. Then we opened the door.

Amara had returned to her seat on Kemwese's chest.

As we entered her tomb, she remained motionless.

The ghastly thought came to me that Maged was wrong, that we were being lured into the tomb by trickery. I found my gaze locked onto that terrible figure. Its eyeless sockets, mere twin pits in the ruined face, seemed to look right into my own two living eyes. Her naked body was brown; wrinkled hideously in parts, elsewhere, as smooth as melon skin. While tumbling in a copper cascade from the skull-like head, down around her shoulder, covering one breast that hung as empty as a poor man's leather purse, was that lustrous hair. How hair could still look lovely and alive attached to that ancient husk of a corpse was beyond me.

A movement beside me roused me from my near-trance. I was tempted to hurry away, but Maged walked forward to shove the thing with his foot. It fell sideways.

'You see, Robert?' he whispered.

I breathed a sigh of relief. 'And you say that it won't . . . get up . . . before sunset?'

'That is what my grandmother told me.'

'Excellent.' With trembling hands, I lit a cigarette. I paced the tomb, smoking it, and thinking. Blue smoke rolled across the walls painted with pig's blood. At last, I said, 'Let's box her up.'

'What?'

'We'll put her back in her coffin and see if we can get it – and her – out of here before dark.'

'Now?'

'No time like the present, my friend. Especially for a nasty job.'

A nasty job it proved to be, indeed. With Amara inside, the coffin was too heavy for us to handle with ease. After carrying it from the tomb, we removed her. I climbed the rope to the tunnel overhead. Below, Maged tied the lidless coffin to the rope. He lifted and guided it while I pulled. Though the coffin was not unmanageably heavy, I had great difficulty hoisting it to my perch and pulling it in after me. It plugged the tunnel's end. I tried, squirming backwards, to pull it along after me. Soon, however, it began scraping along nicely. I realized that Maged was at its other end, pushing. It was a tight fit. Had the tunnel not been perfectly straight, we would never have succeeded.

The going became extremely hard during the final yards when the tunnel slanted upward to the floor of the first pit. I pulled as best I could, and Maged pushed with superhuman effort.

At last, we finished. We fell, exhausted, to the floor as if joining the five old corpses in their rest. When I had recovered my breath, I lit a cigarette.

'The rest of the job will be a snap,' I said.

I was almost correct.

The coffin lid gave no trouble at all. Nor did the four canopic jars. The final stage of the task, however, required us to deal with Amara herself. This was a singularly grim bit of business that set our nerves on edge. As we maneuvered her through the tunnel, we both worried that she might suddenly come alive in our hands. Neither of us spoke of it, at the time. Much later, however, in the safety of my California home, we shared our memories of that day.

Maged, who had been in the lead, confided, 'I was certain her head moved. I couldn't see a thing, of course, but somehow I *knew* that she had turned her head and intended to nip my arm.'

It was with considerable relief that we placed Amara inside her coffin and covered her horrible, naked body with the lid.

We couldn't raise her out of the pit that day. It was not a job for daylight. And yet, we were both loath to deal with Amara at night.

Maged had a solution. We climbed out of the pit, seeing nobody in the vicinity, and pushed the stone into place to conceal the opening.

Maged's solution took the form of a gnarled old man named Ramo who lived not far from Kemwese's hut.

We found him sitting alone in his dark hut. He wore a gray, tattered djellaba and a gold-cloth turban that had seen far better days. I saw at once that something was amiss about his face. The mouth seemed out of kilter, long and stretching across the side of his face. This was due, I later discovered, to an old knife wound that had laid open his right cheek and never healed correctly.

Maged spoke to the man in Arabic, explaining that we had blundered into the tomb of Amara, destroying its sacred seal and so destroying the magic bonds that had contained the creature. Amara had walked. We wished Ramo to use his powers, as a priest of Osiris, to seal the coffin.

He asked to see the broken seal of Osiris. Maged, with commendable foresight, had pocketed the golden disk. He removed its pieces from his pocket and presented them to Ramo. The old man fondled them, grinning. His grin was a hideous sight indeed, as it drew back not only his lips but also the ragged edges of his cheek, exposing what remained of his molars.

He explained that his father had fashioned this very seal, many years ago – a dozen years before Ramo himself had been born. At the time, robbers had plundered Amara's tomb. They had stripped off her winding clothes, stolen her jewelry, and taken her mummified infant from its resting place at its mother's side.

Amara had remained still until the child was taken. Then she had abruptly clutched the nearest robber and killed him. The two survivors, fearing Amara's vengeance, escaped from the tomb, then came to Ramo's father. They paid him well and he fashioned the seal of gold to prevent Amara's escape from the tomb.

We offered to pay Ramo twice the amount his father had received, and he agreed to work the gold into a pair of seals, one for each long side of the coffin's lid. He would bless the seals, according to ancient rite, and their magic would prevent Amara from rising.

They were finished two days later. Just at sunrise, Maged and I dropped a rope into the pit and descended. We expected this. We flashed our lights among the sprawled corpses and found Amara lying beneath one of the naked men.

The sight of it made my flesh crawl. I envisioned all of the bodies stirring in the blackness of the pit, lurching toward the new female in their midst who summoned them with her open legs.

We tumbled a man aside.

I carefully averted my eyes from his privates, afraid of confirming my fears.

We lifted Amara, and put her inside the coffin. We put the lid in place. Then we affixed the twin seals of Osiris at the seams of the lid, hammering small nails through holes made in the gold for this purpose by Ramo.

The job finished, we left the pit and covered its entry with the rock. We would not return until arrangements had been completed to smuggle Amara home.

Conclusion

Many years have gone by since my activities in Egypt. My father died long ago, though not before I was able to delight him with the addition of Amara to our Egyptian collection.

Maged married shortly after coming to live with us. We employed him and his wife as servants until their untimely deaths. Their offspring, Imad, lives with us still.

In 1929, I married the beautiful Sarah Guthrie. Though we wished for children, Sarah was unable to conceive. We bestowed much of our love on Imad, especially after the tragedy that robbed him of his true parents.

That incident took place in 1936 when a house guest named Clive Hargrove opened Amara's coffin. I had spoken to him over dinner about the strange legend surrounding the mummy. As was my policy, I never spoke of what I had witnessed myself. Maged and I had agreed to carry the secrets of our discovery to our respective graves.

In the dead of night, Hargrove entered the Collection Room, and carefully removed the nails holding the seals in place.

Sarah and I slept peacefully through the night. In the morning, we discovered Maged and his wife in their bedroom, mutilated and dead. Their baby, Imad, was missing from his nursery.

I hurried downstairs to the Collection Room, and found Hargrove dead at the foot of Amara's coffin.

The lid was resting upright against a wall, where he had apparently left it.

I found Amara inside the coffin. In the embrace of her withered arms was the unconscious form of the baby, Imad.

The tragedy affected us deeply. Determined to prevent a reoccurrence, I ordered a steel door be installed to make the Collection Room as secure as a bank vault.

That was not enough. Vaults could be entered, nails pulled, seals broken. Only with her infant at her side, however, would Amara's vengeful spirit be still. If I could return the stolen child to her, she would, hopefully, rest in peace forever.

I knew that the child had been taken a dozen years before the birth of the old priest, Ramo. Guessing his age to be near seventy, I calculated that the robbery had taken place during the 1840s.

With luck, the mummy might have found its way into a museum. Otherwise, it had likely disappeared into a private collection, or been destroyed.

My search led me to London, where I spent weeks in the British Museum, searching for references to infant mummies. There I became overly familiar with the work of one Dr Thomas Pettigrew.

'Mummy' Pettigrew, as he was called, astonished London theater audiences with public unwrappings of mummies. He was all the rage. His act went on for twenty years, during which he cut, hacked, and ripped his way through the winding clothes of hundreds of mummies. The morbid business delighted his audiences, for one never knew what treasure or oddity might lurk beneath the crusted bandages.

Among his subjects were several mummified babies.

The London *Times* of 16 March 1843 reported that Pettigrew's audience had been stunned the previous night by the 'strange movements' of an infant he was attempting to unwrap. While many suspected Pettigrew of trickery, he claimed that the child 'stirred as if alive.' Before his claim could be investigated, he 'committed the child to the flames.'

The child, I am reasonably certain, was the missing son of Amara and the god Set.

My search was over. I returned home, disappointed. In the years since then, I have taken exceptional care to avoid a repetition of the tragedy that took Imad's parents. To this date, all has been well.

Sarah and I grow old, however. One day, we shall be gone. I have willed my Egyptian collection to the Charles Ward Museum, which has agreed to house it in a special 'Callahan Room'.

I cannot, however, forget my experience with Amara. Though I intend to leave specific instructions that the seals of the coffin remain intact, I fear that, one day, the hideous crone will walk the night in search of her stolen child.

If Amara should stir from her coffin, Imad (or his descendants) are obligated by the terms of my will to present this memoir to the museum administration. It is my hope that such parties, familiar with the strange ways of the ancients, will believe what I have written, and that my words will help them to understand the nature of the hag.

Robert A. Callahan
Greenside Estates
Burlingdale, California

16 April 1968

206

Chapter Thirty-five

The Memoirs of Robert Callahan.

Memoirs? Or nightmares?

Imad closed the small black notebook that was testament to so much horror and anguish.

This was the first time he'd read the book even though he'd known of its existence. It told him much of the father he'd never had time to know and of Robert Callahan, the kindly man who had adopted him.

He set the book down on a table. Right now, the urge came upon him to shower in water that was near-boiling; to scrub his skin until he bled. Because not only did the memoirs reveal the manner of his parents' death, it told of how he'd been taken by the mummy to its coffin, and how Robert Callahan had discovered the infant Imad asleep in the dead arms of Amara.

He closed his eyes and moaned, the muscles in his face twitching.

Flashbacks.

Memories long repressed . . . of the creature bending over his crib in the dead of night. The withered face, the empty sockets where its eyes should have been; the wash of red hair tumbling onto him like a gush of blood, falling across his face, smothering him.

He rocked on the bed, perspiring, nausea rising in the back of his throat. That smell. Pungent spices. And, worse, the grim odors of the tomb.

Amara had reached out and picked him out of his crib. She'd cradled the infant Imad against her dead skin, pressing the baby's face to her withered breasts. He remembered now. He's seen the blood of his parents still fresh on the monster's teeth. It even glued the hair together into thick gore-covered strings that had brushed against Imad's face.

The mummy had then taken him to the coffin before daylight had broken.

Right then, Imad wanted nothing more than to take a full bottle of gin and retire to bed where he might be able to drown the memories under a torrent of alcohol.

No. There is important work to be done, he told himself. He must obey Robert Callahan's instructions to the letter.

Chapter Thirty-six

In the dark, Ed Lake heard the order.

'Present yourself.'

As he lay there on the panel, pressed tight to the Perspex, he maneuvered his erect penis up through the hole into the receiving orifice. It felt warm and snug. Muscles contracted tight around his organ. That delicious friction again . . . up, down, up, down. There, in the darkness above him, his captor moved, pleasuring herself, filling herself with his manhood.

Don't know how long I can keep this up . . .

Pun intended, Eddie?

Ed was being forced to perform every few hours. And – hell – each performance could last hours. All that friction was taking its toll.

What happens when my strength goes? When I can't pull an erection anymore? They're gonna gash my neck. I'm gonna die in a rush of blood. Just like Marco.

Hell . . .

The body rocked above him in ecstasy. The Perspex flexed. *Gotta be strong.* If it broke . . .

Freedom.

But that stuff was tough. It was made to protect bank cashiers from bullets. Might flex a little. It'd never break. He'd never have it so easy. *Might as well accept it, Eddie boy, you're going to remain a sex slave for as long as you can keep it up. You're going to need to poke to survive. Fuck to live. Otherwise . . .*

Otherwise your nice, soft throat's for the chop.

But he couldn't perform like this forever. One day he'd have an attack of the floppy Joes. *Then it's the big sleep for you, Eddie.*

Don't call me Eddie.

The mind chatter gave way to exhausted rambling. Random thoughts flitted through his head as he pushed his loins upward into the receiving body above.

Didn't a Turkish princess once keep a baboon for this purpose? She was a nympho. Couldn't get enough, so she visited a wise woman who advised her to procure a big buck baboon. Baboons have their own harems to service. Baboons could fuck tirelessly from sunup to sundown.

Nice story.

But where do I buy a baboon at this time of night?

Ed, keep your mind on the job. Nearly slipped out then.

Jeepers creepers, am I losing the erection? I'm bending inside her.

Think sexy thoughts, think sexy thoughts . . .

Panic ripped through him. That didn't help. Didn't help one bit. If he couldn't perform. If he disappointed his captor he was sure he'd lose more than a toe this time.

He pictured Virginia. Pictured her naked and panting hotly over him. In his mind's eye she rubbed her breasts in his face. There were thin, white scars around the nipples. That didn't matter. He imagined they were having great sex. She was moaning. She was crying out his name. Crying louder . . .

Then he realized a cry had escaped his captor. This had never happened before. His captor's orgasms had been confined to a juddering, a breathlessness.

This was a full-blooded shout.

The voice came in a deep booming roar that filled the room.

'Oh, Jesus . . . Yes!'

So loud it sounded like the voice of God. Ed felt as if his skull would burst beneath the avalanche of sound.

Then it cut dead.

Silence.

The body slipped from his cock with a lubricious sucking sound. Then – gone.

Later the lights came on. When Ed at last managed to squirm from between the platform and cage roof he collapsed exhausted to the foam mattress. The hairbrushes, toothbrushes, electric razor and water bottles hanging from the strings tied to the cage roof swung crazily, making him feel even more light-headed. Unscrewing one of the bottles he drank deeply. Man, that was good.

Virginia stared at him through the bars of their respective cages, her eyes wide with astonishment.

'That sound she made . . .' She shook her head, incredulous. 'What do you make of that?'

Ed drank more from the water bottle. The cool liquid felt wonderful. He only wished he could soak his overheated genitals in an ice bath. The relentless friction had left his flesh fiery and sensitive. Exquisitely sensitive. To touch himself could be hell one moment, heaven the next. His nerve endings must be raw.

Taking the water bottle, he sat cross-legged on the mattress.

'You heard the voice?' Virginia's green-eyed stare fixed on his face.

'I heard.' He gave a tired shrug. 'Couldn't miss.'

'Well, what does that tell us?'

He took a mouthful of water. Rolled it. Swallowed. 'Tells us that she's wearing a mike.'

'Can't be wired, so it must be a radio mike.'

'And when she speaks to us the voice is electronically altered. Made deeper.'

'Then instantly relayed back through hidden speakers in the room.'

'I guess.' He let his shoulders sag. 'Sweet Jesus. I need to rest for a year and a day.'

'Lie down,' she told him.

As he did so he glanced across at her. She lay on her side. Not bothering now to cover herself; the blanket had slipped down, exposing one full breast. Copper hair tumbled deliciously over it. A fine sight. Very fine indeed.

Virginia, you saved my life today.

He was going to say the words. Nearly did. Nearly told her that when he'd started to soften during sex he'd thought about her.

Let's say she stiffened my resolve, he thought.

But they needed to filter the facts.

Virginia spoke. 'Let's recap, then.'

'From the beginning.'

'Okay, from the beginning. We know we're being held in cages in a building that's well out of town, in the boondocks.'

'Or is soundproofed.'

'Or both.' She looked round. 'The more I look at this place the more I can believe we're locked up in an old TV studio.'

'The back lot that MGM forgot.'

She gave a wan smile. 'Not a movie studio. Not big enough.'

'So a redundant TV studio?'

'A studio of some kind. Maybe even a recording studio.'

'So, fill in the picture, Virginia. What's our situation?'

This was an old routine now. Using clues and guesswork to figure where they were and what was happening to them.

Virginia continued. 'We're held in some secret location, in

211

a soundproofed room. We're well fed. We're kept in relatively comfortable conditions.'

'A two-star beast house at least.'

She smiled at the little joke. A beautiful smile. A winning smile that warmed his fatigued body. 'A beast house with en-suite bathroom.' She nodded at the sawdust bowl.

'And we can pitch as good a theory as any – that we're kept here as sex slaves.'

'Sounds raunchy, doesn't it?'

'Yeah, but like any day-job it becomes a dull grind sometimes.'

'Say that again.'

'It becomes a dull—'

'Whoa – figure of speech, Ed.'

He grinned. 'I wish I was in that cage with you.'

She grinned back. 'I wish you were in this cage with me.'

'We could keep each other warm.'

'We'd be stimulating company for each other.' She gave a suddenly shy smile. 'What do you think?'

'I think so too.'

She wagged her finger in a mock-scolding way. 'Back to business, Mr Ed Lake. What's our current position?'

'Lying on concrete in a cage.'

'You know what I mean . . . our situation.'

'Our situation. We know that when the lights go out our captors visit us. They move around unseen in complete darkness.'

'How?'

'Because they are wearing some kind of hi-tech head gear. Nightscope goggles.'

'So they see us.'

'But we don't see them.'

'How many?'

He rubbed his jaw. 'How many captors? Let's figure not more than two. Maybe only one.'

'Hmmm . . .' She looked thoughtful. 'I guess two.'

'Oh?'

'It's a lot of work for just one. Supplying food, taking away waste.'

'But not an impossible workload.'

'No, but then there were Marco and the others.'

'I see.' He nodded.

'They were carried here unconscious. Also the corpses had to be manhandled out of the cages and disposed of.'

'That would take one mightily powerful individual.'

'Or two people.'

He nodded again. 'I agree on that point, Virginia. At least two captors, then. But . . .' He shrugged. 'How many do we have sex with?'

'I think I know.' Her shoulders made a little hopping motion. 'Strange what you think about under these blankets, huh?'

'We've got plenty of thinking time, hon.'

She smiled at the endearment. Then: 'I believe there are two captors. We only have sexual contact with one.'

'How can you tell?'

He touched the tip of her nose with her finger. 'Scent.'

'Huh?'

'Sometimes after the lights have gone out and you sense one of them close by you catch a little of how they smell.'

'Go on.'

'The one who moves the sawdust bowls and brings in the meals has a slightly sour odor.'

'You *do* have a good sense of smell.'

'The "warder", as we'll call her, gives off the sour odor. It's like the smell of milk on someone's breath.'

'And the one who . . .' He lifted a shoulder. 'Who pleasures herself at our expense?'

'Smells sweet. She bathes regularly. She uses good-quality beauty products – oils, powders that kind of thing.'

'Anything else?'

'Yes, it might sound odd, but she smells young.'

'You can tell by her body odor?'

'Yes, I think so. Don't you think people in different age groups smell differently?'

'Well . . . I don't know. I guess you're right. But . . .' He shrugged.

'Trust me on that one, Ed: *I know.*' She smiled. 'I was a dental hygienist. It brings you into close contact with people of all ages, all walks of life.'

'Oh . . .' He took a breath. 'OK, but we refer to our captors as "she". Now, I'm sure the one who fucks around with our bodies is female. How do you know the sex of our warder?'

'Brace yourself for this one, Ed, it doesn't sound pretty.'

'Shoot anyway.'

'I've been here long enough to know she has cycles.'

'Huh?'

'She has periods and, like I say, she doesn't exactly devote much time to the bathroom.'

'You mean you can smell her period? Jeez.'

'Like I said. Not pretty. But, yes, I can smell menstrual blood.'

'Wow, I'm impressed, Virginia.'

'Thanks.'

'And that paints a fuller picture. We know our captives are two women below menopausal age. One's our warder.'

'The other our Sex Queen.'

Ed drummed his fingers on his knee. 'But this can't go on, can it?'

'No. But what can we do? We're in the pen, remember?'

'There's got to be some way of hitting them. Some way of doing so much damage that we can escape.'

'How?'

'Wait till they get close, then grab them through the bars.'

'You can't see them. It's completely dark when they come in.'

'But when she fools around with us through the bars. She's close then. You can *feel* her closeness to you.'

Virginia shook her head. 'They always order you to put your hands through restraining loops. What about when you lie on the platform? There's no way of reaching her then?'

'No, there's bulletproof glass between her and me, even though it's only around an inch thick.'

'You couldn't smash it with your fist?'

'Not a hope.'

'And you can't reach round the outside of it?'

'Nope.'

'The hole?'

'What about the hole?'

'The hole you . . . *present* yourself through.'

'Oh.'

'Think about it. She sits on that with her pussy pressed to it. Imagine how vulnerable she is then.'

'You mean that instead of pushing my dick through I should push my hand up and somehow grab her from the inside?'

'Yes.'

'Wouldn't work.'

'Why?'

'The hole's big enough for my dick. Not for my hand.'

'Damn.' Her gaze became downcast.

'Virginia . . . Virginia, look at me. Believe it. We'll find a way

214

out of here. And we're going to hurt these bitches so badly they'll curse the day they were born.'

Ed was jolted awake. Blinking, he opened his eyes. Darkness again. Inky darkness that revealed nothing. But he heard shouting. A male voice: indignant, a throaty anger, demanding to be let out.

'I'll rip your heads off . . . d'ya goddamn hear me? I'll tear you apart!'

Thumping sounds. Someone was hammering cage bars.

'You can't do this to me! D'ya know who I am? I run this neighborhood. When I tells people to do, they *do!* Ya hear me? I said, *ya hear me?*' There was more furious rattling.

'Take it easy,' Ed spoke softly. 'You'll hurt yourself.'

'Hey, who's that?' The voice had a New York accent with a splash of Italian.

'Ed Lake.'

'You let me outta here, Lake, or I'm gonna break every bone in your goddamn body.'

'I can't, I—'

'What ya mean, you can't? Let me out of this freakin' cage. Now!'

The voice had power. People would tremble when they heard that voice.

Ed hissed. 'Ssh.'

'Don't shush me, you asshole.'

'Listen, you've got—'

'No, *you* listen.' The voice raged in the darkness. 'You listen to Romero Cardinali. You open the cage now and you and your children and their children escape with their lives. Got that, asshole?'

'Mr Cardinali, I can't let you out, I'm—'

'You working for the Jamaican Yardie boys?'

'No. I'm—'

'Then it's got to be Ratzioni . . . I tell ya, Fat Ratz is gonna nourish coyotes after this. In fact, I'm going to feed his balls to the coyotes one at a time and he can watch, the double-crossing—'

'Mr Cardinali.' Ed's voice grew to a shout. 'I've nothing to do with Jamaicans or anyone else, I'm trying to tell you that . . .' The lights came on. Ed paused, his face burning as if he'd made a fool of himself, shouting like that. Then he spoke in a near-whisper. 'I'm trying to tell you that I'm in a cage like you.'

A plump, balding man stood in the cage once occupied by Marco. He wore black pants, white shirt, no shoes and could have passed for

215

a wine waiter or even a funeral director. He looked around fifty and was sweating profusely. He also looked very, very angry.

'You sure you're locked in there, kid? You're not puttin' me on?'

Virginia spoke. 'He's not. We're both prisoners here.' Then she added, 'Like you.'

He shrugged his shoulders and adjusted his shirt collar as if composing himself. 'So what's the deal?'

'Deal?'

'Yeah, deal. You stoopid, kid? Deal! What's going down? Why're we here?'

'You should save your strength, Mr Cardinali.' Ed realized he sounded just like Marco the first time he spoke to him. 'Sit down. Save your strength. You're going to need it.'

'Hey, no little schmuck gives Romero Cardinali no orders.'

Ed sighed. 'Suit yourself.' He lay down and covered himself with the blanket.

'Hey, you schmuck. Don't you go to sleep on me. Hey, you . . .'

I tried, Ed told himself. *I tried to help him.*

The man raged on. 'Hey, what's going on here? Where is this place? I'm gonna have my people tear it down brick by brick. I'm gonna find who's responsible for this. They don't know the kind of guy they're jerking around here. Keeping me in a cage, for God's sake. They're dead. D' ya hear? Dee-Ee-Ay-Dee . . . dead! D' ya hear that, ya jerks!'

Ed groaned. He wanted to sleep. But sure as eggs were eggs sleep wouldn't come easy now with Mr Cardinali. *Our new roomie.*

Chapter Thirty-seven

Ed Lake sat in the dark with his back to the cage bars. He listened to the argument. He knew Virginia was listening too.

Shoot, listen to the guy.

Mr Romero Cardinali was saying no dice. 'What kind of freaking guy do you take me for, you jerk? I'm no whore. You—'

The bass voice boomed. *'Lie on the panel. Present yourself as instructed.'*

'You can go preeee-zent yourself, you weird little fuck. When I get my hands on you you're gonna wish—'

The voice thundered over his: *'Cardinali. Do as you are instructed.'*

'So, you know my name, you pervert. You went through my wallet when you knocked me cold. You'll wish *you* were out cold when I start work on you. I'm gonna cook your dick in a microwave. I'm gonna drill through your kneecaps.'

The guy's got balls, Ed reflected. *For now, anyway.*

'Cardinali, present yourself. Otherwise you will be punished.'

'Punished? Ha! Come and face me like a man. Stop skulking away in the shadows, you little freak.'

The electronically altered voice had fooled Cardinali like it had fooled Ed at first. But the more he heard the deep, velvet voice the more he could hear a woman's inflections.

Cardinali raged on.

Once Ed had hissed across at him. 'You've got to do as they say.'

'Sez who, cheeseball?'

'It's me, Ed Lake. Do as they say. They'll hurt you if—'

'Like I'd take orders from you, kid.'

'Listen, I'm trying to save your life. If you don't—'

'Shut it, kid. Romero Cardinali's gonna headline this particular gig, d'ya hear me?'

'Okay, okay.' Sighing, Ed closed his eyes.

Ed heard Virginia whisper to him. 'You tried, Ed. Whatever happens next, your conscience will be clear.'

The deep voice persisted. Maybe the thickset bull of a man interested their sex mistress? Did she have a thing about gangsters? Only he wasn't interested. He wasn't going to play their erotic games and no, he wasn't going to 'preeee-zent' himself through the hole in the Perspex roof of the cage. 'Ya think I'm gonna wave my whang in the air for your appreciation, then ya got another think coming . . . Now do yourself a favor and unlock the damn cage otherwise I'm going to slice you from ass to eyebrow!'

More insults came out to fill the dark void. The guy was in good form. Knew words that Ed didn't, and Ed thought he was a pretty streetwise guy.

The guy was laying it down how he was going to dismantle the owner of the deep voice piece by piece when he gave a sudden, surprised '*Hey!* What did ya prick me with?' His voice grew louder. 'Why don't ya put on the light and try pricking me when I can see ya? You pile of shit. I'm gonna be your own personal hairdresser, do you hear me? I'm gonna shampoo your hair in gasoline. Then I'm going to drop a match. You're gonna get the blow-dry of your life, believe me, you little . . . liffle sh-shit. Hey, wass iss? Wass zisss . . . what ya shot into me? Injected sumfin?'

Ed sat up straight, heart beating. The man's speech was slurred. The volume became lower. The bars clanged as if someone had fallen against them.

'Bash . . . bass . . . bastards. Cowards . . . bast—' Then a deep thump.

Down and out. Someone had KO'd the guy with a hypodermic.

For a little while all Ed heard were the sound of snores.

Then there were other sounds . . . Scraping. Clicks. The sound of panting.

Jesus. Ed strained his ears in the dark. He opened his eyes wide. Wide as they could go, only he could still see nothing in that inky soup. The breathing got louder. Bumps. Scrapes. A grunt. Someone exerting themselves. *Holy shit.* Was someone having sex with the gangster as he lay there unconscious? Maybe this time with his bare butt 'preeee-zented'?

Ed didn't want to allow his mind to roam too far in that direction. His front body parts were sore enough. He didn't want to receive any attention from the rear as well.

The sounds went on. *My God, what're they doing to Cardinali?* Ed didn't like the sounds. He didn't like them at all.

The lights took a while to come back on. For a long time Ed had sat in the darkness listening to the snoring grunts coming from the man. Something had happened. Something shitty. Only Ed couldn't begin to guess what.

After a while: 'At least he's not dead.' That was Virginia's voice.

'But they've done something to him.'

'Given him a shot of some drug. He's out cold.'

'Done something else, too. Heard them working on him.'

'Dear God.'

He heard her breathe deeply. 'Best brace yourself when the lights come on. It's bound to be something bad.'

'I was just thinking the same. Poor guy.'

'He was his own worst enemy, Ed. He should have done what they told him.'

'Maybe he had a stronger sense of self-respect.'

'What's that supposed to mean?' She sounded hurt.

'Nothing,' he replied.

'We're survivors, Ed. We've got to remember that.'

'Sure. I'll remember.'

'Woss . . . 's wrong?'

'Heads up,' Virginia hissed. 'Sleeping beauty's waking.'

'Hey, woss 'appenin? What gives?'

Ed listened to the man's groggy exclamations. He could talk, anyway. Maybe their jailers hadn't punished him harshly after all. Just a shot of some drug to show him who was boss.

A moment later the lights flickered on. Ed blinked against the brilliance. He looked in the direction of Cardinali. He saw him through the bars.

Holy shit. What have they done to him?

The bastards . . . the sadists . . . trussed him like a dead deer.

Almost.

Not quite.

There were differences. Ed looked at the man in the next cage. He was standing on a three-legged stool; one of those old-fashioned milking stools. Around his neck was a noose. The other end was tied to the roof beam of the cage. It had become a gallows.

'Hey, what they done to me?' squealed the guy. 'What's the game?'

No game.

They were serious . . . dead serious.

'Mr Cardinali,' Virginia called in alarm as the stool wobbled. 'Stand still. Perfectly still.'

219

'What they done?' The guy still had a dumbstruck expression on his fleshy face. He couldn't work out what had happened.

But Ed saw.

Saw clear as day.

Their captors had drugged the man. Then, as he'd lain unconscious, they'd somehow winched him upright, stood him on a stool with a noose round his neck and his hands either tied or cuffed behind his back. Ed couldn't tell which because the man was standing facing him on the rickety stool.

But why hadn't he strangled as he'd hung there unconscious? Then Ed saw. They'd supported his body weight with a harness that had been buckled to the roof crossbar. They guy couldn't fall and choke anyway. Even if you kicked the stool from under him.

So what's the deal?

The guy couldn't be comfortable.

But it wasn't as if he was in mortal danger, was he?

Then the light went out again. Moments later, more cursing. A whispering voice. Then a moan in the darkness. *Cardinali?* 'Please . . . listen, I apologize. From now on I'll be good. *Please . . .*' The note of defiance was well and truly history now. Instead: pleading. 'Please. I'll do anything. But don't do that. Please, don't do that! *Don't!*'

Ed heard rustling. Chinks, something like chain links. A frightened gasp.

Then murmuring. Fast, too fast to hear properly.

Virginia said, 'Listen to the guy. He's praying.'

'Oh, hail-Mary-Mother-of-God . . .' Cardinali's voice was low and rapid. 'Please-have-mercy-on-me. Mary-Mother-of-God, I'm-a-sinner. I-ask-for-your-forgiveness-in-this-my-hour-of-darkness . . .'

The light flickered. Brilliance filled the room once more.

Ed looked across at Cardinali.

His heart lurched.

He heard a cry of shock in his own throat.

Bad.

This was bad.

The poor guy didn't deserve this.

'Oh, my God,' Virginia breathed behind Ed.

Ed looked up at the guy through the bars of his cage. They were sadists. They *really* should have their fucking hearts torn out.

Romero Cardinali still stood on the rickety three-legged milking stool. Still had his hands cuffed or tied behind his back. Still had the noose round his neck. But now something was missing.

220

The harness.

Now he'd recovered consciousness they'd snuck down here in the dark and unbuckled it. They'd done it from the top where it had looped over the crossbar, not risking entering the cage with the conscious gangster. His feet were free – he could have delivered a killer of a kick.

The web of the harness dangled down by the side of his waist now like a strappy hula skirt. But it was Cardinali himself who drew Ed's gaze.

He stood there trembling. You could see his knees shaking. In turn, that made the stool wobble.

'Take it easy. Take it real easy.' Ed spoke in a soothing voice. 'You're okay . . . just don't make any sudden movement.'

'Please help me.' Cardinali whispered as if fearing that talking would unbalance him. 'Please. I don't know how much longer I can stand still.' The stool wobbled.

Ed looked up at the man's face. It was a mask of terror. Terror turned his eyes into shining spheres in his head. Perspiration rolled from the crown of his bald head over his face and on down his neck to slick the rope around his neck. The hemp itself was stained dark with sweat.

Ed glanced back at Virginia. She stared in horror at the man.

'What can we do?' he whispered to her.

'What *can* we do?' She echoed the words in a helpless tone. 'We're here; he's there.'

'Hey . . . hey. I know ya talking about me . . . what're ya saying?'

Ed turned. 'You've got to stay as calm as possible. Keep still.'

'Ha.' The sound came as a squeal. 'Keep still? Easy for you to say, kid. But look at me, kid. Look at me!'

The moment his voice got louder his legs wobbled more, making the stool rock.

'Keep as still as possible,' Virginia told him. 'We're working on it.'

Ed shot her a questioning look.

She gave a little shrug. *What can we do?* she seemed to be saying.

Ed turned to the guy. 'Just breathe nice and slow. Keep as still as possible.'

'I think I'm getting the cramp.'

'You're not. Try to untense your muscles.'

'Aw, Jesus, ya gotta be kidding me.' The man sounded close to weeping. His face turned a tomato red.

221

Ed saw him try to move his feet just a little further apart. Just a little. To distribute his weight that bit more evenly. In fascinated horror Ed's gaze traveled up the sweat-soaked body to the noose around the thick neck. The guy was doing his best to balance there. But he was tiring. That stool was rickety. He'd swear one of the wooden legs was loose. *Oh shit.* Watching the guy was unbearable.

What if he sneezed?

Coughed?

Even developed an unbearable itch in the small of his back?

Maybe the noose line was slack enough for him to step down onto the floor. No, not a hope. There was hardly any slack at all. If the guy even tilted too much left or right the rope pulled taut. That in turn tightened the noose around the guy's neck. Already it had started to dig a little into the soft flesh of his throat.

How long could he balance like that on a small stool? Especially with his hands bound behind his back?

Maybe that was it?

'Sir,' Ed said. 'Can you loosen your hands?'

'They're tied . . . with wire.'

The stool wobbled.

The man gave a sharp cry.

Recovered his balance.

Nearly, that time.

Nearly . . .

Virginia spoke up. 'It's the only way, sir. Can you work your hands free from the wire? Once you do that you can just reach up and pull the noose off over your head.'

'Okay, okay . . . I'm trying.' His lips pressed together in concentration, Cardinali worked his shoulders as he tried to slip his bound wrists free of the wire.

'How's it going?' she asked.

The guy sweated hard. 'Purgatory. Freaking purgatory.'

'Keep trying.'

'I *am* trying.'

'Breathe slowly. Deeply. Don't panic.'

'Hey, who's panicking, lady?' Cardinali sounded more like his usual, cocksure self. 'I'm doing it. The loops are slipping down my hands.'

Ed looked at the man's dripping face. Triumph sparked in the eyes. Cardinali raised his face, concentrating hard on those loops of wire that held his hands.

222

'They're coming loose. Once I get them over my knuckles I'll be off this damn perch, I can tell you. Assholes.'

'Careful.'

'Nearly there. Nearly—'

Jerked his elbows. Trying to pull free.

Ed shouted, 'Watch out!'

'Nearly there. Nearly – Ahh!'

Cardinali fell.

The stool shot from under his feet to slam against the bars of the cage. The force of the impact shattered it.

Cardinali didn't fall far. The rope snapped tight. Tongue sticking out. Eyes poking hard from the sockets as he swung backwards and forwards. His legs ran in thin air like a cartoon character who'd run off a cliff.

Then the guy's body started jerking. It didn't last long. After twenty seconds he hung limp at the end of the line. His neck had stretched thin, maybe as much as twice as long as it had been before.

Looks like we're back to two again, Ed told himself as the lights went out.

What now?

When the lights came on what must have been a couple of hours later Cardinali was gone. So was the rope that had hanged him. So was the wreckage of the stool that his death throes had kicked against the cage.

Ed shook his head. 'He didn't last long.'

Virginia shrugged. 'Like I say, you must obey them.'

'But how long can we last?'

'We're doing fine so far, aren't we?'

'Sure.' Ed looked down at the scabbed foot. 'My little toe's made it to freedom. Now I only have to get the other ninety-nine percent of me out.'

'Take it easy, Ed, save your—'

'Yeah, yeah, I know. Save my strength.' He gave a sour laugh.

'Then save it.'

He walked across the cage to look through the bars at the empty cell next door.

Ouch.

The area of flesh from which his little toe had once sprouted burned furiously. He'd stubbed it on something.

He glanced down.

Hey.

Now that might be interesting.

Quickly he bent down, scooped up the object and returned to his mattress. He sat cradling it on his knee.

'What've you got there, Ed?'

'Ssh,' he hushed.

She whispered back. 'What is it?'

'One of the legs from the stool.' He gave her a quick glimpse. *Can't be too careful.* Lights might go out, then his prize would quickly vanish. 'They must have missed it when they cleaned up.'

'What are you thinking, Ed?'

'See? It's more than a foot long. Look how it's broken at that end. It's as sharp as a spear.'

'Oh my God.'

'"Oh my God" indeed. It's miracle time.'

'Don't let *them* see it.'

'Don't you worry. I'm keeping this baby safely wrapped up in my blanket.'

'But what are you going to do with it?'

'Cast your mind back to when we were talking earlier.'

'Go on.'

'Remember we discussed the hole in the cage ceiling?'

'Yes.'

'And how you wondered if I could somehow reach through it?'

'Sweet Jesus. You think you can?'

'Going to try.' He took a peek at the wooden stake cradled in his arms. 'This needs some work first. By the way—' he shot her a wild grin '—have you ever seen anyone harpoon a fish?'

Chapter Thirty-eight

The telephone rang. Susan lowered the paperback she'd been reading and glanced at the clock. Almost midnight. She got up from the couch. 'Expecting a call?' she asked Tag. He shook his head and returned his gaze to the *National Review*. Susan picked up the phone.

'Hello?'

'Am I speaking to Miss Connors from the museum?'

The man pronounced each word with precision; someone educated the expensive way.

'Yes, this is Susan Connors.'

'I must speak to you at once about Amara.'

'Who is this, please?'

'My name is of no importance.'

'I would like to know whom I'm speaking to. This isn't—'

'I saw you on the television news.'

'But you can't—'

'Listen to me, please. This is vital.'

'Do you know where Amara is?' Susan asked.

'I must see you. Then I will explain.'

'Maybe you should call the police?'

'The police? They would scorn me or accuse me. They would not believe. Perhaps *you* will believe. I saw in your face the look of one who understands.'

'What am I supposed to understand?'

'About Amara. May I see you?'

'Well . . .'

'Please, Miss Connors. This if of great importance.'

She sighed. 'Okay, when?'

'At once. You are at 2102 Coral Reef Road?'

'Yes. It's the Marina Towers. Apartment 325. But how did you—'

'I will be there soon,' he said quickly and hung up.

'Who was that?' Tag asked.

'Wouldn't say.'

'Mysterious?'

'Whoever he is, he's coming by.'

'Now?'

'He wants to tell me something about Amara.'

'At midnight?'

'He sounded serious.'

'Could be he's only serious about getting alone with you.'

'I doubt it.'

'That sort of thing happens when you get on TV.'

'We'll see.'

Imad, outside the Marina Towers, heard the buzz of the lock. He rushed to the door and thrust it open before the buzzing could stop. The lobby was plush, with thick carpets, soft lighting, paneled walls. It smelled of pine-scented air freshener.

A little artificial, Imad thought. *Not bad, however, if one must live in the confines of an apartment.*

He slipped Callahan's memoir under his arm and pressed the elevator button. He was surprised that the elevator didn't open immediately. Considering the hour, one would hardly expect to find it in use. After a short wait, a bell rang quietly and the doors slid open.

He was prepared for the possibility of finding a person inside. He was not, however, prepared for a person like this. She simply didn't belong in a clean and ostentatious building such as the Marina Towers: she belonged in a dark, shabby tenement that reeked of stale cigars and urine.

'Going up?' she asked.

Reluctantly, Imad stepped into the elevator. The doors rolled silently shut. Politely, he smiled at the filthy woman. She smiled back.

The smell of her filled the cubicle. A horrid stench like sour milk, sweat and something eminently suggestive of . . . well . . . Imad swallowed to keep himself from gagging. Until the elevator stopped, he breathed only through his mouth. Even then something of her odor secreted itself on his tongue.

The doors rolled back.

He stepped out.

The woman stayed.

Thank heaven.

Relieved, Imad breathed deeply.

A small sign on the wall indicated that apartments 301–335 could be found by following the corridor to the right. As he turned that way, he glanced back at the elevator. Its doors were still open.

The woman must have one of her stumpy thumbs on the 'door open' button.

Was she waiting for him?

Did she have an accomplice hiding nearby?

Feeling uneasy, he quickened his stride. The hallway was narrow and dimly lit. It turned. He followed it, watching the door numbers. He was passing 319 when he heard a sniffing sound behind him. He looked back.

The woman stepped around the corner. She waved at him, wiggling the thick fingers of one hand. The other hand, he noticed, was behind her back.

He hurried forward. Past 321, 323. At 325 he quickly knocked.

The woman was getting closer. She had a peculiar way of walking, head forward and tipped slightly to one side, legs wide apart.

He knocked again. Still the door didn't open. He plucked a scrap of paper from his shirt pocket. He held it at arm's length to catch the poor light. Read it again. Yes, 325 was correct.

He smiled nervously at the woman. She was close enough now to smell.

Her eyes fixed on him. They were dull, filmy, yet he saw some powerful emotion there.

But what?

He knocked again.

Open the door.

Please.

The woman licked her lips. A squishing sound that turned his stomach.

'Who ya want?' she asked.

'The occupant of this apartment,' he replied.

'Me, too.' The woman balled her fist. Then she pounded on the door.

Chapter Thirty-nine

Grace Bucklan looked out through the windshield. The bright lights of Hollywood. They burned in front of her but they might as well have been on the dark side of the moon. As the man said: *So close, yet so far.*

Okay, so tomorrow we start knocking on doors, she told herself. Agents, production offices. Hey, at a pinch maybe even some movie-extra work. That should bring in cash until they could . . .

'I can't sleep,' Pix complained from the backseat.

'Try,' Grace said.

'It's gone midnight,' Cody said, looking at the clock on the dash. 'We should all try and get some rest.'

'Any more salami left, Grace?'

'No, just crackers.'

'There was one piece left. You said that was mine.' Pix's voice got all whiny. 'You promised, you greedy hog.'

'You ate it twenty minutes ago.' Cody made an effort to sound calm. But the kid sister was really starting to eat him up. 'Do you want a drink of water?'

'No, I want some proper food. I'm hungry.'

Grace snapped. 'We've got crackers and that's it.'

'We're gonna starve.'

'We're not going to starve. I'll find some work tomorrow.'

Pix snorted. 'Yeah, Grace. You're gonna be a movie star by the end of the week.'

'I will find work.'

'All you're gonna find is some guy who'll pay you fifty bucks a throw to video you with your jugs out.'

'*Pix.*' Cody's patience was all gone. 'Just cool it, this isn't easy for—'

'I want to go home!' Pix slammed the back of the seat with her palm. 'We can't live like this . . . sleeping in a parking lot? Jeez!'

'We can't go home.'

'Can.'

'You *know* we can't go home.'

'Yeah, because you say Mom's boyfriend took a shine to you.'

'He tried to rape me.'

'Drama queen.'

'Pix—'

'He thought you were giving him the come-on.'

'It wasn't like that. He—'

'If you hadn't flirted with him—'

'He'd have raped you, too. Don't you understand, Pix? We were both in danger.'

'Danger, huh?'

'Yes, in danger. The moment he got you alone he'd have—'

'Danger. We're in more danger here. Sleeping in a beat-up truck in a deserted parking lot. We're gonna get mugged; we're gonna get raped; we're—'

'Pix!' Cody slammed both hands against the steering wheel. 'We're not happy about sleeping rough. But this is the best we can do until we can earn some money. Then we'll book into a hotel.'

'Wuppy-do.'

Grace rounded on her sister. 'That's your problem. You're never satisfied. You just want more and more. Nothing's good enough for you. Why don't you take your things and just—'

'Hey, ssh . . . *Cops.*'

Cody pointed.

A black and white cruiser pulled into the parking lot. Without any fuss or hurry it glided across the blacktop toward them.

'Oh, shit.' Grace groaned. 'They've seen us.'

Pix said, 'So we took a crappy old truck without permission. It's hardly crime of the century. They're not gonna throw us in—'

'*Pix.*' Cody pointed at the sleeping bags. 'Hide under there; don't let them see you.'

'I'll do no such thing.'

Grace pleaded, 'Do it, Pix. Otherwise they'll send us back home. You know what Joe will do to us.'

'Drama queen,' Pix grumbled. Nevertheless, she lay down on the backseat and pulled the sleeping bags over her.

The cruiser slowed down. A brilliant light filled the pickup as the cop shone his flashlight at them. Cody glanced back to see Pix's foot showing from beneath the sleeping bag. Reaching back he thwacked it.

'Hey!' Pix squeaked.

But she withdrew her foot from the edge of the seat. Cody reached

229

back and adjusted the sleeping bag so no part of the sixteen-year-old girl could be seen.

The police car pulled up alongside so they were side window to side window. The cop twirled a finger, signaling Cody to wind down his window.

Immediately a blast of light struck Cody in the eyes. He tried to shield them with his hand but he could see nothing. But he knew what was happening well enough. The cop would be giving Grace and him a close look-over, probably taking a good gander inside the pickup too.

If Pix should move . . .

Maybe the cop would think Cody had kidnapped her?

He'd certainly realize something was amiss when he ran a check on their license plate and found that the vehicle was stolen.

The cop switched off his flashlight. Cody blinked. Looked into the face of a gum-chewing cop of around fifty.

'Okay,' he said. 'Which one of you two is going to confess?'

Cody fixed a polite smile to his face but his insides felt as if they'd just melted and run into his boots.

'Confess, officer?'

'Yeah, confess to criminal insanity . . . or is it pathological stupidity?'

Grace spoke as pleasantly as she could. 'I'm sorry. I don't understand. We—'

'Yeah, yeah,' the cop growled. 'Don't take me for the stupid one. I've seen your plates. You're from North Carolina. How long does it take me to figure out what two kids from North Carolina are doing in Hollywood?'

'We were just—'

'Yeah, taking a nice vacation.'

'We thought—'

'And now you've booked yourself into the luxurious Rodeo Drive Parking Lot.'

'We were just taking a break, we—'

'Kid.' He fixed Cody with a steel-eyed look. 'Do I seem that stupid?'

'But—'

'No, listen to me, kid. I've seen this happen a hundred – a *thousand* times before. A couple of kids from the boondocks decide to make it in the movies, become big stars with a million in the bank and a house on the beach, so they ship out from Wyoming, or Illinois or—' he nodded in the direction of the license plate '—or North

Carolina. They come to Hollywood. They spend all their cash. They live in their car or sleep on a park bench. Before you know it they're into prostitution; into drugs. Guys like me are pulling them off the streets and throwing them in jail. Not long after that the paramedics are pulling them out of some ditch where they've been dumped after being shot or beaten to death. Now, you tell me, am I just stupid and you really have driven thousands of miles to make out in a parking lot, or am I somewhere close to the truth?'

Grace didn't take this lying down. 'But I'm not like the rest. I've got acting experience. I worked on TV.'

He shook his head. 'Sorry to bust your dream, miss. But most of the kids that come here *are* like all the rest. They've all got good reviews when they starred in the school play or they've earned a few bucks appearing in some TV commercial for Mighty Joe's Cattle Feed or whatever. They all come here so full of optimism you think they'd crack open from head to toe.' He wagged a finger. 'But give them twelve months and they wind up blowing some guy with the pox for twenty bucks . . . and guys like you—' he nodded at Cody '—have to learn to take it up the butt or go hungry. Now, am I painting a clear enough picture for you?'

Grace was about to protest, but Cody clasped her hand. Nodded. 'We get the picture, sir.'

'Good. Now, you look nice kids. So do yourself a favor: *Go home*. If you haven't enough money for gas, call your folks, you can reverse the charges: get them to wire the gas money out to you. Whatever heat you're gonna take from your parents for running away isn't going to be one percent of the heat you're going to take out here.' He paused. 'And just if I haven't concentrated your minds on the issue, check out the press. Some fine young people just like yourselves have been going missing from hereabouts over the last couple of years.'

'Murdered?'

The cop shook his head again. 'Who knows? Never been found.' He gave them a relaxed wave. 'Now, remember what I said. You point that truck back east. Don't stop until you've reached your front door. Now you take care of yourselves. Good night.'

With that he drove slowly away.

A moment later Pix sat up primly in the back seat. 'See? What did I tell you?' She folded her arms. 'Now can we go home?'

231

Chapter Forty

Claire Thompson, propped in her bed, watched *Casablanca* on television for the umpteenth time. She knew most of the movie by heart and often mumbled the words in unison with Rick and Ilsa and Victor Lazlo. It was the saddest movie she knew.

She'd first seen it in the old Palace Theater in Charleston, Illinois. The year was 1944. She was seventeen and in love with Junior Clyde. He took her to the movie, to King's Drug Store afterwards for a cherry phosphate, then to the Harrison house. The Harrisons were on vacation. They sat on the porch swing of the deserted house. Kissed. Petted. She let Junior go further than usual that night. He wanted to go all the way, but she refused. She never did let him. Not that night or the next night. And then he was inducted. He became one of Uncle Sam's infantry . . . the poor bloody infantry, they called it. But Junior was proud to be fighting. On the troop ship he enjoyed the camaraderie and used to lead the singing in the mess with his buddies. Even on the ship they trained hard. Physical exercise. Weapon skills: rifle practice, marksmanship, bringing down the seagulls that trailed the ship; learning how to strip a Thompson submachine gun blindfold then reassemble it so it was ready to fire when the sergeant gave the command. And the endless boot-polishing, of course.

In one of his letters to Claire, Junior said he'd been to North Africa. To Casablanca. There really *is* a Rick's Café Americain, he'd written. But where were the Germans? They were pulling back faster than the Americans could advance. At this rate he'd be marching into Berlin still with desert sand in his boots.

But then the Germans did make a stand in a narrow mountain pass in the middle of nowhere. Their 88-millimeter guns lit up the night sky. Stukas screamed down, dropping bombs, strafing with machine guns. Two weeks later, Junior Clyde was killed in action.

On the screen, Rick said, 'We'll always have Paris.'

Claire gasped, a loud sob that made Herb groan and roll over.

She wiped her eyes. Felt her heart give as if this time it would break. Stay broken forever. She thought about the photograph of Junior that she still kept hidden in a drawer.

Then a long, wailing cry came through the open window. The eerie sound made goose bumps rise on her flesh. She pulled the sheet up to her throat. The cry continued. A cat. It had to be a cat.

It sounded so much like a baby, though. Like a baby crying in pain and terror.

Must be in the backyard. Must be close. Just outside her window. Close as that.

Tossing back the sheet, she climbed from the bed. She walked to the window and looked out. Her eyes scanned the moonlit concrete, the lounge chairs, the shimmering surface of the pool. At first, she didn't see the dark figure standing motionless near the diving board. Then it slowly turned toward her. She gasped at the sight of the baby in its arms.

She stared. Shivers in her spine. The dark figure seemed to notice her and stare back. Claire suddenly felt frightened and vulnerable. She wanted to step away from the window, but she was afraid to move – as if the least motion might trigger a horrible attack.

The thing didn't move. Claire felt its cold hatred. In the poor light, it looked like a strange, starving woman. But all that red hair. Pouring in glossy tresses down her back. Down over her shoulders. Such beautiful hair. Yet the legs? Horribly withered. Like dark sticks.

The crying baby couldn't possibly belong to such a creature. It must have been stolen from its mother.

Claire's breath became a quiet, trembling whine.

The baby kept crying.

Kept pulling at her heartstrings.

The thing continued to stand there, staring at her. Hating her.

Claire trembled, clutched the sill for support. Her knees were so weak she sagged.

'For Christ's sake, what's all that racket?'

Herb's voice startled her. She flinched and turned to him. Quickly, she sidestepped away from the window. Then she leaned weakly against the wall, shaking.

'Claire? What's wrong?' He rolled out of bed and rushed to her.

'The window,' she gasped.

He looked out. 'Jesus H. Christ!'

'It's got a little baby!'

'I can see that. Quick, call the cops.'

He hurried to the nightstand.

'No, Herb!'

233

He took out his pistol. Checked it. Six rounds. Man-stoppers.

'Please! Don't go out there!'

'I'll take care of it – you call the cops.'

'No!'

He ran to the bedroom door.

'Herb, please!'

He didn't answer. She heard his bare feet thumping as he ran down the hall.

She grabbed the bedside phone and dialed 911. Then listened to the ringing. Once, twice. Far off in the house a door bumped open. Footsteps sounded. On the sixth ring, her call was answered.

'Operator. How may I help you?'

'I need the police. It's an emergency.'

'Where are you calling from?'

'Westing Vale.'

'Just a moment, please.'

'Hurry!'

She listened to more ringing.

This time no one was going to answer.

The phone would keep ringing. *Herb's all alone out there.*
The police are never going to come in time to—

'LAPD. Officer Kerry, how might I help you?'

'We need help! Quick!' Craning her neck, Claire tried to see Herb through the window. She could see only concrete and a corner of the pool. The wrong corner.

'What's your address?'

'Eight-two-five Ash Road.'

'Name?'

'Thompson. Claire Thompson.'

Herb shouted, 'Stop!'

Dropping the phone, Claire rushed to the window. Her heart beat so wildly against her ribs that it hurt.

'Put it down!' Herb commanded. He was on the far side of the pool, close to its edge, a dozen feet from the thing. 'Put down the baby,' he repeated. His voice had a shrill, hysterical sound that Claire had never heard in it before. His arm was straight out, the gun aimed high. 'Put the baby—'

The creature raised the infant overhead.

Herb fired. The flash lit up the pool area, while the report of the gun snapped as sharply as a firecracker.

The baby shrieked as it was thrown. Claire watched it fly at her husband, its legs kicking as it tumbled through the air. He dropped the gun. Tried to catch the tumbling child, but the force of the impact knocked him backwards. The baby splashed into the pool.

The creature rushed Herb, its long hair flying out.

Claire ran. She ran to the bedroom door, down the hall, into the living room. The poker. She needed the poker. Rushing to the fireplace, she bumped a corner of the coffee table and cried out in pain. But she didn't stop. She clutched at the stand of fireplace tools, knocking it over with a metallic clattering . . . and grabbed the poker. It was heavy – wrought iron – with a hook near the end. She ran through the open glass door to the yard.

Across the pool, the creature was on top of Herb. His arms were up, hands shoving its chest and shoulders. His harsh breathing had a panicked sound, the way it did sometimes during his worst nightmares.

The thing bore down on Herb. Its stick arms reaching out for him, while it tilted its head from side to side. In the meager light the hair gleamed dull copper.

As Claire ran along the pool's edge, she glanced at the water. The baby was floating facedown.

In a corner of her mind, she knew that she might be able to save it. The decision was simple: the baby wasn't hers. Herb was.

The thing's claw fingers tore Herb's face. His arms gave way. Its head darted down.

'No!' Claire cried.

Raising the poker as she ran, she thought she saw the thing kiss Herb. Its head jerked savagely, though. It came up, flesh hanging from its mouth. Droplets of blood spotted the poolside tiles.

Screaming, Claire swung the poker down. It whacked across the creature's back with a resonant thump, as if she'd drummed a hollow log. The thing paid no attention. It thrust its head against Herb's throat. Claire turned the poker hook downward and struck again. She watched the curved spike pierce the back. She noticed other holes already in the dark flesh. Awful, gaping holes. In the moonlight, they looked deep and empty. As if there was nothing inside. Nothing.

She started to bring the poker down again, this time on the head. But suddenly the creature twisted. A hand grabbed the poker. Off balance, Claire staggered forward, almost falling onto the thing. Its other hand clutched her nightgown. It pulled her. Tossed back its head, flicking the red hair from its face. In horror, she gazed into eye sockets as empty as the holes in its back.

Letting go of the poker, she strained to free herself from the claws.

235

The claws were pulling her down to a gaping mouth, its teeth stained red with Herb's blood.

She realized she was only caught by her nightgown. Quickly, she tore the bodice free of the shoulder straps. The gown skimmed down her body. She threw herself sideways, splashed into the pool, kicked away from the wall.

Coming to the surface near the pool's center, her bare shoulder brushed against the baby. She stood in the waist-high water and lifted the child. It was silent. Motionless. Its mouth hung open. Water trickled out. Claire pressed her lips to its mouth and blew in gently, keeping her eyes on the creature.

The thing seemed to be watching. Herb, beneath it, lay motionless. Legs sprawled out wide. In the moonlight the thing had become a silhouette again. Hunched. Predatory.

Slowly, Claire began stepping backwards. She continued to blow into the baby's mouth and ease the air out by lightly pressing its chest. The body felt warm against her bare breasts. She could feel its small chest inflate as she blew, but that was the baby's only movement.

Finally, her back touched the wall. The entire width of the pool now separated her from the creature. It was on its hands and knees, facing her, its mouth hanging open.

Could she beat it in a race to the house? Unless it was incredibly fast her chances looked good. Her main obstacle would be climbing from the pool. Once she was out, she could reach the open back door in seconds.

Keeping her eyes on the creature, Claire turned just enough to set the baby on the pool's edge. In one fluid movement, the thing leaped to its feet and began to run. Its feet made a hard clicking sound against the tiles, as if it were dry bones striking the floor, not flesh and blood. The hair flew up around its head as it moved, a copper-colored halo in the moonlight.

Claire spun around. She flung herself forward, sprawling with a great spray of water onto the concrete. Getting to her knees, she picked up the baby. She looked back.

The thing was already past the diving board, arms out as if reaching for her; its hair flying behind it in the slipstream.

She scrambled to her feet. She ran flat out, the baby clutched to her breast, eyes on the open, sliding door. She felt clumsy and slow. The strength drained from her legs. She didn't think she could take more than a dozen steps before she collapsed exhausted.

If only she'd stayed in the pool!

Her feet slapped the pavement. Behind her, she heard the strange, dry sounds of her pursuer's feet. *Click! Click! Click!* The sound of bones striking the hard surface of the ground. *So close!* And closing all the time.

She even heard the crackle of static in the thing's hair. The rustle of dry skin.

From inside the house came the ring of the doorbell, followed by harsh, rapid knocks.

'Police!' a voice snapped.

She lunged through the doorway and spun round. The creature wasn't far behind.

But far enough.

Claire's left hand grabbed the door handle and jerked. The door rolled shut: a heavy glass partition that would give her time to reach the front door and let in the police.

The outstretched arms of the creature dropped, but it kept coming. Full speed. Those pitlike eyes glaring at Claire. Hating. She watched, amazed.

Its head smashed into the door. The glass exploded. It burst through, that mass of red hair erupting inward into the house like burning napalm. Its bone-thin arms reached for her.

With a yelp of surprise, Claire lurched away.

It caught her by the hair.

'Help!' she cried.

It tugged her off balance. She stumbled backwards. Felt the slice of glass shards underfoot. The piercing of fragments through soft flesh.

A sharp crash. The front door shot open. Just before she went down, she saw a pair of policemen rush in, guns drawn.

They'll save me, she thought as she fell. *They'll save me.* And then something like ice chopped into her back.

Chapter Forty-one

Jason Brown crouched in a combat stance and aimed into the moonlit room. He saw a naked white woman falling backwards – no, *jerked* backwards – by a weird-looking woman behind her. The falling woman had a baby in her arms. As she hit the floor, her body spasmed stiffly as if jolted by an electric shock.

The weird one bent over her, its long hair cascading forward to hang down over the naked woman. The dark figure pulled the baby from her arms.

'Freeze!' Brown yelled.

The weirdo spun away.

Kraus, Brown's partner, fired a warning shot into the ceiling. The weird gal leaped through the broken door and ran. She looked to be naked, too. But horribly bony. Horribly thin. Some disease, maybe.

'Get her!' Brown snapped.

As Kraus ran out, Brown holstered his revolver and crouched beside the fallen woman. She was lying across the broken door, back arched. Her mouth and eyes were wide, her body quaking with convulsions. Brown tried to lift her. No dice. She seemed to be stuck. Bracing himself, he clutched the sides of her rib cage and lifted her straight upward. There was momentary resistance before she came unstuck. He carried her away from the door, set her down on the carpet, and looked back. A broad glass blade remained where she had been. Still upright at the bottom of the door's aluminum frame.

He searched her neck for a pulse.

Found none.

No sign of respiration, either.

With a single shake of his head, he sprang away from her and rushed through the break in the door, barely clearing the dark shard of glass that had ended the woman's life.

Outside, he saw a body across the pool.

'Oh, motherfucker,' he groaned. He started forward, feeling sick, thinking it was Kraus. Then he realized it wasn't in uniform. Relief surged through him. 'Kraus!' he called. 'Kraus?'

'Over here. Quick.'

The voice came from the right, from beyond a high wood fence. Brown ran to it, holstering his revolver. He jumped, caught the top, scrambled over it. Dropping to the other side, he found himself in an alley.

Kraus was standing close to a telephone pole, looking into the darkness of a carport across the alley. There were two cars inside the shelter.

'She's in there, behind the Pontiac,' Kraus whispered.

'Put your piece away. We'll go in with batons.'

'Christ Almighty, Jase, did you see the dead guy by the pool? This gal's a brain case.'

'We don't know she did that. We don't know anything about her, 'cept she's got a baby with her. She still got the baby?'

'Yeah. I'm not so sure it's alive, though. It's been awful quiet.'

'She armed?'

Kraus shook his head.

'We drop an unarmed lady, pal, they'll roast our asses. We hit the kid, they'll fry us in Mazola.'

Kraus holstered his service revolver.

They both slipped batons from the loops on their belts.

'I'll go in, flush her out,' Brown said. He stepped briskly across the alley, eyes searching the darkness in front of the Pontiac. 'Come on out, ma'am,' he said in his best persuasive voice. 'No call to be alarmed. We won't harm you. We just want to talk.'

He reached the rear of the car. Ahead, he still saw no sign of the woman. He walked along the car's side, past its back door.

'Ma'am?'

He stopped beside the front tire, gazing toward a two-foot gap between the bumper and the wall. If she was there, she had to be crouching awfully low, or lying down. He leaned over the hood. Not there.

Not in front of the other car, either.

Could she have crawled under one of them?

Perhaps. From what he saw, she was as skinny as they come.

He got down on his hands and knees, and looked.

Nothing.

He climbed to his feet, dusting his pants with his hands as he did so. Then walked quickly past the front of the Pontiac, angry, daring the woman to show herself. She didn't. Nothing. Not so much as a hair. He glanced down the space between the carts. He stepped past the front of the other car, dropped to his knees, and peered under it. Then he hurried toward his partner.

'She ain't there, Kraus,' he snapped.

'She has to be.'

'You see her run out?'

'No.'

'You see her run *in*?'

'What're you driving at?'

'You fucking well know.'

'I *saw* her go in there, damn it.'

'Which way did she *really* go?'

'I told you.'

'What happened? You figure it ain't healthy, tangling with a brain case? Figure she might do you like she done them?'

'I tell you, I—'

'You've pulled this shit before, Kraus. *Accidentally* losing suspects.'

Kraus backed away, shaking his head.

'This time the sergeant's gonna hear about it.'

'For Christ's sake, Jase . . .'

'Yeah, for Christ's sake,' he said, mimicking Kraus's whine. 'That babe killed two people, looks like. Snatched a kid, maybe killed *it*, too. And she's gonna be walking free and easy because you haven't got a pennyworth of balls in your bag. Now you tell me which way she went, man, or your name's going down engraved in shit. You hear?'

'Jase, you don't under—' Kraus's face twisted. 'I saw her, Jase. Saw her up close. I chased her, okay. I saw her go over the fence. She . . . she had to use both hands on the fence, and she had the baby, so she bit into one of its arms and carried it in her mouth. Christ, man, it was like a dog carrying a bone. The kid didn't . . . didn't cry or nothing. I'm sure it's dead, Jase, or it would've—'

'Get on with it.'

'See, I went after the gal and went over the fence . . . she was standing right there. Like she'd been waiting for me. Close to me as you are.'

'And you let her get away.'

'Jase, it's not a *her*. It's an *it*. I don't know . . . maybe it was a woman once. Not anymore.'

'Just what have you been sniffing, man?'

'It hasn't got eyes, Jase. Just a couple of holes. And its skin isn't

240

like skin . . . parts of it are smooth and like . . . I don't know . . . like shoe leather. Other parts are all dark and shriveled and hard. 'Cause I touched it. See, I didn't know what the hell was going on, maybe it's a guy in a mask, or something. So I told it to put down the baby and turn around . . . I was gonna cuff it, see? But it just stood there, like it was watching me, daring me to go for it. And the head's just like a skull, only there's all this shiny red hair still stuck to it . . . the hair even moved like it was . . . I don't know . . . just weird. Completely weird . . .'

'Then what?'

'Then I took out my cuffs and grabbed one of its hands. I never felt nothing like it. Like a dried-up old corpse, you know? Then the thing . . . it opened up its mouth and I saw all these teeth and I . . . I just backed off. I just backed off, Jase. You would've, too. The thing's not human, Jase. Or if it is, it's been dead a long time, like years and years. I think it's that mummy, the one that disappeared from the museum.'

'Bullshit. Which way did it go?'

'You going after it?'

'Fucking right.'

'Don't, Jase. I'm telling you, it's a goddamn mummy.'

'It's a perpetrator, asshole.'

'Okay, okay. Fine. A perpetrator. Good luck. It went that way.' He pointed south down the alley. 'I'll go to the car, call in for backup.'

'You do that.'

Brown started down the alley at a trot, gaze searching. No sign of it ahead. *It?* Her! *Kraus is out of his fucking mind. Seen too many horror shows. Either that, or he made up all that shit to get himself off the hook.*

Only thing, the asshole hasn't got enough imagination to invent stuff like that.

The gal *did* look pretty weird, what he saw of her in the house.

At the end of the alley, he slowed down and scanned the cross-street, the shadows of trees along it, the lawns and houses.

That thing – that gal – could be anywhere.

Hiding in the shadows.

Waiting.

Then he noticed the street sign to his left. He ran closer to make sure.

The sign read *Maple.*

Holy shit! Some bad action had gone down on Maple while they'd

241

been in the Burger Palace. He didn't know what. They'd got this call to see the woman on Ash as soon as they'd returned to their unit and checked in. Dispatcher was sending all kinds of units over to Maple, though. Sounded like a massacre.

Brown rushed across the street and entered the alley. Ahead of him, nothing seemed to move. He might as well keep going, though. This was the last block before the field. If it – she – headed that way, headed into the field, she might be easier to spot. Long as she didn't hide in the bushes or something.

He walked swiftly, looking into the darkness of the carports, of gaps between garages, of shrubbery along fenced backyards. He was halfway down the alley when a gate swung open. He whirled around.

A dark, gawky figure. Something in its arms. A pale bundle? Or maybe . . .

His hand jumped for his pistol, drew it, aimed. Drew the hammer back with his thumb.

'Freeze, mother!'

'Don't you "mother" me, nigger.'

A black woman. In a dark nightie. And the object in her arms was no baby, just a plastic bag.

Brown holstered his pistol. 'I'm sorry, ma'am.'

'Lady can't take out her trash without she gets jumped by a jive cop.'

'Here, let me get that.' He took the bag from her.

'Why, *thank* you.' Her voice sang with sarcasm. 'What you doing out here in the middle of the night, if I might inquire?'

'Police business.'

'I didn't *think* it was doggy business. But something sure smells not so sweet round here . . . like onions. Or a deli that should be requiring some spring cleaning.'

Smiling politely, Brown dropped the sack of garbage into the can and shut the lid. 'I'm not aiming to alarm you, ma'am, but there's a murder suspect in the area.'

'It ain't me, so I'll haul my pretty tail right on out of here, thank you very much.' She spun away.

He watched her pass through the gate, and didn't like the feel of being alone again. No one to watch his back. Now that's not a good situation to be in for a cop.

He continued down the alley.

He was near its end when he noticed the pale shape on top of a garbage can. He squinted, trying to make out its features. Looked

242

like a kid. A baby. Sitting naked on the lid of the can, arms hanging at its sides, legs straight out, head drooping.

Brown shook his head, grinning with relief.

Just an old plastic doll someone was tossing out.

Hell, Reba might like a doll like this if it was in good condition. No point in letting it go to waste.

As he reached for it, he saw its light, wispy hair stir in the breeze.

'Oh, Jesus,' he muttered. 'Oh, Jesus Christ!'

He drew back his hand quickly before he could touch it.

'Jesus.'

He staggered forward as a sudden weight struck his back. Pain lanced his head. He fell against the garbage can, toppling the baby. It tumbled. Its skull made a hollow cracking sound on the concrete apron of the garage.

Brown went down on top of it.

Chapter Forty-two

It was going to be another of those nights. Loneliness worked at her bones. It became an ache inside of her that could no longer be endured. April Vallsarra turned on the bed, twisting the sheet in her hands.

Yes, there were tricks she used to while away the often sleepless nights. But they were only tricks. Made her feel cheap. Ate at her self-worth.

She'd wake in the morning and rush to the shower where she'd try and scrub away the sense of shame.

Never quite scrubbed herself clean of those particular memories. No matter how hard she worked with the soap.

Now here it was again. The hallway clock downstairs chimed away the early hours. April was lying wide-awake in that desolate, lonesome place between late night and early morning. Those seemingly endless hours when the rest of the world slept soundly and she, April Vallsarra, lay wide-awake and craving.

She craved companionship. A friendly voice. Sometimes she could hug a pillow and make believe that she hugged a lover.

Didn't work tonight.

She shifted position in bed endlessly, trying to get comfortable. No result. The bed was hard right now. Even when she could lie still for more than a moment she sensed that silence pressing down on her. Sensed, too, loneliness haunting the house.

Being blind was no bar to moving around the house at night in the dark. She did this now, walking from room to room, her negligée flowing. Even though she could not see them she knew her father's gold and platinum disks hung in their frames in his den. She couldn't bear to be in the room. She caught the faint scent of him there. It brought back too many painful memories.

She retreated to the kitchen. It seemed vast, an echoing desolate place.

Moments later she found herself climbing the stair. Blind from birth, she moved with confidence, never missing a step or blundering against the stair rail. She climbed quickly to the roof terrace.

The stars there would burn brightly above her. For a while she'd imagine what stars would look like, never having seen them. But she'd heard they were magical lights in the sky.

Wish upon a star.

She'd heard that phrase before.

She stood in the warm night air. A gentle breath of wind tugged at her negligée. Air whispered around her naked calves. The floor tiles were cool beneath her feet. That coolness felt nice. *What if I were to slip out of my negligée and lie on the floor? That cool hardness would press along the length of my body. It would feel wonderful.*

The breeze came again. She heard the rustling of trees out in the canyon. They were whispering busily.

'What have you heard?' she found herself asking them. 'What's going to happen tonight?'

Angry, she clenched her fists.

Now that was the curse of loneliness.

Lonely people talked to themselves. They talked to pets. They talked to their TV. They even talked to the trees.

But who is there to talk to? I'm a blind girl. I live alone. I have no friends.

So what else is there for me to do?

'You could wish upon a star.'

She felt the grim smile on her face as soon as she made the flippant remark. Yes, she could. It wouldn't do any harm. Wouldn't do any good, either. Nothing she did made any difference to her life.

Once, when she couldn't make anything good happen, she'd decided she must make something bad happen. Anything to break the monotony. She'd pulled a knife from the block in the kitchen and cut her finger. Cut so deep that she'd heard the blade scrape across bone.

So she had a choice now. Cut her body again.

Or: wish upon a star.

She moved forward to the wall that ran around the roof terrace and raised her face. Tried to feel the starlight falling on it.

There was cool air, nothing else.

The stars would be up there, though. For a moment she allowed herself to believe in the fairy tale.

Wish upon a star. Then dreams will come true.

245

'I wish . . . I wish someone would come tonight. Someone who will change my life forever.'

The breeze blew harder. Trees rustled, branches creaked. The air moving down the canyon gave such a moan that she looked round, startled. The moan sounded human.

No sooner had she composed herself than she experienced a moment of certainty.

Someone will come tonight. They will change my life.

The force of the premonition caught her by surprise.

Yes.

Someone would come.

When they did come nothing would ever be the same again.

'Please,' she whispered to the breeze. 'Come soon.'

Chapter Forty-three

They only come out at night . . .

That's what Grace told herself as the visitors to their pickup in the parking lot became a steady stream.

First had been the German hooker that tapped on the window.

From a hundred yards away she'd looked great. Slim body. Long legs. Big, blonde hair. Short skirt.

Close up?

Yeuhhh-uckkk.

She looked as if she'd been pulled from a coffin.

Her teeth were as yellow as the whites of her eyes. She'd tried to cover blistering cold sores on her lips with lip gloss that was a ghastly pink. Her throat was as wrinkled as a scrotum.

'You vonna do some business?'

'Pardon?' Cody had said,

'Vont business?'

'I don't think—'

'Mebbe a threesome with your girlfriend there. We can make with the suckling pig, ya?'

'I'm sorry . . . no, we're just staying here overnight.'

'Sleeping here in der lot?'

'Yes.'

'Good luck, honey.' She gave a dismissive shake of her head. 'You're gonna need it.'

Then she walked away, swaying her hips. The backs of her legs were a mass of bruises.

Next up, a laid-back Mexican.

'Okay, bro.' He pulled on a cigarette. 'What's it to be? Smoke, blow or mainline?'

'We don't want anything, thanks.' Again Cody, always the polite one. Never one to cause offence.

'Suit yourself, buddy.' The Mexican shrugged. 'Enjoy the view.'

As the time approached one a.m. the people came and went. Hookers, rent boys, drug dealers.

This was *Vice-R-Us.*

'We're never gonna get any sleep here,' Pix complained.

'It'll quieten down soon,' Cody said. 'Once they realize we don't want anything from them.'

'For once I'm going to have to agree with Pix.' Grace nodded through the window where two tall black women walked toward them accompanying a six-year-old child in stilettos. 'We're not going to get any rest tonight.'

The child turned out to be a dwarf. Aged probably around forty, dressed in black spandex, hair in pigtails. The three turned aggressive when they realized they weren't going to be hired to turn some tricks.

The dwarf kicked the pickup's door.

'This some kinda peep show?'

'Yeah, you got cameras? Is this TV?' The one in the Carma Miranda fruit hat was clearly a man; stubble bristled through face powder. 'If we're gonna be on TV we want five hundred bucks apiece.'

'We're not a TV crew. We only want to—'

'Come out here and I'll scratch your eyes out, mister.'

'That pussy cat next to you, too.'

The dwarf sneered. 'These people from the 'burbs, they drive up here and watch people like us. Then they grope each other and get all horny.'

'Yeah,' said the she-male. 'If you do that, we should get paid.'

'Sex ain't free round here, y' know.'

Cody held out his hands, placating. 'We're just spending the night here. We've got nowhere to stay.'

The dwarf looked at them shrewdly. 'I know a place. Got entertainment, too, if you know what I mean?'

'Here's fine,' Grace said.

'Here's not fine,' Pix muttered from the back.

The dwarf looked them over. 'Hundred bucks a night. You three can watch while we—'

Grace said. 'Please, we just want to sleep.'

'Sleep here ain't cheap either.' The transvestite curled a crimson lip.

'Yeah,' the dwarf said. 'Hand over twenty bucks and we'll leave you to get all warm and snuggled up. How's that sound?'

Cody held out his hands through the car window, a gesture of helplessness. 'We don't have any money. We can't— Hey . . . hey! *My watch!*'

'Cody. *Cody!* Stay in the truck. No . . . don't follow them.'

'But they . . . ah, *shoot.*'

'Great, oh great,' Pix sang out. 'You let a midget and two guys dressed as girls steal your watch.'

'They just grabbed it. I—'

'What's for an encore, Cody, you big lummox, you gonna let someone steal your pants, too?'

Grace rounded on her sister. 'Just shut up, can't you?'

'Why should I shut up? We're thousands of miles from home. We're out on the streets. We're broke. Would anyone shut up when they're up to their ears in this kind of crap?'

'It's only temporary, Pix.' Cody tried to keep his cool.

'Temporary, my butt.'

'I'll find work tomorrow as an extra,' Grace said. 'They pay by the day.'

'"I'll find work",' Pix mimicked. 'The only work we're gonna find is the same as what these people coming up to the truck do.'

Grace fumed. 'Pix, stop causing trouble. Lie down . . . go to sleep.'

'Fat chance.'

'Try.'

'Yeah?'

'Please try, Pix.'

'I don't see it myself.'

'Why not?'

'We've got more visitors.'

Cody sighed. 'Oh, shoot.'

Two men walked up. One black, one white. Both big. Big as pro wrestlers. They wore T-shirts with the sleeves cut off to reveal their bulging biceps. Even though it was the middle of the night and dark they wore sunglasses.

Pix slid down in the backseat. Just before she covered herself with the sleeping bag she murmured, 'These guys don't look friendly.'

'Shhh,' Grace hissed.

'Betcha they've got guns. Betcha they start shooting at us.'

'For crying out loud, Pix,' Cody whispered.

'Just keep quiet, Pix. Please.' Grace turned to see the two men come up to the side window.

Just like the cop earlier they made a turning motion with their fingers.

Wind your window down.

No way. Grace didn't like the look of these men at all.

249

Muggers?

Rapists?

Or maybe they just shot people for fun.

They made the turning motion again. Grace saw the chunky gold rings on their fingers.

'Best wind the window down,' Cody said.

'Cody? No.'

'Just a little,' he said. 'If they have got guns the glass isn't going to stop any bullets.'

'Oh, Jesus, Cody.' A sob caught in the back of her throat.

This pair oozed pure menace.

She opened the window a crack. One of the men leaned closer until his lips almost touched the glass.

The man slipped his sunglasses down so that his penetrating stare could lock onto Grace's eyes.

'Yes?' she said in a small voice.

'Lady. Do you believe Jesus Christ died in order to save your immortal soul?'

'Jeepers creepers!' Pix exclaimed when the two heavies had gone. 'You can't escape Jehovah's Witnesses. Even out in a parking lot in the middle of the night.'

Cody pulled a smile. 'At least they weren't peddling sex or pushing drugs.'

'No, only religion.' Pix folded her arms again, lips pouting sulkily. 'Are we ever gonna sleep tonight?'

Grace sighed wearily. 'Maybe we should move on, Cody?'

'But where?'

'There must be somewhere peaceful in Hollywood.'

'Yeah,' Pix sneered. 'The graveyard.'

'Pix, how many times have I told you not to . . .'

Christ on a motorcycle, Cody thought sourly. *Here we go again.* The two sisters had been at each other's jugulars ever since they'd started this journey . . . this crazy journey . . . yeah, the future wasn't so rosy now. Gloomily he watched prostitutes strutting their stuff on the road by the lot. Johns came . . . then they *came* . . . then they went.

If I have to spend another night in this truck with those two I'll go nuts. Grace is beautiful. She's the one I want to stay with . . . but with that kid sister tied to us like a ball and chain? Oh brother.

Something clunked against the side of the car. Startled, Cody

250

looked sideward to see a brown face looking in at him. He recoiled from the eyes.

Hell.

He'd never seen eyes like that.

Not natural eyes, anyway.

They set his heart racing.

He heard Pix and Grace react in fear, too, giving squeals of fright.

A finger tapped on the glass. A hard clicking sound as the nail struck. Cody looked into the eyes. They shone pure silver. They were alien eyes that made him think of some creature from a monster movie. The voice that came from the mouth wasn't at all extraterrestrial.

'Hey, you guys,' came a drawl. 'It's time we had a talk.'

Cody rolled down the window.

'You've been sitting out here some time,' said the guy with the silver eyes. 'What ya doin'?'

Sighing, Cody repeated their story. 'We're just trying to get some sleep.'

'Sleep?'

'Yes, we don't have anywhere to go.'

'Motels are plentiful, y'know?'

'I know.'

'So rent a room.'

'We don't have any money.'

'That a fact?'

'We only got in today.'

The man with the silver eyes nodded. Cody could see now that the eyes were silver only because of silver contacts. So no close encounter of the third kind tonight.

Not that.

Worse. Far worse.

A close encounter of the Colt .38 kind.

Cody saw the man pull aside the bottom of his jacket to reveal the black butt of the firearm jutting from the waistband of his pants.

'I think maybe you're sussing out Andre's territory.'

'We're not cops,' Cody said quickly.

'Who said you were?'

'But you suggested—'

'I suggested nothing about the police force, man. What I am suggesting is that you might be thinking of moving into my territory.'

He pronounced 'territory' in an easy drawl, each syllable clear and precise: 'Terry . . . tory.'

'No. We're only staying here for tonight.'

'But figuring to do some dealing, huh?'

'No.'

'What? Coke? Grass? Speed?'

'No.' Cody sounded annoyed now. He bunched his fist on the steering wheel. 'Now go away and leave us alone.'

'Oh, big guy.'

'Listen, we've just about had enough tonight.'

'Listen, baby, you haven't had nearly enough.' The man grinned, the silver contacts catching the moonlight. 'If you've come looking for trouble you've come to the right place.'

'Leave us alone.'

'Or?'

'Leave us. I'm warning you.'

'*You*'re doing the warning?' The man's hand went to his pistol.

Pix shrieked. 'He's going to shoot us.'

'He's not,' Cody said, angry.

The guy grinned again. 'So which of you two is right?' He looked at Grace. 'And you, pretty lady, what do you say?'

Cody opened the door, looking as if he was about to take on the guy with the silver eyes.

The guy stepped back, nodding. 'So you *do* want to muscle in on my territory?'

'No, we've just had a hell of a day. We want to be left alone.' Cody growled now.

Grace reached across and grabbed Cody's arm. He was polite, he was slow to anger, but once his fuse was burning . . . well, watch out.

'Leave it,' Grace pleaded.

'But we've been pushed around by every jerk in LA.' Cody quivered with rage. 'I'm not taking it anymore.'

'But he's got a gun,' Pix cried. 'He'll shoot you, Cody.'

'She's right, Cody,' Grace said. 'Get back in. We'll drive away. Find somewhere quiet.'

The man rested his hand on the gun and gave a shrug. *Okay, so what's it going to be?*

'All right.' Cody closed the door. 'We're leaving.'

'You think I'm going to let you just go after you've insulted me? Tried to walk into my territory?'

'I did no such thing.'

'You sure did, baby.'

'Look. We don't want any trouble. We just want to find somewhere quiet—'

'But you've *got* trouble. You're in Andre's territory now. You insult me to my face: "jerk", you called me. I want reparations, you hear? Reparations.'

'We're truly sorry,' Grace said in an effort to placate the man. 'We really are. We're tired. We've driven—'

'Not good enough.'

'Well, what *is* good enough?' Cody clenched his fist again, his face burning with anger.

All that shit today.

Now this.

A jerk.

A jerk with a gun, though. How dangerous is that?

'Tell you what, baby.' The man's eyes glinted silver. 'I'm a reasonable guy. The girl in the back. She gives me a good blow job and I'll consider that full and good reparation.'

Pix cried out. 'No, I'm not doing that.'

'That's the price, babes.' He eased the gun from his pants.

'No way,' Cody said. 'You'll have to put a bullet in me first.'

'Suits me.'

Pix grabbed Cody by the shirt collar, shook hard. 'Cody, you can't let him make me!'

'She's only sixteen, she's just a kid,' Cody said.

'Kids younger than her working these streets.'

'*Cody?*'

'Now I'm gonna unzip my fly.'

'Cody!'

'Moisten those lips for me, baby.'

'No.' Pix bunched herself into the corner of the seat, arms tightly around her knees. Eyes wide and scared, she shook her head, muttering, 'No, no, no . . .'

Andre pointed the gun into Cody's face.

'Listen up, babes. That's the price of you driving away from here. The girl in the back with the tight little mouth's gonna give me the best blow job in town.'

'No, she won't,' Grace said.

'Oh, won't she?'

'No,' Grace said firmly. 'I will.'

253

Chapter Forty-four

Through the peephole, Susan saw a swarthy, black-haired man with a grim face. She opened the door.

He lunged into her. She stumbled backwards, and the man fell to his hands and knees. Susan landed on her back.

In the doorway stood Mable Rudge, hunched slightly, grinning and panting. She held a butcher knife.

'Hi, petunia,' she said and pushed the door shut with the heel of her foot.

Susan climbed to her feet. She stood motionless. 'What do you want?'

The man started to get up. Mable kneed him over. 'Stay down, fella, or I'll slit your gizzard.'

'I'll happily leave,' he said.

'Lay on your back and shut up.'

He obeyed.

Mable stepped past his feet. She held the knife out in front of her, waving its point in small circles.

Susan backed away.

'Know what's gonna happen to you, whore? I'm gonna cut your face – gonna cut your nose off, that's what.'

Susan glanced at the bathroom door. It was open a crack.

'That's for starters. I'm gonna make you look so bad that Tag Parker'll puke when he sees you.'

'Tag!'

Mable charged.

Susan dodged and flung a lamp in her path. Mable kicked it aside. Snarled like a dog. Raised the blade.

'Freeze!' Tag shouted. He stood in the bathroom doorway, pistol aimed.

'Gonna fix her!' Mable yelled. She ran at Susan.

'Stop!'

'*Shoot her!*'

He didn't fire. His attention wasn't on Mable now but on the dark man dashing across the room.

The man sprang onto Mable's back. She plunged forward, arms swinging, blade flashing. Susan leaped out of the way and the big woman plowed into the sofa with an 'Umph!' The man, still on her back, grabbed her right arm. He twisted it. Mable growled and dropped the knife.

Susan rushed forward. She grabbed the knife and backed away.

Mable, no longer struggling, lay motionless beneath the man. She was half on the couch, her face pressed to its rear cushion, her knees on the floor. The seat of her grimy dress was torn, exposing a strip of doughy buttock. It dimpled. Susan looked away.

Tag came forward, holstering his revolver.

'Why didn't you shoot?'

'I might've hit our friend here.'

The small man looked over his shoulder and smiled. 'Imad Samdall.'

'Taggart Parker. This is Susan Connors.'

'Ah, yes. Miss Connors. And this is Mable?' Reaching back, he patted her soft rump. It quivered.

'Hands off,' she muttered.

He smacked the back of her head. 'Shut up. You threatened my life. Because of that I need not be civil to you.' He climbed off Mable's back. 'Sit on the couch and be silent.'

'You fuckin'—'

He slapped her. This time her whole face quivered with the force of the blow.

Mable's eyes narrowed. Her mouth shut. She turned around and flumped down onto the couch. This time she sat there. Said nothing. Her cheek began to burn bright red from the slap.

'You've really done it this time, Mable,' Tag told her. 'Assault with a deadly weapon.'

'I just wanted to throw a scare into her.'

'Yeah.' He stepped toward the phone.

'Oh, you ain't gonna arrest me, Tag?'

'You'll go to jail for this one.'

'I didn't hurt nobody. I just did it for you.'

'I warned you not to interfere.' He reached for the phone and flinched as it rang the second he touched the handset. He picked it up. 'Hello? Yes, she is. Just a moment, please.' He nodded at Susan.

She took the phone. 'Hello?'

'Susan? This is James Blumgard. I'm sorry to disturb you, but I've received a most disturbing call from the police department. I'm sure there's some mistake. They're bewildered themselves. They seem

255

to think, however, that our mummy has been involved in several killings that occurred tonight.'

'*Involved?*'

'They apparently believe Amara *committed* them. I know that sounds ridiculous. I don't know how they could even suggest such a thing. It appears, however, that one of the officers actually confronted the killer. He's sure it was a mummy. What's more, he's *convinced* it was Amara. Now maybe this was someone in disguise. I can hardly believe otherwise, though the officer insists that isn't the case. At any rate, the police would like a representative of the museum to be on hand as a consultant and so forth. I thought you would be the logical choice, since the Callahan Collection falls within your bailiwick.'

'What would I be doing?'

'They'd like you on the scene. I realize this may be an imposition . . .'

'No. You were right to call. I do have a problem, though. Maria's off for the night, and I don't have anyone to leave Geoffrey with.'

'Perhaps you could take him along. I'm sure there's no danger. The police simply want you to interview the officer involved; to establish whether his description does, in fact, fit Amara. They may ask for suggestions and so forth. I doubt it will take more than an hour.'

'Well . . .'

'I would go myself, but you're far more conversant with the subject.'

'I'll go,' she said.

'I appreciate this very much, Susan. Let me give you the address.' Blumgard told it to her and she copied it down. 'Keep me informed.'

'I will.'

'Goodnight, now.'

'Goodnight.' She hung up, turned to Tag. 'That was Blumgard. There've been some killings and get this – the police think Amara's involved.'

'As the perpetrator?'

She nodded.

Imad frowned and walked toward the door.

Susan said, 'I have to go over and talk to the police. Will you come?'

'Of course.'

Imad knelt near the door and picked up a black notebook.

'We'll have to take Geoffrey.'

'Before you leave,' Imad said, 'it would be wise for you to read this.'

'Now? I don't think there's time for—'

'Please. It is important.'

'What is it?'

'The journal of Robert Callahan. I was his ward and companion, you see, before his demise. He left instructions that this must be placed in responsible hands, should Amara walk. Unless I am mistaken, that situation has developed.'

'It's walked before?' Tag asked.

'Indeed.'

Imad gave the journal to Susan. She flipped through it, glancing at the handwritten pages. 'It's awfully long.'

'It tells you many things that you have to know.'

'Why don't you come along and fill us in along the way?'

'I'm sorry, no. I wish to have no further dealings in the matter. If you would permit me, however, I'll assume responsibility for Mable.'

'Can you handle her?' Tag asked.

'Most certainly. We could telephone the police from here if you like. If not, I'll be pleased to escort her elsewhere.'

Susan glanced at Tag.

Tag nodded.

'You're welcome to stay.'

Chapter Forty-five

Cody looked through the windshield. The pickup's headlights revealed the road as it twisted ahead. On either side the rocky walls of a canyon rose up into the night sky. He drove without speaking. Beside him, Grace sat gazing out the side window. Behind them Pix, flat on her back, stared at the underside of the truck's grimy roof.

He downshifted as the road in front ran downhill. The canyon widened a little. Here there were only rocky outcrops and occasional trees and bushes. No houses. No gas stations. This was a dark slice of wilderness tucked away in a corner of LA.

At last Pix asked, 'Grace . . . how could you do that?'

'Pix,' Cody warned.

'Shit . . . you sucked the guy's dick.'

Grace said nothing. Just stared at passing trees, which were becoming more numerous along this stretch of road.

'You didn't even know him. And you let him put his dick in your mouth.'

Grace still said nothing. Jerkily, she grabbed the water bottle and drank from it, her pink lips tight round the end of the wide neck of the bottle; her mouth forming a perfect seal. Cody found himself looking at her mouth, unable to shake the memory of what had happened half an hour ago.

'Afterwards, why didn't you spit?'

'Pix,' Cody said. 'Your sister did what she had to do, okay?'

'I think I'd have chosen the shooting.' Pix shook her head. 'Oh, man . . . he'd even pierced the end of it . . . a gold stud.'

Cody glanced back. 'Don't talk about it. Your sister doesn't need reminding.'

'But to suck a stranger's dick like that. Jeez, Grace, I thought he was gonna choke you, it went in so—'

'*Pix, enough now.*'

Cody glanced at Grace. Still she hadn't spoken. Hadn't spoken since the guy . . . since she'd . . . *Oh, shit.* He didn't want to activate the mental playback.

'Couldn't you have jumped him, Cody? You yellow or something?'

'He had a gun, Pix.'

'Yeah, but he was distracted, you dork.'

'And you think I could have grabbed the gun off him while—'

'Yeah, if you'd got your ass in gear.'

'Hell, you try pulling a stunt with a gun in your face.'

'While he had his dick in my sister's mouth you could have done something.'

'Yeah, slugged him with the cracker box, maybe.'

'But then maybe you enjoyed watching him unload himself into Grace's mouth. I saw you getting all hot and sweaty and—'

'*STOP!*'

Cody's head spun as Grace shouted.

'Stop the truck!'

'Don't worry about, Pix. She'll be quiet from now on, won't—'

'No! It's not that. Look!'

'What?'

'Don't you see?'

'See what?'

'Stop the damn truck, and look!'

He braked.

'What've you seen, Grace?'

'There, through the trees . . . no, further to the right.'

Pix sounded worried. 'What is it? What's wrong?'

Cody looked.

Saw nothing.

Nothing except trees and boulders and the rock walls of the canyon. There were no houses, no buildings, no cars – zilch.

Cody began, 'Grace, I still don't see—'

'I saw a woman in the trees.'

Pix snorted. 'Forget it. We've had enough stranger danger for one night.'

'No, it was a woman. She was holding a baby.' Grace stared into the darkness. 'She was hurrying.'

'But what would a woman be doing out here in the middle of nowhere, carrying a baby?'

'She must be in trouble,' Grace said. 'I'm going to help.'

With that she swung open the door, jumped out of the truck and ran away into the trees.

'Don't let her go, you big lummox. You don't know what's out there.'

259

'Okay, okay.' Cody grabbed the flashlight from under the dash.

'She might get herself killed.'

'I know that, too,' he said grimly.

He climbed out, began to follow Grace. He caught a glimpse of her through the trees as she ran through a shaft of moonlight. He also glimpsed another figure further on. For some reason, it seemed to move strangely. Moonlight glinted on it and he thought he saw long red hair cascading down the figure's back. And was it clutching something pale to its chest?

Too far away to see properly.

But for some reason just that glimpse of the hurrying figure, hunched over the pale bundle, sent a chill down his spine.

Something not-right about it, Cody.

Something dangerous.

'Grace,' he called. 'Grace . . . wait!'

But Grace ran after the figure.

He switched on the flashlight and ran through the trees after her.

Behind him he heard cracking twigs.

Looking back, he saw Pix following him.

'Wait in the pickup,' he told her.

'Yeah, as if.'

'It might not be safe out here.'

'It's gonna be safer out here even with a big lummox like you than alone in that heap of junk.'

'Pix—'

'I'm coming with you.'

'Okay . . . but stay close.'

Together they ran up the slope.

Chapter Forty-six

Knife in hand, Imad watched the door swing shut. He turned to Mable. She sat motionless on the couch, glowering at him.

'Now, Mable, tell me. What is so special about this man whose name is like a game played by children?'

She shrugged.

Her thick lips pouted, sulky-looking.

'What is so special that you would risk prison, even death, to mutilate or kill his girlfriend?'

Her eyes narrowed. She said nothing. Her plump fingers knotted together on her lap.

'Tell me.' He reached for the telephone.

'I like him,' Mable said.

'You like him. Isn't it evident that he doesn't like you?'

'Huh?'

'And he certainly wouldn't like you any better if you harmed Susan.'

'He was nice to me.'

'To protect Susan, he was prepared to empty his revolver into you. He'd have done exactly that if I hadn't intervened, Mable.'

'So?'

'I saved your life, did I not?'

'So what?'

'Isn't that a rather special gift?'

'What do you mean?'

'I gave you back your life when it could have been so easily taken.'

'What do you want from me, you filthy A-rab?'

'Tsk, tsk, so impolite.'

'I don't owe you nuthin', A-rab.'

'And incorrect, too. By parentage I am Egyptian. But legally I am as American as . . . how would you put it? Momma's apple pie.'

'You American? You're putting me on.'

'Oh, indeed I am telling the truth.'

She frowned. 'So what do you want from me?'

'Want?'

'Must want something.'

'Now, let me see.' He rested his fingertips together. 'Mable, it's now in my power to grant you another favor. I needn't call the police, you realize.'

She stared at him. Her glower softened. 'Will ya let me go, then?'

'Oh, Mable, my dear, I can hardly do that. I told Susan that I would assume responsibility for you. To let you go would be the height of *ir*responsibility. You might simply attack her again.'

'I won't. I promise.'

'Words. Mere words. As long as you're infatuated with Tag, you'll continue to be a threat. No, I cannot let you go. I can, however, take you with me.'

She rubbed her hands on her soiled dress. She licked her lips.

'You will be in my custody, much as you would be in police custody should I decide to call them. The difference is this: There will be no handcuffs, no jail, no trial. I'll give you a comfortable room and good food. There will be a TV for you to watch. And books if you should wish to read . . . ah, no books, perhaps. Reading might not be to your taste. But magazines and a radio.'

'What's the catch?'

'Isn't there always a catch?' He smiled. 'This is the catch. You will not be allowed to leave the house alone until I'm satisfied—'

'A house?' she asked, suddenly beaming.

'Indeed. I live in a rather elaborate house. One might call it a mansion.'

'Shoot . . . you want me to live there?'

'For the time being.'

She slapped her knee. Her calf quivered. 'I get it! You're wantin' to screw me. Gee, I've never been screwed by an A-rab before.'

'Screw?'

'Sure. Whyn't you just come out and say it?' Bouncing off the couch, Mable lifted her dress. Her pasty white thighs were mottled with bruises. Her knees were scabbed. There was a fresh scratch from the recent tussle running the length of one meaty thigh.

Imad saw she wore no panties, but her groin was hidden below the roll of her stomach. Her huge breasts quivered as she struggled to pull the dress over her head. Tufts of black hair hung from her armpits.

She talked excitedly. 'No, sir. Never been poked by an A-rab. I've

262

been done by a Mexican and a whole bunch of Cubans. And there was this guy from Austria – or was it Australia? – he tied me up with a clothesline and nailed me good and hard. Couldn't sit down for a week, I can tell you. Here, just help me get this dress off, then we can screw.'

'No!' Imad snapped.

'I know it's what you want, hon. Mable don't mind what you do, or how you do it.' She stretched out her arms to him. 'Come here, hon. Enjoy.'

'No! I insist you lower your dress immediately. Cover yourself, for God's sake. Or I will phone the police. Believe me, I will do that unless you behave with correct modesty.'

'Correct modesty,' she grunted as she pulled the dress down. She scowled at him. 'You queer?'

'Hardly.'

'Wish I was a boy?'

'Mable—'

''Cos if you are that way inclined I can take it like a man.'

'Mable. This is neither the time nor the place for—'

'Good a time as any.'

'It is not.'

'Might as well mess up someone else's couch as your own.'

'You are filthy and you smell like a garbage truck.'

'Can't get it up?'

'I dirtied myself enough when I was forced to subdue you. I certainly don't relish further contact at such close quarters.'

'Fuck you, Charlie.' She dropped to the couch.

'So there'll be no further contact until you've bathed and brushed your teeth. Which you will do immediately after we arrive at my home. Understand?'

One side of Mable's mouth curled upward. 'You *do* want to prong me.'

'No,' he said. 'Not until you are clean.'

'Oh, baby. I get the picture.'

'So what shall it be, the police or me?'

Licking her lips, she slumped on the couch and lifted her dress again. 'Do me now,' she said. 'Show me how you do it A-rab style.'

'You're wasting your time with these antics.'

'Aw.'

'Come along, Mable.'

'What's your name again?'

263

'Imad.'

'Imad.' She stroked her hands down her hips and raised a knee. 'I like you, Imad. Don't you want to put it right in here?'

He set the knife on a lamp table and went to her. She smiled up at him.

Smiled as, moaning, she used her fingers to massage and probe herself. Fingernails became slick.

'Oh . . . Imad. Right here, right here,' she whispered.

Imad slapped her cheek so hard her face wobbled.

'Hey!'

He slapped her again. A loud *thwack* filled the room. 'Get up.'

She got to her feet. Her face was red. Imad saw tears in her eyes.

'Whatcha gonna do? Beat up on me before you screw me?'

'Mable—'

''Cos that's happened to me before when I got gang-banged. They beat the crap out of me, then . . . then one after another they screwed me.' Tears ran down her face. The cheek with the burning red handprint grew slick with them. She used both plump paws to rub her eyes.

'Mable—'

'I thought ya liked me,' she sobbed.

'You must learn to obey, Mable. Once you understand that you will find inner contentment. Understand?'

'But I . . . I—'

'Mable. Learn to obey. Now, follow me.'

Imad led the way across the room. As they passed the lamp table, Mable grabbed the knife.

'No!'

Chapter Forty-seven

Amara held the baby to her dry chest. Her red hair had spilled forward, partially covering the infant. She walked through darkness, her shins whispering against the dry grass.

She'd been walking for a long time now. At first there'd been dwellings. Lights had shone from windows as if they'd been lit by burning torches. But after walking for some time the houses had ended. She'd walked away from the town and into a range of barren hills.

As if by accident rather than purpose she moved down one of the hills and into a canyon. She held the baby tight, her talon-like hands pressing it against her withered breasts.

Amara continued walking through the darkness. She entered an area where trees grew and passed among them, weaving in and out, never pausing.

Never tiring.

Driven by ancient purpose.

It was as she walked some distance from a road yet parallel to it that the truck stopped. Its headlights lit a shining path in front of it.

Then a figure left the truck at a run.

A man's voice sounded on the night air. 'Grace . . . Grace. Wait!'

The figure of a woman ran into the trees. A moment later two more figures left the truck. A man and a second, younger woman. They ran after the first who'd already disappeared.

Amara walked on. She knew the first woman followed her. But that was of no importance. The ancient purpose drove her on. Nothing would distract Amara.

Nothing would get in Amara's way.

Nothing.

No one.

Death came on swift wings to anyone who interfered.

Chapter Forty-eight

'Ed, what're you doing?'

He glanced up through the bars at Virginia. 'I've all ready told you. I'm making a barb. When this baby goes in it's going to *stay* in.'

'You're making too much noise . . . and the sawdust on the floor . . . they'll see it.'

He groaned with frustration. 'Look, Virginia. The point of the stake is sharp enough, but it needs a barb to stop her escaping.'

'But they'll hear you. And they'll see the sawdust when they bring in the food.'

'Virginia—'

'And when they see it they'll know what's happening.'

'I'll think of something.'

'And you'll wind up like Marco and Cardinali.'

'Okay. Lemme think.'

'Ed. The lights could go out any minute, then—'

'Whammo. I know.'

'Move the sawdust bowl so it catches the sawdust.'

His face burned. Seemed so obvious. Catch the sawdust in the wee-wee bowl. *Why didn't I think of that?*

Because you're busy planning on doing some hunting with that harpoon of yours, Eddie, old buddy.

Yeah, gonna harpoon me some fresh meat.

'What's so funny?' she asked.

'I'm just imagining the bitch's surprise when she sits on this instead of on my pecker.'

'Don't get overly optimistic.'

He ran his finger over the wickedly sharp stake. 'Oh, I just know this is going to work like a dream.'

'You've got to avoid being caught with it first. Okay, Ed?'

'Okay, Virginia.'

'We've solved the sawdust mess, so what do you figure to drown the noise?'

He gazed at the edge of the cage bar that he'd been using as a file. It worked surprisingly well.

But noisy as hell.

Squeaked like a chorus of mice every time he ran the wooden stool leg backwards and forwards across it.

'Could you use less pressure?' she suggested.

'Tried. It doesn't scrape away any of the wood when I do that.'

'How much further to go before you've made the barb?'

He looked at the wooden shaft. About four inches back from the point he'd managed to file a cleft. A 'V' shape, it went maybe a quarter of the way through the stool leg.

'Another half an inch. Then I have to work on making the point of the barb sharp, too. When I've driven it into her I need to pull back quick.' He demonstrated, thrusting the chair leg up then tugging back hard. 'So the barb, here, digs into her flesh. Then I've got her like a hooked fish.'

Virginia looked suddenly uncomfortable and crossed her legs. 'I get the picture.'

'Barbaric. But needs must.'

'Yeah, needs must.'

'Let's see if this works.' He licked his finger and ran it along the edge of the bar he used as a file, moistening the metal. This time when he worked on the barb it didn't squeak. He nodded. 'Slippery when wet.'

'It's stopped squeaking now but is it cutting?'

'Yeah, it's cutting. I just need to keep wetting it.'

He worked for a while. Then . . .

He ran his finger along the eighteen inches of hard wood to touch the point lightly. A thought occurred to him. An interesting one at that.

'A bit like staking a vampire,' he told her. 'Only I'm not going through the ribs.' He stabbed upward with the wood. 'I'm going up through the crotch instead.'

'Oh, Jesus . . . You don't have to state the obvious.' She scrunched up her face, imagining the pain. 'You're going to inflict one hell of an injury, you know?'

'I *do* know. But after what she's done to us? Couldn't happen to a nicer person.'

'Well, I'd stuff some tissue in your ears – she's going to scream the place down after you push that thing . . .' She grimaced. 'You know where.'

His grin became wider. 'You know something . . . it's going to be music to my ears.'

Lights out.

All right!

Ed was in a state of readiness.

Ready, Eddie?

He stifled the grin in the dark. They'd see with their nightscope goggles. They'd know he planned some surprise.

He sat on the blanket. He'd slipped the sharpened wooden chair leg that formed the lethally sharp stake down the leg of his pants.

Is that a harpoon in your pocket or are you just pleased to see me?

It was all he could do to stop himself laughing out loud. He'd waited for this. Payback time. Once the bitch had this rammed up inside of her as far as her spleen she'd be going nowhere fast.

She'd scream like a stuck pig, though. Which as analogies went was pretty accurate. He rested his fingers on the harpoon, feeling the thick, hard roundness of the shaft through the material of his trousers.

This is a stickup, honey.

A stickup you're never gonna forget.

He sat there in the dark, waiting for the command to climb up onto the platform and 'present himself' through the hole in the Perspex.

Drafts slipped into the room. A door had opened somewhere. He heard rustling. A whisper of feet moving lightly across the concrete floor.

Nearly here.

Not long now.

Ready, Eddie?

I'm ready.

He stroked the thick shaft inside the leg of his pants.

Then he heard whispering.

'Okay.' This was from Virginia.

Shit.

Oh, shit, shit!

Their sex mistress had chosen Virginia, not him, for this session's entertainment. Maybe he could still stake their captor as she worked on his neighbor. But it was dark. Dark as hell. He couldn't see squat in the darkness. There wasn't a hope of skewering her by sheer chance.

No. Must be patient. Must wait.

He covered himself with the blanket, just in case his captor should glimpse the rod-shaped protuberance in his pants. There was little chance that they'd mistake *that* for his dick.

He heard murmuring from the next cage. Virginia began to breathe heavier. The breathing became panting. Then she moaned.

Oh, that moaning.

Erotic moans.

Sexy moans.

It always fired him up inside. He imagined Virginia standing facing his cage, feet apart. Naked. Her hair spilling down the long curve of her back to her gorgeous butt. Her long thighs. Shapely calves.

And there was a shadowy figure doing great things to her.

Working at her between her legs with slick fingers.

Stroking, parting, entering.

She gave a little cry.

Oh, Eddie. That was the sound she made when being entered. Those fingers were inside now. Finding her clit. Toying, pressing gently, probing. Teasing.

Shit. His heart hammered.

The sounds of pleasure were making him horny.

Horny enough to distract him from what he planned to do with the sharp stake when he got a chance.

He listened hard, his eyes straining into the darkness. Hearing moans, little gasps, muttered 'pleases', 'yessses'.

Then it went wrong.

The note of the whispering altered.

He heard Virginia give a frightened gasp. 'I'm sorry . . . I didn't mean to . . . I'll try harder.'

More whispers. They sounded as if they could be instructions but Ed couldn't be certain.

Their captor's voice boomed. That same deep timbre that made the bars of the cage quiver. *'Stand with your back to the bars. Slip your hands through the loops. Quickly.'*

'Please . . . I'm sorry. I—'

'Do it.'

Sounds of movement. Then silence.

Ed listened. All he could hear was his blood thumping in his ears.

What was going to happen to Virginia? What had she done wrong? He thought of Marco with the grinning slit in his throat. The blood.

269

The image came blasting, too, of Cardinali toppling off the stool to hang by his neck, jerking, choking,

Had their captor grown bored with Virginia?

Then he heard a sound. It was the swish of an object moving fast through the air.

Thwack.

A stick or a belt.

Swish.

Thwack!

'Uh! Please!'

Virginia pleaded with the invisible sadist. But still the beating went on. *Swish. Thwack.* Then came Virginia's sharp gasps. She panted. Moaned. Cried. Still the blows fell. The blistering snap of a weapon against soft flesh.

Later, when the lights came on, Ed saw Virginia lying face down on the foam mattress. She was completely naked. Her hair fanned out across the floor where she'd thrown herself down.

Ed blinked.

Saw the injuries.

Saw a dozen or more cruel red lines that seemed to burn bright across the soft rising mounds of her bare buttocks.

She winced as she moved.

Gingerly raising her head, she looked at Ed. Her eyes brimmed. 'When you get your chance don't hold back. You've got to hurt the bitch. Hurt her. Do you hear me?'

He nodded.

All he had to do now was wait.

It would happen soon. He knew that. Felt it in his bones. *Endgame.*

Chapter Forty-nine

Cody thought: *This is crazy. Who on earth is Grace following out there?* He paused as he ran up the wooded incline. Maybe that's it. Maybe Grace *is* crazy. The incident with the guy with the gun back in the parking lot might have sent her over the edge.

'Slow down, you big lummox,' Pix panted. 'I can't keep up with you.'

'You should have stayed in the pickup.'

'Yeah, and waited for the next oral-fixated weirdo to come ambling by? Think again, Cody, you simpleton.'

'Pix, shush.' He held his finger to his lips.

'What you mean, shushing—'

'Ssh. Pix, I'm trying to listen for your sister.'

He stood for a moment, shining the flashlight ahead through the trees. Listening for the sound of footsteps. Where was Grace? She'd taken off after the strange-looking gal like a missile. Now she was out in the dark alone. *Hell . . . who knows what might happen to her out there?*

This canyon was such an out-of-the-way place.

Might there be bears?

Or Hell's Angels ready for some fun?

Or backwoods boys who were bored with making pigs squeal?

Hell.

Might just get killed out there.

'Cody?'

'What?'

'I don't like it out here. I wanna go back.'

'You should've stayed in the pickup.'

'I wanna stay with you.'

'Make your mind up, Pix.'

'I wanna stay in the pickup with you.'

'We've got to find your sister.' He scanned the forest. All he saw were boulders, tree trunks and a glimpse of stars through the branches.

'Cody?'

'What is it now?'

'Will you hold my hand?'

'*No.*' He looked at her, startled by her suggestion.

'Please.' Suddenly shy-looking, almost demure, she held out her hand.

He shook his head. 'Pix, just stick close behind. I think she went this way.' Without waiting for a reply, he struck off through the trees, shining the light in front of him. He was sure Grace had headed along the path. He walked quickly, not looking back.

He knew Pix was following.

Was positive about it.

Heard her whispering, 'Please, Cody. Hold my hand . . . please . . . *please . . .*'

Grace hurried along the woodland path. It zigzagged down the hillside. She followed the figure that was moving downhill in front of her. The figure had long red hair. It clutched something pale to its chest. Its arms and legs were very thin.

It was difficult to see clearly in this mixture of moonlight and shadow, but Grace was sure it was a woman. What was more, the woman seemed to be clutching a baby.

But the stick-thin woman looked odd. Seemed to move strangely. There was something about the gait. Something stiff-jointed.

And what would a woman be doing out here in a godforsaken canyon at two in the morning? She had to be in trouble. She might be on the run from a bullying, abusive boyfriend.

After what had happened tonight to Grace – how she had been forced into oral sex with the armed stranger – she was determined not to sit back and let innocent people suffer. The world couldn't be such a cruel place. There had to be times when good people did the right thing – they had to help people in need.

She moved down the sharp incline at something like a run, catching hold of tree trunks to steady herself. Her feet raised puffs of dust that showed as white clouds in the moonlight. Sometimes branches caught at her clothes, her hair, but she struggled on, breaking free.

If she could break free of the memories of the past few hours.

Break free of that salt taste that still clung to her lips.

If she dedicated herself fully to helping the poor woman with the child then maybe that would be enough to make her forget. Once she thought she heard Cody calling her name. Only there wasn't time to stop. Once she'd caught up with the woman she could go back.

Grace saw herself in her mind's eye leading the dazed (maybe even battered) woman and babe back to the pickup truck. Then they could drive her to a women's refuge where she'd be safe from the abusive rat who'd made her flee in the middle of the night.

Grace was sure her imagined scenario about the woman was right.

Yet, the woman did look strange. There was something about the round shape of the front of her head. It was almost skull-shaped.

Of course it has to be skull-shaped – you're seeing her head, stupid.

But it's more like a skull bereft of flesh . . .

No . . . that's your imagination, she told herself, panting as she ran down the hill. *Imagination and a trick of the moonlight.*

There goes a woman in trouble.

Your mission? To help.

You're gonna do this. By saving her you're gonna save yourself from those memories. Those dirty, corrosive memories of the . . . of the way he filled your mouth . . . how he pushed in so deep you thought you'd choke on his—

No.

She snapped off the thought.

Save the woman and her baby.

She ran harder through the near-darkness.

And ran straight into the arms of a phantom. They closed round her. A leering face with a twisted nose pressed hard against hers.

The phantom held her tight. Bony fingers pressed into her shoulders, seeking her throat.

Struggling, panting, she fought to free herself.

As she pushed herself away a shaft of moonlight fell through the branches.

Her attacking phantom was a tree. Nothing more. The phantom's arms were branches; its face marks in the bark where a branch had sheered off.

Stupid runaway imagination, she scolded herself. *Stay focused.*

Taking a deep breath, she found the path again. Scuff marks in the dirt revealed that the woman had passed this way. But that was odd . . . Grace squatted down to look closer at the dry dirt. She saw something that made the hairs on her head stand on end. There was a footprint. But it was a bare footprint.

Could the woman have walked all this way along the canyon without some kind of footwear?

Or perhaps she'd lost a shoe walking down the steep slope, only was too exhausted or too frightened to stop and put it back on?

This was getting stranger by the minute.

Grace hurried along the path. Soon she reached a break in the trees that afforded her a better view of the canyon. Up ahead she saw a lone house.

In the distance, she also glimpsed the slight figure of the woman. She seemed to be making for the house.

Okay . . . me, too, Grace told herself.

Chapter Fifty

'It's not gonna work.'

'It is.'

'Not.'

Ed wished she'd shut up. They'd been on this subject for a long time. *Too damn long. Damn pessimist.*

He glared at Virginia.

'Don't look at me like that, Ed Lake.'

'I'll look at you how I damn well please.'

'Look,' she began. 'It's because we're getting tense about the whole situation.'

'I'll say we're tense.'

'Eddie—'

'We're locked up here in cages. We're used as sex toys. We're probably gonna be murdered.'

'Eddie—'

'We're probably gonna wind up in a shallow grave out in the woods.'

'Eddie, you haven't thought it through, you're missing—'

'I haven't. I've got the harpoon.' He brandished the stool leg. 'I'm going to use it.' His face burned. 'And another thing, don't call me Eddie.'

'I thought you might like it.'

'I don't. "Eddie" reminds me of some dog from a comedy show.'

'Okay, Edward . . .'

'Ed. Please.'

'Okay, Ed.'

'That's better.'

'Sheesh.' She touched her forehead as if she'd lost her train of thought. 'You've told me the plan. You impale the woman. The barb holds her in place. You have her trapped, right?'

'Right.'

'But that doesn't get us out of these cages, does it?'

'But she'll be no longer a threat.'

'And you've forgotten something else.'

'What?'

'We think there's two of them.'

'Shit.' He slapped his forehead. *Holy Christ, I'm an idiot. A gold-plated idiot.*

'The one we've nicknamed The Warder. What's she going to do when she sees her partner squirming on top of that pole?' She fixed her green eyes on the stake in Ed's hands. 'She'll probably get hold of a gun and . . . well, for you and me: *Los Endos.*'

'Holy Christ. I just didn't think . . . Virginia, I'm an idiot. But I was so sure about this. I thought I saw a way out.'

Virginia looked him in the eye. 'Ed. I'm not saying *don't* do it. I'm just stressing that the end result might not be what you expect. But . . .'

'But?'

'But if you want to go ahead and do it, do it. Okay?'

'You mean at least nail one of the bitches?'

Virginia nodded. 'And you never know, you might hurt the Sex Queen so bad that her friend panics and runs for it.'

'So then we sit here and starve.'

Virginia gave one of those little jerks of her shoulder. 'Can't say that everything will turn out rosy for us. But you never know. We might get lucky. Sex Queen might have the keys to these padlocks. Then we're free as birds.'

'So you're with me on this?' Lightly he pressed the lethal point of the stake with his thumb. 'Even though it might not work out one hundred percent?'

'Go for it, Ed. It's getting so we've nothing left to lose.'

Chapter Fifty-one

There is someone out there, April told herself with a growing sense of wonder. Someone's coming through the trees toward the house.

Her years of blindness had developed in her an acute sense of hearing. She listened.

Heard the nighttime breeze running in hissing swirls along the canyon to play among the trees. Depending on her mood, it could be such a lonesome sound. Now it had become strangely thrilling.

It seemed to be whispering to April. *'They're here, they're here, they're here.'*

Here is my savior.

Someone to banish loneliness.

She tilted her head to one side, feeling the breeze fingering her long hair. It stroked her neck, tugged lightly at the hem of her negligée, sending a delicious shiver up her thighs.

Concentrating now, she filtered the sounds.

The cry of a bird.

The breeze in the branches. The groan of a tree trunk. Rustling grass.

A whispering through the potted shrubs on the roof terrace where she stood with her hands on the wall that separated her from the twenty-foot drop to the driveway below.

She heard another sound, too. Faint but distinct to her sensitive ears. A rhythmic *scrunch, scrunch.*

That was a pair of feet advancing along the gravel drive to the house. Even though the footsteps sounded very light, there was something purposeful about the stride. She lifted her hand to push back her hair from the side of her head. Turned it slightly, so she could hear more.

Sometimes she could even hear the breathing of a visitor. Occasionally she could even catch their scent, too. But not tonight. The breeze was too strong. It would carry the visitor's scent away down the canyon before it could reach April's delicate nostrils.

April imagined what her caller would be like. From the lightness of their step she pictured someone young and slightly built.

Even though she couldn't imagine their looks she knew one thing.

Her visitor would be beautiful. A divine spirit had brought them here to put an end to her loneliness.

The *scrunch-scrunch* of feet on gravel grew louder as they neared the house.

April Vallsarra waited. Almost here. Almost . . .

Then, a moment later, the footsteps stopped. There was no sound but the breeze in the trees, whispering, sighing.

Her caller – her *savior* – would be standing there below her in that magical radiance that sighted people called 'moonlight.'

April waited. She was patient now. She sensed that her caller might be nervous or even afraid. She didn't want to say anything that would frighten them away. Perhaps they'd spent days trying to pluck up courage to make this trip to the remote house in the middle of the night.

So, nice and easy does it.

Take your time.

Don't rush.

Make them feel comfortable.

She smiled down in the direction of the figure, even though she could only guess at where they stood. But it must be close. She heard a slithering of stones beneath their feet when they shifted their balance.

Even so, they must be standing still. Gazing up at her. Perhaps tongue-tied.

A young man?

Shy, but quite beautiful.

Was he as lonely as she had been? Spending solitary nights praying for a companion? Another person to love and to be loved by?

Softly, April spoke. 'Don't worry. I can't see you but I know you're there.' She paused. 'My name is April Vallsarra. Have you come here to see me?'

There was no reply. Her visitor was indeed so shy as to be tongue-tied. She hoped they wouldn't flee in a fit of nerves.

So she spoke reassuringly. 'It's a lovely night. I wish I could see the stars, but I guess you've already noticed. I'm blind. Can you describe the stars to me?'

No reply.

'Don't worry. I can imagine them. I imagine them as little round

278

cushions that are soft and warm to touch, if only one *could* touch them.' Her laugh came as a light trill. 'That sounds absurd, I know. But I've never seen them, never seen anything, come to that, so when people try and describe what objects *look* like I have to translate it in the only way I can. The sun I think of as being pointed to the touch and quite hard. The moon for me is soft and cool. Stars are soft and warm and if one could touch them they'd tingle against your fingertips.' She smiled downward. 'And I imagined as a girl that if you listened hard enough you could hear them singing . . . small, light voices that sang sweet rising harmonies. See?' She shrugged. 'If something as profound as sight is missing from one's life it's hard to replace it with a substitute.' She paused, thinking. 'The same goes for love. If you don't have someone to love in your life you try to find substitutes. But they're only clumsy facsimiles of the real thing, because there is no genuine substitute for real love . . .' She paused, suddenly feeling awkward. 'See, there I go. You can tell when someone lives alone, they start talking too much. What about you? Tell me about yourself.'

No reply.

'You can't live that close. The nearest houses are three miles away. And I didn't hear the sound of a car . . .'

Silence.

'Did you walk?'

Nothing.

'Then I guess it must be a nice night for a walk. Nice and cool now.'

Again a faint sound as if her caller had shifted their center of balance on the gravel drive.

'It doesn't matter,' she said gently. 'You don't have to talk. I understand.' She smiled. 'It's nice to have someone here. Believe me, incredibly nice.'

She felt the breeze stroke her bare shoulders. It pressed her negligée against her body. It felt like cool hands, gliding down her back.

Lovely sensations.

April shivered. A kind of thrilling shiver that made her tingle all over. Her breasts prickled with goose bumps and her nipples rose.

'We'll talk here as long as you want,' she said. 'Or if you wish you can come inside.'

Grace could see what was happening but couldn't get through. Between her and the driveway to the house was a thicket of

279

thorn bushes. She'd be torn to shreds if she tried to force a way.

Instead, she would have to walk along the path for a further two hundred yards into the trees, then, she figured, double back somehow in order to bring herself to the entrance gates.

But she saw. What she did see didn't make a hatful of sense. Leastways, there was something strange about the scene.

In the moonlight, a good hundred yards or more away, stood the figure she'd been following.

The figure stood at the base of a flat-roofed house. Grace looked up at a second figure. A woman with shoulder-length dark hair.

They seemed to be having a conversation. But it was way too far away for Grace to hear what was being said. She looked hard at the first figure. The moon wasn't all that bright and now some cloud was scudding in front of it, so that the scene went from silvery radiance to deep shadow.

The figure Grace had followed through the wood was a woman. She had a head of long copper-colored hair. When the moon shone at its brightest Grace saw metallic red tints. Awesome hair.

Only the body looked so thin as to be emaciated.

Legs like sticks, Grace told herself. *Thin arms too.* They held the still-silent baby to her chest.

There was some quality about the woman on the driveway that made Grace's skin want to crawl off her bones. Something was wrong about it.

Once, when the moon flickered through the cloud, the figure turned briefly as if to look at Grace.

She recoiled.

That's not a woman . . . that's a dead body. She has no eyes, only empty sockets.

But a dead woman walking?

Surely a trick of the meager light?

And that baby. It never moved once. Never made a sound.

Grace shivered.

She didn't like what she was seeing . . . leastways, she didn't like what her imagination was *telling* her she was seeing.

Corpse of a woman carries dead baby to house in the middle of night.

Snap out of it, Grace Bucklan. You've gone through hell. You're a teenage runaway. You've driven thousands of miles. You've been attacked. You've been forced to go down on a stranger at gunpoint.

Now you're out in some godforsaken canyon alone. You haven't slept properly in days.

No wonder your mind is playing weird stunts on you.

That isn't a dead woman – a dead, naked woman – you see. It's a woman in distress. Now somehow she's reached this house. The homeowner is talking to her from the roof.

Telling her to go away?

Driven by the sense of injustice in the world, and an overpowering desire to help someone in need tonight, Grace walked along the woodland path.

She'd do the right thing.

She'd help the half-starved woman and the infant.

Then her conscience would be clear.

April spoke softly to her caller. She knew they were still there below her on the drive.

'It's late . . . I guess it must still be dark. Are you hungry? Thirsty?'

No reply.

'Surely you must be ready to rest after your walk all the way up here?'

April heard the shifting of gravel as her caller moved a foot. She interpreted that as them being tired.

'Why don't you come in for a while? You can rest. Have a cold drink.' She fingered the soft fabric of her negligée. 'There's no hurry to leave, is there?'

Again a movement of small stones beneath feet. She interpreted this in the affirmative. She'd bring her caller into the house. They'd like her home. They'd like *her*. They'd want to stay. She was sure of it.

Her heart surged with happiness.

For a split second she could hear her father's admonishment: 'Now, now, April, you simply don't invite strangers into the house just like that . . .'

You're not as lonely as I am. You don't know what it's like. Lonely people don't even feel the touch of another's hand for so long that they fear they will go mad. Isolation is cancer. Loneliness, the death of spirit.

She patted the top of the wall in excitement. Anxiety, too. She didn't want her caller to retreat into the woods. Clearly they were incredibly shy.

'Just stay there. Please be patient. It will take me a little time to find my way downstairs and open the door. But please stay a while.'

Lifting the front of her negligée with one hand so she didn't trip, she hurried for the doorway that led to the stairs.

In her heart April was certain. After tonight nothing would be the same ever again.

Cody glanced back at Pix. 'What's wrong?'

She stared at him. Her eyes were bright in the moonlight. Her expression looked . . . it looked . . . well, odd. Cody shifted uncomfortably. He'd just climbed onto the fallen trunk of a tree to see if he could get a better view. Perhaps spot the AWOL Grace.

His girlfriend had acted so weird. But then, she'd suffered stress and a half over the last twenty-four hours.

Only now it was little sister's turn.

She stood with her feet apart so the little skirt was stretched tight. Her arms hung down by her side. Her shoulders were high, though, as if she was tense.

And worse?

It was that stare of hers. She stared right at him.

The moonlight's falling on her . . . she's turning into a werewolf . . . Nope.

Worse than that.

'Cody?'

'What's wrong? Do you feel ill?'

'I've been thinking . . . I'd like it if you kissed me.'

'*What?*'

'I can't get it out of my head . . . I want you to kiss me.'

'Pix, stop fooling around.' He forced a grin . . . a leg-pull of hers. She'd done plenty of those in the past. 'We're looking for your sister. She might be in trouble.' He jumped down from the log.

'She's just using you, Cody. She wanted you to bring her here just so she could be in the movies. She doesn't really love you. Not the way—'

'Pix.'

'I love you.'

'Pix. Stop fooling.'

But she didn't seem to be fooling.

Not by a long way. She lunged forward, grabbed his head in both hands and yanked it down so her lips slammed against his.

'Pix. No. Stop it.' The words came out in a garble. Her tongue

282

was already straining through his lips into his mouth. ''S not right, Pix. Grace . . .'

'Grace isn't here. Hold me tight, Cody.'

'Nn – ghhh.' Her tongue shot into his mouth again, working with a muscular ferocity against his. Her hands went everywhere. *Everywhere.* Cody couldn't believe it.

Was there madness in the Bucklan family? First Grace, now Pix?

'Pix, you mustn't do that, it's . . . *Pix!*'

She pushed herself forward against him. He felt her small, firm breasts against his midriff. She kissed like a demon. As much fury as passion.

He retreated.

Caught the heel of his cowboy boot on a branch. Fell heavily on his rear.

She pounced.

Trying to unbuckle his belt.

Trying to tug down his zipper.

All the time her mouth clamped on his.

'Pix . . . Pix, stop it!'

He reached up, grabbed her by the shoulders and swung her down so that she slammed back against the forest floor.

Even though he heard the 'Uph!' of her breath knocked from her, still she didn't let up.

He rolled on top of her, gripped her wrists.

That was when she melted beneath him. 'Okay,' she whispered. 'You be on top. It'll be nicer.'

'No, Pix. Listen, I don't want you. I love your sister.'

'But I love *you*, Cody.' A little of the old whiny note returned.

'No, you only think you do.'

'But I can't stop thinking about you. I keep imagining you kissing me. I imagine you—'

'Pix, no. It's wrong.'

'Is not.'

'It is.'

'But I can't get you out of my mind,' she whispered.

'When did all this start?' he asked.

'When we left the pickup.'

He looked at her, astounded. 'You mean you've only started having . . .' He searched for the word. 'Having feelings for me in the last few minutes?'

'Yes.' She nodded, solemn. 'Now I can't stop thinking about you.'

'Oh, for Pete's sake, Pix. You don't fall in love as quickly as that.'

'Love at first sight.'

'You've seen me plenty.'

'Cupid's arrow.'

'Lack of sleep, more like.' Still holding her wrists he knelt up. 'Now, I'm going to let you ago. But no weird stuff. Okay?'

She looked up at him with big, gooey eyes. 'Whatever you say, Cody.'

'All right.' Releasing her, he stood up, dusting off his pants as he did so. 'Now you get up onto your feet. Then you're going to follow me as we go look for Grace.'

'Whatever you say, Cody.'

Her meek voice made him uneasy, but at least she was no longer trying to suck the lips off his face.

She held up her hands.

'Help?'

'But no more wrestling me, all right?' He switched on the flashlight. 'Now stick close, d'you hear?'

'I will.' She gave him a shy, girlish smile.

Dear God. This I don't need.

They walked on. In a little while they reached a clearing that revealed a house.

'Sheesh,' Pix breathed. 'If ever there was a haunted house, that's the one.'

In the moonlight Cody could see a figure move cautiously through the open gates and along the driveway. He shook his head, puzzled. 'There's Grace. But what on earth is she doing?'

Pix slipped her hand into his. 'Looks to me as if she's paying a visit to the spook house.'

Grace reached the gates to the drive. They were old and rusted and didn't look as if they were even capable of closing any more. She moved quickly along the driveway in the direction of the house that stood perhaps fifty yards away.

The curve of the driveway meant she lost sight of the front of the house for a few seconds. She walked in deep shadow. The trees reached over her in a way that was nothing less than nightmarish.

What was she getting herself into?

This was trespass now.

Might just get myself shot by a jittery householder.

284

The half-starved woman with the baby might already be inside. This could be her home.

But it had just looked so odd. How she'd stood there clutching the silent baby to her while the woman on the roof, dressed in nothing but a negligée, had talked.

Had to be something peculiar going on here. Mighty peculiar.

Grace glimpsed the roof of the house above the bushes. It was empty now. Whoever the occupant was had gone down into the main body of the house.

She rounded a bend in the drive, gravel crunching beneath her feet. Her heart was thumping: she was close to finding out exactly what was going on here. The urge to answer the mystery was more powerful than the urge to turn back and find Cody.

She needed closure on this. She had to know that the woman and baby would be safe.

But what if this was her home, and the home of her abuser? Grace might land herself in hot water. If she caught the woman's husband, boyfriend or whatever beating up on her what would the man do to Grace to keep her silent?

Heart pounding, she paused behind the last bush before open ground. There was the lawn in front of her. The house. It seemed to tower above her now. A forbidding structure.

More like a castle than a home.

A castle with ghosts. She shivered.

Do it, Grace. Solve the mystery. If you're satisfied the woman and baby are safe, leave. If not, call the cops.

She peeped over the bush.

Nothing was happening. There was the woman and baby. The woman's copper hair cascaded down her back to below her buttocks.

Those thin dark legs. So sticklike.

Like bones without flesh.

As Grace tried to decide whether to approach the woman or wait there came movement from the bottom story of the house.

A door opened. A large one. It could have led to a basement garage.

That was all.

No one appeared to welcome the woman. The door opened and that was that.

For a second the woman with copper hair stood still. She faced the dark opening where the door had been.

Maybe she's afraid to enter?

285

Wondering who's in there?

The pause didn't last long. The woman with copper hair moved forward to be swallowed by the doorway.

Now Grace was alone in the dark. And she was still none the wiser about what had happened to the woman with the baby in her arms.

What would become of them?

There was no movement, but something *was* happening. Grace heard a thin squeaking. A mechanism, maybe.

Metallic clanking. Not loud but definitely coming from the house. Then a rattle as if a shutter was being lowered.

But still the mystery.

What's happening to the woman and her baby?

Now Grace knew she couldn't turn and walk away.

She was involved now. That meant she must act decisively. A life might have to be saved.

Without hesitating, she ran lightly across the lawn, avoiding the noisy gravel. Her feet whispered on grass.

She was at the doorway.

Then she was inside.

Darkness. She could see nothing but the pale opening of the doorway behind her. Finding a wall, she followed it, running her fingers across its hardness, into the depths of the house.

Chapter Fifty-two

'What did Grace go into the spook house for?'

Cody glanced across at Pix. She stood there in the moonlight. Her arms were folded and a mystified expression creased her face.

'I don't know. She had to have had a reason, I guess.'

'Reason, huh? She's gone crazy, that's reason enough.'

'Come on,' he told her. 'We've got to get her out of there.'

'Somehow.' Her expression showed she didn't like this.

'We've got to do it, Pix. She might be in danger.'

'Yeah, that's what I was thinking.' She shook her head. 'I guess that means *we*'ll be in danger, too.'

'*Pix, come on.*'

'Better not be another guy who wants to put his dick in my mouth. That's really gonna send me over the edge this time.'

He gave her a reassuring smile and held out his hand. 'Don't worry, I'll look after you.'

She looked delighted that he'd offered her his hand. Taking it, she walked with him, keeping up with his brisk pace toward the house.

Spook house. The girl's words came back to him as he looked down on the lonesome place. Yeah, Pix might not be far from the mark at that.

Grace tripped on some object in the dark. Why hadn't the owner of the house turned on any damn lights?

She hit her knee on the floor. Bare concrete. *Ouch. That stuff's pretty unyielding.*

Keeping her lips pressed together she got to her feet. Now she kept her back to the wall as she moved on. This was smooth and slippery, almost a wood texture, but her fingertips felt a myriad of small holes, too.

Just what was this place? It seemed way too big for an underground garage. She heard clanks of metal on metal. The sound didn't echo back as she'd expect in a garage. It died instantly as if something had swallowed the echo.

287

This smooth material under her fingers, perhaps.

Even as she slid along it she felt the surface turn to fabric. It yielded slightly as if there were a layer of stuffing under it.

Smooth hard walls. Now walls that yielded under fabric to her touch. Who'd fix padding to the inside of their garage? She frowned. If only someone would switch on the lights.

This wasn't just weird.

It was frightening.

All she wanted was to see if the emaciated woman and her baby were safe. Now this had taken a whole more sinister turn.

She was in a strange underground room.

A bunker?

There was total darkness. Yet sounds of activity. Clanks, rattles, scraping sounds. The squeal of a mechanism in need of some lube. And the sounds were swallowed up somehow as soon as they were made.

Her hip knocked against an obstruction. Racks of some kind? Her hands reached out. Touched objects. Files? Books?

Grace realized the racks and the wall made a kind of gully. Quickly she slotted herself in. Crouched down. If the lights came on she might not be seen.

Not straightaway, anyway.

And suddenly it seemed safer to be out of sight.

Chapter Fifty-three

The deep masculine voice boomed out through the darkness. *'Lake . . . Lake. Move up to the platform. Present yourself. Do it quickly.'* A breathless panting filled the room. It sounded amplified. *'Obey, Lake. You will be punished if you do not hurry.'*

Grace hunkered down between the racks and the wall.

Holy Christ. What kind of place was this? What was that voice? *Whose* was that voice!

It thundered from every direction. She looked round. But could see nothing in that absolute dark.

And where were the woman and child?

Shit. She wanted out. Wanted out now. Before—

Before what?

Before something BAD happens.

She didn't even like the smell of this place. Disinfectant odors hung in the air. Those were mingled with something like the smell of stale herbs and onions. A musty unpleasant smell that worked its way into her nostrils. The kind of smell that made you want to go shower.

'Lake, onto the platform. Present yourself. Hurry!'

Who's Lake? That bass voice was commanding him to go to a certain place. *A platform?*

And to do what?

Present himself. That's what it sounded like. Present himself for what?

Grace scrunched herself down even further between the shelving and the wall.

Didn't want the lights on now.

Didn't want to be seen.

Because this was a bad place.

A mad place, too.

Something terrible happened here.

Right then she knew: Something terrible was going to happen again. Soon . . . real soon.

*   *   *

'*Lake . . . Lake, move up onto the platform. Present yourself. Do it quickly.*'

The moment Ed Lake heard the words he thought: *All right. Let's roll!*

Knowing that his captor – his Sex Queen – could see him through the nightscope goggles she must wear he moved across the cage in a hunched walk, feeling the sharpened stake beneath the leg of his pants. Its cold, hard shaft pressed against his bare thigh.

Here goes, buddy. No retreat now.

He squirmed onto the platform. He lay flat on his back, hearing it squeak as it began to raise him to the Perspex roof of the cage. Toward the hole that he'd slipped himself through so many times before.

He had to go through with this.

Even though it had been different tonight. He'd heard a lot of movement. Clanking sounds. Rattling. The squeal of a mechanism. A door to the outside had opened nearby. Even though it had been dark he'd fancied he'd caught sight of some dim radiance. He'd felt fresh air come blowing through the bars of his cage.

He'd heard Virginia catch her breath before whispering, 'They're bringing someone new in.'

'But they've never done it like this before?'

'No,' she'd confirmed. 'Must be someone special.'

Then there'd been the smell of onions and spices. A musty smell. Stale. Unpleasant.

'*Lake! Present yourself! Hurry . . . Hurry!*'

Okay, here goes nothing.

If it works . . . payback time!

If not, he'd be joining the late Marco and Cardinali before you could say 'RIP.'

He slipped the wooden stool leg from the waistband of his pants. Quickly, he pressed his thumb against the point.

Just checking.

Gotta make sure it goes in sharp end first. And, my God, it's sharp, all right. The barb, too. Wickedly sharp.

Please, Jesus, bless this weapon of vengeance.

For vengeance shall be mine, sayeth the Lord. Vengeance shall be mine.

Ed exulted.

I'm in!

*   *   *

290

April Vallsarra's body burned with exultation. Tonight she'd done it all by herself. She hadn't needed Lettie to help her.

Tell the world blindness isn't a handicap!

Tell the sighted they're not all-powerful!

Because I've done it. I've caught one all by myself.

Exultation melded with excitement. Excitement generated lust. White-hot lust that flamed and burned and seared.

Got to have release. Got to let it out!

As she fastened the belt that held the radio-mike transmitter around her slender waist she recapped the stages of her near-miraculous feat. First, she'd moved unerringly downstairs after telling her visitor to wait.

She'd switched off the lights in her father's basement studio, then moved swiftly down the steps with the confidence of a sighted person in brilliant daylight. There, she'd unlocked the padlocks that held the empty transfer cage in place. This she'd wheeled single-handed to the steel roller-door.

If you could have seen me, Lettie. The times we hauled that together. Today I did it by myself. I don't need you anymore.

I'm self-contained.

I need no one to nursemaid me.

After that it had been surprisingly easy. With the open-ended transfer cage close to the roller door she'd pressed the switch to open it. It had scrolled up.

In the darkness her visitor had unwittingly walked forward. Not knowing they were entering the cage.

Not realizing they were entering the trap. Then it had been simplicity itself. She'd pressed the quick-release lever. The cage door had clanged shut, trapping her visitor. By touch, using her bare feet, she'd located the loops on the floor and had quickly snapped the padlocks in place, locking the cage in position so its occupant couldn't tip it up and escape.

Then she'd returned to the roller-door controls and pressed the button. Seconds later, clanking, it had rolled back, into place, sealing the basement studio from the outside world.

Now she had a third prisoner.

She'd done it all by herself.

April wanted to laugh and to spin round and round with her arms out, reveling in the moment.

Relishing her victory over the world of sight.

Instead, she knew she had to keep silent until the microphone was in place. In a second she'd slipped on the headset. Now whenever

291

she spoke the radio mike would carry her voice to the electronic synthesizer that her father had once used to compose his music. Its circuits would transform her voice into one of those deep male movie-trailer voices.

Her captives would believe they were dealing with some thundering giant of a man. Not a slightly built blind girl.

Now she was so horny she could burst.

She would have loved to pleasure herself using her new guest but that would have to wait, until all the formalities had been gone through, when the new guest would be transferred to the third, static cage and conditioned to obey her orders.

No . . . it would have to be Lake tonight. She would make good use of his body.

She switched on the radio mike, issued the order: '*Lake . . . Lake, move up onto the platform . . .*'

She would enjoy his body tonight. She'd make good use of him, as she had before.

She thrilled at the recollection of his male hardness entering her. How she'd knelt on the cool Perspex and felt his hot erection jutting proud of the hole in the cage roof to work inside her. Exciting her. Making her shudder with pleasure, until she—

No, don't hurry.

Don't rush this.

Take your time.

Virginia and the new guest – the oh-so-silent one – would hear the sounds of love tonight. *Now isn't that an exciting concept? They hear. Only they do not see.*

Tantalizing, isn't it?

Teasing.

Might make them want to touch themselves.

And what of her new guest? April Vallsarra didn't even know its sex. Not that it mattered. Like many an adventurer before her she'd drunk deeply of many different springs.

By sense of touch alone she moved from the elevated walkway that ran around the basement studio and onto the Perspex roof of the cage. Her body throbbed with anticipation. She hungered for Lake's hard member to push deeply into her.

She felt the hole with its smooth edges in the Perspex. There would be Lake lying just below her now. He'd be anticipating, too. She knew he loved this now as much as she did. She'd felt his tremors of excitement through his cock as he entered her. And felt many times his passionate eruption that flooded her with his liquid warmth.

Oh yes . . . yessss. She couldn't bear to wait another minute.

Kneeling down on the cool roof of the cage, April reached down, clasped the hem of her negligée and raised it up to her hips.

When she spoke, her voice came back to her in a boom: '*Lake, present yourself.*'

She went down.

Ed Lake heard the command.

'*Lake, present yourself.*'

Above him a weight settled, slightly flexing the Perspex.

What if she reached down to touch his cock with her fingers first? Then she'd feel the wooden stool leg. She'd know what he planned. His heart hammered in his chest as he lay there, gripping the pointed shaft in his hand.

Because it was too long to push straight up and his own body was still partly in the way he'd have to push at an angle. He clenched his fists around the wooden shaft, ready to force every ounce of his strength into the upward thrust, through the hole in the Perspex and on into the most intimate part of her body.

'*Lake. Present yourself. That is in an order.*'

I hear and obey, oh mighty one!

He drove the point up through the hole. Thrust as hard as he could.

Then flinched at the sound of the deafening scream.

Chapter Fifty-four

Jesus H. Christ! What's that?

Grace smacked her palms to her ears. That screaming . . . hell, it sounded like sheet metal being torn in two.

Her eyes opened wide. But she could see nothing in this darkness. It was black as damnation down here. Not a glimmer of light.

And the place shook with screams.

Deep male ones.

Only they were weird.

There was no single direction to them. Like being in a cinema with surround-sound. The yells came from everywhere at once . . . they were distorted, too, with a kind of electronic overdrive that powered them to a nerve-stripping intensity.

Madhouse.

Freaking madhouse.

Now Grace really did want out.

Had a burning need to bug out of the house. A burning need to run outside and hide in the cool silence until her ears stopped ringing.

'*Aaaaa – hhh – gugh.*' Skull-cracking decibels. '*Lake . . . why? Why?! Uhhhgh!*'

Now Grace heard rushing sounds. The same you get when someone breathes into a microphone. Snapping and deep *umph* sounds, too. A mike being knocked.

Then came the sound of amplified weeping. Someone was in pain. In real pain that Grace couldn't even begin to imagine.

Another voice rang out in the darkness. 'You deserved that, you bitch!'

'*Lake. I loved you.*'

'Yeah, loved me enough to keep me in this stinking cage. Loved me enough to put me in fear for my life every single minute of the damn day . . . that's what I call tough love.'

A third voice; this one female. 'Ed. Can you reach her? Can you find a key?'

'I've got her hooked, Virginia. Got her damn well hooked. All I have to do is twist the shaft a little.'

'Lake, no. Please!'

'What's it like to be on the receiving end, huh?'

'Lake, pleee—'

Grace cringed as the voice rose into a scream.

The one called Lake must have twisted the shaft and caused hurt. Whatever that involved.

'Uu . . . ugh!'

'You took us for a pair of saps,' Lake said. He sounded triumphant. 'We know that you're a woman. We know that you altered your voice with some gizmo.'

Grace had to get away from the madhouse. She started crawling along the floor on her hands and knees.

'Lake, please! I'm hurt real bad . . .'

The female voice pitched in. 'And serves you right. Suffer, you bitch!'

Grace wanted to curl into a ball until the screaming stopped. Only by now she thought it never would.

Gotta get out . . .

Gotta get away . . .

Must be a door somewhere near.

She felt along the wall, fingers hunting for an exit . . . a door . . . even a window . . .

What's that?

Her fingers found something.

Hard. Oblong. Fixed to the wall. Size of a peppermint. Her mind swum dizzily.

It's a . . .

. . . Light switch . . .

Not being able to see in the darkness, Ed Lake could still feel.

He lay on his back on the platform and hung on to the harpoon he'd made from the stool leg.

Fish wriggled.

Fish squirmed.

But let go?

Never!

No, sirree.

He'd caught her. He'd felt the point of the stake punch through skin deep into flesh. In his mind's eye he saw how it was. He was lying flat on the platform, she was directly above him, just inches away on the other side of the Perspex roof panel. The two people were connected by the stake passing through the hole into her— Well . . . go figure.

What made it difficult now was the blood. It ran hot down the wooden shaft.

Blood's slippery stuff, Ed thought, surprised. It made it hard to grip onto the shaft. What was more, his Sex Queen was writhing and screaming. One hard tug and she could pull the slippery thing from his hands.

Then what?

She'd order her accomplice to slit his and Virginia's throats.

Or maybe she'd just abandon them there. Leave the two of them to die of thirst in the dark.

And where was the accomplice?

Maybe she'd panicked when she saw the Sex Queen suddenly convulse in agony.

Ed Lake knew he must hang on to this bloody pole, slippery as it was. Sex Queen could have the keys to the cage. They could bargain. Her life for their freedom.

'Hang on in there, Ed!' That was Virginia shouting encouragement. 'And while you're at it, hurt the bitch!'

Even in darkness, Amara saw.

Amara waited . . .

April Vallsarra writhed in agony. The pain was overwhelming. She could hardly form two words in a row before the sheer *hurt* overwhelmed her thought process. Then she howled in pain.

At first the synthesizer returned her screams to her in a deep bass roar.

Then the microphone headset was thrown clear of her by the convulsions. Instantly, her cries of pain became a high shriek.

But down through the blazing red inferno that was her agony one word roared through her head.

Revenge.

Damned if you do, damned if you don't.

Grace wrestled with the problem. If she switched on the lights she'd be able to see. But then the people doing the shouting and the terrifying screaming would be able to see *her*.

Then maybe it would be the turn for one Grace Bucklan to do all the screaming.

Shit to that, she thought.

But if I switch on the lights, then run for the door, maybe they'll never catch me? Besides, they sound to be too busy doing stuff, freaky stuff, to one another. Just listen to that woman howl. Sounds as if she's making out with a branding iron.

And if I stay hiding in the dark here they're going to find me sooner or later.

What about the woman and her baby?

Uh . . . solve that one when you get to it.

Still keeping her finger on the light switch, she levered herself to her feet. When that light came on she wanted to be running hard.

Away from this madhouse. Back to Cody.

She took a deep breath. *Here goes.*

Grace flicked the light switch.

Still lying on the platform, still gripping the slippery shaft, still praying for a miracle, Ed Lake blinked in surprise as the light came on.

He looked at his hands.

Somehow he was wearing crimson gloves.

Ugh . . . only they weren't gloves.

Contorted with agony, April Vallsarra gulped down lungfuls of air, trying to suppress the pain.

Blind, she didn't see the light.

Grace raised her hands to shield her eyes. The strip lights were dazzling.

She'd meant to run.

Run like lubed lightning for the door.

But she didn't.

Couldn't.

What she saw fixed her rigidly to that square yard of concrete.

She looked at the scene that could have come from a carnival for the damned. In the harsh light were four cages. Three were the size of pickup trucks. One was a smaller wheeled cage.

But Grace's gaze was drawn to the cage nearest her.

Now that was weird.

That was a tableau as bizarre as it was terrible.

A young guy dressed in pants, shirt and with no shoes lay on a platform just below the underside of the cage roof. On the cage roof knelt a beautiful woman dressed in nothing but a flimsy negligée – the same woman Grace had seen on the roof of the house.

She was kneeling with her face down, almost touching the roof that was made out of glass. She was writhing, her two hands gripping a dark stick that protruded from the guy's hands below into her throat.

A splash of ice shivers crashed over Grace's body.

Dear God . . .

She saw what was happening now.

The guy had stabbed the woman in the neck with some kind of spike. The woman couldn't drag herself off the point. She was caught. Bleeding profusely.

Blood ran down the spike, over the guy's hands, dripped down onto the cage floor.

Gross-out . . . she must have been in agony.

Must be dying, too.

Holy shit!

Ed Lake stared up at what he'd done.

Now, in that brilliant electric light, he could see the damage. And what exactly had been damaged.

It wasn't as he'd thought.

She hadn't sat on the hole this time to receive his cock into her. No. Instead, she'd been going down on him when he'd stabbed upward in the dark with his homemade harpoon. The point had gone into her throat just below her jaw.

Gone in deep enough for the barb to hook.

She was going nowhere now.

No escape.

But, Jesus, look at all that blood.

The red stuff gushed from her.

Wet his hands, slicked his chest, pooled on the raised platform. For the first time he got a good close look at his Sex Queen as she knelt above him on the Perspex. He was looking through a rose-tinted smear of blood on the transparent material. But he saw enough.

She was around thirty. Shoulder-length dark hair. Slim. Wore a negligée. Its transparency permitted him a glimpse of curved orbs of breasts tipped by dark nipples . . .

But no nightscope goggles?

'Ed . . . Ed . . .' Virginia called to him. 'Ed. She can't see you . . . she's blind!'

298

Blind?

Holy moly. So that's *how she moved through the darkness.*

The Sex Queen was weakening. The microphone headset that piped her voice through the synthesizer had slipped off to lie on the glass roof of the cage. She still cried out but the noise was softening to a moan.

So when the next scream came Ed was startled by its power.

It also came from another part of the room.

Virginia?

No.

Not from her.

Still holding on to the wooden shaft, he twisted his head. There, outside the cage, was a girl in her late teens.

Who the hell was she?

But there was no time to worry about identities. The girl screamed again. The scream was pure terror. She was pointing, too.

But not at the skewered blind woman.

At something else entirely.

Chapter Fifty-five

Just when it seemed as if it couldn't get any worse, it did just that.

Grace had watched the guy holding the blind woman down in a kneeling position. The spike he held driven deep into the woman's throat. Harpooned.

Sickened by the scene, Grace wrenched her gaze from it.

Only to see something else.

Something far worse.

For a second she'd stared uncomprehending at the figure in the smaller cage, the one nearest the steel roller-door. It was the woman she'd followed through the woods.

Now she stood there in the center of the cage. A dark emaciated body. Long copper hair.

She stood almost casually, as if her surroundings didn't faze her.

Then Grace realized why.

She's dead.

Grace stared at the corpse standing there, motionless. Her gaze swept over the cadaver. It was naked. Ancient-looking. Its breasts had shriveled. Round the neck the flesh was wrinkled, then further down the chest it became smooth. For some reason it reminded Grace of melon skin.

A melon-skin torso; a beef-jerky neck? *Gross.*

Then, framed by beautiful copper hair that glinted in the light, was the most hideous face . . .

Little more than a skull, its lips had shrunk to expose the teeth. There were no eyes in the head. Where they should have been were empty sockets that plunged twin pits of darkness deep into the head. Across the corpse's stomach was a long gash that had been crudely stitched.

Grace's own skin suddenly felt as if it wanted to crawl off her back. Her stomach heaved. Her knees went weak.

Hanging from one claw hand was a dead baby. Held by one leg, it swung gently. Apart from that motion the figure didn't move.

Grace had seen things like this in museums. In history books. On TV.

She was looking at a mummy.

An ancient Egyptian mummy that had been stripped of its bandages.

But why the baby?

Why here?

Why now?

In this madhouse.

She realized the guy lying on the platform and the girl in the adjoining cage were staring at the mummy too. Trying to work out in their heads what was happening.

They seemed to guess. Both wore expressions of disgust mingled with horror.

I wanna go now.

I wanna run from this place. Never look back.

This is a place that should be burned to the ground and the earth sown with salt. That's what you do with haunted houses, isn't it? That's the Biblical way to deal with evil places.

Silence settled onto the big room.

All Grace could hear were soft moans from the wounded woman on top of the cage who'd grown feeble now from the blood loss.

It was the thing in the third cage that had gotten everyone's attention.

It was during this pregnant silence that *it* moved.

The mummy slowly raised its face, as if those eyeless sockets could gaze up at the lights in the ceiling.

Slowly the head lowered. Rotated left. Rotated right.

Looking at its surroundings.

It uncurled its fingers. The baby fell with a thud to the concrete floor.

In no hurry, it moved.

Dear God. The mummy *walked.*

It crossed the cage, long tresses curling down its back, bouncing softly as if they moved with a life of their own. It stopped. Reached out slowly. Fingertips brushed the bars of the cage. The mouth parted slightly as if it said something to itself.

Grace moved with her back pressed to the wall. She'd get past the caged mummy, then race for the roller-door. She'd heard it clank as it rolled down. She knew she could find the control that opened it.

Then she'd be away from here.

She wouldn't stop running until—

301

'Please help us.'

Grace's head jerked back. The girl in the second cage was speaking to her.

'We've been held here . . . we've been prisoners. Find a key to unlock the cages.'

The man nodded furiously. 'Please help. We're dead if we don't get out of here.'

'But . . .' Grace pointed at the mummy that was running a claw finger down the bar of the cage.

'Don't worry about that.' The woman talked quickly. 'It's in a cage – it can't hurt you.'

'But it's dead . . . *it's dead.*'

Only she saw the dead thing move. Saw the copper hair hanging lustrously down from the skull and on down its back. She saw dead, hard flesh that was beef-jerky brown.

Saw holes in the torso.

Bullet holes?

'Please help us!' The guy let go of the spike. Bloodstained, he slithered from where he'd been sandwiched between the platform and the glass roof of the cage and let himself down to the concrete floor. The blind woman flopped down onto the cage roof. Lay still.

The guy reached out a bloody hand through the bars of the cages toward Grace. She looked in horror at the slick fingers, the drips of crimson forming on his fingertips.

'Help us.' His eyes were huge in his head. 'Help us . . . Hey! Where are you going? Don't leave us here. *Please don't leave us . . .*'

Chapter Fifty-six

Grace ran past the cages. She gave the one containing the mummy as wide a berth as possible.

The bloodstained man shouted, 'Where are you going? You can't leave us here . . . we're dead if you go.'

'Come back,' called the woman in the second cage. 'Please!'

Grace ran to a shelf on which stood a metal box. 'I'm not leaving,' she panted. 'I'm looking for tools. I'll need something to break open the cages.'

The woman in the second cage reached through the bars to grip one of the pair of padlocks that sealed the doors. 'These are tungsten. You'd need dynamite to smash them. See if you can find a key.'

'A key? Where?'

The guy pitched in. 'There's gotta be keys somewhere nearby. Look for them.'

'But they could be anywhere in the house.' Grace shrugged. 'It'd be like looking for a needle in a—'

The woman jerked her head at the mummy. 'The padlocks on that one were unlocked sometime in the last half-hour . . . the keys must be close by.'

Grace ran round the room, looking at the walls for a hook. Those elusive keys might be dangling nearby. Or were they slipped into a drawer in the desk that was just around the corner? Did the harpooned woman still have them?

Unlikely. *Sure as hell don't have pockets in a flimsy negligée.*

Even so, Grace craned her head to look at the blind woman. She wasn't moving. Her lips had turned blue and her whole body was a glistening mass of blood.

She turned again, searching through shelves. Dozens of shelves. In seconds she was dizzy with the exertion. Blundering past the cage that held the guy she decided to start her search again at the entrance to this chamber of horrors.

The guy gripped the bars of the cage, shouting encouragement.

Breathless, her head spinning, Grace ran down the other side of the cages, thinking only about the key that must be some-where nearby.

Then something appeared to block her path.

She stopped, blinked. Then screamed.

It was a thin, dark arm.

Hell and damnation!

The mummy had lunged out at her. She'd been focused on finding the key; she'd almost forgotten the monstrosity in the cage. Only now it had suddenly got mobile. Its fingers slashed through the air, reaching out, flexing, trying to grasp her.

Grace screamed again, stumbled back as the fingers swiped down, catching the material of her T-shirt. She looked down – the thing's sharp nails had slashed four vents in the cotton. She glimpsed her own skin.

And, God, that hurts. The monster has scratched me.

Don't let it come close again. Don't!

As the mummy lashed out at her once more, Grace flung herself back against the wall.

'Keep your distance from it,' called the woman in the second cage. 'It can't reach you if you keep away from it.'

Damn right.

I'm not going near that thing again.

Grace stumbled to the far end of the room, her heart thumping hard in her chest. Dazed, she found herself hitting the steel roller-door. The crash reverberated in her head. Taking a deep breath, she looked for what must be there.

And there it is.

Come to momma.

Set in an oblong panel beside the door were buttons marked *Up* and *Down*. With her balled fist she pounded *Up*. Immediately she heard the hum of an electric motor. With a rattling sound the roller-door began to scroll upward. But it was slow . . . too slow.

She willed it to move faster.

Inch by inch it rose.

But at last moonlight spilled between the bottom slat of the door and the concrete floor. A cool breeze stroked her ankles.

I could leave, she told herself in surprise. *I don't have to help these people. I don't have to stay in this place with the dead creature with copper hair and its dead baby. I could slip through the gap between the door and floor now. Then I could run.*

I could leave this chamber of horrors. Never look back.

But . . .

Conscience. She knew she'd have the fates of the two people lying heavily on her for the rest of her life if she ran out now.

Had to help.

Had to.

She backed away from the door, her gaze searching the wall as she did so.

Got 'em!

There by the door was something like a coat hook. Hanging from it was a large steel ring that held a dozen or more keys.

She glanced back at the guy and the girl in the cages. They weren't saying anything. But they were staring hard at her. Perhaps fearing that she would simply run out through the now-open doorway and into the night, never to be seen again.

Instead, she grabbed the key ring.

This time she moved past the mummy's cage with caution, walking with her back to the wall and facing the emaciated creature behind the bars.

Uh, but now that's bad . . . that's really bad.

As Grace walked the mummy rotated its head. It had no eyes, but Grace knew the thing was tracking her. Watching.

In case she got too close again. Got within striking distance of those raking fingernails. The mummy's upper lip curled back. The thing was snarling at her.

'Virginia,' the guy cried, 'she's got the keys.'

'Great,' the one he'd called Virginia breathed. 'But get us out of here real quick, huh? Something tells me time might be running out.'

Grace advanced on the guy's cage. He gave her a winning smile. 'Thank you. You are an angel.' He moved to the cage door as if ready to run the moment she released the padlocks. 'My name's Ed, by the way. My roomie's called Virginia . . . oh, thank you, thank you . . .'

He beamed with such gratitude that Grace felt herself blushing.

'My name's Grace,' she said, studying the keys. 'It looks as if you've got yourself into a situation here?'

'A situation and a half . . .' He nodded at the key ring. 'It's probably one of the smaller ones. Something like a Yale.'

'Make it quick,' Virginia pulled the blanket round her, looking suddenly cold. 'I don't think our new neighbor's gonna be patient for long.'

But which key?

Now that she had them in her hands there looked to be nearer

305

two dozen. The key for the padlocks might not even be in this bunch.

'Try one at random,' Ed suggested. He flashed her a grin. 'Process of elimination.'

Grace tried one with a green fob.

'No go,' she said. 'Doesn't even go in.'

'Okay, go to the next.'

Her hands were shaking. She'd grip a key. Then the thing would slip from her fingers, clinking around the ring.

Got a grip, then tried it in the lock.

'It goes in. But I can't turn it.'

'Must be getting close,' Ed encouraged.

'Hurry it up, guys.' Virginia sounded worried. 'The new girl's making a move.'

Grace started back.

'Don't worry,' Ed told her. 'Whatever the damn thing is it's staying put. It can't bust out of the cage. It's—'

Clang!

The noise was terrific. The sound of a hard object slamming into metal.

All three whirled round. The mummy had moved across its cage. With the flat of its hand it struck the cage door as if to knock it open. The whole cage shook with each blow.

'Don't worry,' Ed shouted. 'It'll hold . . . it'll hold.'

Grace saw him turn back to her. Fix her with his stare. In a calm voice he said. 'Just work through the keys, Grace. It'll be there, trust me.'

Her hands shook so much that when she tried the next key the entire bunch slipped from her perspiring fingers to the floor.

Take your time, she told herself. *Concentrate. Don't panic. You can do this. You can really do this.*

She selected a key with a yellow plastic grip.

Now, nice and easy does it. Slip the key into the padlock.

'This is it!' The words burst from her lips. The key turned easily.

She pulled open the padlock hasp and slipped it from the steel loops that secured the cage door.

'Well done,' Ed told her. 'One down, one to go.' He smiled. 'Knew you could do it, Grace.'

Grace smiled, encouraged. 'Piece of cake.'

Then she did the wrong thing.

She glanced across at the mummy. Her insides turned to water as

306

she watched the creature extend one of its beef-jerky paws through the cage bars. Then, without any hurry, without any fuss the fingers crept around one of the pair of padlocks.

The hand tightened into a balled fist around the tungsten padlock. For a second the hand quivered as the monster applied pressure, then—

Crack!

The padlock snapped like it was made from pastry.

Slowly the creature uncurled its fingers, allowing the destroyed padlock to fall to the concrete floor.

Then it paused.

Grace looked into the twin pits of darkness in the thing's face. And she knew.

That monster's watching me. It's thinking, 'I'm coming for you now . . . I'm going to finish what I started . . .' Grace felt the tingle on the skin of her stomach where the monster had slashed her with its razor nails. *Gonna be more of the same soon. Slashing, scratching, ripping.*

'Grace,' Ed spoke firmly. 'Snap out of it.'

'Uh?'

'You've got to unlock the padlocks.'

As if awakening from a dream she shook her head. Then she selected another key. Tried it.

'Not the right one,' she said.

'You can do this, Grace. We trust you.'

She tried another.

And another.

No luck . . . no goddamn luck.

Her heart began to hammer again. Her breathing quickened.

Beads of perspiration slid down the small of her back.

Next up. A key with a white plastic grip.

She tried it.

Then stood there, blinking. Not believing what had happened.

'Way to go, girl!' Ed was jubilant. 'You've done it.'

He reached through the bars, worked out the hasp, then flung the padlock to one side. He pushed open the cage door. Free at last.

He breathed deeply as if the air outside the cage was so much sweeter.

'Hey, guys . . .' Virginia sounded nervous. 'You won't forget me, will you?'

Grace turned to see the mummy reach through the cage door again. It snapped off the second – and final – padlock that kept it prisoner.

307

Slowly it pushed open the door.

'What the hell's going on here?'

Grace turned sharply when she heard the familiar voice.

'Pix?'

'What's with the cages?'

'Pix, get out of here . . . run!'

Grace waved her sister back as she walked through the doorway. She saw Cody at the girl's side.

'Both of you . . . run! Get away from here!'

Cody started to walk toward her. 'What's the matter, Grace? What's going on here; you—'

Then the thing leaped. Its copper hair flared out behind it as if the monster had somehow caught fire.

Then it was on Cody. Pix screamed.

Grace ran to help. Horror-struck, she saw the thing knock him flat to the ground. Then it was crouching on his chest, its bare, shriveled rump pressing on his stomach as it gnawed at him.

'Leave him . . . let go!' Grace shouted at the creature.

For all the good *that* did.

Grace saw its teeth gnawing.

Cody screamed. His arms flew out to either side, spasming.

Then came a fountain of blood from his throat.

His body convulsed, twitched, then lay still. Eyes staring at the ceiling.

'Cody!' Pix screamed. She hurled herself onto the mummy, punching, clawing.

The creature sprang to its feet, turning as it did so. The savage movement threw Pix clear across the concrete floor. Dazed, she went sprawling.

'Bitch! Murdering bitch!' Grace yelled.

'Grace,' Virginia warned. 'Don't go near it! Keep away!'

Ed moved so the cage was between him and the mummy. 'Grace, come this way round . . . don't let it spring at you.'

'I've got to help my sister.'

By this time, Pix had managed to sit up. She looked groggy from the blow.

'Hey, don't forget *me*, guys,' Virginia pleaded.

Grace remembered the keys in her hand. She threw them through the bars of the cage. Virginia picked them up.

Ed jerked his head toward the mummy. 'I wouldn't be in a hurry to get out just yet, Virginia.'

'Don't worry . . . I'm going to bide my time.'

308

Grace cast a despairing look at Cody. He lay in a growing pool of blood.

He was my first love . . . he was the first man I'd slept with . . . now this . . .

Pix groaned. 'Oh, my head hurts.'

The mummy turned. It must have noticed Pix move.

In a weird way . . . almost gliding . . . it crossed the concrete toward her. Even as it moved it altered its posture. Tipping its top half-forward, hand coming up . . . this was attack mode . . . it was going in for the next kill.

'Pix! Run!'

'Run? Can't even stand . . . my head.'

With a yell Ed charged. Intercepting the mummy, he grabbed it by the waist, lifted it from the floor with it facing him.

Grace watched in disbelief. It looked almost as if he was dancing with the creature. The mummy opened its mouth . . . its teeth dripped crimson. Then it plunged its head downward so fast that its copper hair rippled in the air behind it.

In a few gnawing bites, it had torn most of Ed's face off.

But even with nothing remaining of his visage but a bloody mass, he still moved with the mummy. Waltzing it across the floor toward a cage with an open door.

Grace saw Virginia move fast. With lightning dexterity, she worked through the keys on the ring. In ten seconds she had both padlocks open.

Then the cage door crashed open.

Not stopping to look back, she ran.

Grace glimpsed her face, wild with terror, looming close to her own. Then she was gone through the doorway and out into the night.

'Help me, Grace . . . my legs don't feel right.'

But Grace had to see what happened to Ed. He'd sacrificed himself to save them.

Ed had managed to carry the mummy as far as the cage but didn't have the strength to push it in. He pressed it as hard as he could against the bars. They could have been a pair of lovers necking against a wall. He pressed the creature back hard. The thing held Ed's head in both its hands while pushing its face against what was left of his in a grotesque parody of kissing.

But this was gnawing not smooching. Teeth ripped. Crushed. Tore.

309

Grace heard the ripping of muscles and the cracking of facial bone.

Blood pattered down to the concrete, pooling in a slick mass that reflected the lights above.

Then Ed's legs lost their strength. A moment later his arms dropped by his side.

Still gnawing at his face, the mummy didn't let him go as he slowly folded down to the floor.

'Come on!' Grace pulled Pix to her feet. Then, gripping her hand so hard that the girl cried out in pain, she dragged her outside.

Then she ran.

She didn't stop running until they were both back at the pickup.

When she started the motor Pix managed to rouse herself groggily. 'Where now . . .'

'Home,' Grace panted. 'We're damn well going home.'

Chapter Fifty-seven

While Tag drove, Susan sat beside him. Geoffrey lay snug and asleep in his baby seat in the back of the car. The journal rested lightly on her lap. Susan skimmed it by flashlight, looking for the first mention of Amara.

She was halfway through the journal before she noticed the words 'sarcophagus' and 'mummiform'.

'Here we go,' she said, and began to read. '". . .The mummy beneath him. A portion of its head was visible. I saw its red hair, its eyeless sockets; I had the impression, for a moment, that it was kissing the dead man's neck."'

'Charming,' Tag said.

'"I raised the man's head. The mummy's head also lifted and I realized its teeth were buried in the throat."'

'Same m.o.,' Tag commented.

Susan read silently for a while. '"The bride of Set,"' she said finally. And then: '"She will arise from the dead to seek after the blood of her slayers."' She read more in silence. 'Callahan wants to take her out of the tomb.'

'That was his first mistake.'

'"You have broken the seal of Osiris guarding the doorway. Its magic is destroyed. Without it, Amara will walk the night." The seal. Remember the gold disks on the coffin? Same idea. We had written instructions left by Callahan. They said that on no account should we tamper with them, but they were already broken when the coffin was delivered. Without the seals, she walks the night.'

'Pretty damned hard to swallow, Susan.'

'Your own police officers claim she killed these people.'

'I just can't believe that someone who's been dead for almost four thousand years – or for four seconds, come to that – can be walking around murdering everyone in sight. I mean, can you?'

'I don't know.'

Tag flicked his turn signal. Its quiet clicking was the only sound in the car as he steered up a long, curving off-ramp.

311

'On the other hand,' he said. 'Damn. On the other hand, there wasn't any evidence at all of any human presence. And plenty to support the idea that Gonzalez and Beckerman were attacked by the goddamn mummy. Gonzalez obviously shot it. His fingernail scrapings . . . I mean, there are certainly a few ways to explain all that. We've been through them. But everything falls neatly into place if you accept the mummy as perpetrator.'

'Callahan's death, too.'

Tag nodded. 'The business about the dogs always did sound suspicious. Where was the .22 he used to shoot them? I think the Burlingdale boys just jumped to the obvious conclusion, and didn't worry about the discrepancies when they closed the case.'

'But Callahan *knew* about Amara.'

'Maybe he didn't know the seals were broken. Or maybe he broke them himself for some reason.'

'A form of suicide?'

'Could be. He was old, his health failing, his wife recently killed. Maybe he just wanted to end it all.' Tag shrugged. 'Or maybe he had a different reason for breaking the seals. Could've done it, I suppose, to stick Amara on the robbers.'

'That could be it. Something sure made them leave in a hurry – and empty-handed.'

She shone the flashlight onto the journal and flipped through a few more pages. Then the car turned a corner. Spinning red and blue lights flashed on her face, and she saw four police cars on the road ahead. They were double-parked, blocking half the street. A coroner's van sat in the driveway of a house on the left, its rear doors open. Another van, this one marked *Eyewitness News*, blocked a driveway across the street.

Susan saw people everywhere: in clusters on the sidewalk; a couple strolling directly in front of the house, glancing toward it as if only casually interested; others peering out of windows and doorways of nearby houses.

At this time of night, she told herself. It was the early hours of the morning but the lure of a crime story had drawn enough people out of their houses to fill the sidewalks like it was the middle of the afternoon.

On a lawn, somebody was being interviewed by a TV newsman. The camera lights lit the scene vividly.

'Looks like Vasquez,' Tag said. He drove slowly past the patrol cars and parked.

They climbed from the car. Geoffrey stirred in Susan's arms as she eased him from his baby seat. The lights flashed against his shut eyes. She pulled the comforter so it hung over his face.

They were halfway up the driveway when a voice called, 'Miss Connors! Susan Connors!'

'Oh damn,' she muttered.

Tag grinned. 'You're already a celebrity.'

A short, curly-haired man hurried toward her, followed by a man with a minicam on his shoulder, another with a glaring light.

'Lenny Farrel, *Eyewitness News*.'

'Yes, I remember.'

'Miss Connors, are tonight's killings related to the recent disappearance of the mummy from the Charles Ward Museum?'

'There appears to be a connection. That's why I'm here.'

'Did the police request your presence?'

'Yes.'

'What would be the nature of the connection?'

'No comment.'

'We've heard speculation that tonight's killings were committed by someone resembling the missing mummy, Amara. Do you give credence to such speculation?'

'Do you?'

'According to a reliable source, a patrolman reported over the air from his radio car that he confronted a suspect near the crime scene and that said suspect conformed to descriptions of the mummy.'

'I wouldn't know about that. Now, if you'll excuse me.'

'Before you go, Miss Connors, would you care to elaborate on your role with—'

'Excuse us,' Tag said, stepping between the newsman and Susan. With an arm around her shoulders, he led her away.

They entered the house. Vasquez followed them inside and shut the door. Susan glimpsed several men near a woman's body. She looked away.

'What'd you tell that s.o.b.?' Vasquez asked.

'Nothing. He seemed to know plenty, though.'

'Kraus spilled his guts over the radio. Every bastard in town with a police scanner thinks we've got a homicidal mummy on the loose. The mayor's gonna go crazy.'

'What do you think?' Susan asked.

'I think we'd better get our hands on a suspect fast and it better not be a goddamn zombie.' He looked around. 'Kraus, haul it over here.'

A thin, gray-faced policeman hoisted himself from a sofa. He came across the room, squinting through the smoke of a cigarette pinched between his lips. As he reached the group, he took the cigarette from his mouth. 'Yessir.'

'Kraus, this is Susan Connors from the museum. You want to tell her what you saw?'

'I don't know what I saw.'

Vasquez's eyes narrowed. 'Give it your best shot.'

Kraus dragged on his cigarette. 'I think it was the mummy.'

'We'll be the judge of that,' Vasquez said. 'Describe it.'

'Well . . .' He sighed, blowing smoke out his nose. The skin round his eyes was red, sore-looking. 'I pursued the suspect into the alley. I'd say it was a female, five foot four, red-haired. Long, right down her back. Reached her legs. Very thin, like a . . . like a pile of bones.' His shaking hand poked the cigarette back between his lips. He stared at the bundle in Susan's arms. His right cheek began to twitch.

'Tell her about the eyes.'

'Didn't have any. Just . . . empty sockets. I saw right into her head. Like the head was empty . . . just a shell, you know?'

'What else?'

'Well, there were these holes. In her chest and back. But no blood or anything. They looked like bullet holes. Some of them did. She looked as if she'd been stitched up across here.' He ran his finger across his belly. 'Clumsy-looking job of it someone'd done, too.'

'What was she wearing?'

'Nothing.'

'Nothing at all?'

'She was naked.'

'What else?'

Kraus shrugged. His stare was still fixed on Geoffrey. 'Is . . . is that a baby you've got there?'

Susan nodded.

'Christ, that isn't . . . Not the one *she* had?'

Susan frowned, confused.

'The suspect was carrying a baby,' Vasquez explained. 'The McLeash child. We had three fatalities at their place. Baby-sitter, her boyfriend, and a kid. The baby's missing. Apparently, our suspect grabbed her.'

'Killed her,' Kraus said.

Susan felt sick. She took deep breaths, trying to control her sudden dizziness and nausea.

314

'Okay, Kraus. Tell her what happened after you confronted the suspect.'

He tapped a length of ash into his open palm. The palm was shiny with sweat. 'Well . . . it ran up the alley. South. With the dead baby. Brown went in pursuit, and I returned to the car to call for backup.'

'And made a fine botch of it.'

'Yessir,' he said. The ash turned muddy in his wet hand.

'Where's this Brown?' Susan asked.

'Someone knocked him cold. Probably the perp. The doc says we won't be able to talk to him until the morning.'

'And there's no sign of the mummy now?'

'We've given the alley a search. Our men came up with zip. Right now my men are combing the field by the museum. The alley led right to it. Maybe they'll come up with something.'

Chapter Fifty-eight

Amara held the baby by one arm, dangling it at her side, its feet swinging so close to the ground that they caught the dirt every now and again, raising a puff of dust. Moonlight cascaded down.

Once Amara stopped in one of the silver beams to gaze up at the moon. Her shining hair fell back from her head, cascading down her back. Her eyeless sockets admitted the lunar radiance to her empty skull. Her lips peeled back from the teeth in a silent snarl.

A wild dog howled somewhere in the distance.

Amara stayed, allowing the moonlight to bathe her face. Then she walked on.

After a little while the canyon ended. It opened out into fields. Beyond the fields lights burned in streets. She walked faster; sometimes during her progress through the undergrowth, bushes tugged at the baby. Each time, she kept walking. The baby pulled free.

She joined a trackway that ran through the fields.

She wasn't far away now. She could sense it.

Felt its pull.

Amara walked faster.

Soon.

Chapter Fifty-nine

'Momma's gonna kill me,' Mable said from the back seat. They were her first words in nearly fifteen minutes.

'She doesn't have to know,' Imad told her.

'She's gonna know. That was her best knife. She's gonna kill me.'

'I'll buy her a new one.'

'Ain't the same.'

'A knife is a knife.'

'This knife ain't.'

'Oh?'

'John Wayne gave it her.'

Imad glanced at her in the rearview mirror. 'John Wayne? Really?'

'Back in 1958. She won it as a prize and John Wayne presented it.'

'That's what she told you?'

'Sure – don't you believe it?'

'It's not for me to believe or disbelieve.'

'So she's gonna kill me. It was a genuine Bowie knife like cowboys use.'

'Mable, whatever kind of knife it was, I was not about to let you bring it along.'

'Think I'd stab you?'

'It did, indeed, cross my mind.'

'You're my friend, Imad.'

'Well, thank you.'

'Even if you do call me names and say I stink and won't let me sit in front with you *and* hit me.'

'I'm sorry about that.'

'I don't call you names.'

'I'm aware of that.'

'Or say you stink.'

'I do not stink. I've always been particularly fastidious about personal hygiene. I expect others to be equally fastidious.'

'Huh?'

'I'll teach you, Mable.'

For a few moments there was silence. Imad took his foot off the gas, slowing as they approached the gate. The car's lights shone against the tall ironwork.

'Imad?'

'Yes.'

'How come you're being nice to me?'

'So you'll allow me . . . now, how do you put it? Allow me to prong you.'

She snorted. 'That ain't the reason. How come? Nobody's ever nice to me. How come you are?'

He shrugged. 'To atone for my sins, perhaps.'

'You're a sinner?'

'Indeed I am?'

'You a Catholic?'

'No.'

'Good thing. My momma, she's against 'em.' Mable leaned forward in the rear seat. 'You won't be Jewish, then?'

'No, I am not.'

'Mohammedan?'

'No.'

'Must be something, Imad.'

'My mother's family formed part of Egypt's Coptic Christian community.'

'Coptic Christian?'

'That's right.'

'Good,' she said, satisfied. 'Momma never said nuthin' against Coptic Christians.'

'I'm pleased to hear that.'

Imad pressed the remote button. The gates swung open. He drove through and the gates swung silently shut behind them. Ahead, the house was brightly lit.

'What's that?' Mable asked.

'That, Mable, is home.'

'Whose home?'

'Mine.'

'No shit.'

'It most certainly is.'

'No, it's not.'

318

'It's not?'
'Is it?'
'It is.'
'Well, I'll just squat.'

Chapter Sixty

For more than an hour Grace Bucklan drove the pickup through the darkness. Its nose pointed east.

You shouldn't run from monsters, she told herself. *You should confront them.*

I'm going home. I'm taking my sister home. I'm going to kick Mom's boyfriend out the house. If Mom or the molesting skunk protest then they can just try explaining it all away to the cops.

Grace's head was in a whirl. Images of the last couple of hours fired through her brain like machine-gun bullets.

Pix sat beside her in a daze, eyes staring into space. She had a bump on her forehead where she'd collided with the concrete floor in the chamber of horrors. But she didn't seem badly hurt.

But maybe Grace wasn't thinking straight.

Maybe she should tell the cops about what had happened? About Ed and Cody. They'd been eaten alive back there. Now both of them were dead.

She might tell one day. She could even write the whole thing down in a book.

But not now.

Now all she wanted to do – longed to do – was to drive fast.

They were going home. Leaving the madness behind.

Grace heard Pix give a horrified gasp.

'What's wrong . . . Pix?'

Pix said nothing. Instead, she stared with horror at her hand as it lay open in her lap. Grace glanced down.

She saw strands of copper there, shining in the light from the dashboard.

It was hair from the creature's head. The hank of hair was close on three feet long. Pix must have yanked it from the mummy when she'd launched herself on its back as it attacked Cody.

Hell, there were even shreds of black matter at the ends of the hair where the godforsaken stuff had rooted into the scalp.

Grace wound the window down, snatched the copper hair from

320

Pix's hand and tossed it out. For a second it stayed with them, pulled by the slipstream of the truck.

It's following . . .

Grace floored the accelerator. In the mirror she glimpsed the hair writhing in the moonlight before slowly spinning down to lie on the road.

With the last trace of the thing gone from their lives, Grace eased off the gas. She glanced at Pix. Her sister sat with her eyes closed, a tear rolling down her cheek.

Grace's own eyes pricked. When she touched one with her knuckle it came away glistening wet.

There'd be a lot more tears ahead, she knew that for nothing. But they'd make it. They truly would.

Chapter Sixty-one

It had been a long walk back from the canyon to the edge of town where her destination lay. Amara walked on, untiring, indefatigable. The baby hung by one arm, its feet sometimes catching the grass with a whispery sound.

All the time the moon shone down, sending a silvery light through Amara's empty eye sockets. When she turned her head in that predatory way the copper hair swished in waves down her back.

Once a feral cat attracted by the smell of the baby padded up close behind her as she walked. It closed in, attracted by the faint odor of milk still clinging to the infant.

The cat slinked in closer, its eyes on the silhouette of the figure with the moon shining behind it.

The cat moved noiselessly, confident that its presence was undetected.

Closer, closer. Its nose almost brushed the head of the baby as it swung backwards and forwards.

The silhouette of the human moved quickly, yet with a smooth rhythmic walk. The cat's sensitive nostrils picked up strange scents from the human. It didn't have the same odors that it was accustomed to.

Its nose touched the head of the baby; it risked an appraising lick.

At that moment the figure turned on the cat, the hair flaring out; an explosion of blazing copper. The human head lunged at the cat, lips curling back, baring teeth that smelled of congealing blood.

The cat screeched. Turned. Bolted into the undergrowth.

Presently the mummy neared the brilliant lights of buildings. Before the track ended it turned and walked through a broken section of fence into an overgrown field. She walked smoothly, unhindered by the vegetation.

The field ended.

She walked across the asphalt of the deserted parking lot to the building.

Once there, she scraped at the museum's rear door. Her fingernails left score marks. She found the knob, as if by accident, and pulled. The door stayed shut.

In the distance dogs began to howl. Every animal in the neighborhood raised its snout to the moon. Soon the howling of dogs filled the air in eerie chorus.

Amara pulled at the door again. Then, staggering away from it, she wandered in circles. Now her movements were aimless. Weak.

She pushed her way into a thick border of geraniums. There she lay down on the dirt.

She hugged the baby to her breasts.

Chapter Sixty-two

Virginia returned to the basement where she'd been held all those weeks. Light burned brightly. The cages were empty now. She stood for a moment, breathing the scent of the place. That same smell was in her skin now. She'd smelled it as she'd walked from the house and into the canyon, trying to find her way back to the city.

For some reason she'd found herself sitting on a rocky bluff, gazing at the city lights for a long time. Then she'd turned round.

Returned to her place of torture.

Now she stood in the void of the basement. Two torn corpses lay on the floor. Streams of crimson congealed on concrete.

Without even thinking it through . . . without thinking *what* she was doing or *why* she was doing it she entered the cage that had once imprisoned her.

She sat down cross-legged on the foam mattress. She gazed up at the hairbrush, toothbrush and water bottles hanging from cords tied to the cage's roof crossbars. This was a horrible place. But somehow the outside – and freedom – seemed even more horrible. Here – inside – there were strict rules and order. Outside in the city there was lawlessness and disorder.

She closed her eyes. That was how she stayed until she heard a faint moan.

The woman looked dead. She ought to have been dead.

The stake was a bitch to remove as well. Ed Lake should have been proud of the barb he'd carved into the stool leg. It had worked a treat. The harpoon had gone in deep. It had lodged tight. Virginia had to work hard to loosen it from the woman's throat.

An inch either way and it would have gone either through the windpipe or through the major arteries. As it was, it had lodged in soft muscle tissue.

After a great deal of work the blind woman lay on the bed, her throat wadded and bandaged. A little blood had seeped into the white crepe.

Virginia watched the blind woman sleeping on the bed. Her breathing wasn't at all deep but at least it was regular. The woman's eyelids were black, her lips blue and her skin white as porcelain because of blood loss. But with rest, along with plenty of fluids, she'd make up the lost blood in a few days. The wound would heal.

Virginia walked round the house. She soon saw that the woman lived alone. The one she and Ed had referred to as 'The Warder' was nowhere to be seen. Maybe she just dropped in occasionally to help out.

Letters on a bureau soon gave Virginia her one-time captor's name: April Vallsarra.

Knowing the name was important to Virginia. She rolled it round her mouth, repeating it as she climbed the stairs back to the bedroom. 'April Vallsarra . . . April Vallsarra . . .'

When she reached April's bedroom she went to the woman's bed and sat down on it.

April was beautiful. Her complexion flawless.

Then some thoughts that were startling came to her.

Virginia had never experienced such an intense relationship before as the one with April Vallsara. What was more, Virginia realized she didn't care for her old home, or her day job.

'Hell, I might live to regret this,' she told herself as she gazed down at April. 'But I've reached a decision.'

Virginia leaned forward to kiss the sleeping woman on the lips and whispered, 'I'm staying with you.'

Chapter Sixty-three

The large brown dog named George pushed through the weeds to the edge of the parking lot. He stopped on the asphalt, and sniffed the air.

Then he trotted to the rear door of the museum. He sniffed the seam at its bottom, his tail swishing.

Backing off, he sat down. He stared at the door. He barked impatiently.

A sound in the bushes caught his attention. He cocked an ear toward it, still watching the door. When the sound came again, he got up to explore.

He walked along, nose to the asphalt, sides heaving as he sniffed. Sometimes a snorting sound escaped his mouth as the scent grew stronger.

Near the geranium border, he began to growl. A thick strip of fur bristled upright on the nape of his neck. The growl rumbling deep in his throat, he sprang into the bushes.

For a few seconds, the night's quiet was broken by the clamor of the dog: his barks, snarls, his yelps of pain. The flowers swished, petals flew.

Then he backed out of the bushes, tail down. He swung round and ran across the parking lot, favoring his left foreleg. Halfway across the lot, he stopped and looked back as if to check he wasn't being followed.

Then he broke into a run again, dragging the baby by its leg.

Chapter Sixty-four

'What do you make of it, Mrs Connors?'

Susan shook her head, frowning at Vasquez. 'I don't know what to think. Officer Kraus's description does seem to fit the mummy. Apparently, there's also some evidence that Amara was involved in the museum deaths.'

'Do you honestly believe—no, I can't even ask. It's too . . .' He fished for the appropriate word. 'Outlandish. The fact is, though, that unless Kraus has completely lost his marbles, our suspect has a physical appearance similar to your missing . . . artifact. Do you have photos of the thing?'

'At the museum.'

'All right. I'd like you to go over there and get them. We'll run them by Kraus and see what he has to say. If he gives us a positive make, we'll want to run off duplicates for my men.' He glanced at his wristwatch. 'We'll be here another half-hour or so, wrapping things up. Can you get back here by then?'

'No problem. We can make it in ten, fifteen minutes.'

'Excellent.'

As they left the house, Lenny Farrel of *Eyewitness News* rushed across the yard. 'Mrs Connors! A few questions, Mrs Connors!'

'We're in a hurry,' she called back.

He kept coming. Tag pointed at his face. Farrel stopped and stood motionless as if frozen in place. Only when Tag lowered his arm did the newsman move. He turned away, muttering to his cameraman.

'Persistent bastard,' Tag said.

'It's his job.'

'He can have it.'

Tag opened the car door for Susan and she climbed in. He pushed it gently until it latched. At his own side, he took the same care to make as little noise as possible. He leaned across the seat to look at Geoffrey. Susan uncovered the baby's face.

'Still asleep,' she said.

'That kid'll sleep through anything.'

'Pretty near. Once he's zonked out, he's out for the night. Till daybreak at least.'

Tag started the car.

'Nothing wakes him up but his stomach.'

'I'm the same way,' Tag said, pulling away from the curb.

With the night still warm they drove with the convertible's top locked back. Tag took it nice and steady so as not to disturb the baby despite what Susan had told him about the way the baby slept. The warm slipstream feathered their hair.

Susan reached under her seat and picked up the Callahan journal. 'Wish I had time to read all this.'

'Plenty of time later.'

'Later might be *too* late.' She opened the journal to the page where she had left off and used Tag's flashlight to continue reading above the gentle rush of air through the open-top car. '"She is of the dead who lives,"' she read aloud.

'Great.'

'"The banished god Set, slayer of Osiris, he came in the night to Amara . . . gave her the seed of his loins, that she might bear him a son. In return for her favors, he promised Amara the gift of eternal life."'

Tag shook his head. Concentrated on the road in front of him.

Susan read on in silence.

Then they reached the museum driveway. The car's lights shone on the pair of mock-Egyptian columns that flanked it.

'Go on to the back. We'll take the rear stairs. It'll be quicker.'

'What about the guards?'

'Aren't any. Blumgard decided against it, after what happened last night. I think he feels responsible for those poor guys. Doesn't want any more killings on his conscience.'

Tag drove around the side of the building to the deserted parking lot in the rear. He pulled up to the back door of the museum and shut off the engine.

They climbed from the car into the moonlit lot.

'Look,' Tag said.

In the field beyond them were the distant, sweeping beams of half a dozen flashlights. Far across it, Susan saw the spinning lights of patrol cars.

'Hang on a second,' Tag muttered. He opened the trunk of this car. 'Somewhere in all this junk . . . in case Amara's returned to her lair . . .'

Standing beside Tag, Susan watched him push aside a sleeping

328

bag, a coil of rope, a pack of road flares, a first-aid box, tools, hiking boots, odds and ends of clothing. He pulled out a hatchet. 'Bullets might not stop her, but I bet this will. This was my grandfather's; he'd keep it as sharp as a surgeon's scalpel.' He touched the keen edge. 'I try my best to keep it as old grandpa would have wanted.' Shooting her a smile, he tossed the hatchet's leather sheath into the trunk, then closed the lid.

'Want me to get your keys?' he asked.

She nodded. Tag opened the purse that hung from her shoulder as she held Geoffrey in her arms. The kid didn't peep. He slept the sleep of the innocent.

Tag looked in the purse. 'Phew. A lot of junk in here.'

'Not as bad as your trunk.'

'Ah.' He pulled out the key ring and held it in front of her eyes. 'Third from the left . . . no, your left.'

'Got it.'

He pinched it away from the others and led the way to the door.

He turned the key in the lock and pulled. The door opened noiselessly, releasing a wave of cooler air from within.

He held the door open for Susan.

She entered, the baby held securely in her arms. Her gaze immediately lowered to the concrete floor where the guard named Beckerman had been found. In the light of the new bulb overhead, she saw that the area had been cleaned. A shaded area remained on the concrete, though – it would probably always be there.

She climbed the stairs behind Tag. They reached the first landing. Where Gonzalez had died. His blood was no longer visible on the green paint of the wall, but it lent a rust tint to the porous concrete at her feet.

Turning, she followed Tag up the next flight of stairs. Hatchet in hand, shirttail half untucked, he might have been a maniac in a horror film. Even the shadow he cast became a menacing doppelgänger.

Nicholson in The Shining, *she thought.*

Come and take your punishment, Susan.

Gonna crack your head good and hard, girl.

Gonna feel your entrails tonight . . .

Damn imagination. Slippery as I don't know what.

Every shadow seemed to harbor some waiting demon.

Now she couldn't look at her lover without seeing him as some homicidal maniac with his grandpa's hatchet.

Why isn't Tag saying anything?

What's gotten into him?

329

The spirit of a dead murderer. Redrum, Susan, redrum . . .

She hugged Geoffrey more tightly to her chest, ready to take the hatchet blows to her own back rather than allow them to fall on her son's unprotected head.

No.

Just her stupid imagination.

Tag's probably nervous, too.

Not like him to be so quiet.

'Tag?'

'Huh?'

'You okay?'

'Just hoping the goddamn thing doesn't come charging down at us.'

'Lovely thought.'

'Isn't it, though.'

'Just give the gal forty whacks.'

'Sure.'

'I don't think she can be in here. She hasn't got keys.'

'If a four-thousand-year-old mummy can walk around biting people, maybe she doesn't need keys.'

'Walks through walls?'

'Why not?'

'Yeah.'

'Wish we hadn't brought Geoffrey,' he told her.

'Wish you hadn't said that.'

'If . . .'

'What?'

'If something *does* happen, take him and run. Don't look back. Don't stick around to see how things turn out. Okay?'

She clutched her baby more tightly. Just hearing the words made her skin crawl. 'Okay.'

He reached the upstairs door, opened it.

Peered out.

'Looks all right.'

Susan was glad to get out of the stairwell. Just for a moment back there the walls seemed to be closing in on her. Her heartbeat was so loud she thought the noise would wake Geoffrey as he snuggled against her breast.

She hurried along the corridor, staying close to Tag's side. At the door to her office, she pointed out the correct key. Tag slid it into the lock. Opened the door. He turned on the lights and they entered.

Tag held the baby, supporting its head in the crook of his elbow,

330

while Susan went through the file cabinet. She flipped through the folders, found one bearing Amara's name, and slid it out. She checked it. The photographs of the mummy were inside. 'Okay. Let's go.'

She took back her sleeping baby. Switching off the lights, they left the office.

'Wait here a second,' Tag said. 'I want to take another look at the coffin.'

'What for?'

'See if she's there.'

'Oh, Tag.'

'The old bird might have come home to roost.'

'The museum door was looked. She couldn't—'

'Susan, it's worth just a peek.'

'I'll go with you, then.'

They walked further up the corridor. Tag shone his flashlight into the Callahan Room. 'Wait here,' he said and stepped over the roped cordon.

She watched him cross the room, the beam of his light sweeping its corners, illuminating faces of statues – animals, men, gods . . . demons – the painted eyes stared back. Finally he aimed the beam down into the open coffin.

Suddenly feeling a chill on her back, Susan whirled around. She gazed down the dark hall, but saw nothing.

Nothing but shadows. Nothing but gloomy doorways. Moonlight glinted through window glass.

Faraway, just on the edge of her hearing, she heard a dog howl.

Stepping to the rail, she looked down at the gallery below. There were figures down there, but they were all carved from stone. Nothing moved.

Tag climbed over the cordon.

'Nobody's home,' he told her. 'Coffin's empty.'

'Now can we go?' Susan asked.

'Sure.'

'Let's take the front way. I don't think my nerves can handle the stairwell again.'

'Fine.' He shot her a reassuring smile.

They walked silently down the carpeted corridor, and down the sweeping main stairs. She chose a key for Tag once again and soon they were exiting through one of the big glass doors. Susan breathed deeply of the warm night air. 'Feels good to get out here,' she murmured.

'It'll feel even better, getting home.'

They walked down the concrete steps. She missed one, tumbled forward. Tag reached out for her.

Missed her.

She turned in midair, determined not to fall on Geoffrey. Going down, the walkway pounded her shoulder, her hip. Her neck muscles took a savage yank. She rolled onto her back. Geoffrey squawled.

'You okay?' Tag asked, concerned. He crouched over her, helping her.

'I think so. Christ, what a klutz.'

He helped her to her feet.

She cradled Geoffrey, patted his back. 'It's all right, honey,' she whispered. 'It's all right. There, there . . .' To Tag she said, 'Scared the hell out of the little guy.'

'The big guy, too. You sure you're okay?'

'I'll probably have some dandy bruises.'

Geoffrey continued to wail as they hurried toward the rear of the museum. The sound carried way across the field.

'I've got a bottle in the car,' Susan said. 'That'll calm him.' She kissed the baby's wet face. 'Yeah, you had a nasty shock, didn't you? Didn't know your mom has two left feet.'

'Hope he didn't inherit them. It'd make it tough, buying shoes.'

'Yeah, you want your bottle, don't you? That'll do you just fine, won't it?'

They reached the car. Tag pulled open the door for her. She climbed in. As Tag hurried to the other side, she slipped a plastic bottle out of her diaper bag. She thumbed its cap off, then slipped the teat into Geoffrey's wide, pink mouth. The crying stopped. He sucked on the nipple, the bottle glugging as he drew out its creamy contents. Susan watched the drizzle of bubbles running up through the transparent plastic.

This night journey had made her son hungry.

'There,' Susan soothed.

'Fantastic,' Tag whispered. 'All praise the magic bottle.'

She smiled. 'He'll be asleep in no time.'

Steering out of the parking lot, the convertible's lights blazing, he put his arm around Susan's shoulders. 'It's been a rough night.'

'I wish we could just go home. Go to sleep. Forget everything.'

'We'll just drop off the pictures of old mummy gal and let them worry about the rest of it.'

The long, straight road led through the museum park. It was lined

332

with cherry trees. Beyond the trees, the grounds looked peaceful and deserted in the moonlight.

'This whole business . . . I don't know . . . My life has always been nice. Basically nice, I guess.' She shrugged, sleepy. 'And now all this.' She stroked Geoffrey's head. 'There are horrors all around us. You know? Hell, you're a cop; you know that better than me.'

'Life's like a stroll through the park,' Tag said. 'Enjoy, but beware of the dog piles.'

She laughed wearily.

Tag grinned.

Then he shrieked.

The car swerved wildly. Twisting, Susan saw the head of the mummy behind the seat. The copper hair bloomed around the head, the eyeless face loomed forward, its lips curled back baring the teeth. The jaw clamped onto Tag's shoulder. It began ripping shirt and flesh.

Geoffrey started to howl.

'Hatchet!' Tag cried.

It had been on the seat between them. Now it was gone.

Chapter Sixty-five

A car horn blared. Headlights flooded the scene of the creature grabbing at Tag's face and hair with its shriveled hands. Its teeth snapped, trying to rip his face.

Susan jerked the steering wheel. The car swung right. The onrushing car sped past, kept going.

Careful not to crush Geoffrey, she dropped sideways, her head pressed Tag's lap. She clawed the floor, found nothing.

The hatchet must have slid under the seat when it fell.

Damn.

The monster was going to rip Tag to shreds.

She glanced up to see blood already smearing his cheek. His eyes blazed as he fought to control the car.

And as he fought the attacking mummy, too.

Brakes screamed and the car spun out, throwing Susan against the dash. Head twisted toward Tag, she saw Amara above him, teeth tearing his hair as he tried to bat it away.

And with no roof on the convertible the creature could reach freely over him to attack his unprotected head.

She saw all this. Saw the emaciated cadaver of the mummy now supple and swift, invested with an uncanny life force. Its long hair billowed out behind in the slipstream. Once, twice, three times it ducked its head, snapping at Tag's face. A gash opened above his left eyebrow where the teeth struck.

Then she saw the pistol at his waist.

The car stopped with a harsh jolt. Geoffrey slammed against her breast, the impact making the baby squeal. Her back hit the dash again. Tag was flung forward against the steering wheel, bringing Amara halfway over the top of the seat.

Susan, wedged into the space between the seat and the dashboard, realized she was stuck.

She struggled to free herself. Above her, the withered arms of the mummy flapped, hands savagely pulling at Tag as its jaws worked, snapping teeth shut like a steel trap. It lunged forward again and again. The withered breasts crinkling against Tag's head.

He punched upward, trying to keep the lethal jaws at bay.

Pushing Geoffrey along the seat, she clutched Tag's belt. Got her hand on the pistol.

Tugged.

The pistol was stuck.

'Hatchet!' Tag yelled.

Her fingers worked a strap off the pistol's hammer. She jerked the pistol free. Aimed at the ravaged face with the dark shadowed pits for eyes.

Christ, it's right by Tag's head, biting his shoulder, trying to get at his neck. If I miss . . .

Susan writhed sideways. Knees on the floor, hips against the seat front, she thrust the muzzle toward the mummy's forehead.

Fired.

The gunblast resounded, deafening her. A big, empty hole appeared just below the hairline. A patch of hair blew off the top of Amara's head as the bullet exited. The bullet, still so hot that it glowed, sped into the night sky as a spark of silver.

The mummy, apparently undisturbed, tore off Tag's collar.

Tag's eyes were closed.

Unconscious?

Dead?

Susan lunged forward. Snarling, she rammed the muzzle against Amara's shut mouth, shattering the front teeth. She shoved hard, forcing the head backwards. Her forefinger jerked the trigger. Explosions thundered in the air, one after another, following each other so fast that they sounded like a single roar. Bone and skin sprayed from the exit wounds.

Hanks of hair flew, filling the air with glittering red strands.

Susan fired the last round. The head jerked, wrenching the pistol from Susan's hand.

Now the thing moved for a different target.

The mummy's hands reached for Geoffrey.

'No!' Susan shouted.

Scooping the baby off the seat, Susan hugged him tightly. She lunged sideways.

With her free hand she levered the handle. Threw herself against the door.

It shot open. She tumbled to the road, knocking the breath from her body. Geoffrey whimpered. Not pausing, she scrambled to her feet, then looked back at the car. With the roof folded back she could plainly see Tag in the moonlight. He was motionless, slumped over the steering wheel.

A shadow within the car moved, rising, falling, then rising again. Something that moved in an uncanny, unnatural way.

A second later – *thump*.

The mummy flopped to the road. Its ruined face appeared under the open door. Susan even heard the rustle of the heavy tresses of hair.

Geoffrey's crying was like the scream of a siren in Susan's ears as she started to run.

She ran up the middle of the unlit road, Geoffrey clutched to her breasts, her long legs pumping, her sneakers almost silent as her feet flew. Soon her breathing came in noisy spurts, her heart hammered.

Looking over her shoulder, she saw Amara in the headlights.

On its feet. Running.

Running strangely, arms flapping in the air, long hair fluttering.

Running like a blind lunatic.

Running with awful speed.

Running with dreadful purpose.

Running.

Susan felt a scream in her chest. As she ran, she heard it: her own piercing scream mingling with Geoffrey's howls. The hysteria of the noise added to her fright.

She clenched her teeth, cutting off the scream.

With a glance back, she saw the ghastly creature gaining on her.

'Jesus!' she gasped. 'Oh, sweet Jesus . . .'

She tried to run faster. Her legs felt like stone. They seemed to be cramping, cutting the length of her stride.

Feet now . . .

Growing heavier.

Felt as if the soles of her sneakers were stuck against the asphalt. Each step became a physical effort. Pains ran up her calf and thigh muscles. Her heart pounded. She wanted to scream again, but there was no air left in her lungs.

From behind, she heard the mummy's approach. No gasping from it. No breathing at all. The only sounds, the quick, papery scrape of its feet on the pavement and the faint crackle of its hair as sparks of static ran through it like witch fire.

Pain suddenly seared her shoulder. She heard the rasp of tearing cloth. Felt a tug. Twisting, she whipped her arm across the swatch

336

of fabric torn from her back. The mummy held on tight, but the cloth gave.

Suddenly free, Susan stumbled sideways.

Amara stood motionless, piece of cloth in hand, as if confused.

Scrambling to the side of the road, Susan set Geoffrey down on the dirt shoulder. She stepped back, looking down at him briefly; his eyes were bright in the darkness. Then she turned to face Amara.

The strip of cloth dropped from the mummy's blackened paw. A breeze caught it, tumbling it against her bony leg before blowing it down the road.

With her forearm Susan wiped sweat out of her eyes. She was panting heavily, her heart racing.

The mummy staggered sideways as if to go round her, its hair swayed.

Susan sidestepped to block the creature. She backhanded sweat from her upper lip.

The mummy sidestepped.

So did Susan.

Its mouth opened slowly, lips pulling back like a dog snarling, baring bullet-shattered stumps of teeth.

With a snarl of rage, Susan attacked. She threw herself low against the creature, driving into its belly, throwing it backwards. Like tackling a mannequin of papier-mâché. It doubled over her. Its nails raked her back.

Then its head slammed against the asphalt.

Susan clutched the thing's throat, panting in rage. Through the gaping mouth, she saw asphalt where her bullets had taken out the back of its head.

Her thumbs punched through the brittle windpipe; it felt like breaking dry spaghetti in her fingers.

No effect. *Why should it? The thing hasn't even got lungs.*

No lungs, no brains, no heart, no blood.

Yet she was trying to kill it.

She *had* to kill it. It wanted Geoffrey.

Its flailing hands clawed the side of her face, tore off a front panel of her blouse, scratched gouges in her breasts and down her ribs.

If she could just keep the head down, just keep the shattered teeth away . . . but the pain was numbing. Her strength ebbed with the flow of blood.

And the thing was so strong.

A crooked hand darted at her face. She turned quickly. The fingers

337

missed her eye, but dug into her cheek. The other hand clubbed the side of her head, stunning her.

Susan saw herself falling sideways. Felt the creature move.

This time it seemed to make no effort – as if the earlier battle had just been a simple exercise in toying with her. One-handed, the creature reached round, gripped the collar of her blouse and lifted her from the ground as easily as she could lift a puppy by the scruff of its neck.

The road, trees, moon swung crazily.

Then she was lying winded in the grass at the side of the road.

The mummy had just thrown her ten feet or more.

From her face-down sprawl she lifted her head just enough to see the mummy climb to its feet. Then it lurched across the road, closing in on Geoffrey who lay kicking his legs on the curb.

'No!' she shrieked.

Susan scrambled to her feet.

Swayed.

Moon and trees whirled round her as she tried to keep her balance.

'No!'

The creature kept walking, heedless of Susan's staggering approach.

The copper hair hung down strangely behind the mummy, clumps of it gone. A huge empty hole gaped where the back of the head should have been.

With both hands, Susan grabbed the hanging hair and yanked. The mummy stumbled backwards against her.

She hooked an arm around its head, another across its chest. The skin felt hard and scratchy. The touch of it made her retch – her own skin felt as if it would crawl from her body – but she didn't let go.

She stumbled back, dragging the writhing creature farther away from the roadside where Geoffrey lay sobbing.

A hand reached backwards. Fingernails dug into Susan's belly.

In pain and rage, she cried out. Wrenched the head with all her strength. She heard ripping, crackling sounds – a loud snap – before she fell back to the ground.

Amara stood above her. Slowly turned away. Walked with awkward, staggering steps back toward the baby.

Susan still clutched the mummy's head to her breasts. Shaking violently, she flung it aside. As it rolled from her, she got to her hands and knees. She fell as she tried to stand.

Raising her face from the road, she watched the thing.

338

Headless.

A deep cleft showed where the neck had been torn out. Vertebrae poked up from desiccated skin.

Susan tried to stand.

Couldn't.

She wanted to weep in frustration.

Her baby . . .

A roar filled her ears.

She didn't know what it was. Didn't care.

Then the headlights blazed across the mummy. Tag's car slammed into it, knocking it high off the road. It cartwheeled over the car, bouncing off the trunk. An arm broke off.

Susan watched the torso hit the road. The arm fell nearby, hand first as if trying to break its fall.

The brakes squealed. The car swung into a tight U-turn. Blue smoke from the spinning tires filled the air.

Susan saw Amara stand.

The car started forward.

The mummy staggered toward it.

The car hit more slowly this time, knocking Amara backward onto the road. The convertible turned and its rear tire bumped over the legs.

The car stopped. Tag looked back from its side window.

Susan gazed at the mummy. Its legs were crushed flat, but it used its remaining arm to raise its torso off the road.

Tag backed up slowly.

Susan heard the awful *crunch* as the tire rolled onto Amara's chest.

The car door opened. The hatchet flew out, its head clanking on the pavement. A moment later, Tag hauled himself out. At the end of a bloody arm, he held his pistol. He fed cartridges into its cylinder.

Susan climbed to her feet and went to him. A wry grin reached the corners of his mouth. She kissed him gently, then hurried to the roadside. She picked up Geoffrey. His small hand clutched a hanging strand of her hair and tugged.

'Over here,' Tag said.

She crossed the road.

'Stand back,' he told her. 'Well behind me.'

She stepped farther back from the car.

Two quick shots split the stillness. Through the ringing in her ears, Susan heard a heavy, liquid spatter. A dark puddle began

339

to form beneath the car. The stench of gasoline stung her nostrils.

Amara's remaining hand reached toward Tag, fingers hooking into claws. Clutching.

He lit a match.

Tossed it.

The burning match rose in an arc, then fell toward the pool of gasoline.

With a soft *whup*, like a flutter of a bedsheet on a line, flame engulfed the open-top car.

And Amara's body.

Tag stepped back, moving a safe distance from the car. A few moments passed and the gas tank exploded, sending a ball of fire into the night sky.

In the red light, Tag looked to Susan like a strange, avenging phantom as he picked up the mummy's severed arm and tossed it into the flames.

The hungry fire consumed the dry stick of a limb, blue sparks popping from the crackling bone.

Tag limped across to her. He smiled at Geoffrey, stroked the baby's cheek, then put his hand across her back. She leaned against him, relishing the strength of his encircling arm.

'Awful thing to do to your car,' she said in a small voice.

'After that passenger it'd have never been the same again anyway,' he told her. Then he laughed wearily.

Susan jerked. Gasped with pain. Looking down, she screamed.

The head of Amara was clamped to her ankle, gnawing, its copper hair stretching out behind it like the body of a snake.

'Christ!' Tag yelled.

Susan shook her leg. The teeth worked, biting deeper. Grinding. Embedding.

'My God! Get her off! Get her off me!'

Tag ran for the hatchet.

'Hurry!' Pain burned her leg like fire. She couldn't shake free. She couldn't use her hand to try and pry the head loose – not without putting down Geoffrey. She clung to him tightly. '*Tag!*'

He ran to her. The hatchet chopped into Amara's head. Split it. But the teeth didn't loose their hold. He chopped again . . . again. Each blow knocking off clumps of the head, each blow jarring the teeth so that they ripped more flesh from Susan's ankle.

'Shoot it!'

'The bullet'd hit your foot,' he panted.

With a final blow, he broke one of the jaw hinges. He worked the wedge of the hatchet head between the bones.

Then pried them apart.

The teeth opened. Loosened. Susan felt them leave her skin. She limped away.

Though only one hinge of the jaw was still connected, the teeth gripped Tag's hatchet relentlessly. He tried to shake them off.

Couldn't.

Without leaving Susan's side, Tag hurled away the hatchet and the biting remains of Amara's head. They disappeared into his flaming car.

The long hair caught fire. It crackled fiercely.

Red sparks swirled high into the night sky where they faded and – at last – died.